OCTAVE MIRBEAU

THE 628-E8

Translated and with an Introduction by
COLIN BOSWELL

THE 628-E8

OCTAVE MIRBEAU (1848-1917) was a prolific French journalist, novelist, playwright and art critic. In the latter capacity, he was an important early advocate of Vincent van Gogh. Mirbeau is nowadays deemed to have been a significant member of the Decadent Movement, largely because of his classic phantasmagoric fantasy *Torture Garden* (1899). Among his other novels of note are *Abbé Jules* (1888) and *The Diary of a Chambermaid* (1900).

COLIN BOSWELL studied French Language and Literature at University College London. Whilst completing a PhD he began his career lecturing in French at Goldsmiths University of London and later at the University of Kent, where he was also Development Director. He then created and served as Executive Director of the first European office of the US-based Council for Advancement and Support of Education (CASE). He has published books and articles on the French language and on Émile Zola, and his translations include Petrus Borel's *The Treasure of the Arcueil Cavern*, and, in a joint translation with Sue Boswell, Gustave Kahn's *The Mad King*.

CONTENTS

INTRODUCTION

In 2023 some readers may experience a curious if guilty enjoyment at the lack of political correctness of Octave Mirbeau's *The 628-E8*. How so? First because the work is a paean of praise to its central character, a petrol-driven motorcar. Even if Mirbeau does not manifest the exaggerated exuberance of the petrol-heads vaunting the merits of cars on TV programmes such as *Top Gear*, it is clear that he is a serious fan of motorcars. One imagines that in 1907 he could not have foreseen that slightly more than a century later, as a result of worries about climate change, greenhouse gases and global warming, the sale of new petrol- and diesel-powered cars would become illegal in many developed countries and the world would be encouraged to switch entirely to electric-powered vehicles. Mirbeau made clear his view of electric cars in the chapter 'Ships': "As for the electric car, it is just an illusion, not yet knowing where to rest its strength…"

But not only does Mirbeau admire the sophistication of the design and engineering of the car, particularly his car, for him it is also a symbol of progress, not only increasing the ease of travel and thereby breaking down national barriers, but also creating jobs for thousands of workers. However, he is also clear that this progress is not without its casualties, mostly animal but sometimes human. Towards the end of the long section entitled 'Fauna seen on the Road' Mirbeau comes across another motorist who has run over and killed a little girl and who is remarkably hard-hearted towards the girl's mother, telling her to console herself that her daughter has died in the name of progress.

As far as political correctness is concerned, one also wonders what the *#MeToo* movement would make of the episode in the chapter 'The half-open Door' where Mirbeau's fictitious English friend Gérald B—— blunders into the wrong hotel bedroom and seduces, or should we say rapes, a woman who is definitely saying no to his initial advances even if she finally voluntarily succumbs. It is interesting that Mirbeau refers to himself as a 'cad' for relating this imagined episode.

And one could wonder whether Mirbeau is a homophobe as, in the chapter entitled 'An Evening at the Music Hall', he wittily describes the German officers 'wiggling their buttocks' as they leave the theatre. In his humorous treatment of homosexuality in the chapter 'Berlin-Sodom' Mirbeau has Albert D—— say: "Instead of making love amongst men simply through vice, they are pedantic in their homosexuality..." So is it their pedantry that is more focused on than their homosexuality?

What sort of a work is *The 628-E8?* In the section 'To the Reader' in the chapter 'Departure' Mirbeau tantalises us: "Here then is the Journal of this journey in a motorcar through part of France, part of Belgium, part of Holland, part of Germany, and, especially, through part of myself. Is it a journal? Is it even a journey? Are these not rather dreams, reveries, memories, impressions, tales which, most frequently, have no relationship to, no visible link with, the countries visited, and are born and reborn, in me, quite simply, by a face met, a landscape glimpsed, a voice that I thought I heard singing or weeping in the wind?"

It is clearly not a novel. At about the time of perhaps his best-known work, *The Diary of a Chambermaid* (1900), Mirbeau was abandoning the realist novel, a change that he explained in a letter to his friend Claude Monet. He was becoming increasingly interested in writing for the theatre. In 1903 he wrote his comedy *Business is Business*, a play that was commercially successful and which, along with its central character Isidore Lechat, is frequently mentioned in *The 628-E8*.

The 628-E8 is a mixture of autobiography and fiction. It is therefore arguably autofiction, a term coined in 1977 by Serge Doubrovsky. The characteristics of autofiction are (1) that the writer whose name appears on the book's cover is (2) the same person as the narrator and is (3) also the character whose adventures and misadventures are reported. These adventures may be real or fictitious as may be the characters.

Where the characters of *The 628*-E8 are concerned, all the writers, painters and musicians mentioned are clearly identifiable and real. But we know that other characters are not. As has already been mentioned, Mirbeau's English friend Gérald B—— is fictitious, as is Mirbeau's 'so-called old friend' Weil-Sée. The reader cannot even be sure whether Mirbeau's driver-mechanic Brossette is real or not. Mirbeau's German friend von B—— was a real character, Baron von Bunsen, whom he had met on the Côte d'Azur in 1889. But by the time of Mirbeau's real trip to Germany in 1905 von B—— had been dead for some years and therefore their conversation is entirely fictitious. Also probably fictitious is the chapter 'The Funeral Meal' but it is an excellent vehicle for Mirbeau's wicked sense of humour, particularly with the sting in its tail as he gives to the coachman the address of his inebriated friend so that he may be delivered safely home only to discover later that he had erroneously given him the address of a brothel.

Where most of the real characters are concerned Mirbeau adopts a quasi-binary attitude. If they are *Dreyfusards*, that is to say on the side of Albert Dreyfus in the infamous Dreyfus Affair, as was Mirbeau along with Emile Zola and the majority of intellectuals, then he approves of them. If they are *anti-Dreyfusards* he disapproves of them, with the possible exception of his driver Brossette who reads an anti-Dreyfus newspaper. It is interesting that Mirbeau had also portrayed the central working-class characters in *The Diary of a Chambermaid* as anti-Dreyfus.

A particularly curious example is the writer Paul Bourget. Bourget and Mirbeau had been friends for over ten years until 1889 when they fell out over a review article that Mirbeau had written criticising Bourget, although Bourget was not actually named in the article. Throughout *The 628-E8* Mirbeau is consistently critical of Bourget, particularly in the chapter 'German Women and M. Paul Bourget'. Since he was a writer and intellectual Bourget might have been expected to be a *Dreyfusard,* but he was not. Mirbeau is also very critical about the negative influence that he felt Bourget was having on Maupassant's writing.

The 628-E8 shows us two contrasting aspects of Mirbeau's style: vitriol and humour. The clearest aspects of Mirbeau's vitriolic style are when he deals with anti-Semitism, including in the context of the Dreyfus affair, and colonialism and colonial exploitation. The most powerful denunciation of anti-Semitism is in the chapter 'Pogroms'. The end of this chapter is so moving that the final paragraphs are almost impossible to read aloud without the reader choking up.

Colonialism is the main theme in the chapters 'King of Business' and 'Red Rubber,' in which Mirbeau produces vitriolic criticism of King Leopold II of the Belgians and the barbaric treatment of slaves in the Congo producing the rubber that increase his personal fortune. Mirbeau's criticism of colonialism goes much further than that found in Gustave Kahn's *The Mad King* (1896), published in an English translation in 2021 by Snuggly Books. Although Kahn's colonisers come ostensibly from some vaguely Germanic state, Hummertanz, he had spent time in Belgium and was probably actually referring to Belgian colonial activity in *The Mad King*.

Mirbeau's humour can be sardonic. In the chapter 'A Family of Motorists' he describes a French family whose motorcar has broken down. Mirbeau treats the whole family, father, mother, daughter and son, with comic disdain. But throughout the book there are little comic cameos such as a furniture-cart driver who has fallen asleep and who will be surprised when he wakes up the next day to discover that he is back where he started as, in the meantime, the horse has decided to make a U-turn in the road and head for home.

The funniest section is the one entitled 'The Fauna seen on the Roads'. As Mirbeau works his way through the various categories he ends with the motorist's biggest enemy—the cyclist. Mirbeau may here be making a joke at the expense of the three owners of the company that had built his motorcar who had all been racing cyclists. But the joke has a particular resonance for readers in the twenty-first century who have become used to 'Mamils' (middle-aged men in Lycra) and the angry reaction they can provoke in motorists.

On its publication in 1907 *The 628-E8* provoked two scandals. The first was that Mirbeau's treatment of Belgium had been too hostile. The second was that Mirbeau had originally included three chapters about the death of Balzac loosely linked to the fact that in the chapter 'Memories and Daydreams in Cologne' Mirbeau recounts staying in his hotel bedroom to read a copy of Balzac's *Correspondence* he had bought that day. In these chapters Mirbeau alleges that whilst Balzac was dying, his Polish-born wife Madame Hanska was not at his bedside but was instead making love to the painter Jean Gigoux. Mirbeau was quickly persuaded by Madame Hanska's daughter to leave out these three chapters, but they were reintegrated into *The 628-E8* in 1939. They are omitted from this translation, not on grounds of propriety, but because they have already appeared in 2018 in a translation by Brian Stableford (Snuggly Books).

If *The 628-E8* has an overriding theme it is more implicit than explicit. With the exception of the peasants in the Jura in the 'Dedication', described by Mirbeau as sensible and level-headed, elsewhere in the book he treats the French harshly, particularly in comparison with the inhabitants of the other countries that he visits.

Born in 1848, Mirbeau had in his early twenties experienced the horror of the Franco-Prussian War (1870-71), which saw the defeat of France and brought to an end the reign of Napoleon III. Immediately after this defeat Mirbeau was initially drawn to Bonapartism, before being attracted to anarchism, as a form of anti-authoritarianism, and then to humanism.

The book comes out strongly against xenophobia. In the chapter 'Hymn to Peace and to The Hague' Mirbeau writes: "I can understand why Holland was chosen, and, in Holland, The Hague, to set up the court which, one day, despite the jokes and the pessimistic denials, will replace the pleasure of Emperors, of Kings, of Parliaments, to take account of international disputes and find solutions to them which will no longer be massacres, and finally establish peace, not between men but between peoples." Here we see a sort of embryonic European Union. It becomes particularly pertinent for, as these lines are being written, a sovereign, democratic country, Ukraine, is being invaded by Russia.

I would like to thank my wife Sue Boswell for her extremely valuable comments on an earlier version of this translation and to Brendan Connell, for his always helpful advice and skilful editing. Any imperfections that remain are, of course, entirely my responsibility.

—Colin Boswell

THE 628-E8

DEDICATION

To Monsieur FERNAND CHARRON[1]

To whom else can I contemplate dedicating the tale of this journey other than you, my dear Monsieur Charron, for it is you who designed, built and animated with such a marvellous life the marvellous motorcar[2] *in which I am accomplishing this journey without fatigue and hitches?*

I owe you this homage for I owe you multiple delights, brand new impressions, a whole gamut of precious knowledge not to be found in books, and months, whole months of total freedom, free from my usual business, from my major cares, and free from myself, in the middle of countries new to me or only poorly known to me, amidst so diverse beings of whom I have better understood, for having got closer to them, the enormous and slow strength which, despite local discords, despite the resistance of interests, of appetites and of privileges, and despite themselves, is pushing them invincibly towards great human unity.

---

1 Fernand Charron (1866-1921) began his career as a racing cyclist and bicycle salesman. In November 1897 he joined forces with two other businessmen, Laiton Girardot and Émile Voigt, both former racing cyclists. Their company was called C.-G.-V. and in the first year of production built 75 motorcars. Eventually the factory was located at Puteaux and the garage and salesroom on the Avenue de la Grande Armée.

2 *628-E8*, the title of the book, is the registration number of the C.-G.-V. that Mirbeau had purchased. At the time this indicated that the car was registered in Paris. The car had a thirty-horsepower engine and would have cost the equivalent of about €75,000 at the time of purchase.

Yes, what is new, what is captivating, is this. Not only does the motorcar carry us away, from the plain to the mountain, from the mountain to the sea, across infinite forms, contrasting landscapes, from the ever-changing picturesque; it takes us also through hidden customs, ideas that are forming, through history, our living history of today...

At least, one is quite happy to honestly believe that all that has happened. Then, to make them bearable for us and free from remorse, should we not ennoble all our distractions a little?

Six years ago, I remember having left Aurillac in the morning in one of the first motorcars that you had built, and I arrived in the evening, at about four o'clock, in Poligny in the heart of the Jura.

It was the end of a market day. All was quiet in the streets. There was no noise in the bars, which were nearly empty. Beasts and humans were departing peacefully, the former to their cowsheds, the latter to their homes. A few groups still stayed chatting in the square, where the traders had taken down and folded away their stalls... Just by walking around it, the town seemed congenial to me. It had a feeling of decency, of health, of welcome, very rare in France.

In the inn where I stayed, I sat at table between two farmers, very handsome, very strong men, with thick, black hair on powerful square heads, their faces energetically shaped: especially attractive. They were talking about their business whilst I, eating delicious trout washed down with an excellent Arbois wine, was listening to them talk. As they showed none of that sectarian and mistrustful nationalism, with which, normally, farmers receive people they refer to as 'strangers', they very kindly allowed me to take part in their conversation.

They revealed themselves to be perfect agricultural technicians, curious about progress, informed about matters that went well beyond their calling. I no longer had before me the Auvergnat, bitter and cunning, talkative and superstitious, ignorant and lyrical, that I had left behind, that very morning, not without pleasure I must confess; I was finally seeing men, calm, reflective, realistic, precise, who believe only in their own effort, rely only on themselves, know what they want, have the very clear feeling of their economic strength, demand that the social and human dignity of work be respected in them. Not a trace of superstition in their speech, not the slightest hesitation about progress. They did not have one word of hatred against motoring. Quite the opposite. They had a great admiration for this novelty and credited it for still only being a sport—an experimental sport—for the wealthy, and of which they were waiting confidently for democratic applications.

Several times they showed their pride that, of all the départements in France, theirs was the one where education was the most developed.

One of the two said to me:

"Here, we all want to learn. Unfortunately, they don't teach us much. Clearly, we don't have the ambition to be scientists like Pasteur.[1] But we would like to know the basics. Well, the education that they give us needs total reform. It is a clerical education which continues hypocritically in the guise of a lay education. Our minds are still stuffed with useless myths... But we are still unaware of the simplest elements of life: for example, what is the water we are drinking, the meat we are eating, the air we are breathing, the seed we are planting in the ground... basically, all natural phenomena and ourselves... So, like our forefathers, we feel our way, in the same routine, and we are incapable of taking advantage of the immense riches which are everywhere, in nature, within reach."

The other, who agreed, in his turn said:

"All the time the socialists are making speeches about emancipation, about liberation... great, dammit!... but, liberation, emancipation from what, if to begin with one does not emancipate and liberate our brain?"

---

1 Pasteur was originally from the Jura like these peasants.

I quickly understood that the past had no influence over these sensible men and that they would defend, with tenacious will-power and tranquil self-assurance, the conquests, the poor little material and moral conquests, that they had managed, on their own, to snatch from society and from the disagreeable soil of their mountains…

And here was the miracle… In a few hours, I had gone from one human race to another human race, travelling through all the different types of terrain, of culture, of customs, of humanity which link them together and give them meaning, and I was experiencing this sensation—so much did I seem to have seen things—of having, in one day, lived months and months.

And this sensation, which only the motorcar can give, for the railways which have their imprisoning tracks, always the same, their captured populations, always the same, the enclosed towns that are the yards and the stations, always the same, do not really travel through the countries, do not put you in direct contact with their inhabitants,—this totally new sensation of which I sometimes tasted the force and the charm, during this exquisite journey, during which I am constantly reminded of my admiration and, I may say, my gratitude for this ideal moving house, this docile and precise instrument of forward motion that is the motorcar, and especially—since one must end by bringing it back to you—the motorcar created by you, dear Monsieur Charron, to satisfy my curiosity and my stray reveries…

That is why I love my motorcar. Henceforth, it is part of my life; it is my life, my artistic and spiritual life, as much as and more than my house. It is full of constantly renewed riches, which cost no more than the joy of catching them as they pass by, here, there, everywhere that I am taken by the whim to see and the desire to study. In it I sense things and beings living with intense activity, with prodigious emphasis, which speed confirms rather than erases.

It is dearer to me, more useful, more filled with lessons than my library, where the closed books sleep on their bookshelves, than my pictures which, now, bring death to my walls, with the unchanging nature of their skies, of their trees, of their waters, of their faces... In my motorcar I have all that, more than all that, for all that is stirring, teeming, passing by, changing, vertiginous, limitless, infinite... I foresee, without worry, the disposal of my books, of my pictures, of my objets d'art; I cannot get used to the idea that, one day, I might no longer own this magical beast, this fabulous unicorn which carries me away, without jolts, the brain more free, the eye more acute, through the beauties of nature, the diversity of life and the conflicts of humanity.

❋

Well, should I tell you this, dear Monsieur Charron? I hesitated for a long time before putting your name at the front of this little volume... I confess that, for a few hours, courage failed me... That is a pompous way, is it not, of saying something which is very natural and very simple... It is just that I know my contemporaries, especially those from my milieu. Their so well-known benevolence, their indomitable morality and the uncompromising nature of their virtues, actually terrified me... But the very vivid feeling that I have of my freedom, the horror no less vivid, that I have of received customs and current practices, my immorality, in fact, rapidly overcame this fleeting and absurd terror... If one listened to them, these good people, one would never do anything one wanted to or that one liked... Let them have their say...

Let them have their say, but let us benefit from this situation to risk a few observations...

To begin with, a little anecdote, if you will allow me?... It has a message...

You are aware that, for nine years, I was a contributor to Le Journal[1]... *How could I, without abandoning my ideas, without*

---

1 A daily newspaper with a wide circulation.

hypocrisy and without intrigue, keep working for so long for this public broadsheet?... Here is not the place to say, and in any case, I do not know. One day, I submitted an article in which, writing about a recent scientific discovery, I elaborated on showing the social utility the results could provide in the future. M. Eugène Letellier[1] was very offended by it... He said to me:

"I cannot publish your article."

"Why not?"

"But, my dear Sir, do you wish to take the bread out of my mouth?"

This had not been my idea. It would also have been a very painful operation for which I had no taste at all... I replied simply:

"I do not understand..."

"But this is advertising!" M. Eugène Letellier cried... "front page advertising!... I could get five thousand francs for your article..."

"Seven thousand!" said the administrator who was present at the interview...

"And you were imagining that I was going... like that... gaily..."

"Excuse me!" I interrupted... "could you tell me, Sir, what are, in your opinion, the topics which are not close to advertising?"

M. Eugène Letellier thought for a long time... He was very embarrassed by this question... Finally, he decided to reply: "There are... I assure you... there are lots of them..."

"Which ones?"

"Good grief!... listen... you can write about literature—on condition, of course, that you do not refer to any author's name, or to any book title... Yes... we are a literary magazine, are we not?... And art. My dear friend,—art, in general, of course—there

---

1 Eugène Letellier, patron of *Le Journal*, was thought to be the main model for the character Isidore Lechat in Mirbeau's play *Les affaires sont les affaires* or *Business is Business*. The character and the play are mentioned a few times later in the book.

is another topic for an article… I do not claim that it is ideal… no… you know, art, for me!… But with talent…"

And then suddenly, striking his forehead…

"Ah!… Why not pornography?… An admirable subject!… Limitless!… Pornography, for a writer with imagination… well, there you are… Ah!"

I did not try, with any remark, to diminish the majesty of this exclamation… I simply continued to look, with increasing attention, at M. Eugène Letellier… He was handsome… he was powerful… he embodied the century… The poor man!

And later I learned that the Republic had placed, on the chest of this educator of the crowds, the red sign of that honour… of which, moreover, there are legions[1]…

The age, dear Monsieur Charron, is terribly resistant to the admiration that we owe to progress, to the gratitude we should show to people who work, struggle and discover. Admiration and gratitude are only understood and accepted if they are valued and rewarded according to current prices, proportional to the enthusiasm with which they are expressed. The press has become so universally venal, it obliges everything in life to fill its coffers, in order to be recognised as valuable, an increasingly heavy tax, so that writers today, for fear of dishonouring themselves, are no longer entitled to draw attention to an important scientific discovery, or to admit to a pleasure, an emotion, unless that emotion, that pleasure arises from a fabricated object that can be sold. For a time, the end of which we can see is not far away, writers may still—except, of course, in Le Journal—*admire a book, a picture, a statue, and state, almost freely, their impressions about what are called works of the imagination. A rather arbitrary and comical classification,*

---

1 Mirbeau is playing with words here. The 'red sign of that honour' is the rosette of the *Légion d'honneur*.

for I have always thought that statues, pictures, books are sold with more ferocity than machines; and machines appear to me, more than books, statues, pictures, to be works of imagination. When I look at, when I listen to, the life of that admirable organism that is the engine of my motorcar, with its lungs and its heart of steel, its vascular system of rubber and copper, its electrical nerve supply, do I not have a differently moving idea of human genius from when I read a book by M. Paul Bourget, or look at a picture by M. Detaille, a statue of Denys Puech? Does not the smallest mechanism that transports motor energy, heat, speech, image, using slender networks of metal wires, or by invisible waves, imply a greater sum of study, observation, effort, superior faculty?… And yet, the banal, infinitely useless book by M. Paul Bourget, the statue—if one can call it that—of M. Denys Puech, the picture—euphemism—of M. Detaille, is admitted, is honourable, elegant, and I may extol them as much as I like, and everybody will praise me for having uttered, in respect of them, the aesthetic stupidity that ferments in the brain of an art critic. But I will be formally forbidden to describe a machine which, like the motorcar, for example, is already revolutionising and will revolutionise even more in the future the conditions of social life.

Well, I protest with all my strength against this pedagogic concept of newspapers which allows them—because it is art—to tell you, in four columns, about the latest vaudeville at the Variétés, and which means that we never know—because it is business— about the admirable work, by means of which so many obscure scientists are struggling to acquire, for us, every day a little more happiness.

I am not claiming this freedom, dear Monsieur Charron, to declare, up front, that you invented the motorcar. But because you were passionate about it, motoring owes you a great deal. Amongst French carmakers—I am pleased to recognise—you are certainly

the person who brought the most notable progress to this industry. Ingenious, practical and tenacious, you never stopped looking for and finding improvements, you never stopped creating devices, adopted universally today, thanks to which our engines have reached that degree of quasi-perfection, where we are at the moment. And what surprises me the most, and I praise you to the skies for this, is that you also took the trouble to give them a harmonious shape, and to endow the machine, like an objet d'art, with its share of beauty.

I have followed you, with increasing interest, from the day when, in the basement of the avenue de la Grande-Armée—at that time you did not have a factory—you summoned a few people to come and see the pieces of the first chassis that you were going to construct... I was there... I remember a curious character, an American, who is not an unknown and who is king, like quite a few citizens of his republic, king of steel, M. Schwab,[1] in fact, was there as well... I still see him, taking hold of each piece, one after the other, and having examined it, weighed it, evaluated it, smelled it, saying:

"That really is steel... Great!... That is steel!..."

So much so that before he left, he ordered two chassis for himself, ten others for Americans, kings of something evidently, of whom he gave you the names and addresses.

And he added: "If they don't want them... too bad for them!... I'll take them for myself... Go on!... Go on!... That really is steel..."

And I, who am king of nothing, induced by the example of M. Schwab, ordered one for myself as well.

"Good!" cried M. Schwab. "Perfect!... And if, at the last moment you no longer want it... I'll take it... it's real steel!"

❋

---

1 Schwab was the President of the Carnegie Company.

During the journey of which I am undertaking the account here, M. Schwab reminded me of that day, one evening when I saw him in Delft, where I had just arrived…

It was a fairly comical evening, and a very American one.

After dinner, during which we had talked a lot about cars—for among other benefits of motoring, it is remarkable how the normal course of our conversations about the immortality of the soul and about women has been so radically changed—we went out. We strolled in the city.

A curious and delightful city, and so different!

The moon was illuminating with a mother-of-pearl light the hemmed-in canals, the bridges that cross them with a single arch, the thin trees that line them like lace curtains. And the silhouettes, against the sky, of the tall gables, took on an aspect of an outdated yet charming romanticism… Then, between blue spaces, enormous towers suddenly rose up into the silvery sky… I say that they rose up; they looked more as though they had fallen from the sky and had kept the oblique angle of their fall once on the ground. Then we were walking in front of palaces, dark and silent, where the light picked out, here and there, an ogival door, the gap in a battlement, trellised windows… Nobody in the streets, almost no lights at the windows… sleeping shops whose radiance seemed to be shrinking, weakening and dying, like that of lamps which are going to go out in a sanctuary… And, suddenly, we were breathing in, amidst the musty smell of the water trapped in the stone, the violent perfume of hyacinths that was rising up to us, from the little barges full of flowers, moored at the quayside and waiting for the next day's market.

We were not talking… M. Schwab was energetically smoking one of those awful cigars that are only smoked by millionaires… And I, transported in this medieval décor of the evening, seemed to be far away from everything, far from steel and the kings of steel… so far, so far, so far!

But M. Schwab had not left behind this century, nor America, nor the Avenue de la Grande-Armée… He insisted on puffing on his cigar which left an appalling odour behind him… And it made exactly the same noise as carp in a pond, when they come up to breathe, their snout out of the water, the air of fine summer evenings. I heard him, in the gap between these noises, saying:

"This fellow Charron... Hey? He's a one!... He knows what real steel is..."

Two women, with long, black cloaks, passed by with quiet footsteps, as silent as flights of bats... Where had they come from?... Where were they going?... Were they even women?... Were they not rather souls, ancient souls, the nocturnal souls of all this past?... I saw their cloaks disappear into the night...

M. Schwab had not looked at them... He went on:

"You know... in America... this fellow Charron, he would also be a king... king of the motorcar..."

And then, in the distance, very far away, it was like the sound of a bell, a tiny sound of a bell, with a unique ring, with no lasting vibration, a sound similar to the so attractive, so melancholic sound of a toad, in the stifling gardens during August... Then other sounds of bells, also far away, in the east, in the west, replied... I imagined that I saw the insides of convents, cloisters, pale faces beneath veils, hands clasped together, candles... And, close to me, a voice to which I was no longer listening, and of which I was only receiving words interrupted by the silence that these little peals of bells, over there, were making so moving, so mysterious, a voice was saying:

"Carburettor... gear box... clutch... magneto... steel... steel... steel... steel...

And this word 'trust... trust... trust...' which vibrated, tickled me, annoyed by ear like the buzzing of an insect:

"Pruut...Pruut... Pruut!..."

It was very late when we got back to the hotel.

I thought that you would be amused to know that you had pre-occupied the mind of a man like M. Schwab so much that, during a calm evening in Holland, in the décor of an old city, illustrated by so many memories and which, since William the Silent,[1] had scarcely changed, he crowned you King of the Motorcar!...

---

1 William the Silent (1533-1584) was assassinated in Delft.

DEPARTURE

To the Reader.

Here then is the Journal of this journey in a motorcar through part of France, part of Belgium, part of Holland, part of Germany, and, especially, through part of myself.

Is it a journal? Is it even a journey?

Are these not rather dreams, reveries, memories, impressions, tales which, most frequently, have no relationship to, no visible link with, the countries visited, and are born and reborn, in me, quite simply, by a face met, a landscape glimpsed, a voice that I thought I heard singing or weeping in the wind? But is it certain that I really heard this voice, that this face, which recalled so may joyful and melancholic things, was one that I really did encounter somewhere; and that I have seen, here or there, seen with my own eyes, this landscape to which I owe pages of such a sharp lyricism, and which, suddenly,—by what association of ideas?—made me think of M. André Theuriet's academic botanist?

There are moments when, in all seriousness, I wonder what is, in all this, dream, and what is reality. I have no idea. The scary thing about the motorcar is that you know nothing about it, that you can know nothing about it. The motorcar is whim, is fantasy, is incoherence, is oblivion of everything… You set off for Bordeaux and—how?… why?—in the evening you are in Lille. Besides, Lille or Bordeaux, Florence or Berlin,

Budapest or Madrid, Montpellier or Pontarlier… what is the difference?…

The motorcar is also the deformation of speed, the continual rebound upon oneself, it is vertigo.

When, after a twelve-hour drive, you get out of the car, you are like a sick person who has fainted and who is slowly regaining contact with the external world. Objects still seem to you to be animated with strange grimaces and disordered movement… Only gradually do they regain their shape, their place, their equilibrium. Your ears are buzzing as though they have been invaded by thousands of insects with sonorous wings. It seems as though your eyelids are lifting with effort to take life in, like a theatre curtain rising on the illuminated stage… What has happened?… You only have the memory, or rather the very vague sensation, of having travelled through empty spaces, through infinite whiteness, where little tongues of fire were dancing, twisting… You have to shake yourself, feel yourself, stamp your foot on the ground, in order to notice that your heel is touching something hard, something solid, and that there are around you, in front of you, houses, shops, people who are passing by, talking, hurrying… It is only in the evening that you compose yourself, after dinner. But you still have a sort of nervous agitation which will grow tenfold and will swell your dreams in the night.

"So," you will be telling me, "it is the journal of a sick person, of a madman, that you are going to give us?"

"Alas!… dear Monsieur Thureau-Dangin,[1] what man—even amongst those who have the smallest amount of genius—can boast that he is neither mad, nor sick?

---

1 Paul Thureau-Dangin (1837-1913) was a Catholic and Orléanist historian elected to the Académie Française in 1893 in preference to Émile Zola.

Thanks to memories which are perhaps only dreams, and dreams which are perhaps only real impressions, it is possible, after all, for me to take you from Cologne to Rotterdam, from Rotterdam to Hamburg, from Hamburg to Antwerp, from Antwerp to Delft, from Delft to The Helder, from The Helder to Bremen and to Dusseldorf, and that to arrive at these different stopping places, we were travelling through America, Russia, China, the African lakes, the frozen mountains of solitary polar regions. But do not be sure. In any case do not expect me to give historical, geographical, political, economic, statistical information, parliamentary, town council, military, university, judicial documents… No, I despise them, as you can imagine… But where and how was I able to collect them? You have to inhabit a country, live among its institutions, its daily customs, its morals and its fashions, in order to sense its benefits and its offences… Well, I have only been able to drive on its roads, like a cannonball on the arc of its trajectory.

Let the demographers and the sociologists abandon here all their hopes! In no way am I pretentious enough to offer them a serious and full work, comparing the state of peoples, enumerating their wealth, predicting their fate, and which—providing that in addition to this respectable and fanciful knowledge I had intimate knowledge of the concierge or the corset-maker of Madame de X———,—would get me the praise of the Institut, and, perhaps, this prize—ah! which I have often longed for—this prize which responds to the very gracious, to the very gallant, to the very decorative name of Queen Pou!

I know people who have the gift of writing, in the margin of their guide books, on a daily basis, their emotions from the journey, or what they think are their emotions; who go from room to room in museums, a fountain pen in one hand, a notebook in the other, their *Baedeker* in their pocket, their eyes elsewhere and their mind nowhere; and who stop their car at a historic ruin, a recommended viewpoint, the site of a former battlefield, to note immediately an 'idea and sensation', which is frequently no more than the reminiscence of something read the previous day; who never go to sleep without having scrupulously made a detailed note of their enthusiasms at the same time as their expenses.

For example, this one, which I read in a notebook left behind by a tourist in a hotel bedroom:

"Visited the Château de Chambord (see the description in the *Baedeker*…) They do not build castles like that any more… Forgot the disgraces of the present (Combes, Pelletan, Jaurès, Hervé)[1]… Lived the whole day amongst the noble glories of the past… (François Ier, Diane de Poitiers, the Duchesse d'Étampes)… Felt consoled, and better… (to be developed)… Gave two francs to the attendant, which my wife found excessive… Bought twelve sous' worth of illustrated postcards (show how today these postcards are bad for the budget of a journey)."

I genuinely respect these people. Perhaps they feel a superior joy of which I am unaware. But I stand by not knowing them, being perfectly happy with my own joys, even though I am not entirely sure if they are joys.

I shall write randomly of my memories and my dreams, without distinguishing too much between them. You will sometimes see, I imagine, contradictions that will shock your delicate and ordered soul, will exasperate your mind, with its strict logic… What is to be done? It is just that I am a man, like everybody, and that nothing of the infirmities, the incoherence, the human errors, is alien to me. Just like all my fellows,—who boast, with such comic pride, that they are but heart, brain, nothing

---

1 All people that Mirbeau admired.

but wings,—I have a stomach, a liver, nerves and as a result, digestion, melancholy and rheumatism, on which the sun and the rain, pleasure and pain exert inimical influences. What M. Paul Bourget calls 'states of mind' is never more than 'states of matter,' which affect in diverse ways our moral sensibility, the movement and direction of our ideas, like the meteors which pass over the sea, changing a thousand times, its colour and its rhythm. Depending on whether my organs are working well or badly, I sometimes end up hating today what I liked yesterday, and liking the next day what, the previous day, I had violently detested. Far from complaining, I am pleased about it, for it is that which gives life its infinite interest... "There is something that I prefer to beauty, and that is change," writes Ernest Renan, unless it was M. Maurice Barrès.

Finally, I shall try to follow, in everything, the advice of Boileau, so stupidly defamed, according to whom a fine disorder is an effect of art.

How happy he must be, today, Boileau!

Speed.

It has to be said—and this is not the least curious thing about it—that motoring is an illness, a mental illness. And this illness has a very attractive name: speed. Have you noticed how illnesses almost always have charming names? Scarlet fever, tonsillitis, measles, beriberi, adenitis, etc. Have you also noticed, the more these names are charming, the more serious are the illnesses?... I rave about repeating that the name of ours is... speed. Not the mechanical speed which sweeps the machine along on the roads, through more and more countries, but that sort of neuropathic speed, which sweeps man along through all his actions and distractions... He cannot keep still, hectic, his nerves as tight as springs, impatient to set off again as soon as he has arrived somewhere, desperate to be elsewhere, always elsewhere, further away than elsewhere... His brain is an endless track on which thoughts, images, sensations roar and race at a hundred kilometres an hour. A hundred kilometres, this is the benchmark of his activity. He passes by like a whirlwind, thinks like a whirlwind, feels like a whirlwind, loves like a whirlwind, lives like a whirlwind. Everywhere life rushes, jostles, animated by a crazy movement, a movement like a cavalry charge, and cinematographically disappears, like the trees, the hedges, the walls, the silhouettes at the side of the road... Everything, around him, and in him, jumps, dances, gallops, is in motion, in motion inverse to his own motion. Painful sensation, sometimes, but strong, fantastical and intoxicating, like vertigo and like fever.

For example, I go to Amsterdam... When I have a problem, a revulsion, quite simply, in order not to hear any further talk about M. Willy[1] and M. Bernstein,[2] I go to Amsterdam. I decide that I will spend a week there, a week of forgetfulness, a week of joy... I need a full week to see once again, rather superficially but calmly, this admirable city. If a week is not enough, I shall take a fortnight... I am free both where I and time are concerned... Nothing is keeping me here; I have no urgent business elsewhere.

And I set off.

I arrive in Amsterdam... Despite the smoothness of my C.-G.-V., and the soft, lulling elasticity of its unique springs, I arrive, a little shaken for having driven over the horrid, barbaric cobblestones of Belgium, where so many poor chassis came to grief, badly prepared to confront these stone obstacles which turn Flemish roads into something resembling interminable moraines... So, I arrive one morning, for I had slept in The Hague where I had seen again the Fishpond and its Swans,

---

1 Willy was the pen name of Henri Gauthier-Villars, the husband of Colette. Many of his novels were written by ghost writers.
2 Henry Bernstein (1876-1953) was a popular dramatist disliked by Mirbeau.

where I breathed once again this gentle calm, this gilded calm which is supposed to cure me of all vain agitation... Finally... finally... here I am back in Amsterdam... I am happy... Undoubtedly, a week, a fortnight... will not be enough... I shall stay three weeks.

I say to my mechanic:

"Brossette, my friend... we will be staying here a month... Maybe longer."

Brossette smiles and replies:

"Understood, Monsieur... So, shall I unload the luggage?... All of it?"

"Yes, I think, all of it, all of it..."

"Understood, Monsieur..."

"And for you my dear Brossette... some days off... I shall not need the car here..."

Brossette's smile gets wider...

"Very well!... Very well!" he says... "In any case I shall wait for your orders this evening, Monsieur."

"No, no... Go to bed... Enjoy yourself..."

And he sets off for the garage.

As soon as I was out of the car, having taken a shower and rubbed essence of sage and rosemary all over my body, from head to foot, and joyfully with a spring in my step, I walk through the city... First of all, slowly... like a tourist who wishes to enjoy the things he is rediscovering, that he loves... Ah! what a city!... What joy!... What tranquillity I have!... For the one hundred thousandth time, with phrases which I know, and you know so well, I bless the invention of the motorcar and its incomparable benefits... I tell myself:

"What a wonder! You set off when you want to. You stop where you want to. No more tyrannical timetables, which drag you from your bed too early, which have you arrive at ridiculous hours of the night in filthy and dangerous stations. No more promiscuity, in tight cells, with intolerable people, with their dogs, their suitcases, their smells, their quirks... Would

I come so often to Amsterdam, if I had to suffer, for a whole night, in a carriage, the horror of this proximity and the danger of this breath, when one can have the vivifying air of the grassland or the forest? Oh no!… And the free strolls, the beautiful, delightful strolls!… The polder, the polder!…"

And as I say that, without really noticing it, with each step that pushes and pulls me, I am walking more quickly… still more quickly… My loins are as elastic as new rubber; the soles of my shoes, on the cobblestones, on the pavements, rebound, before me, behind me, like tennis balls… I run to catch them… I run… I run…

Do I begin with the museums?… with these magnificent museums in which, before the genius of Rembrandt and of Vermeer, I came to forget Parisian art exhibitions, the aesthetically poor, breathless and mad exhibitions of our aesthetes… Rooms, rooms, rooms, in which I seem to be motionless and in which the paintings pass by with such speed that I can barely glimpse their muddled and mingled images… And a moment later, without really knowing how it happens, I find myself walking along the canals, the canals with their dead waters, bronzed and feverish, on which glide, similar to Chinese junks, these massive and beautiful Dutch barges, which project on the black surface, the green, acid and moving reflection of their convex prows.

Now, here I am in squares, in streets, in alleyways, which criss-cross one another, these prodigiously coloured streets, in which there are strings of cantilevered houses, of such a supple design, tall facades, narrow and pointed, which lean towards one another, strangle one another, crush one another. Twice, three times I crossed the Dam… I am still walking, and, in front of shop windows, I catch myself looking at a mad image passing by, an image of vertigo and speed: my image.

And now we have gardens, with beds of tulips… enormous brick monuments… banks that look like citadels, the Stock Exchange, completely red, more canals, canals, bridges, bridges, and more houses that dance and collapse, and, two strides from the Kalverstraat, I have the little Catholic beguinage, invisible, silent, completely lost amongst the lively and busy shops, with its tiny church, its narrow triangular gardens, so sad to be without greenery and flowers, its little houses with green gables, on the threshold of which, sitting and crammed beneath their flat headdresses, very old women, who do not look at you, who never look at anything, who have never looked at anything...

I continue walking... And now, I am at the harbour...

It is now evening... A damp, very cold wind is blowing. In the mist all I can see are twinkling red, yellow, green lights, very pale, over the canal... The sirens do not stop sounding out, like lost dogs in the night. Then, I get deeper into the almost unknown districts of the harbour, where one can find down-market hotels, noisy music cafés, a whole strange, dirty and frozen Indies, a half-Northern, half-Javanese carnival, which grates on your nerves with its shrill and creeping music, grabs your throat with its odours of marine salinity, of tar, of alcohol, of opium, of petroleum, of fetid rags, of black or coppery skin, where, here and there, around a raised arm, an ankle in the air, a gold circle glistens... What do I know?...

For everything is new, in Amsterdam, everything arrests your progress, with its multiple, tragic and far-off aspects... But I do not stop... I do not stop anywhere... I push away a negress who has clung to me and, with her fat lips reddened with betel, is whispering in my face words of licentiousness, a smell of death... And I walk... I walk without knowing where I am going... I retain the vague memory of dark, obscure brasseries, with chapel-like ceilings, in which faces of shadow and silence watch crowds continually passing by, beneath blinding lights, like the projections from a magic lantern... And then nothing... nothing except things which slip by... which disappear... which twirl like curls... and sway like waves...

Once back at the hotel, tired out, exhausted, my head bursting with the pressure of all the truncated images I have crammed in, images which are vainly trying to link to one another, I have but one obsession: get away, get away… Oh! Get away…

Brossette is waiting for me there… He is chatting with the doorman. He is playing the part of the hero… With expressive gestures, he is describing bends, extravagant speeds, is recounting admirable journeys that he has never made, and during which his sang-froid, his courage, his knowledge as a mechanic saved me from death… I am so happy to see him there, that I want to kiss him.

"Well, my dear Brossette… Is the car ready?"

"Yes, Monsieur."

"In that case… tomorrow morning… at seven o'clock on the dot, Brossette… We will be leaving… we will be leaving…"

Brossette is not surprised… he is used to the sudden changes in my plans… Besides, he cannot prevent himself—but discreetly—showing how pleased he is… I know that he does not like Amsterdam. He told me one day, when he was feeling down:

"It is not a city for a driver…"

He prefers Trouville, Dieppe, Monte-Carlo, Ostend… That's where there are real garages… He especially prefers the Avenue de la Grande-Armée, the driver's real homeland.

He asks me:

"Is Monsieur returning to Paris?"

"Yes, yes… And non-stop, Brossette… non-stop…"

"Monsieur is right to do so."

As he steps away, he shrugs:

"And please let Monsieur not talk to me about a country where they fill you up with petrol from a barrel."

And then doubtless he also suffers from vertigo when he is not in his machine, his hands on the steering wheel… That is where calm returns to his soul and to mine…

He knew what to expect, this cunning Brossette, for in spite of my orders, he had only got my suitcase out of the car…

Ah, what shall I do whilst waiting for tomorrow? For I feel that I shall not sleep… In spite of the calm of this hotel, all my nerves are vibrating and trembling… I am like the engine one has put in neutral, without switching it off, and which is still vibrating…

The Garage.

Charles Brossette? He is well worth a digression…

But before talking about him, I must say a word about the milieu in which was born and developed this new zoological species: the mechanic.

Motoring is a trade different from all others, a trade which slightly resembles that of gambling dens and all-night restaurants. When it began, it appealed exclusively to the world of pleasure and luxury. And so, inevitably, automatically, it gathered around itself roughly the same cast of characters: hollow-faced partygoers, gentlemen always asking for money, sporty puppets straight out of the albums of Sem,[1] teasing kept women and pimps, the whole brilliant fast society, that whole underworld in flowery waistcoats, living off thousands of obscure, unholy activities resulting from gallantry and gambling, of which powder rooms, salons are the commonplace offices. The 'great names of France,' those propping up dead religions and disappeared monarchies, who would blush if they conducted legitimate trades, indulge the most gladly in the world in the worst, clandestine trades, provided that their elegance does not suffer too much thereby, publicly, and that their traditional principles are thereby reassured. For it is false to say that they are decaying, these gentlemen; they are continuing. And so, they frenetically rushed into motoring. This duke, this viscount, who was painfully eking out a living, procuring for

---

1 Sem, real name Georges Goursat, was a caricaturist.

Americans, for rich bankers, fake old furniture, tarted up old knick-knacks, paintings of doubtful provenance and, sometimes, ladies to sleep with or to marry, began to sell motorcars, to embellish, with their financially remunerated presence, the garages which were set up, a little everywhere, for the exploitation—what I really mean is—the robbery of the new client.

These garages trained teams of mechanics. They taught them vague knowledge about driving and the maintenance of engines; above all, they skilfully taught them how to make them go wrong, in the same way that the coachman of a great house makes his horses' harness go wrong, so that it has to be replaced and he can thereby make large profits from the sale of the old and the purchase of the new. They taught them admirable methods, the most varied tricks, which gave rise to increasing one hundredfold the supply of tools, of spare parts, to making money from oil and petrol, to exploiting the fragility of tyres, just as the coachman I mentioned makes money from oats, hay, straw... It was a school for downgrading morality in which, each one dragging the other down, the old rascal encouraging the timid newcomer, each one gradually lost the proportional sense of money, the most basic notion of the value of raw or worked junk. It was so mad that what once was worth two sous, here was worth, without anyone being too surprised, twenty francs. I remember a bill in which a motorcar headlamp-maker was charging me one hundred francs for simply welding a headlamp, a job which could not have been worth more than three... This spare part, priced at that time at eighty francs, is nowadays priced at seven francs in the catalogues—illustrated by Helleu[1]—of the dearest companies. The rest, in proportion.

There was no risk either for the mechanic or the garage, for they were certainly banking on the ignorance of the client, who could be easily rendered silent with a fine technical expression:

---

1 Paul Helleu (1859-1925) was a painter and printmaker and also a friend of Mirbeau.

"But, Monsieur, it's the sliding gear. It's the camshaft… It's the clutch cone… It's the differential… The differential, Monsieur… just think!"

Confronted with these terrible words, what could he do?… He paid… And paid… He was even proud enough to say to his friends:

"I am delighted with my car… It's going very well… Yesterday, I had a problem with my differential…"

Nowadays when the motoring business is developing everywhere, is attracting fantastic competition, is tending to revert to the normal conditions of other businesses, the garages want to restrain the evil they have unleashed… Thus, the established crooks, the aging kept women aspire to the respectability of a decent, regular existence. In the hope of ending part of the abuses which were beginning to discredit even them, the association of constructors of motorcars has decided ruthlessly not to pay commissions to mechanics for the repairs of the cars that they bring in. A little everywhere precautions are being taken, to reduce to admissible percentages the rate of these usurious profits. One sees in garages those who were the most tenacious yesterday, in teaching mechanics the best methods of banditry, preaching to them today, with conviction, the beauties of moderation and unselfishness, the enthusiastic respect for morality. The garages are shouting to them:

"It is not enough to be honest, my friends, and to have a clear conscience."

It remains to be seen whether people, in the habit of having earnings which, even if they were immoral, have none the less increased their standard of living, improved their well-being, created a caste which is the envy of other workers, will give them up so easily…

One day, Brossette, with whom I was discussing these matters, said to me:

"Well, Monsieur, so what?… So what?… These are all stories about rich people… So what?"

And yet Brossette is conservative, nationalist, Catholic. Apart from *L'Auto*,[1] he only reads *La Libre Parole*[2]… Even to-day, like any decent man, he still firmly believes that Dreyfus was a traitor.

My Driver.

Brossette—Charles-Louis-Eugène Brossette—was born in Touraine, in a little village near Amboise. Until he was twenty, he worked with his father, a farrier, and there he learned at the same time his love of horses and his love of 'mechanical things': the two things which have made him. When he had finished his military service, and with his father, one of the noted drunks of the region, having died, young Charles Brossette went as a carter to a large farm, then as a coachman with a rich bourgeois family. He really liked horses, knew everything about them, drove them and looked after them himself, but he hated the livery. His various bosses always endured the fact that he said he was 'trussed up like a chicken'. He has not changed, in fact.

When people begin to talk about the motorcar, Brosssette understands immediately that there is something to be done 'in that business'. He has savings—for, contrary to the laws of heredity, he is sober and even a little miserly—he goes off to Paris to learn this new trade, in a garage. He is intelligent, skilful; he is passionate about it. This provincial clodhopper is soon teaching the cheekiest Parisian rogues. He goes from factory to factory, from garage to garage, familiarises himself with all types of cars, drives around kept women, stockbrokers, dukes, goes on journeys, takes part in the abduction of girls and in the trials of tourism.

---

1 *L'Auto* was founded in 1900 as a sporting daily newspaper by Henri Desgrange. As a publicity stunt it organised the first Tour de France in 1903.
2 *La libre parole* was a nationalistic, anti-Semitic daily paper. It was opposed to the campaign in favour of Dreyfus.

He had just come back from America, rather disillusioned, when I met him. He was looking for a car and I was looking for a mechanic. During our discussions, I asked him what he thought about America.

"Nothing to write home about, Monsieur," he replied. "America? Well… it's like Aubervilliers… on a grand scale!"

First of all, I found it difficult to get used to him… Then I did get used to him, as one does to a vice.

Brossette is the product of the garage system.

He has difficulty distinguishing what belongs to me and what belongs to him, and readily confuses my wallet with his. For three years, the extraordinary thing is that the petrol tank of his cars, thanks to a diabolical fate, always has holes, invisible holes, through which fuel flows and disappears, and which cannot be stopped… By a regrettable example, and an even rarer contagion, the oil sump perfectly imitates its neighbour.

At the end of each month, when Brossette brings me his ledger, each time we have the same conversation…

"Let's see, Brossette, I don't understand this at all. On Tuesday 17th, you put down fifty-five litres of petrol."

"Yes…"

"Good. On Wednesday 18th, another fifty-five litres…"

"Of course…"

"Good… But do you not recall?… On Wednesday we did not go out…"

"That's true… nevertheless!"

"And I see that, on Thursday 19th, there is another fifty-five litres…"

"Naturally… Monsieur knows… This blasted fuel tank!"

"And oil? You are not asking me to believe…"

"The sump as well!… It's easy to understand… They are both escaping… It's all running away…"

"Well, repair them, for goodness' sake!"

"But that's all I do, Monsieur! It's killing me… It's killing me… It's not possible!"

It is painful for me to catch this decent boy in the act of lying and stealing… And yet, what?… That's just stories about rich people… I remain silent and I pay…

Moreover, Brossette has virtues which make me excuse his professional practices. He is an excellent travelling companion, cheerful, resourceful, attentive without being servile, and if one puts his slight accounting fantasies on one side, very faithful. He amuses me, and with him I enjoy the most complete security. He has an imperturbable sang-froid, prudence, and, when necessary, boldness. He never gets tired, and maintains his good humour in all circumstances… You should see him arguing with cycling policemen and gendarmes, that he dazzles with his picturesque politeness, with the result that he nearly always gets away with the most obvious traffic offences…

And then, he loves his machine; he is proud of it; he talks of it as of a beautiful woman.

Last month we were coming back from Bordeaux at night. Between Blois and Chartres 'we punctured'… four times…; beyond Versailles, near Ville-d'Avray, for the fifth time, a tyre burst. I was annoyed, anxious to get home. Besides, I was feeling really sorry for poor Brossette.

"Too bad!" I said to him… "Let's drive on like that!…"

He had stopped the car:

"No, Monsieur, that's impossible…" he said. "That puts too much pressure on the differential…"

And he began working, helping his spirit along with a song.

In the imagination of lady cooks and maids, mechanics have a prestige that is almost as irresistible as that of the military. This prestige has a noble cause; it arises from the very trade they judge to be heroic, full of dangers, and which they compare to that of warfare. For them, a man continually cast through space, like a tempest or a cyclone, has something of the superhuman about him. They remember having seen prints in which warlike angels are blowing long trumpets, to excite the murderous frenzy of armies, or little chubby-cheeked gods whose breath was lifting the sea, bringing down the trees in forests, carrying mountains away, like straw foetuses… I think that they have a similar idea about the motorcar mechanic.

Yet Brossette is not handsome. His look has nothing exciting about it, and which might arouse, in the mind, such allegories, such prodigies. He stoops, has a flat chest, his legs are thin and slightly knock-kneed. It looks as though his very short moustache is suffering from hair loss. If he did not have quite an attractive smile, which sometimes gives him a look of jovial malice, a look of witty and jokey gaiety, his face would offer no special charm to amorousness. His untidy dress, his clothes the most frequently dirty and dishevelled, his cap pulled down at the back over his neck, his heavy and stiff workman's gait, do not create dreams of voluptuousness and glory…

Well! He has plenty of fans in the household.

The cook adores him, and the maid is mad about him. He is looked after like a pasha; he is spoiled like a child. One fills him with little dishes lovingly concocted, and treats; the other is solely occupied with looking after his wardrobe, his linen… He is overwhelmed with all sorts of gifts, and my boxes of cigars go that way, one after the other. He goes along with it, good-naturedly, cheerfully, without too much enthusiasm, as someone who is blasé about all these favours. As a result of taking care of his strength and his marrow, Brossette does not have a lover's temperament. In love, he prefers rather light-hearted escapades, which do not commit you, and little gains. He willingly gives up the rest.

Of course, this does not happen without terrible scenes of jealousy. Often the two rivals threaten one another, grab each other's hair. There is such a noise of saucepans and crockery, that to stop these mad women, I am obliged to dismiss them:

"Listen, Brossette… you are a nightmare… You are turning everything upside down in my home. I no longer have a house. Henceforth, you will lodge and take your meals elsewhere."

And he replies philosophically:

"Monsieur is correct… At least I will be able to read *L'Auto* when I want to… But you know!… nothing will change… That's what they are like, Monsieur… Ah! these blasted women, how annoying they are!…"

When we are on a journey, he is bombarded with letters… He scarcely reads them, shrugging his shoulders… He never replies to them… But he does write copiously to his friends, to whom he recounts his moving adventures, more and more extraordinary feats, and he keeps for them a book of 'average speeds', never actually attained, do I have to say?

What I admire in Brossette is the strength of his eyesight which allows him to see, from kilometres away, the smallest obstacle in the road; what I especially admire is the astounding, mysterious sense of direction. This faculty which seems a miracle, may be explained, is explained by very clear physical reasons for pigeons, wild ducks, swallows… But how can you explain it with Brossette? And he, who likes boasting about everything, on this point shows a modesty that surprises me… I do not think about it… do not talk about it… That's how it is… He has always been like that… There you are… Often I observe him, his hand scarcely touching the steering wheel, his face serious and wrinkled, keeping an eye in turn on the grease pump, the voltmeter, the pressure gauge, the countryside… his ear listening to the smallest noises of the engine, he drives, without ever worrying about the milestones, or the signposts on which the arrows show the way… At crossroads he raises his head a little… He looks at the horizon, sniffs the wind, then resolutely takes one of the four or six roads in front of him… It is always the right one… He never makes a mistake…

Two years ago… We were returning from Marseille. We had stopped in Lyon one day… Brossette was particularly cheerful… I had never seen him so cheerful. I remarked about it to him.

"It's the machine, Monsieur… It's going like an angel… That gives me pleasure."

We left Lyon early in the morning. I thought about return-ing via Dijon, where I intended to lunch at a friend's house… I soon noticed that we were not on the right road… But Brossette said to me with tranquil assurance:

"Please don't worry, Monsieur!… It's fine… It's fine."

He was so sure that he was right that I did not dare insist any further… However, I did not stop saying to myself: "We are on the wrong road… We are on the wrong road."

The weather was cool… almost cold. No sun in the sky… no mist either… a limpid, grey atmosphere in which everything took on delicate colorations… My heart rejoiced… The ma-chine was ardent, excited by a regular, strong carburation… And we were going… we were going… There were landscapes, villages, towns, hills that we passed by at top speed, which I was sure we had never encountered before; at least, never encoun-tered between Lyon and Dijon… Two hours… three hours… four hours. From the shape of the terrain, from the type of faces, I felt that we were getting close to Touraine, or that we were already in Touraine, that perhaps we had already passed through it.

We had to stop in a town to fill up with petrol. I looked at the map… Blimey! What was I saying?… Triumphantly I showed the map to Brossette, happy to catch him in the wrong for once.

I was so surprised that it did not cross my mind to ask him for an explanation… Besides, as soon as the car door had opened, Brossette had disappeared…

What asylum?… Why this asylum?… what was he going to do in this asylum?… Had my mechanic suddenly gone mad?

Through the gate that was ajar I saw gardens and, at the bottom, a large, completely white house… Old people were in groups in front of the house. Old folk were walking with little steps along the paths in the garden…

Brossette appeared again, a broad smile on his face. He was supporting a very old woman, fat, short, wrinkled, bent over, who was walking painfully with the help of a stick. He led her right up to me, and said to me with a look which was asking to be forgiven, at the same time as his face lit up with happiness:

"Well, I really did want you to meet my mother, Monsieur… It's my mother, Monsieur!"

And speaking to the old woman:

"Look, Mam… It's Monsieur… Say hello to Monsieur!"

The old woman seemed worried by our wolf skins, our goggles raised on to the visors of our caps… Round, haggard, her eyes went from me to her son who, in truth, she did not recognise beneath this apparel bristling with white and black hairs… Finally, she warbled, indignantly:

"My goodness is it possible!… Ah!… Masks!… Masks!"

Brossette burst out laughing, but a nice laugh full of tenderness.

"Mam! Oh! Mam!… That amazes you, hey?… And look… that… that's a motorcar… It's me, your son… who drives it… Just look at it a bit… You have perhaps never seen them, motorcars?… Look at this…"

He started up the engine, made it give out a terrible roar. The old woman, terrified, wished to go back in. She was crying:

"My goodness!… My goodness!"

Brossette calmed her down by kissing her and slipping two louis into her hand.

"Come on, say goodbye to Monsieur… We have to be on our way… But we will be back soon… We will come to see you again…"

He confided his mother to a supervisor who was waiting, near the door, kissed her again, tenderly…

"Keep well, Mam…"

And he jumped into the car:

"Seventy-seven years old, Monsieur!… And crafty… crafty!… You understand?… all on her own at that age… so I put her here… she is well looked after… she is happy…"

Then:

"Monsieur has been good to me… I thank Monsieur… Truly… Monsieur is a fine gentleman…"

He added, after he had checked his grease pump:

"If Monsieur is hungry, we can lunch in Amboise… It's ten minutes from here…

As we drove through the village slowly, he was pointing out the houses… calling to the people.

"There!… That's Prosper… Good day, Prosper!… There is my father's forge… Now it's a café… There, Monsieur. In Tivoli… yes that's where it was… Well, old Vazeilles… you have caught the sun…That's my uncle, the short, fat man in front of the grocers… Good day, uncle!…"

Touched and in his glory, he sat up squarely in the motorcar.

When we had driven past the last house, he turned to me and said as 'he put his foot down':

"A pretty spot, isn't it?… It hasn't changed…"

That month, as I examined his ledger, I discovered without too much surprise and without the slightest irritation that Brossette had easily got back the forty francs given to his mother. I must say, to be fair to him, that there had been a struggle in his mind. Very fresh surcharges visibly indicated that he had only decided on this recovery quite late… I was grateful to him. But habit had been stronger than gratitude… Once more, his self-interest triumphed over his emotion. But, after all, was he not right?… It's just a story of rich people, isn't it?

Good old Brossette!…

Borders.

It was not without apprehension that, one fine morning in April 1905, we started off, my friends and I, in our marvellous, ardent, supple C.-G.-V.

Not far from Saint-Quentin, where we were supposed to make the obligatory little pilgrimage to see the pastels of La

Tour, stones were thrown at us… At La Capelle, gendarmes, hiding behind glasses of absinthe in a café, arrested us and menacingly demanded the car's papers. After an interminable discussion during which, once again, I admired the fine uniform, the fine language, the impeccable logic of the French authorities, despite Brossette's verve, we got two traffic offences, the first for speeding, the second because the number at the back, the 628-E8, had, on the road, gathered a little dust that partly obscured it. I suppose that gendarmes do have to enliven a little their gloomy time spent in cafés… As we were arriving in Givet, a raised fortress against incursions by Belgians, an urchin, from the top of a mound, caused a large log of wood to roll down beneath the wheels of the car, making us skid dangerously to avoid it…

And yet we were in France, gentle France, the France of progress, of generosity, of wit! Comforting ideas! What could happen to us in Holland, my friends were thinking, or especially in Germany, where it is acknowledged by the most learned historians of *La Patrie*[1] that the shapeless beings that people these two countries are still savages?…

In vain did I reassure them… They were not so calm.

They had been told:

"Ah! you are going to have problems!… In Holland, the Batavians consider you to be curious, evil beasts, get roused, become excited, set traps… And then push you into the canal… As for Germany, it's an even more dangerous country… Remember the war of 1870… It's terrifying what's going to happen to you!"

They had been told terrifying anecdotes about the hostility of populations, the implacable strictness of regulations, the bloody tyranny of the authorities… It seemed that it would have been easier and less dangerous to go to Mecca, to the Peterhof Palace or to Lhasa, than to Cologne or to Essen…

---

1 An anti-Dreyfusard, anti-Semitic daily paper.

"And the roads!... They are positively pre-historic... No highways authorities in those countries... no civil engineering!... Just imagine, for a moment, that you are not murdered by the people; that you emerge, almost intact, your motorcar and you, from the clutches of the authorities... you will never escape from those roads... Cesspools... bogs... abysses... A certain accident... probably prison... possibly death... That's what lies in wait for you... But you don't know the Germans. Remember, during the war, in the country, we had to house a squadron of uhlans... Do you remember what they did?... They ate the sludge from our carriages... Yes, indeed... that's what they are like, my friend..."

They had therefore hesitated for a long time about coming with me on this journey, which, for all sorts of reasons, attracted them... Therefore, before we set off, they had armed themselves copiously with all the political, diplomatic, military, customs advice...We had wallets stuffed with certificates, attestations, and admirable letters written in a very fine hand, decorated with impressive red seals. The Dutch papers said: "We request the authorities, etc." The German ones said: "Order is given to the authorities." In that there was a fairly reassuring nuance... But when the time came to put them to the test, how much weight would they have in the face of so much barbarity?...

The German Customs Post.

Which happened, when we crossed the German border, at Elten...

We had spent a wonderful month, an enchanted month, in Holland, in gentle, bright Holland, still delighted by its landscapes of sky and of water, by its sloping towns, by its museums. Nothing unpleasant had happened to us. Quite the opposite. Here a reserved but benevolent welcome; there, enthusiastic hospitality. Even in Friesland, where a motorcar is an almost unknown animal, where Dutch curiosity can sometimes appear awkward, we aroused a sort of respectful astonishment... At least, I preferred to call it astonishment... When you are driving along Frisian roads, all the time you see men passing by with placid faces, leading their admirable horses, whose beautiful, round forms are captured in Dutch paintings, these very black horses, with high necks, with shiny coats, which fit in so well with the countryside and which decorate our Parisian hearses with so much majesty... They would stop to look at us, letting their surprised beasts run riot... I still have the memory of the man who we made, by sounding our horn, turn round in the distance and who no longer worrying about his horse who had left at a gallop, at top speed, on the polder, remained petrified with admiration, motionless at the side of the road, with his hat in his hand...

I was also remembering that at Edam, having left Brossette in charge of the motorcar, so we could take the water coach to Volendam, we had been suddenly surrounded by the inhabitants of the whole village; there were pretty, smiling girls, adorned with jewels and lace; we were especially uneasy about the men. These colossuses, calm and clean-shaven, very handsome in their lambskin bonnets and their ample, puffed breeches, made me think of those peasant heroes, their ancestors, who kicked out of their Republic our hot-headed Louis XIV, his dashing cavalry squadrons, his well-trained infantry regiments, his kitchens and his ladies, not without retaining a few banners and flags, and a few decorated cannons. I imagined that they examined these trophies with the same proud and conquering look as their descendants gave to our machine... When we got back from Volendam, I learned from Brossette that he had been treated royally and that these decent people had offered him a banquet.

"Only," explained Brossette, "...I had to take some of them for a drive... the local notables... and give them a little lecture about the mechanism..."

"So, you speak Dutch?" I asked him…

"No, Monsieur… But one can use gestures… It's the same… they are characters, you know!… I wouldn't trust them…"

Yes, but Germany? Its roguish customs officials, its terrible officers, its pitiless police? The trials would soon begin. I regretted! Oh! How I regretted, at this moment, that I did not have the quixotic soul of M. Déroulède,[1] so that I could, with one gesture, wipe this barbaric country from the map of the world!

Coming from Arnhem, we arrived at Elten at about four o'clock in the afternoon. For a long time, I looked to see where the customs house might be… I was shown a small, modest and familial building, and we were surprised to find it empty… I knocked on the doors and called out in vain several times… With difficulty I finally discovered a woman, sitting in the corner of a room and peacefully mending her stockings… She had large spectacles, a venerable, gentle face. She was deaf. Near her a ginger cat was sleeping, curled up on an old cushion… An earthenware pot was singing on the stove. In vain did I inspect the room, not the slightest military equipment anywhere… no rifle rack full of rifles… no pointed helmet… not even a portrait of Kaiser Wilhelm on the walls… I thought that I must have made a mistake. With much difficulty, I made the woman understand what brought me there.

"Yes… yes," she said, getting up with difficulty… "This is the right place…"

She put her spectacles and her sewing down on a table laden with papers, registers, accounting books. The cat woke up and stretched voluptuously… Smiling, she said:

"It's fine weather to be travelling… Na!… Come with me… It's close by…"

We crossed the street. She bade me enter a pub where a fat man, with a very red face and short legs, was smoking his large

---

1 Paul Déroulède (1846-1914) was a poet and nationalistic politician as well as an anti-Dreyfusard. He founded the *Ligue des Patriotes* in 1882. Mirbeau fought a duel with him in 1883.

pipe, sitting in front of a pint of beer… Although he was on his own, he seemed to be having an extraordinarily good time. Was he thinking perhaps of our defeats, of his victories? For what else can Germans think about? The woman spoke a few words to him.

"Ah, ha!" said the fat man… "Very well… very well! We'll see about that…"

I noticed that, on his head, he rather comically had an English-style cap, which stuck closely to his skull, and that his faded clothes only looked like a uniform because of three copper buttons and a border where remnants of the red colour appeared with long gaps between them… We went out.

He walked around the car, examined it with happy curiosity… Brossette followed him, ready to open the trunks as soon as he was asked to… I took the famous wallet from my pocket… And this was the dialogue that ensued between a French citizen and a German customs officer:

"Does it drive well?

"Quite well…"

"Quickly?"

"Quite quickly, yes."

"Thirty kilometres an hour?"

"Oh, more than that… more than that…"

"Good Lord!… It's beautiful… beautiful…"

He passed his hand over the bulb of the klaxon, puffed out his cheeks, blew:

"Parp? Parp?…"

"Yes…"

"It's nice… and you are going to Krefeld?"

"No… to Dusseldorf…"

"To Dusseldorf?… Good Lord!… Well, get a move on… Parp!… Parp… Parp!"

He touched me on the shoulder in a friendly way:

"French, hey?…"

"Yes…"

He shook me warmly by the hand and, indicating the road:

"Dusseldorf… the first on the right… At Emmerich you cross the Rhine on the ferry… Parp! Parp!"

I asked:

"Is the road bad?"

"Bad?… It's like waxed parquet flooring… Parp!"

Before making our turn, following the instructions of the customs officer, I looked back… I saw him standing in the middle of the road, waving his cap in the air as a signal of bon voyage.

It took us a long time to recover from our surprise.

"That must be hiding something terrible," said one of us… "Be careful, Brossette… And not so fast!"

And that is how we came into Germany.

Towards Rocroy.

For the moment we have not even crossed the Belgian border, and we are still driving towards Givet.

The first disagreeable day.

After Compiègne the wind had suddenly got up, a north wind, bitter and strong, which did not help our progress and was sending in twists towards us, on the road, small cyclones of dust… As long as we were driving along the Oise, leaving it only to come back to it, with the freshness of its valley, the surprise of its charming ports, the movement of its river boats, everything was fine. But beyond Saint-Quentin, where our patriotism contented itself with admiring Latour and never thought for one minute, alas! of paying the slightest attention to M. Anatole de la Forge,[1] the landscape became morose. And so did we. Scarcely more than fields of beetroot, sparsely plant-ed… It seemed as though the countryside was becoming wrin-

---

1 Anatole de la Forge (1820-1892) had successfully organised the defence of Saint-Quentin in October 1870.

kled, shrivelled, colourless beneath the aridity of the wind… It looked ugly, like a bedroom that has not been tidied for a long time… A few villages, no towns, except Guise which did not seem to me to be the industrial Eldorado, celebrated by good old Fournière and created by good old Godin.[1] Away in the distance, sleepy hamlets, dozing farms; here, a brickyard; there, an abandoned distillery… and the road, the monotonous road, idle, almost deserted. We scarcely encountered anything other than the tall, heavy carriages of the liqueur makers, who were off, with a noise of rattling bottles, to bring to the rare humans living in these regions sadness, illness and death.

The less a region works, the more it would seem that one meets these moving liqueur providers. No doubt this comes from the fact that they are the only ones we meet.

I noticed that almost all the old châteaux are deserted… Their owners can no longer make a living out of them. Some are being used as sanatoriums for poor people, or children's holiday camps; they have returned to the common people, and that is the best thing for them. Others fall into ruin and die in their circle of brambles. Nobody wants them any more. Times are hard for the idleness of knights. On market days, on Sundays, at mass, you still see them strutting in the town, with their breeches of worn velvet, riding whips, boots, spurs which they still make ring proudly on the pavement. But they no longer have a horse, because oats are dear; and they no longer have anything, because to have something, you have to earn it by working. They content themselves with the pretence of luxury and chic, with which they can still feed their fallen pride, their quixotic faith… But happy, when returning from the fair, on the road, they meet a peasant who agrees to bring them home in his cart, along with his pig!… I am talking about Brittany, Le Perche, the Nivernais, where there are still châteaux dirtier

---

1 Eugène Fournière was a socialist writer and Godin a factory owner whose factory was based on the socialist principles of Charles Fourier.

than pig sties, inhabited by knights, poorer than beggars… But here it seems that there are no more knights, who have come back with their whips, their spurs, their King and their God, in the great whole that is the past.

Sometimes, on a hilltop, stands a brand-new château, made of brick or stone, with towers, turrets, battlements. You can be sure that it belongs to a successful shoemaker, a rich grocer, who has finally succeeded in realising the anachronistic and lordly dream, which haunted the mind of the proletarian…

A Dead City.

Rocroy, a sonorous name which, in itself, seems to trumpet the youthful glory of Louis XIV.

I have seen dead cities—there are plenty of them in France—but as dead as Rocroy I do not think there are any anywhere in the world. Rocroy is more than a dead city, it is a graveyard; more than a graveyard, it is the graveyard of a graveyard, if such a thing may be imagined. The highway authority which, through national modesty, wished to spare foreign travellers the appalling sight of this decay, downgraded the road that leads to Rocroy. The only thing now leading to Rocroy is a sandy, bumpy path, taken by nobody, and on which greyish grass is growing: the old road. The new road bypasses it by a few kilometres, serving villages that are more alive and countryside that is less gloomy. Yet, Rocroy still exists on maps, by habit, I think, or perhaps through charity, just as sometimes in the budgets of the State, there continue to be grants allocated to services that have been discontinued, or to dead people… I cannot get my head round the idea that the government can find civil servants useless enough to be sent—deputy-prefects, judges, tax collectors, etc.—to this necropolis. I imagine that they are recruited—still with difficulty—amongst the former concierges of historic châteaux and caretakers of disused cemeteries... As far as the few minor characters are concerned, whose role is to play the part of the locals, where are they from? From which hospitals? From which mortuaries?... From which wax museums?

And note that, through an audacious irony, Rocroy is given, in our system of departmental geography, the title of the centre of the arrondissement... Perhaps one should rather call it the centre of shrinkage...

We arrived there by chance, or rather by mistake, for in spite of Brossette, who is never deceived by his instinct, I desperately wanted to believe that the afore-mentioned bumpy road had to be a short cut, and that, by taking it, we would save distance and time in order to get to Fumay.

Unfortunately! It was Rocroy.

But I have no regrets. Agreeable sights are not the only useful ones, and we have learned, from Roman history, that nothing excites the mind, elevates the heart, more than meditating about ruins.

Rocroy still has its ramparts and its two gates. Although they were built by Vauban, who after all had imagination and a sense of the picturesque, they are not tremendous, nor are they decorative. The city is, so to speak, no more than a square, a small lugubrious and silent square, around which houses, which do not even have the prestige of ancient architecture, are falling apart, are peeling away, are exfoliating like poor faces suffering from dermatitis. It is black, mangy, frighteningly empty. I cannot recall having seen a tree, a fountain, a kiosk. In vain would you search, even in a shop or a café, for a memory of the great Condé[1]... Ah! The Spaniards can come to Rocroy without the slightest humiliation. Nothing here recalls the memorable thrashing they got here; no trophy in the town hall, no cannon on the ramparts... But what would Spaniards come to Rocroy

----

1 Louis, known as the Great Condé, won a victory over the Spanish in Rocroy in 1643.

for? They have enough dead cities, at home, old Saracen cities, porcelain cities that the sun, each morning and each evening, animates with marvellous, flaming reflections.

When we crossed this square, we saw a few phantoms, sitting on chairs or on benches, on the threshold of doors, in front of shops, the majority of which moreover were closed. They were not moving, not talking, not looking. They did not even raise their heads at the noise of the motorcar.

In the smallest villages, deep in the countryside, a stray dog, a vagabond passing by, a vendor's cart, a flight of wild geese, all these are a considerable event. And even more so, a car… people are worried, people gather around unusual sights which, for a moment, interrupt the monotony of these trapped existences.

In Rocroy, they were worried by nothing, looked at nothing, and were so perfectly still that we thought they might be rag dolls and that, if we touched them lightly, they would fall on the pavement with a dull sound… Our surprise increased when we discovered that the shop fronts were decorated with signs such as these: "Parisian grocery… Parisian bakery… Parisian delicatessen…" I do not know what idea these ghosts have about Paris, whether, for them, Paris symbolises life or death… What I do know is that everything was Parisian, in Rocroy, and that everything was dead.

To begin with, one only sees the funny side of things; it is only after some thought that the tragic appears.

It did not take us long to feel that this ruin and this death were the perfect and painful image of ruin and death, that were the political and military works of Louis XIV, eternally harmful works, later completed by Napoleon, by which miraculously France did not die, but which continually burden it with such a heavy and stifling weight…

Today, respectable and wise historians are undertaking to revisit the history of that abominable century, which, in democratic schools and liberal salons, is still called the great century. Truly, we no longer need to be ashamed of our own century, despite the Academies, severe guardians of the lies of the past.

What are our vices, our corruption, our venality, our poor little Panama scandals, compared with the vices, corruption, bribery, treachery of this famous court that is still held up to be the model of honour, of patriotism, of elegance and of virtue? Scarcely schoolboy pranks... My thought was turning, with a sort of grateful piety, towards our good old radicals and radical socialists who, like the nobility of former times, make up the privileged class of today, the class which, eternally, with different titles but with similar appetites, is stampeding towards, so it is said, the same quarry of honours and money... What decent chaps! And how I love them!... They are affable, polite, moderate in the public expression of their passions, totally against scandal, which is always ugly, against noisy intrigues which are sometimes dangerous. Excellent patriots, solid capitalists, skilful intermediaries between savings and banks, conventional property owners, who then could better defend the immortal principles of social stability, share out more equitably between the big businesses they protect, and the slender needs of the poor to whom they administer the manna of state budgets?... Furthermore, they have education, decency and virtue, a middling culture which makes them capable of carrying out all the brilliant and fruitful mediocre affairs, a moral refinement which makes their conduct of business pleasant and without surprises, electoral habits which bring them close to the people, and which teach even the grumpiest their benevolence and familiarity towards the poor...

Ah! how fine they look, when you compare them, in their severe black jackets, with these great lords, dressed in silk and lace, brutes and cads, ignoramuses and thieves, servants and pimps, whose so vaunted, so regretted elegance consisted of belching in each other's faces, receiving people with their breeches down as they sat on their commodes, daubing themselves with sauces like dogs which poke their nose in their food, cultivating, bacteriologists without knowing it, disgusting vermin beneath their wigs: walking graves, walking filth, who left behind them as they walked through the corridors of Versailles, of Meudon, of the Petit-Luxembourg, a persistent smell of musk and of shit… Prestigious servants of the monarchy and of religion, all they thought about was trading their roles, pillaging the treasury, the general taxes, the salt taxes, the public shops, cheating at cards, betraying their country, bringing their wives, their daughters, their mistresses, to the royal bed, their sons to the august sodomites of the House of France, and, better than on the battlefields where, it is true, they fought like lions, their chivalric pride was enhanced by presenting the chamber pot to the king, to changing his shirts, his breeches, his sheets soiled by the droppings caused by his purgatives…

A monstruous and fetid reign, of which the smell of the latrines, of the brothel, catches in your throat, and makes you feel so sick that you wish to vomit!… Neither the beauty of the palaces, nor the grace of the gardens and parks, nor the glory of de la Rochefoucauld, of Pascal, of de la Bruyère, of Corneille, of Racine, of Molière, nor—which is finer and greater than all that—the powerful, constructive genius of Colbert, nor—the accusatory strength of his confessions, of the portraits of the immortal Saint-Simon, could wipe away the shame and the crimes of it.

And since I was not forgetting that we were in Rocroy, I lingered more obligingly over the features of Colbert the Great, who, according to history, was the most wearisome, the most stupid, the most heroic brute of this century of brutes, and who always sold his sword to the highest bidder, who even sold it to France… Oh glory of Chantilly!

As we left Rocroy where, among so many dead people, I had been reminded of so many memories of a hated past, with what enthusiasm did I dive again—this is an image—into the bath of your refreshing and hygienic virtues, fine radicals and radical socialists of our epoch, so peaceful and so refined!… With what purifying joy, with what consoling devotion did I enjoy evoking your virtuous top hats and your respectable black jackets... of still evoking, always evoking, crowded around M. Fallières—at that time it was M. Loubet[1]—in the finally aerated, finally disinfected apartments at Rambouillet, the elegant features of our contemporary Court!... How reassuring M. Loubet seemed to me!—today it is M. Fallières, a fine, fat winegrower from his land in the South of France.—How charming, moving, antiseptic, I found your new elegance, fine radicals and radical socialists! The fine affair that a vile, frivolous, morose mind observes, so inappropriately, all that this elegance owes to the perfumery of hairdressing salons, to the familial cut of the hairdressers of La Belle-Jardinière!...

Rocroy's death has spread to the surrounding countryside, as gangrene spreads to a neighbouring limb... It gives off a sinister feeling... One thinks one is going to breathe, one chokes even more. Before we got back to the balsamic life of the earth, the splendour of the forest, the turmoil of the Meuse, beside the slate-works of Fumay, we had to cross a wide plateau, a sort of funereal zone, where the ground is stony, lugubriously sterile. In this place the only things that grow are dry, discoloured grass, skinny birch trees no higher than dwarf bushes, and, here and there, gorse bushes without a single flower... Finally, we have a pleasure good enough to sing out in joy, it is like a resurrection, when we get back, through the hairpins in the Ardennes, to the busy river, and we hear the sirens of the tugs pulling the long lines of boats... And everything becomes green again, everything shimmers, everything smells good, everything is toiling, the earth is in flower, the trees in bud, the water, the hills, the houses, the people, the sky; it is all magical as far as Givet.

---

1 Fallières and Loubet were two radical senators.

A Strong City.

What crazy terror did the Belgians instil in us for us to turn Givet into such a fortress?

The city almost disappears beneath the accumulation of its military defences… Small forts nestling on the tops of peaks, fortified terraces, ramparts, fortified casemates, moats, drawbridges, machicolations, watch-turrets, half-moons over the courtine walls, sentry walks, everything that had been invented by ancient and modern science for fortification, Givet has them all… Through the posterns and the covered walkways, one expects to see armed men, encased in iron, suddenly rush out… Ah! the Belgians must be proud to be Belgian as they look at Givet… Through it they are aware of just how redoubtable their military power is… I can easily imagine that, for them, Givet is the best school in which their national arrogance is increased. On Sundays, fathers must bring their children to Givet, and I can hear them telling them:

"Look how we make the world tremble with fear!"

On the other hand, a French officer to whom I was expressing my surprise at this warlike extravagance, explained it to me in these words:

"We have to prevent anyone shouting out, during future wars: 'Ah! here come the Belgians. We are done for!'"

And so many barracks!… What vast esplanades for troops to parade!… So many soldiers!

I have seen battalions and battalions of infantry march past. In battle dress and with bugles sounding, no doubt they were returning from a reconnaissance, perhaps from a combat. And I admired their martial gait, their supple drill… We are certainly well protected!… Everything makes me think today that, faced with such a deployment of force, such a bristling of defences, the Belgian army will, in the future, leave us alone.

"If you wish for peace..." says the Stupidity of nations.

For Nancy they conjure up only a third of the patriotic works carried out at Givet... But it is, of course, true that it is only the Germans...

A Family of Motorists.

Once our surprise was over, and when we were sure that we would not be disturbed by a sudden attack by Belgian army corps, we spent the evening quite cheerfully in a clean hotel, highly recommended by the Touring Club, where we were served a simple, modest meal, a siege meal. The Meuse trout, on the menu, were, at the last moment, replaced by humble deep-fried roach, and roast beef was replaced by cold meats; but all done with such grace that we were delighted with our dinner.

Near to us a whole family were sitting at table: the father, the mother, the daughter, the son. They had also arrived by motorcar, just before us... They had been on the road from Paris for three days and had been stopped, in rather uninhabitable places, by all sorts of mishaps... They were talking about them with acrimony... The mother, especially, was complaining bitterly about the machine:

"It's nothing... it's nothing..." explained the father. "It's a bit sluggish, that's true... It'll warm up..."

She insisted:

"I always said that you should have bought a Charron, like the Levasseurs, or a Panhard, like the Tripiers... They're not fools, are they?... Ah! It's not very pleasant to have breakdowns all the time!"

"It's going to warm up... I tell you again, it's going to warm up... It has to be run in... Of course... You are not being reasonable... It's like a pair of brand-new shoes... they are only comfortable after a week... Ah! women... they want the moon straight away!"

62

"Well, I'm telling you that we'll never get to Brussels in that clog."

He began to laugh noisily and turned to us as if to call on our support:

"Clog!… A Brulard-Taponnier, twelve horsepower! Ha! Ha! Ha!"

"You'll see… you'll see!…"

She had blotchy, flabby skin, was striking poses, and pessimistic. To show off that she had arrived in a motorcar she had kept on her awful goggles, clearly seen on her beige velvet hat. He, short, fat, with round clean-shaven cheeks, a pointed beard, a jovial, vulgar, and decent chap, was proudly wearing a Russian cap decorated with the badges of the Touring Club. It would have been impossible to be more awkward, more stupidly dressed than his daughter. With no freshness, no grace, her pale, prominent ears, poor hair, she already had signs at the front of her mouth of teeth beginning to rot… Where the son was concerned, with a low forehead, receding chin, yellow and very thin, his body weakened by solitary habits, he was a complete moron… A typical French family, as we can see.

As we are travelling, we never cease, we French people, to make fun of German, English, Italian families that we meet on the road and who often give us an example of physical health and good education. With a fierce pleasure and a foolish pride, we enjoy judging, always to our advantage, what we call their ridiculous features, their flaws, which perhaps are only virtues… But it is understood that nothing is as beautiful, elegant, dazzling, witty, nothing is as intelligent as France. The great names from other countries are no more than plain copyists, shameful plagiarists. Dickens owes everything to Alphonse Daudet, Tolstoy to Stendhal… All of Ibsen may be found in *La Révolte*[1] by Villiers de l'Isle-Adam… What would Goethe have been without Gounod and without Thomas?…

---

1 A one-act play withdrawn in 1870 after only five performances.

And, where Heinrich Heine is concerned, please let us not talk about him!… that old spy in the pay of Guizot… The spirit of being French was completely summed up for me by Brossette's exclamation when, one day in Koenigsberg, he said to me:

"The Germans, Monsieur?… what a race of savages!… They don't understand a single word of French…"

Ah! if however, we sometimes thought about looking hard at our own families, our racial inferiority, our alcoholic and syphilitic descendants, our dullness, our hateful or gullible stupidity?

This time, as I looked at this French family sitting at table near us, I thought about it with what painful humility!

They were heading to Belgium. They had never been out of France, and the idea that, the following morning, for the first time, they would cross a border, would enter a country that was not France, this idea was impressing them, was especially disturbing them… They did not know whether they should be afraid, or be happy…

After dinner, once the table had been cleared, the father got into a long conversation about local industries with the owner of the hotel; the mother took a pack of cards from her bag and began a game of patience; the girl riffled through the *Baedeker*, and the son, slumped on his chair, with his mouth open and arms dangling down, was in a deep sleep.

Suddenly the girl asked:

"Mother!… what is the Mannekin-Piss?"

"Please be quiet!" whispered her mother, looking anxiously at us… Please don't say things like that, wretched child!"

But the girl pressed on, ingenuously:

"What things?… But it's in the *Baedeker*!"

"That's not polite, there you are!"

"Why?"

"Because…"

"So, won't we see the Mannekin-Piss?"

"Yes, you will see it… You will see it with your mother… Only, be quiet!"

The father was continuing his education from the owner of the hotel.

"We have here," the latter was saying, "fine limestone quarries… a large factory producing strong glue… tanneries…"

"Tanneries?… Ah!… That's interesting… And canning factories?"

"No, we don't have those… However, we do have a fine rubber factory…"

"Good Lord!… Tell me!… No canning factory?… That's curious!…"

At that moment we realised that this fat gentleman owned, somewhere, a food preserving factory… Despite his decent appearance he must have poisoned people! And perhaps, he had brought up his children on these products and that explained their earthy, unhealthy complexion… Satisfied with this information and these hypotheses, we were just about to retire when the mechanic came in, in his work coat, his hands black with grease…

"Ah! Ferdinand, tell me!… The motorcar!… It's running fine, isn't it?… We leave tomorrow at eight o'clock, my boy,… eight o'clock on the dot… Tell me!… Fill her up… Let's see… Namur!… Sixty kilometres, roughly, hey? No… half a tank-full… That will be enough…"

The mechanic seemed embarrassed, scratched his head:

"It's that," he said, "the machine won't go at all… It won't go any more…"

"Good heavens!… Tell me!… Is it serious?"

"Yes, Monsieur… it's irritating…"

The whole family, including the son who had woken up, were listening to the mechanic…

"How?… What are you saying?… a brand-new machine!"

"Of course… but Monsieur has to understand… once it won't go…"

"I understand… of course, I understand… but… Tell me!… That's not a reason… Look here… Get back to work…"

"You can't work… There is no inspection pit here… and now it's too dark… Tomorrow morning, we'll have a look at it… Ah! I'm really afraid…"

"But no… but no… eight o'clock, hey!… Ah!… only ten litres… We will fill up again after the border…"

He uttered the word 'border' with in a majestic tone. When the mechanic had left, he walked up and down in the room for a few minutes with a furrowed brow… But to hide his worries, with his thumbs tucked into the seams of his waistcoat and nodding his head, he was going on:

"No! no! no!… No! no!"

The mother had an evil smile on her face… she said:

"You'll see… you'll see!"

The daughter asked:

"Father what does that mean: 'it won't go'?"

"My child, it means…"

He stopped, tried for an explanation and not finding one:

"It's nothing…" he said, "nothing at all… With a little bit of grease, it will be alright…"

"Yes! Yes!… count on it…" sniggered the mother, as she stood up.

We went to bed.

The following morning, in the courtyard of the hotel, there was a tragic scene.

The family, all dressed up for the journey, was standing around the Brulard-Taponnier, with its twelve horsepower… We arrived just at the moment that Brossette, from whom his colleague had asked for assistance, was coming out from beneath the car.

"Well?" asked the gentleman, who had put his final hopes in the knowledge of our mechanic…

"Well…" he replied, dusting himself down… "there's nothing to be done… The clutch cone is bent out of shape, and the leather is burned… It will have to go back to the factory."

They were so surprised, all four of them, that they did not even think about protesting or getting annoyed. The silence which followed this judgment was quite poignant… I felt pity for them… Truly, they looked like people condemned to death.

Ferdinand approached his master. I was struck by his devious air. He was verbose.

"Well, I did tell you yesterday evening, Monsieur… Ah! it's very frustrating… I'll take the blasted machine back to Paris, and I'll come back to find Monsieur in Belgium, wherever Monsieur tells me… you can really call that bad luck… but Monsieur can take the railway for a few days, five… six days… a week at most… the time to carry out the repairs!… Unless Monsieur would prefer to wait for me here… It's entirely what Monsieur wishes…"

The owner of the hotel, who was walking round the car, said casually:

"There are some very fine walks around here… Good horses… Comfortable carriages… Moderate prices…"

After a new silence, the gentleman looked at Ferdinand with a timid, begging look:

"Are you really sure?… There are no means?… Tell me… no means?"

"Please listen to my colleague, Monsieur!…"

Brossette, who was washing his hands at the pump, turned his head, and repeated:

"There's nothing to be done…"

Ferdinand moved the bonnet of the engine. They looked at it as though they were hoping for a miracle… But the engine remained silent…

"Well, that's perfect," said, through pinched lips, the lady whose blotchy face, beneath her veil, was made worse with purplish patches… "It's pretty, the Brulard-Taponnier, twelve horsepower!… It's pretty!"

More and more dazed, the gentleman sighed.

"To arrive in Brussels by rail!… Tell me… that's a bit steep…"

The daughter had tears in her eyes. Farewell, perhaps, the Manneken-Piss!… The son was opening and closing the door with an angry and stupid gesture

Listening to the gentle regular noise of our engine that Brossette had just started up, the gentleman in his distress became bold enough to speak to me:

"You are lucky… Ah! you are lucky…"

"The gentleman has a decent car, that's all…" the woman corrected him bitterly… "The gentleman does not have a Brulard-Taponnier, twelve horsepower!…"

Our 626-E8 departed with loud revving up, that Brossette, maliciously, had contrived to make as noisy as possible.

"Poor people!…" I said to Brossette once we were out of the town.

First of all, Brossette did not reply. Then, with a shrug of his shoulders and unable to prevent a little smile which I saw playing at the corner of his mouth:

"What fools, Monsieur!… You know, there is nothing wrong with the car!… Only Ferdinand thinks his wife is cheating on him… He can't get it out of his head… he can't get it out of his head… he wants to go home and catch her out… And since these people know nothing about cars…"

I criticised Brossette strongly for becoming an accomplice in such a horrible deceit.

"Oh! Monsieur… as far as I'm concerned, I think Ferdinand is in the wrong… you don't do things like that… it's better to be a cuckold… But he was stubborn… All the same, I couldn't refuse helping out a mate… And also, people shouldn't be as stupid as that!"

There was a chill in the air; it was an exquisite, fragrant morning… A large boat was sailing upstream on the Meuse, with red splashes… We were driving along quite fast… Gradually I felt my indignation weakening. When we stopped in front of the customs post, the bad instincts that are present in the soul of the motorist had done their work. And it was with a sort of evil joy, of barbaric pleasure, that I enjoyed conjuring up the image, in the courtyard of the hotel, crowded around their silent machine, that distressed family to whom the owner of the hotel was no doubt continuing to say:

"There are nice walks around here!…"

BRUSSELS

There are plenty of reasons to be annoyed for having driven, since we crossed the border, on horrible cobblestones, on immense waves of cobblestones, for having driven through the Borinage which is black and smoky even when the sun is shining, with metal slivers, and which, every night, inflames the night with its bubbling forges, its hellish flames, just to arrive in this city that is so perfectly useless, so completely a parody: Brussels.

Brussels!

Truly, it is intolerable, and a little humiliating to find oneself in this capital of tramway systems for the whole world, the queen of the industry of early-growing asparagus, of bitter chicory and of tasteless hothouse-grown grapes, when Bruges with its lace, Liège with its steel, Louvain with its prayers, Ghent of former times, with its so ancient streets, its painted gables, its coloured roofs and everything recounted to us by the facades of its churches, whispered to us by the old walls alongside the canal; when the tremendous quaysides of Antwerp, Mons swarming with ferocious jaws, Charleroi and its slagheaps crossed by little aerial railways; Furne where those processing from the Saint-Sang walk past, bearing iron crosses, as heavy as their sins, when all this quaintness, all this art, all this tragic movement of travail, all this tumult of the Meuse and the Escaut, all the deathly silence of the béguinages, all these memories of fêtes and of massacres, are just a few turns of a wheel away from here.

And precisely Brussels!

Finally, I am here… I must stay here, if only to heal my bruised ribs and my back injured by so many bumps and jolts by the torture of these roads…

✳

And yet, in the end, you can like Brussels. There is nothing discreditable about so doing.

I know people, poor people, people like everyone else, who live here happily, at least who think that they live here happily, and what's the difference.

Previously I have told the story, I think, of this friend, a resident in a provincial lunatic asylum, who from his bedroom could only see a barracks on the left; on the right, the prison and a works manufacturing chemical products; in front, the hospital and the lycée; nothing but grey stone, sentry walkways, bare courtyards, no greenery, barred windows; he would point out to me, tenderly, above one wall, a small, sick, twisted cherry tree, the only thing that was barely alive, in the midst of this landscape of damnation, and he would say:

"Look, my friend… It's nice here, isn't it?… It's like being in the country."

There are people who think that Brussels really is what a city should look like.

I even know some who would prefer to live there, who regret not living there, for example these joyful lawyers from our thrifty provinces, our amiable financiers from the Rue Pelletier, who currently, at the Dépôt, at Gaillon, at Poissy, at Clairvaux, are reproaching themselves bitterly for not having been able to finalise—legally finalise—those dangerous operations involving breach of trust and forgery. But their species is becoming rarer and rarer. And now that we have had prison reform, instead of Brussels, they prefer humanitarian Fresnes,[1] where comfort and hygiene are not illusory, where work seems recreational and educational, where the modern décor of the cells, the courtyards, the recreational rooms, is bearable, sober and does not bring about nightmares: the first prison where one can chat.

✳

It is possible not to like Brussels. This is actually the case with many of the people who live here, including not the least insignificant.

Just look at King Leopold[2] who is never here, who multiplies his chances of never staying here, who is everywhere, in France, in Italy, in Switzerland, in Germany, in England, who is on a railway train, a yacht, a motorcar, but never in Belgium.

"That is how," he gaily confessed, one evening at the Palace of the Elysée, to one of my friends, who knows how to speak to kings, "I have managed to keep the liveliness of my mind, the assuredness of my taste, and this youthfulness that impresses the ladies so much… And then, besides I have major business activities, in so many countries…"

"And even in Belgium, Monsieur…"

"Yes… I am aware of that…" he said, with a nod, "… in Belgium, I have a people… But I also have an enormous fortune causing me lots of problems… I have to administer it…"

Just look at all these poets, all these writers, all these writers from Brussels and Ixelles who, from an early age onwards, in serried ranks, hurry to desert their capital, and come to Paris doubtless to bring there a little of this savoury accent which our literature still lacks, and there rapidly to obtain their reward in decorations and money so lacking in their own…

And how right they are.

----

1 A large prison near Paris.
2 Leopold II (1835-1909) was King of the Belgians from 1865.

They are right, for I find almost everything in Brussels ridiculous, it makes me and them want to laugh, but a dull laughter, but a stifled laughter, an icy, sad laughter which suddenly makes everything so sad, sad, sad like its wintery sky, its circular boulevards, M. Edmond Picard's[1] books, M. Ivan Gilkin's[2] poems, the book covers of M. Deman,[3] the furniture of M. Vandevelde.[4]

However, Brussels is comic. There are no two ways about it, it is extremely comic, is it not, dear M. Lemonnier,[5] who was, in turn, and with equal enthusiasm and equal joy, Alfred de Musset, Byron, Émile Zola, Chateaubriand, Edgar Allan Poe, Ruskin, all the pre-Raphaelites, all the romantics, all the naturalists, all the symbolists, all the impressionists, and who, today, after so many different glories and so many universal successes, is submitting your old age and your always youthful works in the protection of naturism, and of its young chief M. Saint-Georges de Bouhélier?[6]

❋

At the time of its pomp, at the time when the Dukes of Burgundy were displaying here their barbaric and magnificent luxury, when the infantas and archdukes reigned here on behalf of the Emperor and the King of Spain, Brussels was the shining city of cloth of gold, of velvets, of silks, of furs, the poetic and

---

1 Picard was a left-wing Belgian poet.

2 Gilkin was also a Belgian poet.

3 Deman was a Belgian publisher.

4 Van de Velde began as a neo-impressionist painter but became a furniture designer.

5 Camille Lemonnier was, in his early career, a naturalist novelist.

6 Saint-Georges de Bouhélier was a leading light in the literary naturist movement, proclaiming the end of symbolism.

74

amorous city of lace, which are the most beautifully feminine luxury, the art which is most exquisitely a slave to sensuality. It was the capital of the good life, of good drinking, where comfortable bourgeois, wealthy merchants, well-rounded ladies of easy virtue, boldly enjoyed themselves and in their unsteady dances banged into the walls of the narrow streets, where the most opulent foreigners felt poor and denuded before so much lavishness and so many feasts…

The only witnesses left to this picturesque and frantic life are the Town Hall, touched up too many times, regilded too many times, Sainte-Gudule with its pretty name, but one which not a single lady wished to have as a patron saint, the Mannekin-Piss, sadly anachronistic, and a few alleyways with leaning gables, with sonorous names of good food.

Now, all we have are women who are almost pretty, almost well-dressed, chubby nymphs from the Parc, the Monnaie and the Cambre, almost elegant gentlemen, who are the ornament of Spa, the adornment of Blankenberghe, and the royal glory of Ostend. There are only false Havana cigars which all come from Antwerp or Hamburg, and frightful false lace, frightful mechanically made lace, despite the fact that a hundred lace houses—just as formerly a hundred Greek cities did with Homer—fight over the pitiful honour of having provided the trousseau of Princess Stephanie.[1]

And all there are now in Brussels are scholarship holders without notebooks, founders of *The Twenty*[2] with no pictures, the inventors of *modern style* without customers, and here and there, a few symbolist art critics, alas, out of work, a few poets bitter because they were not able to get away to somewhere else, melancholics left on behalf of literature, of art, of brewing, and what is worse than all that—oh! How I can understand better every day, dear Baudelaire, your painful sarcasm!—about the inhabitants of Brussels.

---

1 Princess Stephanie was the daughter of Leopold II.
2 The *Circle of the Twenty* organised an annual exhibition of avant-garde paintings.

✳

During the Empire, which was the second and will be the last—for we have nothing to fear from a prince[1] who could live in the Avenue de Louise for twenty years,—Brussels was still something... At least it is said that it was... Today it is no longer anything.

Ah! How inspired they were, the day they kicked Victor Hugo out![2]... What rather providential good fortune for the great poet, and for us! He would certainly have lost all his genius if he had remained there; we would have lost all his glory, insufficiently replaced by that of M. Viélé-Griffin.[3]

Moreover, they have never been able to keep a top-notch exile. They needed exiles relative to their size, poor little exiles of no consequence... They need Boulange, Boulange, Boulange, Boulange!... Yes, they needed General Boulanger... They had him... They were proud of his unpolished boots his white plume smeared with the mud of nationalism... They surrounded him with attentiveness, sent him flowers, played him M. Gevaert's music... And yet, after a very short time, sick and tired of the rue Montagne-de-la-Cour, of the wood at La Cambre, full of boredom and disgust, the poor devil finished up blowing out what remained of his brains... He too!... In which case, who?

I do not think that there exists today, anywhere, in Aurillac, in Le Puy, even in Briançon, cashiers who are so poor that they wish to retire to Brussels. As a testimony I give this moving, sad story told to me in confidence, one evening, by an honourable cashier of a major French bank:

---

1 Prince Victor, grandson of Jérôme Bonaparte, lived in Brussels after his expulsion from France in 1886.
2 Victor Hugo was expelled from Belgium by royal decree on 30 May 1871 for having suggested that he would house Communards.
3 An American poet who wrote in French and who was despised by Mirbeau.

"Several times, Monsieur," this wise man confessed to me, "I thought about running off with my till... What can one do?... I have a large family and a small salary... I can't... I can't make ends meet... Oh, that would have been easy, I assure you... From Saturday evening to Monday morning... I had all the time I needed, you see!... But then I reminded myself: 'I'm going to have to live in Brussels from now on... Good heavens, no... I prefer to remain an honest man.'"

And he gave a deep sigh...

Despite my goodwill—for I think that I have made it clear that I have no prejudices where Brussels is concerned,—I am unable to find any character in these rows of little houses and these tiny parks. They only seem there to prove that London is a fine, unique city. Here and there, brand new buildings, wide, morose avenues, in which the King is insisting on swallowing up the millions belonging to his daughters, these evoke the sad wealth of Berlin... But Brussels, with its civic guards, is not the capital of an Empire of cannons and business, in which there still remain the memory of the great Frederick, and the charm of its phony eighteenth century.

No, Brussels is well and truly the comic capital, the capital of operetta, the capital of Vandepereboom!

Behind the Museum, in a street bordered by thin acacias, I noticed, through its railings, between a courtyard and a garden, a house that was certainly too small even for Little Tich[1]... In front of the house, a pond, round and scarcely larger than a plate, from which emerge two arum-lilies, crossed, who knows why, by a green-painted arched bridge. A few plants, keeping

---

1 A circus dwarf.

themselves to themselves, are drying out at the bottom of the walls, along which clematis and virginia creeper are obstinately refusing to climb. To the right one notices something tawny, rusty and peeling which was once, perhaps, a lawn.

The owner of this villa has two swans, one white, the other black, but the pond is so narrow and the water so shallow that the two unfortunate birds, since they are unable to swim, have taken refuge on the bridge. And that is where, exhausted, spread out, sometimes with their beak under their wing, sometimes with their neck stretching out towards the water, they spend their days dozing, daydreaming of blue lakes and pools full of reeds…

I am not saying that this is a bucolic characteristic special to Brussels. One can encounter it, observe it, in all the suburbs, in Chatou, in Le Vésinet, no doubt, no less than in Villeneuve Saint-Georges and at Choisy-le-Roi, everywhere, around cities where he who retires from his business has desires that are greater than his house, his garden and his pond, and believes that he is creating a universe, whilst making animals and plants suffer…

Which makes me think that Brussels is not a city, but the suburb or a city that one day may be created…

Let us hope so… Let us hope so!

I have been to the railway station to collect the luggage we had had sent on by train.

Above a door I saw this notice, in two languages, which still said:

Exit for passengers with luggage, and for others also.

We went to the station to meet a friend who is coming from Amsterdam… And we are waiting on the platform for the train to arrive.

An employee says to us:

"It's for Belgians here."

He points out to us another part of the platform:

"Over there… you see… that's for the others!"

✳

The same evening, at a street corner, a woman—a Flemish woman with quite a fresh face but large and heavy,—is soliciting a passer-by. The conversation begins; the passer-by asks:

"And where do you live?"

The woman replies proudly:

"Rue Montagne-de-la-Cour."

The passer-by objects:

"It's too far away."

Then the woman replies:

"Come on!… I have a beautiful bedroom,… very *soft and comfy*… You will see, young man, how *soft and comfy* it is… I *upholster* everywhere."

✳

Gérald B—— one of our friends, recounts how he spent the night with one of the prettiest cocottes in Brussels…

"Very pretty, indeed!… and a nice girl… And a tasteful apartment… which really embarrassed me… At the moment of supreme pleasure, the pretty cocotte begins to sigh, to sigh, and then suddenly, she cries out: 'There's some really good stuff here… can't you see… there's some really good stuff!'"

✳

There are many motorcars driving around in Brussels, and which all seem to be formidable machines. The majority copy—if one is not mistaken—our most famous French brands. Despite the fact that they look like monsters, they do not go fast, they go very slowly, they do not go at all.

"Out of prudence," is the explanation given to me, "Belgians are very careful mechanics… Otherwise!"

This morning I saw, parked in front of a private house decorated—as with all private houses—with stained glass, mosaics, with burnished copper, designed by M. Théo Van Rysselberghe,[1] I saw one of these monstrous cars, even more monstrous than any I have seen so far… My whole body trembled, just when I looked at the huge bonnet protecting the engine… It is a prodigious cube of sheet metal, flanked by steamship sirens, armed with gigantic, lenticular headlamps. Moreover, an electric spotlight, capable of illuminating the whole of nocturnal Belgium, is attached to the steering bar. I tell myself, with a feeling of terror mingled, however, with much admiration:

"A machine of at least five hundred horsepower, these Belgians, who do not look like much, are quite extraordinary…"

Very impressed, I approach this terrible war machine. It is resting… it is sleeping… Ah! that is how I prefer it… Neither is the mechanic there… what carelessness!… No doubt, in a bar close by, he is drinking beer that is not really beer, unless he is drinking gin which is not even brandy made from potatoes… But, in any case, he is not there… So, I am curious enough to lift this terrifying bonnet… I feel as though I am holding a bomb in my hands, with its fuse already lit. My heart is beating, beating…

First of all, I see nothing, nothing but a void… Then, by looking harder, I finally see a sort of tiny, single-cylinder mechanism, about as large as a Chinese coffee cup, of which the power cannot be greater than one and a half horsepower…

---

1 A neo-impressionist painter and designer.

The mechanic comes back. Pride on his face… he gives me a pitying look. Then he begins to turn the starting handle… I depart…

An hour later, I am once again in this street, in front of the little house. The mechanic is still turning the handle, without success… Bare headed, his face dripping with sweat, his clothes on the ground, he is turning… turning… turning!…

※

After a number of revolutions, rather like ours, of course they went off to find in order to install it in this useless capital, a dynasty of petty German princelings, bastardised from what?… from the house of Orléans.[1]

What funny people.

It is no less admirable that they are pursuing their paradoxical attempt to create an autonomous nationality from the residues of so many poorly amalgamated races, at the same time as they are trying to create an official language from a patois.

Let people speak Flemish in Flanders, Walloon in Wallonia, but I beg you Monsieur Picard, please let them continue to speak, in Brussels, this Belgian that you speak so well!

For, if the whole of Belgium is wonderfully Flemish, Brussels is nothing but Belgian, irreparably Belgian. Nowhere else does one encounter effigies in stone, in marble, in bronze, in lard, in gingerbread, effigies of this lion who is neither heraldic, nor zoological, of this lion who is not evil, who is not a lion, not even a puppy, who has such a strong resemblance to the lion of the famous Magasins du Louvre, and for whom is doubtless reserved by a decree ordained by Leopold the fate of becoming the shop sign for the famous Magasins du Congo.

------

1 The second wife of Leopold I, the first King of the Belgians, was Louise-Marie d'Orléans, eldest daughter of Louis-Philippe. She was the mother of Leopold II.

'Unity makes strength,' is repeated everywhere on bilingual inscriptions. It is the union of all imitations which makes the strength of their comedy.

✳

But Brussels seems to have no doubts about all that, nor about this scattered, obsessing humour, nor of what Brussels was in former times. And this sort of small city has the air of still being satisfied that it is only the Brussels of today and—what is most comic—sees this to be to its own advantage.

If there is a charming Brussels, and one with which one may fall in love—after all, why not?—I am sure, at least that it is an invisible Brussels. The traveller, who passes by, never sees what is there to be seen. The souls hidden in cities, rather like flowers hidden in grassland, are always the most attractive. Ah! I really would like to see what is hidden in Brussels...

Let us keep on looking...

The King is Involved...

We stayed at the Hotel Bellevue. It is being repaired. From the cellar to the attic, it is being renovated. Planks, ladders, trestles obstruct the corridors. Huge props are supporting the crumbling ceilings. You are swimming in plaster, in rubble; you stumble over pots of adhesive. It is going to be, so it appears, an orgy of modern comfort. At least this is what we are told, in English, in German, in Russian, in French, by little notices which are very prominent in the bedrooms.

The waiters tell you with well-informed airs and to boost your confidence:

"The King is involved."

Good Heavens! The King is involved in everything in Belgium; except, he is never in Belgium. Moreover, in a few days, when I pay my bill at the cash desk, I shall see that the King is involved… Maybe, too involved.

Whilst we are waiting, in the hotel we meet more painters, bricklayers, plumbers, carpenters, upholsterers, than tourists… Scarcely four or five American women going to Holland, or coming back from there, they are not quite sure; hardly three poor Englishmen who are going, tomorrow morning, to the battlefield at Waterloo.

The service is completely disorganised. You cannot get anything, not even water. This morning, by way of breakfast, I had this conversation with the waiter.

"No doubt, Monsieur is going to Ostend?"

"No, my friend… if it is alright with you, I shall not be going to Ostend."

"Monsieur is making a mistake… Monsieur should go there… It is something that just has to be seen… It's curious… Since gambling was abolished, in the Casino at Ostend there are four roulette and thirty-two baccarat tables… They are going night and day, Monsieur… And then there are the little horses for the little people… There are lots of them!… Lots of them!… And the women… the women!… Ah! Monsieur probably knows that nowadays Ostend is open all year round…. Once gambling is forbidden, there are no further problems, are there?"

Then, discreetly:

"The King is involved!"

And, because I remain silent, the waiter explains:

"Oh, he doesn't hide away… He doesn't care what people do or don't think about him… He's quite a fellow… And as long as there's cash involved!… Arm in arm he walks on the sea wall with Marquet, the Director of the Casino… There's a lucky chap!… Not long ago he was a waiter… a simple waiter… in the station bar in Namur… Many a time has he served me a coffee between two trains… He wasn't proud then… And now look at him, almost a minister… more than a minister… a business partner of the King…"

I went out.

In front of the hotel, on the hotel forecourt, I see a very pretty young woman, with infinite grace, who is playing with her two daughters. The young woman is very elegant, and is dressed in supple, soft, gentle white; the two daughters are dressed in white too, with bare legs, huge straw hats and lots of lace… All three are playing at chasing one another around a green box in which a large oleander is flowering. Very stiff, very dignified, dressed all in black, the governess is sitting on a bench, near the door, a pile of umbrellas and coats on her lap, a closed book in her hand. They are probably waiting for a carriage they have ordered, and which is not arriving in the same way that my breakfast did not arrive… The doorman, with his gold-coloured coat, is looking up and down the square and the streets feeling worried.

I pause to look at this young woman, who is acting in a more childish way than her daughters. I have never seen such beautiful blonde hair, blonde as, on certain days, can be blonde the so marvellously blonde North Sea. I have never seen a nape of neck, better curved, of silkier flesh. Her blue eyes are of an adorable, childlike frankness. Ah! how unaware of Nietzsche these eyes are, and how they are indifferent to this Rembrandt, whose *Night Watch*, they find inexplicable and ridiculous, because you do not see in them little girls, dancing, one evening, in a garden… Each movement of the bust, the arms, the legs which can often be guessed at beneath the embroidered cambric of her dress, each swaying of the hips, each fold of her skirt is an elegance, a caress, an invention of beauty, a moving festival of life. Although her outline is slender, of an almost delicate appearance, one senses that she is round and firm with a skin which certainly radiates light, as do, at twilight, the great white irises of Florence…

Suddenly, she lets out a little bird-like sound, stops running, reaches up on the point of her bronzed slippers, divinely stretches out her arm, tenses her elastic bust, and takes I know not what from the oleander.

The two little ones are stamping, clapping.

"Give it here... give it here... Mummy."

And I see in her hand, in a suede glove with the same blonde colour as her hair, the shell of a little snail, dry and empty.

"Ah! The poor little thing!... It's dead..." she said with an air of delightful consternation. "It's dead!"

I am sure that it is dead, this poor snail... He has been dead for millions of years, for it is a fossilised snail... With infinite care, with maternal tenderness which were prodigies of sculptural grace, she puts the snail shell back in the fork of a branch. It is as though she is saying to it:

"Sleep, little one, sleep!"

Then she starts running again, pursuing the two girls, crying out:

"Jeanne... Gabrielle... my darlings... here comes the big lion... the big lion... the big lion!"

As Jeanne, Gabrielle, pretending to be frightened, begin pretending to cry, the young woman bends down, crouches down, pulls into her arms the children she consumes with caresses and kisses:

"Oh! the silly little things I love!... The silly little things I adore!"

It did not escape my notice that, feeling herself watched, admired, she possibly lavished, for the doorman of the hotel, for the passer-by in the street, perhaps for me as well, the multiple charm of her gestures, the subtle or exaggerated grace of the winks she made. But I am in no way vain about it and take no hope from it. I know all about this coquettishness and where it leads, or rather, where it does not lead.

Besides, it would be completely supernatural that, in a hotel in Brussels, I could have adventures which I have never had in any other hotel in the world.

Let us not think about it any longer, as M. Gounod sings, and let us gallantly go to see the Manneken-Piss, since that is where everything finishes, here…

All the same, in the evening, I wanted to get some information from the waiter:

"She's a lady from Paris…" he explains, "she comes sometimes… she is called Madame X—— but we know that's not her real name…"

"Ah?"

"Yes…"

He gets closer to me and, very quietly, with a sort of confidential seriousness:

"The King is involved!…"

The Belgian Accent.

Their theatres, except for the Théâtre du Parc, which is totally French, are almost the Comédie-Française, almost the Opéra, almost the Les Nouveautés, almost the Olympia, but with an accent. Now, this accent is both sad and comic, like something artificial.

Not only the ingenues, the great coquettes, the rising starlets, the waning stars, the lovers, the noble fathers, the female singers, the members of the choir, the prompters, the stage managers, scenery makers, the gymnasts, the seal tamers, the horsewomen, they all have this accentless accent which makes you both laugh and cry, but—and this is the most fantastic thing—the ballerinas as well, above all the ballerinas who, since they cannot express their accent with their mouths, express it in their legs, in their smiles, in their exercises of disarticulation, in all their poses, even in the airy trembling of their flying tutus.

I went to the Palais de Justice, where they have jumbled, as far as they could, memories of monuments on monuments of memory, which has ended up with a monument of improbable ugliness. In it they have piled Assyrian on Gothic, Gothic on Tibetan, Tibetan on Louis XVI, Louis XVI on Papuan... It is so ugly that it, as a result, it becomes beautiful...

In the court there was being judged a poor devil of a Frenchman, who, not thinking he was in the wrong, and to take possession of the money which she was making no use of, had strangled an old lady in Brussels. I was struck by his happy, simple, naïve expression. M. Edmond Picard was defending him, for, not only does M. Edmond Picard write, but he also speaks the purest, most refined Belgian.

When the judge read out, in an accent which, this time, seemed to me to be strangely, sinisterly comic, the sentence condemning him to a lifetime in jail, M. Edmond Picard's client starts laughing, he bursts out laughing. Several times, he claps his hands frantically.

In the evening, he said to his barrister, who was criticising him for his unseemly conduct:

"I didn't realise that it was for real... I thought that I'd been taken to the theatre, to amuse me a little, and for me to see the best comics around here. I was happy... I was having a good time... Ah! what a good time I was having!... It's true.... I love impersonations..."

And he added, in a disappointed voice:

"So, it wasn't an impersonation?... It really was a judge?... And you really are a barrister?... And I really am a murderer?... Ah, goodness me!..."

The Funeral Meal.

I had to go to the funeral of Mme Hoockenbeck, the wife of my friend Hoockenbeck. He knew that I was in Brussels. Besides, a Belgian funeral, I would not have missed it for the world.

My friend Hoockenbeck, a renowned businessman,—he had a brilliant success in business,—an important politician—he is a member of parliament,—protector of the arts—he is in all the artistic societies created by and presided over by M. Octave Maus,[1]—my friend Hoockenbeck is one of those poor devils about whom it is said that they 'do not exist`. And if my friend Hoockenbeck 'does not exist' in Brussels, I leave you to imagine... Hoockenbeck has never had an opinion, a taste, a habit, not even a mania capable of withstanding, for more than five minutes, another which has been, I do not say put up in opposition, but proposed to him. Nothing was easier than to make him change his mind, especially on matters that he really cared about: *poohlitics*, and independent art. For example, he is intractable where puns are concerned. He makes puns tirelessly, unbearably. This comes from his good nature. He likes to make people laugh. And because he does not always have the choice, the most often, he makes jokes about himself. He often reduced me to tears, I who do not have such a pure soul. I find him talkative, bitchy, curious, vain, as much, on his own, as I find all other men. The only advantage that he has over them is that he is all that, but more ingenuously... Hoockenbeck is possibly the only man in the world with whom, not one single time, have I been able to have a serious conversation; the only man, as well, I have never been able to listen to without becoming annoyed, to the point of having a mental breakdown... Nevertheless, I like him.

His wife has always been as insignificant as her face, as colourless as the faded blond of her hair. Never did I hear her

---

1 Octave Maus (1856-1919) was a leading art critic.

say an interesting word, express an idea, any sort of feeling. Exceptional in her banality. I liked her as well.

I found poor Hoockenbeck in tears, desperate. It was pitiful to see him. He was sniffling, crying, embracing me, multiplying to such an extent his demonstrations of grief that sometimes I looked at him, secretly, fearing that it was a comic performance.

He was adamant about taking me to see his wife's coffin, and through his sobs he told me the story of his wife's death.

"Cancer of the uterus!… Yes… yes… Who would have thought it, looking at her? I… I never noticed anything… And she… Ah!… she never said anything to me… She was so brave!"

And he sobbed:

"My poor Louise! What a loss for me!… She so much loved to enjoy herself!… We were supposed to go to Paris… Oh! Oh!… next month… She wanted to go back to the Abbey of Thélème… to the Abbey… sob! Sob!… of Thélème… Poor Louise!…Oh! Oh!… She was so brave! And now… there you are!… Cancer of the uterus… there you are!… No… no… never… I…"

At this point, my friend Hoockenbeck really broke down sobbing, and during this time I caught myself playing, to keep my composure, with the silver fringe of the shroud… Then, suddenly, I saw him throw himself face down on the carpet, and begin to give himself a beating on the backside as if he either wished to punish himself for his grief, or for not being sufficiently grief-stricken…

"She was so brave!… She was so brave!"

I had to dab his temples, massage him, get him to drink, finally get him to lie on a divan, and hold his hands until, like a child, he calmed down.

Fortunately, other visitors arrived. He recovered completely, in order to welcome them, and then, as he was starting again to wet their cheeks with his tears, I slipped away.

The following day, there was a magnificent mass, but a Belgian mass… In a sonorous Latin! And a very Belgian French!… At the graveyard, funeral orations in Belgian, condolences in Belgian. I remember that during the pathetic speech of a small old blond man, bald, strangely spherical, who, very pale, was sweating profusely and whose voice was thundering out in Belgian, always in Belgian, I let out a cry which made heads turn and I had to stuff my handkerchief in my mouth. My hope was that it was mistaken for my tears…

After the ceremony, I could not refuse Hoockenbeck's invitation, who tearfully insisted that I stay for dinner.

I thought it would be just the two of us for dinner. But great was my surprise to find in the drawing room, from which they had quickly cleared away the *chapelle ardente*, a large number of people. A smell of faded flowers, incense, and another ambiguous one, persisted and they were dreadfully annoying. I was presented to aunts, to female cousins from Louvain, to nieces from Liège, to friends from Antwerp, to a family from Verviers, and to a number of Bruxellois. The men were in jackets, with white ties, the women in silk dresses. One woman, corpulent and over-made-up, had her corsage open. On these types of occasion one never really knows how to behave. To find the right balance is very delicate. After all, a dinner, even a funeral dinner, is not a funeral… But neither is it a normal dinner…

A copious, succulent meal washed down with those Burgundies and Bordeaux which are only produced in France, but which are only properly aged in Belgium. It began sadly. A massive uncle, in a funereal voice, reminded us of the childhood of the deceased. Little by little, from memory to memory, they arrived at tender little stories which had us gently weeping, then to joyful anecdotes which had us laughing a little before rude jokes that had us guffawing.

"She was so brave!" my friend Hoockenbeck, who moreover was not saying much but was drinking a lot, kept on repeating, sometimes sadly, sometimes joyfully.

After one rather saucy joke, Hoockenbeck, trying to stop himself laughing, had a large mouthful of lobster go down the wrong way and, worrying that he might choke, everyone started beating him on the back with their fists. From that moment on the entertainment increased and soon the funeral degenerated into a fête. The men's hooters became violently red; the women's eyes filled up with their troubles. And the jokes, the plays on words, the smutty stories set off, criss-crossed, rebounded from one end of the table to the other. And, under the table, God knows what was going on! A fat, female cousin was placing, with a more and more frantic persistence, her hand on mine… Couples were disappearing,… were coming back…

"It's not every day that you bury such a woman…" thundered the massive uncle… "such a woman!"

And nodding, with slurred speech, Hoockenbeck was stammering:

"She was so brave!… so bra… a…ve!"

Despite the wines, despite the sauces, despite the evaporated perfumes of the clammy skins, the smell of the faded flowers, and the other one, were predominant. But this did not seem to stop anyone's joy.

When I wanted to go, Hoockenbeck apologised,—it seemed to me regretfully,—that he could not drive me back. But his brother-in-law, a captain returned from the Congo (unfortunately he was not in uniform), claimed that the air would do him good… Helped by a young household from Liège, he easily overcame the scruples of the widower, who, normally red-faced and blotchy, had become purple as a result of congestion.

The five of us set off.

What can one do in Brussels towards ten o'clock in the evening other than make the traditional round of the cafés? From brasserie to brasserie, from café to café, our group swelled with friends we had met… One was becoming sad:

"Oh! My poor old chap!"

"Oh! Poor Louise!"

"Just like that… so quickly!… what was it?"

"Cancer of the uterus… You would never have thought it, looking at her!"

Sometimes Hoockenbeck was remorseful.

"If she could see us!" he said timidly.

To this the captain replied:

Don't be silly! Louise was a fine woman… She liked to enjoy herself, without appearing to. How happy she would be to be with us now!"

"She was so brave," became the leitmotif, in a more and more indistinct voice, of the unfortunate widower.

It finally happened that, having exhausted all the cafés and all the cheap pubs, we ended up in an all-night restaurant… It was noisy… Women with their dresses undone, young drunks, were singing and dancing to the music of Romanian *laoutars*.

"Champagne! Champagne!" ordered Hoockenbeck, who, once he was in the room, with his tie undone and his hat on sideways, had his arm wound the waist of a pretty brunette… But I think it was only so that he could maintain his balance… as a consequence he collapsed onto a bench.

At six o'clock in the morning,—I am ashamed to confess, but it has to be confessed,—I woke up in a cab, at the door of my hotel. The widower was snoring beside me. I got out quietly and gave Hoockenbeck's address to the coachman. I only noticed later that I had made a mistake: it was the address of a brothel.

Bravo Hoockenbeck! Perhaps he is still there.

Long live the Belgian Army!

The most comical thing of all—everything is always the most comical thing in Belgium—is the Belgian army. The Belgian army is more terrible to behold than the German army, not because of the number of its soldiers, but the rich decoration of its uniforms. It recalls—but more like a race track—the most splendid moments of the Napoleonic epic. All that is missing are its wars and its victories, and Monsieur d'Esparbès,[1] to sing their praises. The Belgians have not dared to go that far.

On the square in front of the Hôtel de Ville, this morning, there are six cavalry soldiers. Large, fat, heavy, with long, thick moustaches, their chests puffed out beneath a green dolman, embroidered on the front, on the sides and on the back, with enormous orange frogging, the sleeves with so many stripes that one does not know whether one is dealing with corporals or with generals, amaranth trousers hugging their thighs and corkscrewing on their boots, a police-style cap also with frogging, jauntily placed on their ear… And so martial, so conquering, that they look as if they have vanquished the world! I thought I saw survivors of the old imperial guard… There were six of them.

The crowd, happy, very proud, surrounds the six cavalry soldiers… From what I am hearing around me they are dressed down… in almost their uniform for carrying out fatigues… A bourgeois is saying to a foreign friend that he is taking for a walk around the city:

"And if you saw them in ceremonial dress, you know!"

A short time after, the same bourgeois, still radiating enthusiasm, says again:

"A hundred thousand men like that… Just imagine!"

My Lady Accomplice.

I only spent one agreeable day in Brussels: the day I spent there with Mme B——— arriving from Monte-Carlo on her way to Ostend. It is always a pleasure to see her and to hear her laugh.

I was able to talk to her about Brussels, totally freely, and it is her complicity that is partly responsible for the memory I still have of this last visit.

---

1 Georges d'Esparbès (1863-1944) wrote widely about the Napoleonic era.

She has the wonderfully coquettish gift of making the most stupid men feel proud when she laughs at everything they say, as if she was totally unaware that she manages to look even a little prettier when she is laughing, that her eyes become deeper and change colour, like velvet touched by one's finger, and that her top lip not only shows her teeth but also uncovers the gums of a pussy cat. If I had not been cured of loving love, and capable in any case of only being attracted to an ugly woman, I would envy the friend who is so in love with her, and would envy him more than her, who can only make fun of him.

It is doubtless not this poor, attractive, little Mme B——— who invented the Belgian accent, especially the Belgian accent of Brussels; nor is she responsible for Belgian art, or Belgian fashion, or Belgian morals, or Belgian imitations, nor the comic, posh look of the men and women from Brussels. But, certainly, if the compatriots of M. Francis de Croisset, né Wiener,[1] still seem to me to be so comical or, which adds up to the same thing, are so comical, it is that I exaggerated their ridiculous features only so that I could hear again, always hear giggling with laughter and crying with laughter, and snorting with laughter and singing with laughter, this pretty little Mme B——— whose natural character has the exquisite taste of very pure water, and whose absence of hypocrisy would have delighted Stendhal, like the Italian women she so resembles.

With the result that, if these pages meet a happy fate, if they last for a few days, if I am accused of having slandered Brussels, if henceforth I am forbidden to show my face here, without running the risk of being stoned to death, it is your fault, in vain do you laugh, you are right to laugh, it will be your fault, Madame.

---

1 Francis Wiener was the real name of the poet Francis de Croisset (1877-1937). Mirbeau had been persuaded to write a preface for his *Nuits de quinze ans*.

In the Restaurant.

One evening we were in one of those restaurants where one eats well, either in the Rue Chair-et-Pain or the Rue des Harengs, and we were the guests of a gang of Bruxellois[1]…

Do I need to say that they are excellent chaps and that they wear their hearts on their sleeves? After all, it is not their fault if they are Bruxellois. With a noisy amiability, almost as you find in Marseille, but without the picturesque nature, the spiky, flowery grace of Marseille, they call themselves the Parisians from Brussels, or the Bruxellois from Paris… I cannot remember which exactly.

That evening we were all, especially me, tired of museums and art galleries, tired of fine painting, even tired of Flemish painting and of the purest Dutch masters… I could no longer hear, without becoming neurasthenic and wanting to devour colour, the venerated names of Van Eyck, Jordaens, Rubens, Bouts. Readily I would have given up, perhaps not a Vermeer from Delft,—I hate exaggeration—but perhaps four Memlings, and surely the whole output of Wiertz, Gallait, Leys, Van Beers, Jef Lambeaux, the two Stevens and Rops, and even more the work of Henri de Groux added to that of Knopff, and many more besides, ah! I swear to you, without forgetting, of course, the Japanese lanterns of M. Théo Van Rysselberghe, just to be able to eat quietly without hearing talk of art and of Paris… especially of Paris… But the Bruxellois, when they push the boat out, and so that they can display their culture, and to show that they are from Brussels, only have two topics of conversation: art and Paris… Paris and art.

Unfortunately, that evening our hosts were especially lovers of art, and lovers of Paris, and particularly prolix. After five minutes when we had scarcely made a start on our hors-d'oeuvre—how did they manage it?—they had ended up

---

1 Translator's note. We are using *Bruxellois* to avoid the constant repetition of 'people from Brussels'.

disgusting me with their museum, which is a fine provincial museum, disgusting me with all museums, just as much those in Dresden and Berlin as those in The Hague, Madrid and Florence… Where Paris is concerned, each time its name came out of their mouths, the effect was such that I began to bark painfully, as a dog barks when you play the piano before it… Must I make a full confession? They had ended up making me disgusted with their wonderful cuisine.

They listed, as an old soldier does his campaigns, the Parisian first nights they had attended or which they would attend, they were returning from the openings of exhibitions, of auctions, from the Salon des Indépendants, they would go back for further salons, other exhibition openings, other auctions, for the Grand Prix, to the last first nights of the season, to the autumn Salons, of Bernheim, of Vollard, of Moline, of Durand Ruel[1]… I was ashamed that I did not know nine-tenths of the illustrious Parisians with whom they were clearly on very friendly terms, and more than ninety-nine per cent of the authors of whom they were able to quote whole pages, in free prose and in free verse.

I just wanted to get away.

But these were our hosts, and we were irrevocably sitting at table.

Oysters that had fed on the fattest seaweed from Zealand were followed by fish whose flesh gave off the strong smell of the North Sea; slices of meat running with juices, flanked by sautéed pasta, were followed by all sorts of birds, golden, crispy, overflowing with truffles from every orifice; rare vegetables, marine cabbages, hop sprouts, which had imbibed the most subtle aromas of the earth and the most perfumed ethers of compost, mountains of crayfish, lakes of cream, patisseries from the *Thousand and One Nights*. And then fruits, that had ripened in paradise, were added to cheeses that must have rotted away

---

1 Parisian art dealers who principally sold impressionist and post-impressionist paintings.

in hell. The Meursaults, the Haut-Brions, the Château-Lafittes, the Clos-Vougeots, the Chambolle-Musignys, the Ruchottes, the Romanées which were the pride of Professor Albert Robin's[1] wine cellar, Champagnes harder than nickel-steel, the brandies more than a hundred years old, all the liqueurs of Holland, all the rotgut from England and America only excited even further the aesthetic verve and the nevertheless so exalted Parisianism of our hosts, whereas where I was concerned, as I became drowsy, I no longer even had the strength to express, nor the faculty to feel, all the horror that art inspired in me, and Paris as well… ah! Paris!

I was no longer thinking about leaving… I was no longer thinking about anything.

Towards the back of the little room, with its paint peeling off, with its stripped panelling, in the middle of a table full of Flemings, whose faces were becoming red like brick dormers in the evening light the more I looked at them, a couple did not stop kissing, kissing passionately, kissing all the time, still kissing… They were certainly not thinking about art, those two… They were not talking about art, those two… They were not talking about art, nor about Paris, I can assure you… What happy people!… And how I envied them… not because they were kissing but because they were not talking!… I was focusing desperately on the sight they were presenting as one does on an image, flowers on a carpet, rays of light from a venetian blind, a fly crawling on a white wall, in order to get rid, far away from oneself, of a painful idea and which obstinately keeps on returning.

She was almost too blonde, almost too pink, almost too chubby, with that unhealthy fat with pink tinges found in our good pâtés from Strasbourg, and she was wrapping herself round an attractive boy, with black eyes, thin and dark-skinned like a Spaniard… Whilst their friends were eating with silent

---

1 Professor Albert Robin (1847-1928) was Mirbeau's doctor. *Dingo*, about Mirbeau's dog, was dedicated to him.

gluttony, all they did was to embrace, embrace so closely that it looked as though they were turning, turning… Beyond her long, suede gloves, turned back, the rather short, chubby little hands, not pretty, sensual, but with a rather crude sensuality, these little hands on which shone the fires of a ruby were clenching, to increase the pleasure of the kiss, by touching a corner of the moustache, the shoulders, the back of the neck, the collar, the thick hair of the boy, whose hands were wandering beneath her skirts, as though they were in a village fête of Rubens. It was not at all indecent, because it was so open, naïve and clumsy.

Moreover, nobody was paying attention to the loving couple, neither their table companions who did not miss a mouthful, nor my overwhelmed friends, nor our indefatigable hosts, nor the cashier leaning over her bills, nor the old head waiter, with his dirty and too ample jacket, his shiny head, his thinning grey hair, who was circulating with a heavy tread amidst the tables carrying dishes… Oh! This old servant of *Joy inspires fear.*[1]

When the small, passionate woman stopped to draw breath, you could see at her neck the gleam of a cross made of diamonds… she quickly patted her hair, at the side of her hat, no less quickly sucked the claw of a crayfish and, finally, pulled her gloves back over her elbows… Then they embraced again, more boldly, as freely as if they had been on their own in a bedroom… Their hands hidden beneath the table were imparting invisible, but precise caresses… I admired the fact, clumsy and heavy as she was, that she was only graceful and light when she was kissing… They were still not saying anything, nor were their table companions, as if words might spoil the joys, equally passionate, equally fleeting, of eating and lovemaking.

And I heard the cashier, very pale and very haughty, beneath her black headbands, repeat, as she wrote in a large ledger, as though writing the words of a dictation:

---

1 A reference to a one-act play by Girardin *La Joie fait peur.*

"Four grilled lobsters… four snipes in Champagne."

And I heard the old head waiter shout out in a broken voice:

"Cigars… there you are, Monsieur."

And I heard our Bruxellois, more and more enthusiastically, proclaiming, one:

"Paris!… Paris!… Paris!"

The other:

"Art!… Art!… Art!"

A third was punctuating this sentence, in which M. Camille Lemonnier *asserts*, as they say, in such a poetically just autobiography:

"'And since then, my soul, evaporates amidst the moving grace of the reeds, in the frivolous nature of dragonflies'."

And I heard a furious voice arising from the depths of myself:

"Blast it! Blast it! Blast it!"

So much so that, towards two o'clock in the morning, dizzy, tired out, my brain dreadfully liquified, my heart turned upside down, my legs staggering, I went to bed as well informed about Parisian things as the least amongst these Parisians from Brussels, or these Bruxellois from Paris… I still do not know.

> And more competent in art
> Than their Monsieur Edmond Picard
> And more than my dear Mendès
> Than your Dujardin-Beaumetz
> Who is not from Brussels, but
> In a speech totally Belgified
> Refocused aesthetics
> Of France and of Belgium.

And noticing that I was speaking in verse… in Belgian verse, I fell asleep in a dreadful temper.

AMONGST THE BELGIANS

Catholicism.

It is not by spending a few days in a country that one may judge its morals, its tendencies, its ideas, its institutions. One's observations are clearly rapid and superficial; they are only related to an infinitely restricted order of things, an order of little importance. One does not get to the intimate soul, the secret soul, the profound soul of a country unless one actually lives there… And so, we have to be content with appearances, which are often deceptive. For this reason, I beseech my readers to excuse the somewhat frivolous and unfair tone that you will find in these pages of mine.

However, as soon as you enter Belgium, you are struck by the sort of religious malaria prevalent there. It makes this little country strangely sad… It is possibly what turns so black the greenery of the countryside that was so hated by Baudelaire… Just as in our wild and sorrowful Brittany, where religious feeling has, as it were, turned everything to stone, just as, in the Austrian Tyrol, where, at every turn in the road, at every crossroads, everywhere, stand images of sainthood which could serve the local highways agency as distance markers, so is it that, in Belgium, religious superstition is the sovereign mistress of souls, countryside and laws. I am not talking only about the convents which pullulate there, just as barracks do in Germany; I am not talking of the béguinages, which are moreover nothing more than souvenirs, retained only by Ghent and Bruges, for tourists seeking the picturesque and the blind sheep of tourism. I am talking about all of this country over which Catholicism spreads its thick, unhealthy shadow. On the roads, pathways and in the towns, one encounters, in their thousands, faces showing stubborn faith, faces in prayer, aggressive and sombre, that we see in the triptychs of Flemish primitive painters. Centuries have passed over them, progress and science have passed over them, without softening their hard and obtuse angles.

I remember, a few years ago, that suddenly feeling ill in a village inn, I asked for them to fetch me a doctor, from the nearest town, which happened to be Ghent.

"Oh! Lord Jesus," cried the maid, seeing me so pale. "Perhaps he's going to die... Please say a prayer quickly, Monsieur... And wait for me."

She rushed out without bringing me any further help.

A few minutes later, I saw the arrival, let into my bedroom by the little maid, of a fat priest, out of breath from too much running... He tried, with all his strength, to administer extreme unction to me. And because I refused to arm myself with the Church's sacraments, he insisted violently, and only left after he had called to be brought down on my miscreant's head all the maledictions of heaven and all the furies of hell.

Everywhere processions, peals of bells, extravagant and medieval religious ceremonies, altar decorations in private rooms, stooping backs, clasped hands... and insolent, bawdy, thieving priests, and terrible bishops with faces reminiscent of the Inquisition. And everywhere, this literature of which the mystical eroticism associates itself so well with pious fervour and glorifies it... He who has not been present at the festivals of the Holy Blood, in Furne, turned that day into a genuine lunatic asylum, cannot conceive into what disorders, what insanities, religion, when it is taught like this, may lead the poor souls of men… It was this bellringer from Rodenbach[1]—moreover a historical figure—who engraved on the sonorous and blessed bronze of his bells the most monstrous obscenities… (It appears that these bells may be seen in Bruges, if you know the right people in ecclesiastical circles…) It is Philippe II, covering his notebook with demonic images, whilst surrounded by his bishops, his monks, his torturers, with a nun sitting on his knees, who shed the blood and tortured the flesh of the heretics, in the torture chambers.

The working-class centres themselves, the industrial districts, which are often grumbling with the seeds of revolt and riot, do not always evade this contagion. I once saw a strike in Ghent. It was in no way a flood of people released and beating, like a raging sea, against the walls of the city… It was a religious procession that was progressing silently, with religious attributes, church banners, standards, women disguised as Holy-Virgins, children, as little curly-haired angels… And I shall always remember this workman, with a wild face, walking in front of the crowd, carrying something that looked like a monstrance.

Belgium cannot get rid of the Spanish blood that flows in its veins.

Ghent's Democrats.

A charming friend of Maeterlinck, we met in Brussels, tells us this anecdote:

"In our country, Ghent specialises in bizarre riots. Do you remember those that took place in Belgium twelve years ago?[2] The common people were demanding universal suffrage. They also

---

1 An allusion to a novel by Rodenbach, *Le Carillonneur*, in which the bellringer, obsessed with the obscene images around his bell, ends up hanging himself.
2 A protest in 1892 after universal suffrage had originally been rejected.

wanted to be a sovereign people. This idea had come to them suddenly, it is not clear how. They already had a constitutional Monarch and doubtless were finding that that this did not bring them happiness. They wanted more, much more, kings in civil dress, and they wanted to choose them… So, the common people came down into the street bearing arms and letting out the usual shouts. The bourgeois, protected by the troops, made fun of this spectacle they deemed to be without danger.

"In Ghent, it seemed that, after a little time, things became tragic. Shouts, barricades, bloody fights, revolver shots, cavalry charges, discharges of musketry, the festival lacked for nothing, not even deaths. There was an ordinary apotheosis… Since these skirmishes risked continuing, the civic guard was summoned. I was part of it. I was obliged to line up beneath the flag of law and order, amongst the defenders of society. In my company there were only two genuine bourgeois, a painter friend of mine and me. The rest?… workers, clerks, shopworkers, all of them, or almost all of them, sharing a perfect communion of ideas with the rioters. In the ranks, they were discussing amongst themselves, quietly, and this phrase of 'universal suffrage' was constantly on their lips.

"They were promising, even swearing, that if they were ordered to fire at the people, they would fire in the air.

"'They are right,' said one, 'they are fighting for our happiness.'

"'Better than that,' added another, '…for our sovereignty.'

"'Yes, yes! We all want to be sovereign, as they are in France.'

"'To lay down our laws, as in France.'

"'Patience! Just a few more days and we will be masters of everything, as in France.'

"Another was saying:

"'They can give me as many orders as they like. I won't fire… First, because I don't want to, second because my brother is with those who are fighting, for our sovereignty. I would have fought with them too… but I have a wife and two children.'

"'I too would have fought with them... but my boss, who is not on the side of the common people, would have sacked me, and I would have been out of work... Yes, but when we are sovereigns, we'll sack the bosses.'

"A small man who had not yet said anything began, suddenly, to repeat several times, casting sharp, jumpy, threatening looks in my direction:

"'Me, I know who I'd vote for.'

"And, since I remained silent, standing in my rank:

"'Yes, yes... you would like me to vote for you... But I'm not a total fool... I won't vote for you... I know who I'll vote for... I'll vote for someone... And when I have voted for the person I have in mind... ah! ah! ah!...I know what I'll say... And you...You are not saying what you know.'

"'At least,' I thought, 'they won't fire.'

"Our captain was walking up and down in front of the company, anxious, nervous, listening to the still far-off shouting of the riot. From time-to-time horsemen galloped across the square. The shops were closing; pale bourgeois were returning home, hastily, out of breath. Gradually the roaring of the populace got closer; shouts, cries, calls, became more distinct. Two shots cracked in the air like whiplashes, in a disturbance of carriages... the captain turned towards us. He was a tie merchant from the city... He had a round, pink face, a fat, pacific tummy, gentle eyes.

"'Boys,' he said to us, 'things are getting worse. They'll be here in a few minutes. There are no two ways about it. I'll be obliged to pronounce the statutory legal commands and then order you to fire. It's really irritating... for I know them... they are hot heads... they won't listen to me... to fire on people from the city, people that I know... it's very irritating. On the one hand, the rule of law must prevail... It has to... It's very irritating... If only they had set out their claims peacefully!... The King is a decent chap; the ministers are decent chaps... They too, good grief, are good chaps... It could have been sorted out one way or the other!… But that's got nothing to do with it… Duty comes before everything… it's very irritating… Soldiers… listen to me carefully… We have to create the least amount of misery we can… When I give the order to fire, the front rank will not fire… Only the second rank will fire… And perhaps it's not necessary for the whole of the second rank to fire? No. No. Finally, we just have to frighten them… Three or four dead,… three or four wounded… It's very irritating… But it's not a big issue…And perhaps that will be enough to stop them, those so-and-sos… You, over there in the second rank, attention!… Ready! Are there, amongst you, ten men… ready to fire at the people on my order?… Are there only five of you?… Let's see, good heavens!… are there four?… Four? Reply!'

"To my stupefaction, from the right to the left of the rank, I heard on each lip, jumping from each lip, this word:

"'Me… me… me… me… me!'

"Out of the fifty men that were in the rank, only two had remained silent… Only two decided not only not to shoot at the men, but to raise their rifle butt in the air, as soon as the death order was given… And these two men were not at all the proletarian members of the company, but the two bourgeois ones, my friend the painter and me.

"Fortunately, they shot very badly… There were only ten poor devils killed, and twelve wounded."

Constantin Meunier.[1]

For the whole day—a sad and rainy day—I have revisited the work of Constantin Meunier.

Constantin Meunier is an interesting and worthy artist. Because of his talent, his blameless life, he is entitled to our entire respect. His work is redolent of important human meaning.

---

1 Constantin Meunier (1831-1905) was a painter and sculptor whose career Mirbeau had promoted. His primary subjects were people at work.

Like so many others, who found fame and profit by so doing, he could have created waxy figures of Diana, undulating Venuses and voluptuous fauns. He could have raised, as many others did, monuments of sugar and lard, in memory of great Bruxellois, and populated the Bois de la Cambre with a whole crowd of painters, of poets, of orators and of soldiers... But he had a prouder ideal.

Born in the heart of a land of work and of suffering, living in a murderous atmosphere, always in sight of the lugubrious hell of the coalmines, the red drama of the factory. He created workers.

First of all, he painted them; then, he moulded them.

He was keenly passionate about their travails, their miseries, their revolts. He understood the rough tragic beauty of their torsos, the taut musculature, violent with their gestures, the gasping, wild, hard sadness of their underground faces. He tried to stylise, to reduce to the linear simplicity of antique dress, their leather aprons, their tight-fitting blouses, their poor work attire. Above all, he was moved,—for he had infinite goodness, and always dreamed about justice,—by the social injustice, the bitter capitalist and political exploitation, found in the fate of these outcasts, whose fate is to find their meagre daily existence only in terror, or in the slow wear and tear of a trade, after which the sweatshop almost seems sweet release.

Out of all this he was able to create quite noble accents, quite strong sculptural semblances, of pity. We owe to him three works that are almost entirely beautiful: a *Figure of a peasant woman*, with a worn-out face, dead, eyes, dried up breasts; the *Pit Pony*, the *Woman in the firedamp*, the latter being especially an ample and simple composition, showing a tighter workmanship. That is already quite a lot.

Unfortunately, he had come to sculpture too late in his life. It is a very difficult art, the enemy of cheating and of the smokescreen, and Constantin Meunier, despite his genuine gifts, his passion, his deep understanding of working-class life, did not really understand his trade. His shaping is poor, sometimes lacking in unity, his form often heavy, his planes not numerous enough, not sufficiently coloured, his outlines dry… He does not always know how to combine harmoniously a monument, create the architecture of an ensemble, group the figures… His effort shows too clearly in everything he does. The suppleness which gives life, movement to matter, is what is most lacking in his work. By itself, the piece is worth what it is worth, and, most frequently only has a value,—consequently, an illusion—of literature.

✳

I was told the following dramatic story.

The Human Rights League, chaired so firmly and with so much devotion by M. Francis de Pressensé,[1] set up a special committee charged with creating a monument in memory of Émile Zola. This committee chose Constantin Meunier to carry it out. But the latter hesitated for a long time, said he had qualms. He said he was ill, was feeling very old, had another important work that still needed to be finished, the work of which we have admired several fragments at our exhibitions, and which he wished to see erected in one of the public squares in Brussels before he died. But after repeated entreaties, certainly flattering for him but doubtless clumsy, for he was the only person who could know what he could or could not carry out,—he ended up accepting this onerous project, weakly, on condition that they gave him a French collaborator, who was chosen immediately, or rather who chose himself: M. Alexandre Charpentier.[2]

After a very long year, Constantin Meunier and M. Alexandre Charpentier presented a model to the committee,

---

1 Francis de Pressensé (1853-1914) was a journalist friend of Mirbeau who had fought for the cause of Dreyfus alongside Mirbeau.
2 Alexandre Charpentier (1856-1909) was a naturalist sculptor.

108

truth to tell not a very good one. It was judged to be inadequate. Besides, the two artists confessed that they themselves were not happy with it. They realised that they needed to look for and find something different.

This was what the monument looked like. An Émile Zola, standing, in an oratorical, dramatic pose, in a tight-fitting workman's jacket, tight trousers, a Zola lacking in nobility and without genuine life, where nothing captured that physiognomy, mobile, ardent, purposeful, timid, so conquering and so fine, cunning and tender, jovial and sad, enthusiastic and downcast, and which simply seemed to breathe life, the whole of life, with such a strong passion. Behind this Zola, banal and poor, a naked Truth was stretching out her hands. On the right, a coalminer; on the left, a serf. The imagination left much to be desired. We can see that it did not go beyond the mentality of official artists. And the group was poorly put together.

"Good heavens!" said M. Alexandre Charpentier, as they made this rather tardy discovery. "This is upsetting… For they are right… It's worthless… I think that it's Truth which is our problem… She is very pretty… but not in her rightful place, behind Zola… She should be put in front… What do you think?"

"Let's try her in front," agreed Constantin Meunier.

"Let's try."

Placed at the front, Truth now produced an even more deplorable effect. Then it obliterated the serf, the coalminer.

"By the devil!" cried out together with more unity than in their work, the two terrified artists.

They thought for a long time.

"If we dressed her up," Constantin Meunier suggested.

"Truth?"

"Yes, why not?"

"A Truth with clothes on? It wouldn't be a Truth any longer… No, let's try her on the right."

"Let's try," agreed Constantin Meunier.

They moved Truth to the right.

"No, no. That's terrible! Take her away."

Constantin Meunier hides his face… Everything in the monument is becoming unbalanced… It is all collapsing… it's all 'buggering off,' as they say in the studios.

The problem was getting more and more difficult.

"Well, on the left," M. Alexandre Charpentier suggested for the second time.

Poor Constantin Meunier no longer had any faith. He replied weakly:

"Let's try her on the left."

Truth was moved to the left.

"Impossible!"

This was the cry that Constantin Meunier and M. Alexandre Charpentier let out simultaneously

Unfortunately! Neither at the front, nor at the rear, nor on the right, nor on the left. A tricky situation with no solution. What Truth must have been hearing, but that was usually her situation!

During the work the two sculptors had fallen out quite painfully on a number of occasions. This last adventure was not likely to dissipate their misunderstandings. Those who understand the heart of men, especially the heart of artists, who are men twice over, may imagine what went on between Constantin Meunier and M. Alexandre Charpentier. They arrived, in their relationship, at such a tension that the Belgian artist, irritated by the dominant meddling of his collaborator, and thinking that his influence might have had a depressing effect on him, ended up dispensing with his services. Perhaps he ought to have started out like that.

Left by himself, the poor great sculptor was rather handicapped. Should we believe, as some people affirm, that the atmosphere in Brussels, today, is inimical to all artistic creativity? Or was Constantin Meunier just too old? Did he now lack that spark of imagination that had so many times made up for his poor craftsmanship? He tried all sorts of combinations, none of which worked. Finally, after days of effort, after painful days spent with his work and with himself, he arrived at this stupefying conclusion: that, aesthetically at least, the two figures of Truth and Zola were mutually exclusive, that a choice had to be made between Truth and Zola, and that one should not try to bring them together, in bronze. And he chose Zola, saving Truth for an unknown destination.

It is claimed that his irritation, chagrin, the constant struggle he had had with M. Alexandre Charpentier, the disappointment, all contributed to his death which happened soon after. And the monument to Émile Zola, despite the opposition of the family of Constantin Meunier, reverted to M. Alexandre Charpentier, who, henceforth, worked on it on his own. Where has he got to with it? What is it like? I have no idea since I do not have an inside track.

This story is sad, and, like all sad stories, it has its comic side, a bitter, dark humour, perhaps the most tragic thing in the world. But when one looks more closely at it, one sees that it is very characteristic, and also very harmonious with life.

Before finding peace in immortality, the fate of Émile Zola was strangely troubled. As with all men of genius—especially men of a tough, tenacious and humane genius—Zola always created a storm around himself. It is not surprising that the squall is still blowing.

His work was decried, insulted, cursed, because it was beautiful and bare, because it opposed to poetic and religious lies the shining, healthy, strong truth of life, and the fertile, constructive realities of science and reason.

He was hunted like a wild animal, even into the temples of justice. He was jeered at, beaten in the street, and sent into exile: and all that because in place of triumphant social crime, of Catholic ferocity, of nationalistic barbarity, he had wanted, on one day of great duty, to substitute justice and love.

His death was a terrible and stupid drama.[1] The man who, in front of the roaring of men, before their crowds drunk with murder, had revealed such an intrepid heart, such magnificent and tranquil courage, could do nothing against the cowardly and cunning imbecility of things, for one could say that things themselves can have hatred, an atrocious hatred, a human hatred, for what is just and beautiful.

And here we have one sculptor, two sculptors, whose intentions cannot for a moment be regarded as suspect, who liked Zola, who admired him, and who, because they were impotent to interpret the genius of a body of work and the heroic beauty of an act,[2] cried out in their language of artists who have lost their way:

"Clearly, Truth and Zola don't make a whole."

I am aware that the fact, taken by itself, is slender evidence and that one should only see in these words a poor joke, in their trade jargon.

However, that evening, as a result of this story, I returned to the hotel terribly sad and discouraged. I spent a very feverish, agitated night. In my nightmares all I saw everywhere were public squares, parks, gardens in which fanatical crows were erecting formidable and derisory monuments to Lies, Hatred, Crime, Stupidity.[3]

Fortunately, the following day, I recovered thanks to Brussels. As I came out of the hotel, I saw again the pretty woman with the oleander, more ingenuous, more childlike than ever… She was no longer pretending to be a big lion with her girls; she was playing at being a wicked tiger. And the Bruxellois were drawing me into their round of comedy.

---

1 Zola died of asphyxiation from a blocked chimney in Paris on 29 September 1902. There are still arguments about whether it was an accident or murder.

2 A reference to Zola's famous article *J'accuse*.

3 A fundraising campaign had been launched by those opposed to Dreyfus to finance a statue of Colonel Henry who had been accused of forging the documents which led to Dreyfus's guilty verdict.

On the bridges
Of Brussels…

What on earth am I singing?… There are no bridges in Brussels… They once had a river, a river which through a spirit of imitation and to justify their Parisianism, they had called, whilst reforming the spelling: the Senne. But, for a long time, they buried it underground and covered it with a canopy… Perhaps also they did it so as not to have competition for the Manneken-Piss, whose puerile pee satisfies them, satisfies their love of water, their love of reflections in water.

An Industrialist.

I have met a great industrialist. He was, however, quite small as is often the case with great writers, great artists, great barristers, great doctors… He was quite small, with a very red face, very blond beard and hair, and portly, with a very fat gold chain, or rather a very fat gold cable, slung across his stomach.

"Things are bad… things are bad," he groaned. "It's impossible to get on with your work… There are always strikes!… When one ends, the next one begins… Why, for heaven's sake, why? Oh, I don't know what's happening to our poor industry… It's very sick."

And suddenly:

"It's your fault!" he cried.

"My fault? How can it be my fault?"

"Yes, yes… well the French socialists' fault… the French anarchists' fault… Yes, indeed… You don't know our workers… Good men… very good men… Deep down, they don't want anything… are not asking for anything… are very happy with what they earn. They don't earn much, that's true. But it's enough for them… Plus, what would they do with more money? Nothing… nothing… nothing. I'll make you laugh. Last year I gave twenty francs to a worker who had saved my daughter's life… my only daughter… who had fallen into the canal… Do you know what he did with his twenty francs? He bought a samovar, dear Monsieur, a samovar! Okay, he was a Russian, but nevertheless."

And he repeats, raising his arms:

"A samovar!… A samovar! They're all like that!… Good Lord! They go on strike, from time to time, like the others… But so what? That's the fashion, today, in the workers' world… At least, in our country, strikes are not serious… the strikes are jokes… a few days strolling about… then back to work!… Our strikes? They are the modern form of the village fair… Yes, but as soon as our workers are on strike, there arrive, Lord knows where from, a horde of socialists… of anarchists… finally of Frenchmen… They shout out: 'Rise up, rise up! Down with the bosses!… Death to capitalism!…' They are inciting violence, rioting, pillaging. And now we see our nice little Belgian lambs, changed immediately into ferocious French beasts… And so, it's all going wrong… it's a mess, isn't it?… Sometimes we have to put wages up… Well, putting wages up, do you know what that is? It's quite simply the ruination of our industry… Yes, Monsieur, our industry… you are quite simply ruining our industry… Ah! without you!"

I tried to explain to my interlocutor that our great industrialists in the North of France were expressing the same praises for the unselfishness of their workers, and the same complaints about the Belgians coming to stir them up. It is easier than to research the real causes, let us say, so as not to irritate them, of an evolution of an economic disease, and to find its remedy. I tried to get him to understand that, until working conditions had been reorganised along fairer lines, it would always be like this… But the little great industrialist is obstinate about not coming to his senses.

He protests, fusses, stamps, shouts:

"No, no… There is no economic evolution, no economic illness… There is nothing economic at all… There is work… Work is work… What is work?… Nothing… What should it be?… Nothing… That's the only principle that I know… Leave me alone… It's you, you!… You have always been the spreaders of the propaganda of revolutionary spirit amongst the people… It's disgusting… Ah! I can see what you are dreaming of… I can see what you're waiting for… Belgium belonging to France, that's it, isn't it?"

"And you, France belonging to the Belgians, aren't you?"

The small great industrialist looks at me with a strangely brilliant gaze:

"Ho!… Ho!" he says, clicking his tongue. "Don't laugh… I say!… I say! With our good, our excellent friends the Germans!…Ho!… Ho!… But I say!"

Then he rises on tiptoes, puts his hand on my shoulder and gives me protective little taps.

"Ho! Ho!… Good Lord… I say!… It would be really good luck for you."

Waterloo.

The same day I went to see the battlefield of Waterloo. Perhaps I was encouraged unconsciously to make this ridiculous visit by the no less ridiculous idea of making myself used to the notion of defeat, of denationalisation, of Belgification, that is evoked in my mind by the single name Waterloo.

But I saw nothing at the battlefield of Waterloo… At the battlefield of Waterloo, by the Auberge de Belle-Alliance, where a few English tourists were exchanging small yellow pebbles for small black pebbles. I only saw, standing on a table, wearing boots, a panama hat untidily on his head, an enormous lorgnette in front of his eyes, I only saw M. Henry Houssaye,[1] who was looking at… what?

Crows were flying here and there over the dull plain[2]… And I told myself melancholically:

"He still thinks they are eagles."

In the Museum.

I shall not say anything about my visits to Museums. I want to keep secret to myself, entirely to myself, the pleasures and musings that I owe you, Van Eyck, Jordaens, Rubens, Teniers, Van Dyck!… As a respectful admirer, I wish to spare you all the thick, sticky nonsense hideously secreted by art critics, when they are in the presence of works of art, any works of art, permanent stupidity, which, better than the accumulated dust and the clogged varnish, clog for ever your masterpieces and end up disgusting you with yourselves… Ah! it was hardly worth taking the trouble to be great men and decent chaps!

One evening, in the Museum in The Hague, I genuinely heard Rembrandt's *Homer* say to me:

"Send away from me,—I implore you, you who seems to be appreciating me silently,—send away from me all this muffled buzzing of mosquitoes, all these painful stings of flies, which make my life so intolerable, in this museum, that I often regret—on my word of honour—not having been painted by M. Dagnan-Bouveret,[3] do you understand?… then everything that is said about me would have had its raison d'être… and I would not be suffering because of it… a moment! Look at

---

1 Henry Houssaye (1848-1911) published four volumes about the events of 1815, one entitled *Waterloo*.
2 A reference to the line in Victor Hugo's poem *Expiation*: "Waterloo! Waterloo! Waterloo! Morne plaine."
3 Dagnan-Bouveret (1852-1929) painted religious scenes in a realist style.

116

this fat lady… yes, over there… to the left… that fat lady in pink… in front of the Vermeer… A moment ago, she gathered her whole family around me—four boys, four girls, and just as many nephews and nieces—and she said to everybody, pointing at me with a hat pin: 'Look carefully at the old man, children. He looks just like your grandfather!' And the children cried out, clapping their hands: 'It's true! Grandpa…Grandpa!' Well, I prefer that. I don't know why… I enjoyed it… it moved me to know that I looked like somebody, somebody living, even somebody in Brussels;… for it was clear that she was from Brussels, the fat lady in pink… But if you had heard the other day M. Thiébault-Sisson?[1] Well, I no longer looked like anything… And what about M. Mauclair?[2]… Did he not assert that I represented 'static painting?' What pity, my God, what pity!"

Is it not curious?… Is it not humiliating for our mentality, that there are still in the twentieth century so many people who are sufficiently idle, sufficiently lacking in ideas, sufficiently denuded of the meaning of life, sufficiently disrespectful of the meaning of beauty, that they give themselves the ridiculous mission of explaining things, which actually are inexplicable, which they do not understand and will never understand, when it is so easy just to let everyone enjoy what they see, freely, in their own way?

But there you are… Everybody has, in their heart, a sleeping Mauclair.

If only, he was still sleeping, this blasted Mauclair! Isn't that so, my poor Homer?

---

1 Thiébault-Sisson was an art critic who did not like contemporary styles of painting.
2 Camille Mauclair (1872-19450) was also an art critic who did not like impressionist painting.

He is Improving the Breed.

The Belgians are important breeders of hens and of rabbits. They created a breed of rabbit which has a grandiose name: the giant of Flanders, and which, for a rabbit, not a particularly lyrical animal, is indeed a giant, more than a giant, a veritable monster. The giant of Flanders can weigh up to twenty-two pounds[1] of meat.

But it is especially the hen, which constitutes, for Belgium, an interesting and very prosperous business. It has to be said that the Belgians are incomparable masters where aviculture is concerned.

Amongst the very numerous breeding farms around Brussels, I visited one that had been specially recommended to me. It belongs to M. de S… Half-peasant, half gentle-man-farmer, with a rather rough welcome, but deep down a good man, M. de S… ended up getting to know me almost to the point of indiscretion, to the point of joyful punches, taps on the stomach. And his laughter is so deafening that, each time he laughs, one instinctively wishes to block up one's ears, as one does when a whistling locomotive goes by.

His installation is wonderful. Nothing is left to chance… Everything is put together, foreseen, regulated, disciplined: food, care, hygiene, physical exercise, selection, in view of the constant improvement and the most perfect happiness of the race… I have never seen, anywhere, anyone do as much for human beings.

"I am strict…" confesses M. de S…, "that's true… But I don't upset them… You should never upset animals… Quite the opposite, they should have a good time… When they are not having a good time, they decline… And then, goodbye to eggs!"

They have two types of hens in Belgium: the Coucou de Malines, and the Campine. A very well-established product of

---

1 A metric pound is half a kilo.

a cross between the ermined Brahma and the Campine, the Coucou de Malines is resilient, fat, not very shapely, with a pretty pebble-grey colour, and with an abundant, delicate flesh. It is essentially a commercial bird. It is exported to the whole world. The Campine is the national bird. It is said that, more than a century ago, the breed had almost disappeared; at least it had astutely dispersed itself among other breeds. Gradually, it has been bred back to its original purity. It is small, but extremely elegant, lively, pretty. M. Paul Bourget would say that it has aristocratic features. Slim and a little jumpy, at least that is how I remember her, I think that it would be fairer to attribute to her the airs of a cocotte, of a dandy. A white mantle, deliciously white, accompanies its white and black well-fitting coat, which picks out her outlines with a rather bold grace... a slender bright-red comb sets off her head in an exquisitely insolent manner. Like our Bresse variety, it has blue feet, which is a sign of good breeding. Blue blood, naturally.

And as he walked me around his clean, gleaming, luxurious hen houses, like those to be found in private houses in Saint-Germain and in l'Isle-Adam, he confided to me, in verbose terms, his ideas about breeding.

To what extent did I admire the vitality, the robustness, the good humour of his animals:

"Ah! there you are!" he stated. "You have to be pitiless and scientific... I am pitiless and scientific... I eliminate the cockerels that don't sing well... whose voice is not sufficiently sonorous or loud... It's all in that, dear Monsieur... I have observed that, the more a cockerel sings loudly, the more he is ardent, and, as a result, good for reproduction. A fine voice, in cockerels, just as in men, is a good sign of... well, you know what I mean!"

"What about the tenors?" I could not help saying... "now there's a new point of view."

"No, not tenors, of course. Tenors are powder-puffs... Ha! Ha! Ha!... Tenors, on the spit!... In the cooking pot, the tenors!... Of course, I only keep the baritones... serious, well-fed baritones… You see, the hens are not wrong in this… They know perfectly well that the more a cockerel sings in his baritone voice, the better served they will be, larger and more abundant will be their eggs… and more vigorous their offspring… for everything is linked together in nature… I can tell you, I have founded a Club in Brussels, charged with propagating around the world these biological truths… A fantastic success, my dear Monsieur… We now have newspapers, lectures, laboratories… lots of money… We organise terrific exhibitions… with singing competitions… a genuine conservatoire… but not of music… no, holy mastiff!… a conservatoire of… you know what I'm going to say… it's thrilling."

He taught me that there was only one way of reconstituting a breed that had degenerated: incest.

"Thus, you take, for example, two wild Cochins… They have inadmissible, ignoble, disgusting, criminal flaws, for example grey, black or white feathers… tight trousers, not baggy enough… tails that are too long… Finally, they still have the relics of ancient mixtures, of disparate influences… Well, you isolate them in a hen house… Well… they have broods… Good!… You choose, without any weakness, the hen and the cockerel, in other words, the brother and sister that you bluntly encourage to reproduce… And so on, from brood to brood… Gradually the foreign influences are attenuated, the mixtures disappear… After five or six generations, you have got back to all the well-defined characteristics, all the original virtues, all the initial purity of the breed! It's so exciting!"

He added:

"Where men are concerned, goodness me!… I haven't tried."

He nudged me gently:

"Ha! Ha! Good heavens! Perhaps it should be tried… in France where the breed is disappearing… disappearing."

I saw, in a hen house, extraordinary birds that, first of all, I mistook for birds of prey. Standing as straight as men, and perched on tall, dry feet, nervous, armed with terrible spurs, their chests jutting out, in a jerkin of blueish feathers, a short, pointed tail, turned up like a sabre, with fierce eyes, a curved beak, sharp like a vulture's, they produced on me the effect of those quarrelsome knights of the past who, for nothing at all, would draw their sword and leave you stretched out, with a rapier thrust, at the side of the road.

"They're Combattants de Bruges," the gentleman-farmer explained shrugging his shoulders. "They're nothing at all… nothing at all… Yes, they pretend to be brave… it makes them seem impressive… but, deep down, they are scaredy cats, my dear Monsieur, the worst scaredy cats in the world. Don't talk to me about these impressive birds, that would be frighted off by a robin… and who have to be raised in cottonwool."

We were still walking from hen house to hen house and still the great aviculturist was talking, talking, explaining, commenting:

"The hospital!" he told me suddenly.

He stopped, showed me a large area, divided into five or six compartments, enclosed by wire mesh, where, well exposed to the sun, were standing genuine little houses. A strong odour of carbolic acid rose from the carefully raked soil… A few hens were walking about, with a low wing, and with that sad, slow and broken walk that old women have in the countryside. I saw some that were limping, that were jumping on their little feet, covered in bandages. Others, stupid, with dull and puffy feathers, discoloured crest, not noticing anything happening around them. And others, crouched in a row, on the sulphated grass, nodding their heads and telling each other little stories, were no doubt talking about their illnesses, as convalescents do sitting on benches on a sunny day in the garden of the nursing home.

And M. de S… told me this:

"One morning, I hear from my head man, that I have two hens with diphtheria… How had they managed to catch this disease, here, where, every day, the hen houses, the floor, the mangers, the water, even the food, in fact everything is disinfected? I am still asking myself that… But there was no doubt about it, they had diphtheria… Ah! Good heavens!… Immediately I ordered that they should be isolated in one of those little houses that you can see… And they are looked after… Three times a day an employee came with nurse's equipment… He began by scraping the hens' necks, then, with a little paint brush daubed a generous layer of petroleum on the open wounds, and since the sick have to be supported during the progress of this disease, he would give them two or three patties of a special and tonic composition… This diet was extremely difficult and painful for them. But so what! There was no point in their protesting, it had to be done… Now, this is what they thought up… You won't believe this! I myself would have treated as a jokester anyone who had told me this, if I had not been, a dozen times, an astonished witness… as soon as they saw their torturer coming with his kit, they would try straight away to get up on their feet, would beat their wings, pretended to be really happy, then, rushing to the mangers containing a little millet, they would pretend to eat… Yes, dear Monsieur, with comic ostentation, they would pretend to eat, greedily. And looking up at the employee, with an air of cunning, they seemed to be telling him: 'You see, we are really hungry, we are completely cured… So, go away with your scraper, your petroleum brush, and your patties'… Ah! the crafty beasts!… It's fascinating."

"And to think," I cried, "that, in college, I was punished with a week's detention for having written, in a presentation in French these sacrilegious words: 'the intelligence of animals'!"

"Well! Me too, in a Latin prose," exclaimed the aviculturist, "…with the Jesuits."

And his huge laugh shook the whole poultry yard.

But this was not the last of my surprises.

In the centre of a hen house, a small man wrapped in a long blouse of unbleached canvas, a white apron tied around himself, a round skullcap on his head—the classical look of a hospital intern—was methodically setting out on a table, pots, phials, tapes, rolls of cotton wool, and was heating up thin steel instruments in a metal container.

"What's he up to?" I asked.

For a moment the aviculturist seemed embarrassed:

"Nothing… nothing," he replied.

Then suddenly:

"Okay!… you seem to be a decent chap… but not a word to anyone, please… Well, he is preparing the hens for an upcoming exhibition… He is getting them up to scratch."

And, with his joyful character getting the better of him:

"He's improving the breed," he added, with a loud laugh. "Do you understand? I have competitors that have good qualities… but which also have faults… Nobody is perfect! Well, I increase the good qualities and I get rid of the faults… I make younger the spurs that are too old… I paint in pink or in blue, depending on the breed, the yellow feet… I dye the defective feathers… I get rid of toes, or I add some more, depending on the case… I shape poor crests and put them in order… It's delicate, very complicated, you know!… But there you are! That's how it is!… You have to act like everybody else… And if I told you that two years ago, in Liège, I took First Prize with a bad group of wild Cochins, that had been completely dipped in carbonyl!… To heck with it!… Ah! it's fascinating."

And with this strange confidence, we ended our visit.

King of Business.

Dining with friends from the overseas colony, I asked a notable Belgian, who has the reputation of knowing everything about Brussels, especially all its scandals, to tell me a few typical anecdotes about King Leopold.

The notable Belgian smiled and then said to me:

"Well, there's no point... You know him better than I do...
Leopold is Isidore Lechat.[1]"

And then wittily:

"Perhaps a Lechat who has had a better cat-lick," he corrected himself.

"Very well!" I replied, "I give you Isidore Lechat... But that
does not give me any detail... I always hear, when the King is
talked of: 'The King is this... the King is that'... but of stories
that illustrate these vague affirmations, I do not hear the slightest one. Or else, they are stories you hear in the streets, the
theatres, the boudoirs, the restaurants of Paris, and that I really
cannot take seriously... No, I need concrete facts... character
traits... even documents... in the case of such a man, there
must be thousands of admirable, extraordinary ones."

Then they began to chat about the King, saying many different things.

But you never learn anything... People pass near you, things
happen around you; no one has eyes, no one has ears.

They did not get beyond lyrical generalities which told me
nothing about this interesting character, other than their own
opinions which left me cold.

I finally discovered, what I had known for a long time, that
the King is refined, cunning, devious, voluptuous, without the
slightest scruple or the slightest pity. He is extremely harsh and
miserly, megalomaniac as well, more importantly with a strange
type of megalomania which compels him to build, to build
houses, palaces, shops, with no other aim than to turn Brussels
into an enormous city, rather like a New York or a Chicago. An
absurd project, for he has doubtless not reflected on the fact
that it is to Belgians—in fact to Belgians from Brussels—that
he is addressing himself, not to Americans. At the same time,
to satisfy his avarice, his pleasures, his megalomania, all he can

---

1 Isidore Lechat, the businessman, is the main character in Mirbeau's
comedy (1903) *Les Affaires sont les affaires,* [*Business is business*].

think of is money, more money, money all the time. He considers all means of getting it to be good, especially the worst ones. In business, his imagination is marvellous and inexhaustible. He takes folk in, even whole peoples, with a sovereign masterfulness. He never lacks for good tricks to play. In vain does he empty his bag; it is always full. His daughters, whom he fleeced in no time at all, found that out to their cost. England and Germany, who are not suckers that it is easy to *take in*, paid the price of his magicianly superiority, during the infamous negotiations about the Congo… He has turned his throne into a sort of supremely well-organised commercial counter, a business office, where he trades everything, sells everything, even scandal. In another epoch this man would have been a genuine scourge upon humanity, for his heart is totally inaccessible to any feeling of justice and goodness. Beneath external features that are polished, likeable, witty, elegantly sceptical, even familiar, he hides a soul of such complete ferocity that no pain can soften… How much he made his wife, his daughters suffer, will probably never be known… Ah! the poor creatures!… And they were envied!… There was a stupor in the whole of Belgium when it was announced that the Queen—the best, the gentlest, the most resigned of women—had died, on her own, totally on her own, like a beggar woman, in that sad palace at Spa. The King, of course, was in Paris… He took his time to come, begrudgingly, buried his wife informally, quickly, quickly, and, once the formalities were over, that very evening, took the train back to Paris in order to return to his pleasures… On this occasion it seems that people were not grateful to him for his lack of hypocrisy… I think that they were really in the wrong because it is good when men—even kings—show themselves as they really are. Perhaps he had enough esteem for his people not to pretend to be touched by a bourgeois sadness that he was not feeling; this was too idealistic for our notable Belgian and he did not agree with the theory… No, on that day, all one saw on the King's face was boredom, the irritation of having been disturbed for so trivial a matter… This funeral mass, no matter how quickly expedited, was not worth the disappointment of a missed business meeting, of a postponed lunch, in the Pavillon d'Armenonville…

The wife of the notable Belgian spoke next:

"If he is indulgent towards himself, he is ruthless towards others. His Court is strangled, stiff, with a stilted and old-fashioned protocol, an outdated and comical hierarchy… He wants virtue and religion to predominate there… You are bored to death… He does not care. He does not live his life there… He only comes to his Court to rest after he has tired himself out in Paris and to recharge his batteries… he uses us as a period of Lent… Besides, beyond this health cure for which we all pick up the bill, I think that his evil egotism is enormously amused at seeing others shrivelling up with boredom… Ah! you have no idea what a celebration is like at the Court of King Leopold, that old lecher, that friend of all pleasures… It always feels as if someone is being buried there."

I objected:

"But they say he is charming, gallant with women."

"With women from other countries, Good Lord!" cried the lady angrily. "But what about us?… With us!… he has only one joy… an infernal joy: to embarrass us, to hurt us, to mortify us… All we get from him is irony and… what shall I call it?… contempt… yes, that's it, contempt."

"And yet…" I began to imply, "what about, you know, she who…?"

The wife of the notable Belgian quickly cut across me:

"I know what you mean… you are wrong… She isn't Belgian… she isn't Belgian… she is… well, she isn't Belgian…"[1]

And she went on:

"I have only ever seen him unpleasant with Belgian women… with a coarseness of spirit which he is able, better than

---

1 An allusion to the dancer Cléo de Mérode.

anyone else, to dress up in light badinage, in sharp witticism, but which only increase the cruelty of the wound… What can one do?… Answer him back?… Get angry?… Then he takes his revenge on the husbands, for positions and honours are down to him… So, you remain silent, you smile, you accept all the humiliations… Life has to go on… I tell you… here is a very recent trait of his character, of what one likes to call his wit… At the last Court Ball, I was in a small drawing-room with one of my friends, the Countess of M ——. She's a charming woman, who has been a widow for four years… quite pretty… well, not very pretty… very good and very lively… whose life is, I recognise, a little free… a little free… But so what!… She does what she wants and what she does is nobody else's business, after all. The preceding evening, at the Ball of the Cercle de la Noblesse, the Countess had danced a lot with M. de K—— who, rightly or wrongly, is taken to be her close friend… But so what, she had danced decently, and nobody saw anything objectionable about it… Look here, Monsieur, I am asking you… if M. de K—— is her lover, nothing could be more natural than that she dances with him."

"Evidently."

"And if he isn't?"

"Then nothing could be more natural," I said in approval, "so that he does become her lover."

"Evidently."

She noticed that this adverb, where she had placed it, was perhaps rather quick… She hastened to resume her narrative.

"We were both languishing in the small drawing room, when the King, after the procession of the diplomatic corps, came in. Nothing depresses him, puts him in a bad humour, more than this ceremony which he detests… He came towards us… I am obliged to confess that, despite his years, the King has a fine look about him… he is slender… graceful… Well, he is good-looking… But from his small slanting eyes, frightening when you see them from close to, from a certain shape of his mouth, I know that there is an air of malice about him… And there was."

"'Well, Madame,' he said, addressing the Countess, '…are you enjoying yourself today?'

"'Yes, Sire, very much,' she replied, making a deep curtsey.

"'But not as much as yesterday… not as much as yesterday, is that not so?'

"My friend was embarrassed, and stammered:

"'What do you mean, Sire?'

"'I was told,' insisted the King, '…I was told that you danced a lot yesterday… at the Cercle de la Noblesse… danced a lot… With whom did you dance so much?'

"My poor friend blushed:

"'But Sire,' she stuttered, "I… I… I… can't remember.'

"'Ah!… Well… well.'

"And turning suddenly to me, he said to me:

""And you, Madame? Is it indiscreet also to ask with whom you danced?'

"The King waited for my reply… But as I remained silent, he saluted and, laughing with that spiteful little laugh which covered us with confusion, he slowly walked away."

The lady seemed outraged as she told this anecdote. She ended up with his conclusion with a rather rough energy:

"I don't care what you say… he's a cad!"

Then a senior Belgian civil servant protested gently:

"Lots of bad things are said about him… We have a regrettable tendency to demand that kings should be above and outside humanity… But, no… they are men like other men… Leopold is just a man like all men… that's all… He has our faults, our desires, our passions, our wickedness, our vices, perhaps also—who knows—our qualities as well? For example, why should his household be better than yours?… And that he should practise tedious and pompous virtues that you are sensible enough to repudiate for yourselves? Are you reproaching him for the boredom of his Court? Where do you think people are having a good time, where is it possible to have a good time anywhere in Brussels?… The boredom of his Court?… But it's the boredom of Brussels, it is just Brussels… The King can't do anything about it… He does what we all do, according to our means and preferences… when he is bored at home, he goes off to find pleasure elsewhere. And he's right to do so… And where Belgian ladies are concerned, one cannot use the Constitution to oblige him to sleep with them all."

At this point there was an explosion of fury which I shall not bother to describe here, because you can easily imagine it for yourselves, but also because it had no effect at all on the senior civil servant, who all the same continued his panegyric.

"As far as I'm concerned, I am infinitely grateful to the King for not taking his royalty too seriously. He will have served—much more than anarchists did—to demonstrate to the people that Royalty, in our time, is completely useless, completely out of date, almost as grotesque as the old chivalric armour which still furnish, here and there, the anti-chambers and the corridors, in a few castles belonging to wealthy shoemakers… it should only exist in operettas, even though librettists think that this theme is worn out. Seriously, don't the Courts of Austria, Germany, Spain, with the buffoonery of their ceremonial, the carnival-like splendour of their disguises, now look more like stupid theatre sets, lamentable staging, racecourse productions?… Whenever I meet Leopold, he never gives me the impression that he is the King of the Belgians. I tell myself: 'Ah! there's the Chairman of Belgium & Co!'… And that is enough, I can assure you, to satisfy the demands of my national pride… And then, I actually like him… He is witty, speaks charmingly, with modesty… Do you want me to prove it?… There was a time when all the newspaper and flower kiosks, all the windows of bookshops, all the stationers, were full of postcards, showing—in Lord knows what poses!—the King and Mlle Cléo de Mérode. I remember having seen some that were absolutely obscene… he was really annoyed by it… and what annoyed him more than the lèse-majesté that they revealed so audaciously, it was their clumsy and crude stupidity… Although he never complained, their display was strictly forbidden, but not their sale which continued, under the table, as they said at the time of Andréa de Nerciat."[1]

The senior civil servant interrupted himself to ask me:

"I am sure that you certainly know your compatriot, M. B——… don't you?"

"The spitting image of the King?"

"Yes."

"I think so… the same height, same elegant appearance, same square beard, same eyes… It's extraordinary!"

"You do know him… Good… Well, one day last year, in Ostend, the King was walking on the harbour wall… with a few friends… He mixes with the crowd to such an extent that nobody takes notice of him… When he passed by near me, I had stopped in front of a kiosk which, unusually, was covered, from top to bottom, with the postcards I have already mentioned… Imagine my surprise when I saw the King turn round, leave his group, and head for the kiosk!"

"'Good day, good day, dear Monsieur C——,' he said to me, in a very friendly voice as he saw me. "Ah! I am pleased to see you… I was told that yesterday, at the Cercle, you won… a large sum of money… a very large sum.'

"'Good Lord, Sire… that's true… I was quite fortunate… quite fortunate.'

"'So much the better… so much the better… One must earn money, dear Monsieur C——, much money.'

"He bought a newspaper which he put in the pocket of his overcoat and… raising his head he looked at all the postcards of which the least improper showed him, with, on his knees, Mlle Cléo de Mérode, almost naked and who was pulling his beard. I was anxious, but also a bit amused, I must say.

---

1 Andréa de Nerciat (1739-1800) was the author of racy novels.

"Once he had looked them over, he showed me these horrors, with perfect ease, and in the most natural tone:

"'What about this kiosk?' he said. "What do you think?… This poor M. B——! He must be really annoyed with all this filth. I know that he will be coming to Ostend soon… Please have all that removed, but discreetly…'

"Having shaken my hand, he left to join his friends."

The anecdote was successful.

"That's quite charming," they murmured with nods of approval, "that's not bad."

The only person not to be disarmed was the wife of the notable Belgian. With an expression of hatred, she looked at the notable Belgian who was now not talking and taking, with the tips of her fingers, a praline from a box of chocolates… then shrugging her shoulders so strongly that a rose fell from her corsage, and rolled on the carpet:

"Oh! You… really," she rasped.

They talked no more about the King… They talked about Paris, and about art, and about art and Paris, and Paris and art.

Of course!

And, of course, I stole away as best I could.

Red Rubber.[1]

I stop in front of a little shop with a very strange window display: pyramids of small whetstones, small cubes, small cylinders, small parallelepipeds, small bread rolls made of a dull material, alternately grey or black. Nothing else. No indication. No label. With my face pressed to the window, I can see, in the

---

1 *Red rubber* was the title of an anti-slavery work by E.D. Morel that appeared in London in 1906. In a work published in 1998 *Les fantômes du Roi Léopold* Adam Hochschild calculates that, between 1880 and 1920, 10 million Africans died, about half the initial population of the Congo, working on the rubber plantations. Although the true figure was undoubtedly large, Hochschild's evaluation is disputed.

shop, a thick-set man, in a frock-coat who, with a cigar in his mouth, is reading a newspaper. The shop sign bears this single name, written in red letters: "Blothair[1] & Company."

I go in; I ask.

"What is all that?"

The man in the frock-coat has stood up. He puts the newspaper down on a chair, his cigar at the edge of a table, bows, smiles and says:

"Samples of rubber, Monsieur."

The shop is empty. On the walls, permanent cupboards, in waxed mahogany, all closed. To the right, a table, on which are repeated the samples in the window. To the left, a counter with ledgers. At the back, an open door, through which I glimpse a sort of stockroom, piled with raincoats, sections of cables, engine gaskets, galoshes, protective covers and tyre covers, and a whole family of rubber dogs, with some of them, lying on their backs, revealing a small round wound under their stomachs, with metal lips. It is all very old, *worn out*, as you might say.

Pointing to the pyramids in the shop window and on the table, I ask:

"From the Congo, I suppose?"

"Yes," replies the man, simply but with an expression of pride.

This shop window is quite inoffensive; the shop seems placid. However, gradually, I become fascinated by the samples. It comes to the point where I cannot take my eyes of these pieces of rubber. Why are there not any explanatory pictures, photos, in this window?… My imagination quickly makes up for their lack.

I am thinking of the forests, of the lakes, of the enchantment of this paradise of sun and of flowers… I am thinking of the childish negroes, charming negroes, capable of the same kindness and same fierceness as the children. I remember this phrase of an explorer: "They are as pretty and as gentle as the

---

1 It is possible that this name is a reference to Hubert Lothaire a Belgian officer who had unjustly hanged an English arms dealer.

rabbits you see, in the evening, at the edge of the woods, washing themselves or playing in the scented grass." Which, however, did not stop him killing them… I can see them, as they laugh, showing their shining teeth and chasing one another, becoming exhilarated at the sound of their fifes and their bass drums. I can see the perfect bronzes of the female bodies, and the little ones running about, with their swollen bellies. I can see great devils, as handsome as ancient statues, smiling at a loincloth, at strings of beads; reaching out their arms towards liqueurs; jostling one another, pawing the ground around watches, phonographs, all the poor rubbish we manufacture for them; arching themselves, prancing about, as if they are making fun of us, or are making fun of themselves; moving their heads like embarrassed children. I can see, in their women, susceptible to the caresses of white men, the awkward gesture of a peasant woman made to blush easily by a city dweller.

And so suddenly, I see above them, and threatening them, the whip of the trafficker, of the colonialist, of the civil servant. I see them only being forced to work, at revolver point, treated as badly as our soldiers are in the penitentiaries in Africa, and coming back from work, exhausted, their skin slashed, less numerous than they were when they set off. I can see executions, massacres, tortures, during which are screaming, a mish-mash of bleeding, trussed up athletes who are crucified, women whose tortures provide a horrible voluptuous spectacle, children who are fleeing with their arms over their heads, their tiny legs disjointed beneath their prominent bellies. Clearly, in a grey patch, in a black lump, I have picked out the too pretty torso of a negress who has been raped and decapitated, and I have also seen old men, mutilated, dying, with their dried-out limbs crackling. And I have to close my eyes to evade the vision of all these horrors, which these samples of rubber, in front of me, so motionless, so neutral, have suddenly provoked in me.

These are the images that should be evoked by almost every passing tyre and almost each cable, sheathed in its isolating jersey. But you cannot always know where rubber comes from. Here, you are aware: it comes from the Congo. It really is *red rubber*. There is not a single gramme of it, landed at Antwerp, that is not covered in blood.

In South America, in Malaysia, in the Indies, the cultivation of rubber plants is simply an agricultural industry. In the Congo, it is the worst human exploitation imaginable. They began by making incisions in the trees, as they do in America and in Asia, and then as European merchants and industry increased their demands, and because greater profits were required for the companies on which King Leopold's fortune depends, they finished by uprooting the trees and the creepers. The villages never provide enough of the precious matter. They thrash the negroes whose slow work makes them impatient. Their backs are striped with bleeding tattoos. Expeditions are organised which travel everywhere, pillaging, demanding the payment of tributes. Hostages are taken, some of the youngest women, children, with whom it is permitted to have a little bit of fun to pass the time, or old men whose howls of pain provoke laughter. The rubber is weighed in front of the gathered negroes. An officer consults a notebook. All that is needed is a discrepancy between two figures for blood to flow freely and for a dozen heads to roll between the boxes.

And still more tyres are needed, more raincoats, more networks for our telephones, more insulation for engine cables. Therefore, just as one makes incisions in vegetable matter, one makes incisions in the deplorable native races, and the same ferocity which uproots the creepers is depopulating the country of its human plants.

Down with the English who are jealous and who do not forgive King Leopold for having tricked them and stolen from them! Down with the scribblers on paper, creators of embarrassment! If the pitch on all our tyres, on all our cables, is made of negro blood, then big deal! How better may we associate the inferior races of our civilisation, than to mingle them more closely with the needs of our trade and our life?… And then Leopold's palaces, his whims, his pleasures, are expensive. Is it not necessary to increase the shareholders' dividends, to pay the newspapers for them to remain silent, give shares to the Belgian parliament, so that they will vote the right way, disengage other governments so that they will shut their eyes to these atrocities?

It is all the same. The next time I meet King Leopold dragging his leg in Monte-Carlo, in Trouville, or in the rue de la Paix, when I see his eye shining, beneath the looking glass, as he looks at a jeweller's caskets, staring at the corsage or the lips of a woman passing by, when I see the too mature lady companion of a pretty young woman whisper in the sovereign's ear, in a restaurant on the Champs Élysées, I shall think of this shop window and will not be inclined to laugh.

"We also have fine ivory," the man in the frock-coat said to me, leading me to the door.

Remorse.

I notice that I, who so bitterly criticise the French for their aggressive irony and their injustice to other peoples, have just been very French where the Belgians are concerned.

Is it because they are from Brussels?

Do we not have Toulouse? Do we not have the spirit of Toulouse, which is as much a caricature of France, at least as much as the spirit of Brussels is a caricature of Belgium?

No doubt the Belgians have their ridiculous characteristics, just as we do, as do all nations. They also have qualities, virtues that many others do not have, and which I wish the French had, who are so proud of their frivolity and vain riches. They work. They know how to awaken old cities from their ancient torpor. Even Bruges is finally emerging from its long mystic silence. The noise of hammers, the whistle of factories are nowadays louder than the sounds of its bells and the funereal whispering of its béguinages. Despite all its religious flaws, a glimmering of new life is shaking and animating this little country. Finally, M. Edmond Picard and M. Camille Lemonnier do not represent Belgium any more than M. Drumont and M. Bourget represent France.

And then I do not forget that I like Maurice Maeterlinck, that I like Émile Verhaeren, that I did like Franz Servais, the gentle and tender Rodenbach. And this last holiday in Brussels, and everyone I encountered there, everyone I rubbed shoulders with, I like them more and more and admire them with greater faith. They owe nothing to France which, on the other hand, was happy to welcome them, to honour them and to derive honour from them. And Brussels, where they are not from, and where they could not be from, and through which they have only passed, has taken none of their genius away from them. They are from where they come from, for they have been able to incarnate in their so different works, with a strength and a grace that are very rare, the very soul of the places where they were born.

I encountered Maeterlinck again in Ghent, beside the canal, and I also rediscovered in the dead waters of the canal all the mirages, all the reflections, all the magical melancholy of his youth. And in the garden of the family home, I saw again the hive, whence departed the divine bees which went off to feed on the beautiful flowers of wisdom and of life.

What about Verhaeren? I heard his eloquent voice, his word carried away, in the wind which blows over the hard plains of the Escaut… and I collected, on the old doors of Flemish dwellings, on the old Flemish houses in the villages, his fine verses sculpted with such a certain gouge, with such a powerful and such a passionate chisel.

I searched, as if he were still living, for Franz Servais, in the fertile countryside around Halle and the sad streets of Ixelles. I hear him laughing joyfully and tarrying as he spoke of the music of Liszt, and of the proportion of Flemish influence there is in the work of Beethoven, and, once again, of that admirable poem about Joan of Arc, that he was going to set to music, and which died with him.

And I surprised Rodenbach in an old lace-like house in Bruges, with its intimate silences, sitting, behind this transparent screen that vaporises faces, listening to the pealing of the bells, and weeping for the souls of men, watching the swans glide over the bronze water of the Lac d'Amour.

They are from where their home is because thought always needs a fulcrum, a certain springboard, from which to fly away and fan out throughout humanity. They are from where their home is, but they are at home with us, and they are from everywhere, like those privileged beings who were able to bring a truth, an emotion, an eternal form of beauty, to the world which takes pleasure from them.

And perhaps my bad temper—for which I will be forgiven because of my love for Maeterlinck, for Verhaeren, for Franz Servais and for Rodenbach—is uniquely linked to the childish fact that we have been too often forced, despite ourselves, to climb up and go down the rue Montagne-de-la-Cour, and to drive for much longer than we would have wished in the Bois de la Cambre… That is all it takes.

Scarcely, indeed, after a week, had we finished driving in Brussels when, just as we left, right in the middle of the Boulevard Anspach, our four tyres burst simultaneously.

I nevertheless thought, despite my remorse, that it was quite funny.

ANTWERP

Towards the Port.

A gentleman had done, I am not sure what, something that contravened the laws of the Principality of Monaco; for not only are there roulette wheels and cocottes, in the Principality of Monaco, there are also—may justice forgive me—laws. Perhaps this gentleman had been indiscreet enough to win too large a sum at Trente-et-quarante; perhaps he had allowed himself to cast doubt on the princely virtues of oceanography; perhaps he had attributed an expiatory character to the seismographic equipment, installed at each street corner of Monte-Carlo by the generosity of the Prince. Nevertheless, one morning he saw the commissioner of police come into his hotel bedroom who, solemnly, in the name of his Most Serene Highness, brought to his attention a decree for his expulsion. To which, as was the custom, the commissioner added:

"You have twenty-four hours to reach the border."

The gentleman replied, with a smile:

"Oh! Five minutes should do me!"

There are scarcely any more distances in Belgium than there are in Monaco. Which means that in Belgium one is more aware of the chaotic state of the little roads.

And with what fervour do I invoke Leopold!

"Oh Leopold," I begged, "sovereign Master of the Commission, of Brokerage, and of Banking, Prince of Trading,

King of Business and of love affairs, incomparable *Businessking*, you, who understand so well, where your personal life is concerned, all the economic necessities of modern life, the woman-chaser King, you who so well sow gold and roses on all the roads leading to Venus, can you not move a few of your scandalous profits from the sands of Ostend and the negroes of the Congo, into your metropolitan roads, which break your ribs and backs as cruelly as the artistic sentences of M. Edmond Picard damage your brain?"

Vain prayer.

But I get the impression that an ironical voice, a well-known voice from the private rooms of the Restaurant Paillard, replies:

"Why do you want me to give roads to these Belgians for whom I am the always absent King? Do as I do. French roads are magnificent."

Then, since after the energetic efforts of Brossette our four tyres had stopped making fun of us, we set off for Antwerp. Do I need to repeat that it is always the same cobblestones, waves of hard stone? But, at the risk of breaking our springs and disembowelling our crankcase, in our joy to be leaving Brussels, we reach an average speed of fifty-five kilometres an hour. We will be in Antwerp in three-quarters of an hour. And yet I am cross that the engine is not running harder and that the Flemish countryside which, with its flat fertility, feeds an industrious people, the trees, the low houses, the dark greenery, the regular multi-coloured villages, are not passing by quickly enough, as I would wish, anxious to get to a port.

Near Malines, what a joy, teams of workers are removing the cobblestones. From now on, I suppose, we will be driving on the elastic silk of a brand-new tarmac. And then, suddenly, a violent shock throws us against one another. The car has plunged, down to its axles, into a quagmire. It rages, grumbles, and steams, powerless… A burst waterpipe has softened and weakened the ground at this spot and transformed the road into a lake of deep, sticky mud. We need the rather humiliating assistance of two horses, pulling as hard as they can, to haul the car from this bog.

And the cobblestones begin their torturous undulations once again.

Ah! these roads!… these roads!

Fortunately, the good old C. G.-V. is miraculously robust, and so well built that not a bolt is missing, after this audacious foray… not one has come loose… She is furious that we had to get help from horses, she is uncontrollable. At times she is no longer on the ground. She is flying, flying in the air like a balloon. We will be in the port in a few minutes… unless we are lying in the road, crushed and with our bellies slashed open!

A Harbour.

What a wonderful and always new sight is a great harbour! A scary world in which the whole universe is at ease between the docksides of a berth, in which, in a prodigious display of colour come together the implacable realities of money, of trade, of warfare, and the most delightful enchantments! Black and rolling masses which are transporting in their holds the imagination, the genius, the fertility, the filth, the riches, the death of the whole world!… Turmoil, on the lapping waters, of the small, furious tugboats and of the heavy barges, around which the seagulls surge in their whiteness, like flecks of foam around a reef! On the quaysides, between the bales, the tons of grease and of lard, the wools and the pelts, with their odours of decay, there is a swarming of naked torsos, bending under the strain, and poor open-mouthed faces twisted with fatigue and revolt! The work of machines which, continually shrieking, raise and move about in space, at the ends of their iron arms, the heavy loads, as soft as if they were clouds!… Light, airy silhouettes, sails, masts.—"Your hair is like masts… Your dress slips onto the lawn in the garden, like a little, pink sail onto the sea…"

And between all that is creaking, panting, howling and singing, the silent heap of a city, and the vaporisation, in the sky, of gilded domes, of blue spires, of towers, of cathedrals, of Lord knows what… And beyond that, still, infinity… with all that it awakens in us of sleeping nostalgia, all that it unleashes in us of new and passionate desires!

✳

There is scarcely a harbour where I do not feel moved… I am enchanted by even the little, tucked away ones like curlews' nests, in the depths of rocky creeks, and from which a barque scarcely sets sail… My heart jumps and bounds in the large ones… It is there that the rivers which are human join the supernatural sea.

For me the largest cities are almost always small, closed worlds… A moment quickly arrives when I feel I am in prison there… and I bump into the walls there… I stifle in the mountains; I am unable to breathe their atmosphere, their clouds, which always steal the sight of peaks and the sky, and crush me like heavy, like thick pieces of lead. The forest clasps my heart, makes me anxious, tightens my throat into a sob… I cannot stand this sort of religious terror, which it accumulates beneath its canopies and which fills its darkness, where, sometimes, wild animals are letting out deathly howls…

But there is not a quayside, a jetty, a breakwater, a wharf, there are not *piers*, as they say here, alongside which boats are swaying, in which I do not genuinely feel at the edge of the universe, and joyful, and free, and light… The whistles which make railway station windows vibrate, even the largest ones, are only lacklustre warnings; they do not really appeal to my imagination… The call of sirens has a different meaning, a different eloquence, a higher reach. When it sounds out in harbours, it has the sonority, the depth, the poignant emotion of news arriving from the ends of the earth, and each time I have heard their accents continuing, from the farthest off part of myself, I heard replying to them my insatiable desire for unknown seas, landscapes of fire and ice, of flora and fauna, of humanities I would like to know and whom, no doubt, I shall never know.

The song of the sirens arouses, to the point of delirium, my curiosity about the whole world.

Ships.

But just the very look of ships gives me a complete and gentler satisfaction.

I like them all.

It is the boldest of human machines, the one with the greatest natural elegance. I often think, tenderly, about the bold and charming soul of he—whose name history has not retained—who, one day, sitting at the edge of a pool and watching an adorable little teal with a red head swimming on the water, invented the boat.

Ah! He was right to invent it, the boat, this kind unknown person, for I think that, if not, I would have invented it myself, so much do I love it… Do not be surprised!… When I was a child, without knowing anything about physics and geology, without knowing anything about the famous principle of *connected vessels*, I invented fountains. And because, as happy as a sandboy, with the ingenuous faith of ignorance, I tried to explain, sketchily, this discovery to my teacher:

"But it's an artesian well!" he cried out with a look of scornful pity that I will never forget… "Little imbecile, off you go!… And Moses, who made the waters gush in the desert with the tip of his wand? What do you say about Moses?… And gunpowder, you invented that as well, I suppose?… You will copy this sentence out a thousand times: 'I invented artesian wells'."

It is to this punishment, no doubt, that I owed the fact that, later, I did not invent gunpowder… I would have been too ashamed.

The taste that I have for motorcars, the less kind but more knowledgeable sisters of boats, for skates, for swings, for balloons, sometimes also for the fever, for everything which raises me up and carries me away, very quickly, away from here, ever farther away, higher, always higher and always farther, all these tastes are closely linked together… They have their common origin in that instinct, restrained by our civilisation, which drives us to participate in the rhythms of the whole of life, of free, ardent and alas vague life like our desires and our destinies.

✳

I did once like locomotives, but I do not like them now. They lack imagination, grace, personality, they are too subservient to the tracks, too much the slave of stupid timetables and tyrannical rules. They are administrative, bureaucratical; they are poor, solid, joyless souls with no dreams like those of the functionary who, all day long, puts down the same writing on the same paper and inserts the same sheets into pigeonholes that never change. On their fenced-in tracks, between their embankments of sad grass, they give me the impression of prisoners, only allowed to walk in the exercise yard of their prison.

Too clumsy to bend their crude assemblies, their stiff joints, to the pretty curve of the bends, too heavy, too quickly out of breath from climbing gradients, for no apparent reason they plunge into tunnels, like a frightened rat into the darkness of his den.

And yet they are not so old, and already they are as nothing. Just like so many regressive forms, which no longer meet the needs of today's man, they are fated to disappear… But in how many centuries?

But let us be fair towards them. They had their hour of glory and, when one travels from Zurich to Innsbruck, pulled by them, through the bold gorges of the Arlberg, their glory still continues. It is true that the greatest part of that glory goes to the audacious engineers who managed to carve for them, in the rock, on the sides of the gorges, paths where until then neither mountain goats nor shepherds dared venture.

⁕

Man really only surpassed himself when he constructed machines to which he gave the virtue of free movement, at the hour of his need, at the very minute of his whim.

Such as, the motorcar.

Balloons, of which I am dimly aware, almost as dimly as I am of M. Santos-Dumont,[1] but much better than M. Lebaudy,[2] still make you think of disproportionate beasts, in which nature was stumbling towards its first attempts at creation. These prehistoric monsters, of which we still have a more and more weakened survival, amongst those curious animals called nationalists (see Millevoye, Déroulède), had to make useless great leaps forward, and only their stupidity prevented them from being surprised by their enormous clumsiness.

But the motorcar is beginning to take on the supple beauty of beings that have been reasonably built, reasonably balanced, and the organs of which correspond to the needs of its functions

⁕

However, let us here show our indignation just a little bit.

There are irritating imbeciles, quite lacking in imagination and in taste, who plonk on the chassis of a small mo-

---

1 A famous Brazilian pioneer of aviation.
2 A wealthy businessman who invested in dirigible balloons.

torcar Lord knows what stupidity of sedan chair; others, no less irritating and no less imbecilic, who are proudly haunted by memories of horse-drawn carriages with windows, preserved in royal armouries, and which could still be seen a few years ago being used at carnivals on racecourses… There are motorcars, crudely squatting like Buddhas, swelling out their hideous bellies above insect thin limbs… There were, and there still are, radiators so poorly attached that the motorcar seems to be losing, along the way, its intestines as a poor horse does during a bullfight… There are stingy bonnets that do not entirely enclose the engine and make you think that it is not finished. There are, in fact there are many, which look like moving larders, others which look like coffins already eaten by worms, and even others which look like tombs, prematurely built to receive the mutilated limbs of their unfortunate drivers… and still more, of which the rather dull ambition is limited to pretending to be, through I know not what analogy, a modest tube as if it were a stove lying on its side… And there are some of which the accent, very Italian and, as we have seen, very Bruxellois, is comic in developing the scale of a gas bell around empty chambers in which thunder no more than the power of eight cab horses. There are also motorcars which, when they are at rest, seem logical, stable, from the desired curved front to the rear that is rounded like a barge's stern and which, once the machine carries them away, jump, twitch, lose cohesion and rattle lugubriously, for the sole reason that their master, inappropriately ambitious, has not understood the irreparable lack of balance and taste that comes with a counterfeit. It is the same wealthy entrepreneur, fortunate commissioner, who thinks that he is displaying seigneurial pomp by installing a driver at the wheel of his motorcar, shaved, booted, belted in, derisorily kitted out with a top hat, with a resplendent and obscene coachman's livery.

As for the electric car, it is just an illusion, not yet knowing where to rest its strength…

And I have no bed on which to rest my head…[1]

✳

But finally, it has to be said, a shape became established, particularly in France, which has what is necessary to satisfy us.

If, for example, I am touched by the fine outline, the fine curve, so full, so well modelled, so perfectly harmonious of the bonnet of the Charron, it is because it encloses the whole of the engine and gives it its exactly fitting epidermis. I am no less so by the layout of the motor, by the studied coiling of its copper scrolls, by the quadruple branching of the intake so practically mechanical and so attractively ornamental, by the whole apparatus bringing together the metals most appropriate to their task, to the anatomical distribution of the pieces which, not only animate the motor and capture its energy, but which also give it a genuine beauty.

Yes, a beauty, dear Monsieur Mauclair de la Lune…

If there is a beauty in beings and objects which is no more than the fact of fully, exclusively, corresponding to their fate and to their use… well, Monsieur Mauclair, I am like you, I do not know what beauty is.

The aesthetic nature of objets d'art is infinitely more mysterious and, as a result, infinitely more confused… But as is the case that with all sorcery, a book of spells is needed.

✳

Between the machines that man's sensitivity and imagination have created to free himself from his thousands of servitudes

____

1 Possibly a reference to *Luke*, Ch. 9, V. 58.

and to get closer to the elements, it is thus the boat and the motorcar that I prefer.

Carried away by one or the other, I taste the same cosmic pleasure; I am exalted by the same intoxication… Aboard them, I am at the edge of space. Each revolution of the wheel, as each turn of the screw, or the simple effort of the sail, beneath the propulsion of the wind, infinitely multiplies the circumferences of air or water, concentric as I look at them, with its scope as a radius, and their vertiginous addition creates my notion of moving space… Then, gradually, I am aware that I am myself a little of that space, a little of that vertigo… Proudly, joyfully, I feel that I am an animated fragment of that water, of that air, a particle of that motor force that animates all organs, coils and uncoils all springs, turns all the cogwheels of that unimaginable factory: the universe… Yes, I feel that I am, to say it all with a wonderful word: an atom… an atom becoming alive…

I am enchanted by the fact that the shapes of the motorcar and the boat are related; that the wind cuts off, when we are under way, the always so useless words, just as the sea imposes silence; that the sailor and the driver do not only share the taste of remaining silent, that they have, one at the steering wheel of his machine as the other at the tiller of his vessel, the same spirit of quick decision-making in the face of the obstacle that suddenly appears, the same cold tranquillity in the face of death. I like the fact that, in their eyes, the continuous observation of spaces deepens the same quality of colour, sharpens the same acuity of vision…

And the siren in the countryside, the siren in the mountains, almost as moving as at sea and in the harbours, the siren of which the prolonged warning teaches the fearful beasts, the villages in turmoil, the sleeping motorcars, hostile humanity, that the roads are made so that everything may pass by, even the storm, even progress, which is a storm, since it is a revolution.

The City.

For a long time we had driven along the meanderings of the Senne—the road and the water were dodging about like children playing a game—we had gone through a few nondescript small towns, almost dead villages, a sad and black countryside, across which the wind howled, we had raced through Malines and its mud bogs, gone past the forts which defend Antwerp, slowed down in the suburbs, before stopping for lunch in the centre of the city, in the Place de Meir.

If the beauty of a city may be judged by the excellence of its restaurants, then Antwerp does not hold a candle to Brussels. In Antwerp, which is undoubtedly extremely rich, where bourgeois life is, so it is said, intense and lavish, where vast numbers of travellers arrive, to go forth to the four corners of the globe, the restaurants are indifferent, and so are the hotels. No comfort, no luxury; scarcely the bare necessities. Meals quickly prepared, quickly swallowed, and then off one goes. One would think that as you see their agitation the citizens of Antwerp do not have time to eat. Their agitation is less strolling about, less dawdling, less chatty, less literary, more expressive than in Brussels.

The Place de Meir is packed full of people moving about. Hurried crowds do not tarry in front of shops, at the smallest of incidents in the street, they crisscross, mingle, disappear and continually reform… They are going to work, to their business activities… It recalls, with less hectic feverishness, activity in London, in the streets of the City, or even better, the calmer, weightier activity of Berlin, in the *Friedrichstrasse*. First of all, not much personality in the varieties. In vain do I seek in the women the plump beauty, the blond beauty, the luxuriance, the lyrical blossoming of the fleshes of Rubens… But that is not immediately evident, you only see it in villages, in the countryside, on the thresholds of doors, and I have noticed, with only a few exceptions, that cities, especially cities of work and of wealth which, like Antwerp, are outfalls of all humanity, have quickly unified into one single type the characteristic features of faces... It seems now that, in large cities, all rich people look alike as do all poor people.

It does not take much for gawping to win over the crowd that initially seemed so busy. All that is needed is a motorcar stopped in front of a restaurant. Must I believe that in Antwerp there are so few motorcars or so few which pass through that ours is such a new or rare sight? That would be surprising. It is a sensation, no two ways about it; it is even a scandal. It is looked at with a sort of troubled curiosity, like an unknown animal, and they do not know whether it is gentle or vicious, whether it bites or allows itself to be stroked. Urchins, first as they do everywhere, then women, draw closer, are examining it with a look that is both uneasy and delighted. They form a crowd which still keeps a respectful distance from the machine... Each one is saying:

"If suddenly, it began to roar, move, rush at us!"

Then, after a few minutes, it is a genuine crowd which, minute by minute, is getting bigger and bigger. They get bolder, want to play with the gear lever, the brake lever, the clutch pedal, even lift the openings of the bonnet. Soon, all you see is a confusion of heads, undulations, eddies, a moving tempestuous surface, from which murmurs are emerging.

Brossette has a lot on his plate. I worry that he may let out too rude a word, that he might make an inappropriate gesture. And if so, what will happen then? You never know with crowds, more impressionable, more jittery, madder than women. Brossette, as much as the machine, is the object of general curiosity. Because the wind was cold this morning, he has put on his wolf skin. And this wolf skin, worn by a man, produces huge astonishment. Some are laughing and poking fun, others are outraged, others are almost terrified. They have never seen a human being dressed like an animal... They all want to feel his skin, to see if it is alive, to stroke the hair to see whether this hair really belongs to this strange and fabulous man… A joker, amidst the laughter, asks Brossette whether he eats cows and sheep alive, and why he does not walk on all fours like a dog, instead of showing off on two legs like a man… Ah! finally! Parisian wit, as I find again on our banks of the Escaut… I find it again in all its traditional purity of fear of change and of practical joke… And I will find it again even more so, this evening, at the theatre, in a satirical review: *A twerp in Antwerp*, which seems, without its obscenities, to have been conceived, written, directed by a Monsieur de Gorsse of crudity… And that is probably all that Antwerp has retained from us, from our so short influence, from our so ephemeral domination, although Lazare Carnot who governed here did not have the reputation of being a very Parisian wit, nor a playwright for music halls in Parisian theatreland.

I do not know how all this will finish, how we will be able to get back in the motorcar, in the middle of this crowd which always seems to be getting bigger and bigger, and which is getting more and more twitchy. I voice my anxiety to the owner of the restaurant… He is smiling, officious, proud to be receiving us in his establishment. He says to me:

"It's nothing, nothing, have no fear… they are having a good time… they don't see those very often, do you understand, but they are decent people, decent people."

And then, scratching his head, he adds with a grimace:

"All the same… it would be better if your driver were to take that off… yes… you know… his pelt… Ah! his pelt! It's that pelt, do you see, that pelt!"

This curiosity, which was sometimes annoying, stayed with us from then on… It will follow us through the whole of Holland, except for Amsterdam and The Hague, and it will reach its high point in Volendam where, however, the men, giants with brick-red faces, with a gentle look, wear large fur bonnets, like Circasians…

✳

I no longer like old cities, or the old stinking districts of old cities, or the dark old alleyways which tumble one into the other, nor the old Gothic gables, the weekly site of the erudition of local art societies which meet on Sundays, scraping and re-scraping the hitherto sculpted doors, the door frames and the beams with their embellishments that have disappeared… I no longer like the old porches opening up to courtyards in ruins which never saw the sun, and flowers which never encountered moss or lichen… And I no longer like the old bridges under which sleep black, putrid waters. If first of all I like the picturesque; if I am first of all seduced by the supple and complicated shape of these arabesques, by this patina, of accumulated dirt polished and modelled by time; if this false 'artistic feeling' which I owe to a regressive education retains me for a few minutes in front of this spectacle of distress, of decay and of death, another feeling—a feeling of revolt and human dignity—pulls me away from it in horror. For in it I see the triumph of filth, of illness, of laziness, in which there crouches all the poetry of the past, in which the realities of the present are miserably petering out.

Is it not curious, is it not discouraging, this persistence that poetry has of liking only what is morbid, what is old, what is dead, and of condemning in the name of a stupid and sterile beauty, the youthful and magnificent effort made by men to-day, to put into a creative power the untamed element and all the wild forces that nature only used for destruction?

When you go through the gorges of the Romanche and you see, squatting beside the torrent, at the foot of an abyss of rocks, that little factory which has captured the waterfall, which has transformed it into motor energy, into light, into an infinite source of work which it distributes through its networks of copper wire, across a vast country, do you not experience an emotion that is just as poignant in its way, do you not feel a poetry just as grandiose in its way, as you do when you look at eroded stones?

But no, poetry retains us and will still retain us for a long time, for it is one of the elements which make up our Latin and Catholic race. Just look! As soon as it is a question of demolishing a block of rotten old houses, of bringing the pickaxe to bear on the alleyways full of the filth of centuries, to let in some air, some light, some health, then all we hear are protests, shouts, furies. Artistic and historical protection societies are created, commissions buzz about and work, newspapers are given over to the craziest propaganda, stimulate one another, the radical, the socialist, the royalist ones, to preserve, against what they call an act of vandalism, what they call the treasures of our national heritage. Finally, the government takes a step back in the face of the electoral danger that is always there, in France, in attempting to carry out a work of cleansing. In order to honour poetry, art and history, it will preserve these awesome hotbeds of infection. It will do better than that: it will appoint, to curate them, a curator.

Ah! I sometimes wonder, despite my admiration for the splendour of his verse, whether Victor Hugo was not a great Social Crime? Is he not, all by himself, the whole of poetry? Has he not engraved all our prejudices, all our routines, all our superstitions, all our errors, all our stupidities, in the indestructible marble of his verse?

I shall not take you to old Antwerp, not even to the Musée Plantin in which we will leave these gaggles of English people walking interminably through the interminable galleries, listening to the guardian recount the life and the career of this famous printer, as they listened to the guide who made them count on their fingers the echoes of the no less famous Cave of

Han, and on the battlefield of Waterloo the bemedalled historian who taught them the history of Napoleon, finally defeated by the Belgians. Let us race past the cathedral where it irritates me that Rubens is bored, on those dark and cold walls, behind the curtains of glossy green silk, and also in the Zoo, those poor condors who, in order to please Leconte de Lisle, and to authenticate his verse, are asleep, no longer in the frozen air of the Andes, but in their cages,

… their wings spread wide.[1]

And, if you like, we will go, to the Museum another time, tomorrow perhaps, when I shall feel disposed to confide in you my thoughts about Rubens, about this bountiful, shining, magnificent Rubens, of whom M. Ingres—Oh my dear Hélène Fourment![2]—wrote that he was but the 'drunk butcher,' the pork butcher covered in grease and in blood, of painting.

Let us drive rapidly, without stopping too much there, through the new town, with its wide, lively and busy roads, its gardens that Holland, nearby, would embellish with tulips and daffodils; let us speed along the boulevards, quickly, quickly, for nothing is holding me back there. I am anxious to get to the harbour from where I can already sense, in large gusts, the good, strong, delicious, intoxicating odours of saltiness and of coal tar.

Antwerp is a large city. It would even be the only genuinely large city in Belgium, if it were not, in reality, a German city. Germans, all the major ship owners, the major bankers, the major merchants, the engineers; German, the brokerage houses, the arbitrage houses, the companies of maritime insurance, of shipping, of emigration; German, everything which undertakes anything and works towards self-enrichment, everything

---

1 A line from *Le Sommeil du Condor*.
2 Rubens' model who was also his second wife.

which draws up a plan, makes a blueprint, adds figures together, is manipulating business and money.

At least, that is what is affirmed with ostentation, with brilliance, by the gilded signs resplendent on the facades of the houses and by the houses themselves, the stations, some public monuments which display that proud monumentalism that Germany has taken from America, and which gradually America is bestowing on all modern capital cities except Paris which, as an artist, elegant, an arbiter of taste, is stubbornly multiplying in our streets the heavy, parodic aspect of an eighteenth century of junk and of caricature.

It was in Antwerp, in a business building, that I saw for the first time in Belgium these German lifts, sorts of moving, perpendicular pavements that you walk on to and walk off from and which, without stopping, take up to the roof and bring back down to the street level those busy people who are either running from the Stock Exchange or running there.

The King obtained millions in order to fortify Antwerp. These fortifications have poise. The Belgians are very proud of them. They claim that the city is impregnable. The misfortune is that it has already fallen. I willingly believe that the Uhlans would have more trouble getting in than they would getting into Nancy. But why would they commit this useless folly of forcing their way in? Their families are proliferating there, are dominant there, solidly installed in places from which the civic guard will not dislodge them easily.

But here are the black streets, roadways that look like they are made of coal dust; dirty, salty houses, a crowd of louche little restaurants, one-eyed little inns, small shops, strange little counters, pressed one against the other… a whole hectic movement of tooting trams, whistling locomotives, heavy lorries… And smoky faces, exiled faces, faces from elsewhere, from nowhere, from everywhere… piles of sacks, piles of chests, rolling barrels… busy customs officers, suspicious, martial, who stab their probes into these poor dead things, as they would their bayonets, by virtue of the principle that commerce is war...

And all of that smells of soot, salty fish, alcohol, beer, thick oil, new wood, old leather and orange...

And here are the docks, above which yardarms and masts are swaying, along which fat chimneys are sending out into the sky the black trails of their smoke... and here and there, through an escape of light, between heavy planks, between dark, fat silhouettes, there is the lapping, the foaming of the yellowing waters of the Escaut.

It is the harbour.

On the Quaysides.

Less joyful and diverse, less colourful than Marseilles, the port of Antwerp is almost as imposing—not as magical or sinister—as the monster that is Hamburg. But there is only one Hamburg.

No other port has its extraordinary colour, its variety, its extent, its technology, nor its powerful avenues of water, lined as far as the eye can see, like huge trees in winter, by ships. No other has its twisting alleyways, by means of which it divides, spreads, in countless canals in the city, and running alongside parks, lawns, palaces, hills with flowers, re-joins the beautiful surface of the Alster. No other has its moving crannies in which the Elbe, so difficult to tame, infiltrates itself, strangles itself and roars because it cannot conquer the whole of the earth. Nowhere else, these huge, surprising silhouettes, these floating islands, these magical gardens suspended in the mist, these enormous and interminable towns that are the docks, and this impressive red cliff created in the fog by the tall brick houses of Altona. Nowhere else these fantastic nights lit by a prodigious constellation of signal stars, of lighthouses, of floodlights, of multicoloured electric lights, illuminated portholes... In this harbour, on a small but very fast yacht of the *Hamburg-America Line*, I sailed for a whole day and a whole evening and yet I only saw a tiny part of it. No large English port has ever given me, as much as Hamburg, the crushing, almost painful sensation, of the formidable...

The monumental clock of Saint-Pierre, in Beauvais, is so complicated that it has ninety thousand mechanical pieces which are set in motion by a simple little copper weight weighing only fifty grammes... Here it is just a small man, a small very old man, almost as old and scarcely heavier than the weight in the clock in Beauvais, M. Ballin,[1] whose genius is the moving force behind this gigantic instrument of commercial distribution. All by himself M. Ballin has done more for German grandeur and wealth than the cannons of Moltke, the lies of Bismarck, the universal agitation of Wilhelm II.

After Hamburg, Antwerp also is capable of satisfying and diverting us.

Goods from the whole world are unloaded there. The double network of the channelled river and the railway rhythmically carry out there, like the beating of a human organ, bales of wool, of metals, of ivory in exchange for clothes, toys, machinery; fruits, exotic plants, spices, petroleum, tons of rubber, precious woods, in exchange for coloured calico, perfumes and the glass beads so prized by the negroes... Dashing, fresh vessels set off gaily, whistling cheerfully, and swollen hulls, exhausted, eaten by rockweeds and barnacles, return, whimpering, and lying down in the docks to recuperate... Like the sailors... They too set off, their heads full of hope about the unknown and adventures... They went towards the miraculous... Many stayed there... There are some who return who are no longer recognisable, who no longer recognise anything and anyone... who do not recognise themselves... They are strangers.

---

1 Mirbeau exaggerates as Ballin was not that old as he was only 50 years old in 1907.

Ports are the most perfect, the most exact image of man's dream. They contain it, they carry it away, in its entirety, towards all chimaera... Dream of happiness, hope of making a fortune, putting degradation behind one, illusion of adventure, rejuvenation of unlucky energies... Departure makes joyful the worst distress... because for sick people, the remedy is never there where they are suffering... it is over there... It is that one has space before oneself and for oneself, one also has time, and at the end of space and time there can only be happiness... Travel is a numbness, a sleep peopled by our happy dreams... But a nothing may wake you up and make these dreams fly away... all that is needed is the first shape encountered in this vague enormity cradling you; all that is needed is the first city where you land, the first human face in which once again our implacable egoisms are encountered... and when one arrives, one is recaptured by reality, everywhere... everywhere... everywhere!

The limbs which, on all sides, as they creak, are being moved about by cranes, multiply the efforts of the human arms. The manoeuvres, the dockers with their hairy chests, their bent backs, their haggard eyes, their faces of exhausted animals, who seem condemned to carry out some useless torture from antiquity, are unloading the holds, which they are then going to refill, then unload, then refill, without respite. It is as though the ships only sail around the world in order to occupy interminably the effort of these fierce Danaids.

Tapirs.

There is something better than an odour of the sea on these quaysides… You get the smell there of the Islands and a whole feverish perfume of Africa. You see shivering negroes pass by, birds displaying, with raucous cries, an infinity of colours, troops of monkeys, curious, chatty, in which we always like to stare at our own grimaces, animals of every type.

I was present at the unloading of twenty tapirs. Admirable and very modern beasts, although one feels that their evolution, of which the ideal end point is perhaps the pig and perhaps the elephant, has come to a standstill. They do not seem to be surprised either by the crowd or the city… Nothing seems to surprise them. They were looking around with a heavy tranquillity, an impassive, hard assurance. They looked like twenty bank directors—a whole board of directors—returning from a study trip, from an economic investigation, and who were returning to their offices, heavier with new business.

Minstrels.

Surrounded by onlookers, workers, agents, small ships' cooks, there were two negroes… two poor negroes, dressed in black, with comically dented top hats, red scarves around their necks. One was dancing, the other was singing.

He was singing:

In my homeland, there are forests,
In the forests, there are trees,
In the trees, there are branches,
In the branches, there are birds,
And in the birds, there is music
A sort of little flute that goes: "Pipi… pipi… pipi…"

The Evangelist.

I was shown, sitting on a pile of luggage, in front of a departing steamer, a compatriot. He was a missionary. Bearded, booted, with leather belts, a colonial helmet too hastily placed on his head, his greasy cassock turned up like a soldier's greatcoat, he is investigating the mechanism of a Browning revolver, of which the holster is fixed to his belt, near a rosary with large beads. His bronzed face is lively, his laughing eyes are very gentle. When he laughs, he opens the mouth of a sufferer from quinsy, all black and with no teeth. A decent man, no doubt, but who looks more like a bandit than an apostle… I am reassured by that. I approach him. We chat… he is leaving for Fiji… with him he is taking a whole cargo of gramophones.

"You can't imagine," he tells me, "how limited, how stubborn those blasted negroes are!… It's curious… I can't succeed in evangelising them… I have tried everything… Nothing… nothing works… walls… the Good Lord, the Virgin, Saint Joseph, the joys of Paradise!… Yes indeed… They couldn't give a damn… you have no idea… I have seen plenty of negroes in my life… I have seen them, but not of this type… never… would you believe that alcohol, or nothing at all… it's all the same to them!… And yet Lord knows, it's an excellent method of conversion!… Ah! Good Lord, they get as drunk as pigs… And then, nothing… unbelievers after just as they were before… You know, that's unheard of… it's even unique… So, this time… I'm going to try gramophones… Yes, indeed!… What am I risking? Besides, it seems that gramophones operate genuine miracles… I have a friend in Africa, and they worked wonderfully well for him… And no worries… no fatigue… no catechising… He gathers his negroes around the instrument and, after the third record… bang… they are Christians… Their state of grace comes from listening to the gramophone…

Ah! ah! ah!… I am only half surprised by that… I have always noticed that negroes love music and singing. Therefore, I am going to see whether, with the military marches of the Republican Guard, the waltzes of Strauss, the comic songs of Yvette Guilbert, the bel canto of M. Caruso, I shall be more successful than with the Good Lord, the promise of Paradise, and the little tots of rum. In any case…"

He begins to laugh, an honest, sonorous laugh:

"In any case," he continues, "I shall not have set off yonder for nothing… For I give you my word of honour that, if I do not succeed in converting them… and even if I do succeed… well then!… ah! ah!… they will pay me for these gramophones, and at a price… ah! ah!… a genuine price… What do I risk? I am taking a thousand of them with me which I have thanks to the generosity of an old and very pious dowager… Ah! the decent woman, the holy woman!"

He puts his revolver in its holster, whilst turning his rosary on which crosses, hearts of Jesus, are clashing:

"It's fortunate," he concludes, "that from time to time we meet generous souls, souls like that… because religion, don't you see… nowadays, is becoming a lousy job… ah! Heavens above… a really lousy job! Still, there you are!"

Emigrants.

Workers from Hungary, from Romania, Serbian peasants, Bulgarian proletarians, whose tastes are like those of negroes, groups of Russian singers, all are setting sail for America… Already, their lassitude makes you feel sorry for them… brilliant women and yet suffering from worms, in red rags, with poor copper jewels, are dragging, as though they were bundles, children crying from tiredness, hunger, surprise. One wonders how it will all lead, and whether they will ever arrive at the end of their exile… Brutally they are made to go down to the bot-

tom of the holds where they are piled up like the merchandise
that they actually are and where, for days and nights, they will
be stacked, higgledy-piggledy, in the stench of their poverty
and their filth, with no air, almost no light, scarcely fed, subject
to the most severe discipline… They will not even have that
sort of respite that travel provides; they will not know that sort
of numbness, that anaesthetic brought to the most desperate
people by this enormous rocking vagueness that is the infinity
of sea and sky.

But the worst emigrants are these Jews from all countries
seeking, once again, a small piece of land, that they do not
hope to be hospitable, but where they may free themselves, a
little, from the scorn which follows them, and break the chains
of this appalling millstone of infamy, which they drag around
everywhere… I followed a group of them in sombre rags, who
were not left indifferent by any sight and who were gesturing
energetically… Despite their distress, one sensed in them a love
of life, an intelligence of life, something ardent, strong, tenacious rarely seen on the faces of other men… One truly felt,
just by looking at them, what useful energy, ingenious work,
progress, is stupidly destroyed when one massacres them, as
was done in Russia, or boycotts them as was done in civilised
countries, like France.

I said to myself:

"It is no doubt very sad and absurd; it touches your heart
and confounds reason… But what can you do? The poor Jew
is paying for the rich Jew… the ostentatious, insolent, voluptuous, all-conquering Jew who, more and more, is losing all
the ancient virtues of his race… And he is no longer using his
real name, of which he is ashamed and which he renounces,
he is using borrowed names, meaningless names which have
no odour, now that he is working towards the dispossession,
towards the ruin of others… His hand is everywhere, he walks
on everything, he is trampling everything underfoot. As soon

as he settles somewhere, it is not only to create a space for himself, which would be a legitimate thing to do, but to drive everyone else away… He has invented philosophies, systems of morality, in which those virtues most indispensable to man, conscience, trust in the given word, are scorned and treated as prejudices and nonsense… 'I don't give a damn about anything' is his motto… He is hated, but he is also feared for, in a society uniquely founded on the power of money, his money protects him."

The hatreds that he unleashes are not in the slightest way detrimental to him; they are blunted and broken on his golden breastplate. They only hit full in the heart, full in life, the small, poor people, as they always do. Vengeance is taken on them, innocent as they are, for the excesses of this brigand who seems—following the example of ousted aristocracies, of which, through shameful alliances, he endeavours to burnish the tarnished escutcheons, to refill the empty coffers—to have learned nothing and forgotten everything. He who formerly, throughout his beautiful yet terrible history, was one of the noblest elements of human progress, he who owed it to himself and owed it to his race, always the outcast, to be the eternal rebel, now he has become the accomplice, and, most frequently, the treasurer of all reactionary forces, even anti-Semitic ones, the most hideous, the most barbaric of all reactionary forces… And that is why these unfortunates, bowed down with his crimes, are setting off in search of a free country—does such a country exist?—where to be a Jew is not an irremediable shame.

And amongst these poor devils that I heard talking, with a bitter pity, how many, from continent to continent, will pursue their wandering path, without a single one of the five sous,[1] will follow their hope, with which the Providence they have

---

1 A reference to a story in which a man, in order to obtain an inheritance, must go round the world with only 5 sous.

invented for themselves continues to deceive them?… Out of a thousand, one will come back aboard a magnificent steamship, in a gilded cabin. He will come back ostentatious, insolent, all-conquering, and he will betray his former companions in poverty, and will contribute to making worse their eternal misfortune.

Pogroms.

On a sack of clothes, a little away from the others, sat a man who held my attention a little longer. He was an old man. He had a very long beard. Like most of his companions he was wearing an ample frock-coat, which had once been black, down to his calves, and like the others he was wearing a peaked cap, except that his was a cloth one. He was not talking to anyone and was looking straight ahead… like someone looking into the depths of himself. His serious face was expressing more distress than any face, even one of an old man in tears, and all the fatigue of human misfortune. And yet, his eyes had retained a moving youth and gentleness. I reproached myself for my indiscretion but did not succeed in diverting my gaze from this ruined face in which this youthful gaze shone out.

It was a little time before he saw me and then he began to look at me. I feared he might shout at me, or at least scowl, and what I feared most of all, when he stood up, was that I might lose him. But he smiled and I was delighted hear his voice sing out:

"Bonjour, Mossié!"[1]

I held out my hand to him. He shivered. His limp hand stayed in mine for a few seconds, clumsily, and I was so affect-

---

1 Translator's note. We are keeping Mirbeau's spelling "Mossié" to indicate how the character mispronounces "Monsieur." Throughout this chapter Mirbeau has his character make mistakes in French. Some of the translations reflect these errors.

ed that I did not immediately hear what he said to me. I was listening, as one listens to the noise of the wind, the noise of the sea, to this accent in which the 'r' sounds were rolled and the final syllables sung… He was comparing himself to Job and repeating:

"Yobb! Yobb!"

I sat down next to him on a black wooden trunk with two pigskin straps.

Where had he learned French?

As a young barrister who had married, against his parents' wishes, a poor girl, he had been obliged, as a result of an altercation with an anti-Semitic magistrate, to leave the little town in Russia where he had been eking out a living. He had come to France with his wife and the three children that he already had… His eyes shone as he talked about Paris. Despite a number of promises he had not been able to find an appropriate position… The family had found lodgings near the Hôtel de Ville and was living meagrely from a variety of trades, including selling confetti.

"Who wants some confetti?" his voice chanted rhythmically.

This cry and his artificial gaiety were ridiculous, on this quayside in the midst of this crowd wearing rags, and these ships on the point of leaving.

"Who wants some confetti?"

It made me ill at ease.

A business associate "not a Jew, no, Mossié," he had met "on the Boulevard Ornano," had robbed him and, on a rainy Shrove Tuesday, had brought about his ruin. Tired of not being paid his rent, the landlord, one winter day, had broken down the door and, helped by two thieves, dragged his pregnant wife from her bed, sent the children flying to the floor, and threw them all out on the street.

He had lodged a complaint but, in front of the tribunal, the landlord who had brought witnesses with him immediately won his case against someone without witnesses. Poor people never have witnesses… He had to stop the trial in order to avoid being found guilty.

"I wept tears of rage, I wept, Mossié."

This man who, since then, must have encountered so many misfortunes, griefs, ruins, violence, this pitiful monument to bad luck was obligingly stopping over the smallest details of this injustice.

"In France, Mossié! In France!… Ach!"

A small amount of drool was soiling the corner of his lips. I was repelled by his breath. And this insistence troubled me to the point of anguish.

He had left Paris to return to Russia with the help of an Israelite charity, and he had succeeded in setting up as a clothes merchant in a small town in the South. His business only just broke even, but he lived happily with his wife and six children… That lasted for sixteen years.

I remember that at that point in his story he had suddenly stopped… And he was looking… A vessel was passing by hooting; handkerchiefs were being waved on board… what was he looking at, so far away?

He had managed to get his wife's brother to come and live with them. He was a rabbi and from that moment on he was obliged to spend all his savings on the education of his five sons… Two were supposed to be "lawyerers," one a "midicale doctor" and the two youngest "inginieurs." The daughter was working "in embroodery". He seemed to me to be almost smiling but a grimace twisted his face into which his long nose almost completely disappeared.

"But what's the point, Mossié?… Ach! What's the point?… What stupidity!"

One evening,—it was right at the beginning of the Revolution[1], the town had been in a state of siege for months; the whole family was dying of hunger,—on one sabbath

____

1 A reference to insurrections that happened in Tsarist Russia in 1905.

evening, the governor authorised the Jewish shops to remain open until ten o'clock. The whole district was overjoyed. As it was the day before an Orthodox festival, perhaps they would be able to earn a little money? They had spruced up the window displays and gone to the expense of lights to attract customers… Suddenly at a quarter past nine, "a quarter after nine, Mossié, just a quarter," a band of soldiers burst into the little street containing his shop, and a volley of bullets broke all the windows.

"Why? Ach!… Why?"

His youngest son—and his dirty hand with its black nails was trembling as he formed the shape of the small one—a boy, "such a witzy boy" had fallen into his arms, vomiting blood, and, laden with this body, the father had seen a drunken dragoon plunge two fingers into the eyes of his eldest son, of the son "who was going to be lawyerer, Mossié… lawyerer!" And then he had fainted.

When he had come round, his beard had been torn off, one ear nearly cut off by a sabre blow, but it was his chin that was painful… It was dark in the shop; he was stumbling over bodies, and he only stopped crying out in order to listen to the salvoes that were getting further away and the groans that seemed to be coming from the street, that seemed to be coming up from the floor, from within the walls, from below the ground. By the light of a candle, he had been able to establish that not one single garment remained in the displays. The robbers had ransacked everything, taken everything… On the shelves of the counter, at the back of the shop, amongst the empty drawers, the broken drawers, the bloodied things trampled underfoot, his wife was lying and, to begin with, he thought that she had fainted.

"I pulled her skirt back down," he added quietly… And his eyes closed.

And then, even more quietly,

"It was pulled right up, Mossié!… A voman more than fifefty years old!"

He then recognised that his wife was dead, strangled, her eyes open.

He looked at me for a moment in silence… A flush ran beneath his yellowing skin which was scarcely reddened by it… Again, I saw the grimace which caused his beard to rise and his nose to wrinkle… and he began to talk about his wife, his beloved wife.

"So brave a voman… so thrifty!"

He became animated. His breath was becoming unbearable. I noticed that he was speaking almost without anger and as though without pain… Perhaps he no longer had the strength to express those emotions!… And it was my eyes that I felt beginning to fill with tears.

"That wasn't all… They took the bodies… they wouldn't give the bodies back, buried them, at night, dead and injured, higgledy-piggledy, ve don't know where… They massacred the Jews and they pillaged for a whole week… We couldn't resist… How could we have, Mossié? They slapped us in the face… and they punched us in the stomach… and they spat at us… why?… ach!… why?"

Fires broke out that were not extinguished… The largest part of the poor district was destroyed… Another of his children died, in the hospital, from a blow with the heel of a boot that had split open his skull… And from the family of nine they had been before, just about happy in their poverty, five of them left this accursed town, robbed of everything, in mourning for ever.

"You just don't know how evil those soldiers are, Mossié… how evil they are… evil."

He shook his head and repeated:

"Nobody… no… nobody knows how evil they are."

I listened to the account of these hardships, iniquities, privations and long peregrinations, from town to town, towns where Jews were banned, villages from which they were driven with volleys of stones or blows with a scythe… He no longer knew from what nor how they had lived, during this frightful time… Finally, the old vagabond managed to find a job in a little bank… with a fellow Jew… Of the remaining children, his two sons, one of whom had married and had a daughter, worked as porters at the railway station.

"So weak, Mossié, so weak… and sick!"

The daughter began to sell oranges and garlic.

"Oranges!… oranges!… poor Sarah!"

But they saddened him. They had all joined the Bound[1] in open revolt against government and society.

"Reds, reds, Mossié… all reds!… Ach!"

Whenever he had stubbornly repeated during interminable arguments that Jews are black by vocation, that they are supposed to be black, it was the rabbi who came to the assistance of the children.

"Yes," he said, "Jews are naturally black, they are supposed to be black, but when you boil them, they become red… as red as crayfish."

And the rabbi chuckled, pleased with his comparison.

"It had to end badly… It did end badly… the governmenti has so many rifles, and even cannons… And they, they had rivolvers… poor rivolvers… What stupidity! For a policeman injured, a general who jumps from his car, a hundred Jews killed… three hundred Jews bleeding!"

One evening when he was helping his boss to do his accounts with a gentleman who had come to transact a piece of business… they heard salvoes of rifle shots, first of all in the distance, then closer… then very close, in the same street… and through the shattered windows, a volley of bullets had whistled into the room on the first floor.

"A different town, Mossié… but the same bullets… the same bullets!"

They threw themselves on the floor and tried to crawl into the room next door which looked out over the courtyard. A

---

1 Founded in 1897, an association of Jewish socialists in Imperial Russia.

new volley of projectiles knocked down the wall hangings. In the darkness they heard the footsteps of the soldiers resounding on the stairs. Shouts… muffled blows.

"Open up!… Open up!"

And the door, which the boss had barricaded, gave way to the blows from rifle butts… A sergeant was carrying a lantern… Soldiers rushed in, howling like savages… The gentleman shouted that human creatures should not be killed like that. He had succeeded in making himself recognised and in slipping a hundred rouble note into the hand of the sergeant who marched him away. And at that moment, whilst soldiers were trying to break into the safe, the old man had felt the point of a bayonet on his neck.

He pushed his scarf aside to show me the scar.

"Why am I still alive?… Ach! Why? These *dragonns*, Mossié, and these gendarmes… (he pronounced the word as *djandarmms*)… Ach! They're worse than wild animals… God knows what they get them drunk with… And then they throw themselves on women… on children… they can't even tell the difference between a Jew and anyone else, nor between a woman and a young boy… It's horrible, Mossié… And always killing, shooting, and they laugh about it!"

In the hospital he had found out that his two sons had been shot dead, in the station, by soldiers summoned to help with the massacre… His brother-in-law, the rabbi, had been arrested at home… He had been taken to prison… From that time, there had never been any news of him.

"There… Mossié… there… in the snow… in the coalmine!"

He had also learned, a little later, that poor Sarah, his daughter, had been found on her cart, dead amongst the vegetables, the crushed fruit, and that they had had the courage to push her severed legs into the open wound of her stomach… Why had the lady who lived nearby told him the details of this horror? He would have preferred not to know… And now, he would always have this nightmare before him, always, until he sighed his last!… He added that his daughter-in-law had died, as a result of blows with a rifle butt to her chest.

"Why am I still alive, I'm the oldest one?… Why, have I surfifed all that?… Ach!… What stupidity!"

The only person who remained from his whole family was his granddaughter, little Sonia.

"Pretty, Mossié, pretty!… And her little hands, and her little mouth in my beard… Ach!… And her eyes!"

She was the daughter of his favourite son.

"Why did I prefer him?"

He was no longer talking to me but to himself… And he only responded to himself by sketching a little smile… Once again, he was looking into the distance… And I heard him say quietly, without looking at me, that this son was called Jacob. Slowly he repeated the word: "Yacobb" nodding and as if he would have liked to caress him with his trembling lips:

"Yacobb!… Yacobb!"

My throat was dry… but such was the bewilderment this sequence, this improbable accumulation of crimes caused in me that in truth it seemed as though I no longer felt them.

He had gone away with his granddaughter and miraculously, amongst so many out of work wretches, he had managed to find a job, in another region, in a hotel where he ran errands and sometimes helped the cashier with her accounts.

In this region, as well, everything was going wrong… Strikes… fires in the countryside… searches… round ups… murders… streets full of soldiers, full of gangs of looters. Cossacks swishing the crowds with their nagaïkas,[1] which were worse than the iron of their sabres and the bayonets of their rifles… Everywhere a pogrom was being predicted. For two months he had waited, as though in a trance. He was no longer living… It was not that he was frightened on his own behalf. It was because of little Sonia that he was frightened…. Were soldiers coming? He trembled. With each attack he trembled…

---

1 Leather whips carried by the Cossacks.

An unusual noise in the street, a door opened too violently… footsteps in the night… he trembled… As soon as he was sent into the town, he would run home,—a dirty hovel where he would leave Sonia to be looked after by a neighbour, the widow of a policeman killed by the reds… Finally, the sinister news became clearer… One evening, he found out in the hotel that the town was closed.

"So, there you are… Once again."

That evening, in the large dining room, the assembled travellers were complaining about not being able to leave. However, they were reassured when they saw, at one table, drinking and quietly chatting, four dragoon officers, some Mossiés from St. Petersburg, guards officers, one of whom, the youngest was, so it was said, a cousin of the Emperor.

Suddenly a loud bang, a revolver shot, put an end to all the conversations… And it was during a tense silence that, a minute later, there was the crackle of a fusillade, which seemed to be replying to it. The officers continued to drink, to chat, as though nothing had happened… At their table, away from the others, they were leaning close together… At other tables, anxious people were pointing at them. Someone plucked up courage to speak to them… They replied politely, with evasive gestures, as though they were people who had no idea what was going on. There was no provocation, no irony… just indifference… Women were calling out… As a child had begun to cry the old man had wanted to run to his granddaughter… But, once again, a revolver shot silenced everybody. In the street, shops' shutters were closing, were banging to in a sinister manner… People were running by as they escaped, people were asking for Lord knows what!… Still, nobody had dared to talk again in the restaurant when a hundred further rifle shots went off together… Then, outside, horses galloping by, the clicking of firearms… orders, ranting.

A man who looked as though he was made of wax, bare headed, his clothes in rags, stumbled into the restaurant. He was surrounded… Leaning with effort on a table he said that the massacre had been organised, that the soldiers were being ordered to attack Jewish shops, Jewish houses… They were taking money, valuables… they were taking the women… they were killing… they were throwing the mutilated bodies through the windows into the street.

And, suddenly, the man who was speaking fell silent… turned round, and fell flat on the floor, pulling with him, in his clenched fingers, the tablecloth laden with crockery.

It was only then that they saw that his shirt was bloodstained and that there was more blood, in long blackish threads, in his hair and on his beard.

There were cries of horror… indignant protests… The four officers had disappeared.

During the tragic evening, the robbers, despite the orderly who was on duty, invaded the restaurant; but the same evening the colonel ordered that part of the spoils should be brought to the hotel, cases of Champagne, all sorts of victuals, that the men had stolen.

The poor old man, making the best of a respite, had managed to run home… The road was covered with cartridge cases… Drunks were snoring, resting on dead bodies… Wounded were writhing and groaning; others were crawling to find a shelter… A young man, with a ginger beard, his face smashed in, was trying to drink, like a dog, in the red mud of a stream… But he did not stop, he ran and ran.

Finally, he had found his little Sonia, fast asleep, and leaning over her mattress "with no noise" he had wept, wept until daybreak.

"It is the last time in my life that I have wept, Mossié!"

The firing began again the next day… The governor had ordered that they should not shoot at the pharmacies or the hospital, but the commanders were no longer in charge of their troops. There were scenes of savage horror.

"You can't imagine, Mossié!"

Towards midday the artillery regiment from a neighbouring town brought its cannons. The prominent Jews, summoned to the governor's castle, learned that the town would be razed to the ground if they refused to hand over the terrorists of the *Bound*… They lamented but there was nothing they could do.

"What was to be done?… Mossié."

Two prominent people were held as hostages and hanged that very evening in the courtyard of the prison.

"We were relying on the 'artilleryists' who are more enlightened, less evil… Ach!… Stupidity."

The cannon fire rumbled on for two days.

The old man had stopped talking… Even he seemed exhausted from recounting all these horrors… He was speaking in a soft, low voice, as though far away… And he was looking at the ground beneath his feet, or rather he was not looking at anything.

I took his hand… He did not move… I squeezed his hand… Then he raised his gaze at me, and smiled a dazed smile… but his hand remained soft and cold in mine, like the hand of a dead man… He only withdrew it to trace on the ground, with the tip of his tattered umbrella, the plan of the house where he had taken refuge.

The façade was on the street; in the middle there was the carriage entrance door, thick, massive, with heavy hinges and big iron nails… On both sides a building at right angles to the façade shut off the courtyard, the fourth side of which was closed by a garden. Whichever way one went out was to expose oneself to certain death.

In the house there lived about forty poor people who pooled their provisions… But the first time that a woman went to get water from the well, which was at the far end of the courtyard, she was shot dead… In the neighbouring houses also, access to the wells was forbidden and guarded by sentries… The unfortunates got to know the tortures of thirst… For example, they were suffering less from hunger… They were allowed to eat…

Towards the fifth day there was hope that calm was going to return… The soldiers must have left the garden… they were no longer seen around the wells. In town, firing was dying down.

"To drink, Mossié!… To drink, drink!"

They were drunk from thirst; they were mad from thirst.

"To drink!… To drink!"

Two men had the courage to move forward, with buckets, to the lip of the well. All faces were turned towards them, in a delight of hope… They hooked on their buckets. The noise of the chain going down sounded like music…

"We heard it going down… going down… Ach!"

But, as the water carriers were returning, the dragoons who had remained hidden until then suddenly revealed themselves… They killed one of the men with a carbine shot and the other, terrified, fled leaving behind his bucket and its water spilled out into the courtyard.

"But we knew ze dead man. Everybody loved such a decent boy… But… and this is terrible, but it has to be said… we felt sorrier about the water."

That evening, the well was filled with mud, manure, all sorts of filth. They also threw in the body of the poor boy…

Then, madness overwhelmed the beleaguered… They gathered together in the courtyard, and spent the night there groaning, praying, howling, sleeping, hugging…

"I have never seen anything so sad, Mossié… mothing like it."

In the morning—had their presence been denounced?… or was it only a patrol doing the rounds?—whatever it was they heard the sound of horses in the street and soon furious blows smashing down the carriage entrance which soon yielded… With one bound a horse jumped across the wreckage, carrying an officer who stopped a few metres away from the terrified prisoners and, with his revolver in his fist, barked out the usual order:

"Hands up!"

The old man thought he had to explain to me:

"Officers and policemen always shout: 'Arms in the air!… Hands up!' because they are afraid of rivolvers and bombs… So, they shout: 'Arms in the air!… Hands up!'…"

All the hands went up…. Except for little Sonia who hadn't understood… who couldn't understand, who could only smile, and was looking at the officer, with a smile, her little hands by her side… Her grandfather tried to warn her with a gesture:

"Do it like that… Like that!"

And the old man imitated with his trembling hands the gesture that could have saved her.

He did not have the time. Already the officer was aiming at the child and, despite the cry of horror filling the courtyard, he shot her…

I can still hear, I shall hear for a long time, I shall always hear the strangled voice of the old man:

"With a rivolver shot, Mossié!"

She did not let out a cry. She had a few contractions, scratched the paving with the tips of her little fingers… A little bit of blood on her… a little bit of blood around her… And then it was over… Like a little bird…

"I was alone, completely alone in life… I was alone on this earth…"

I understood that he would have liked to cry… He couldn't… He bit his lips… with light jerks his beard twitched, his nose wrinkled… But he did not cry… The well of his tears had dried up for ever in him…

He repeated, joining his hands together:

"A littul thing… like that… littul… littul… nothing, Mossié… nothing… like a littul bird… Ach!"

Rocking his head, he said, after a silence:

"Why I going? I don't know… Why I going there?… Ach!… I don't know!"

He said again:

"Stupidity!… Stupidity!"

I looked at this unfortunate man and was incapable of the effort needed to look away from him… I felt even less capable of saying a single word… I was full of horror… I was paralysed with horror… And then what good was there in talking? What could I have said that would not have been ridiculous and icy in the face of such an appalling example of human misfortune? The old Jew was not asking me for consolation nor for pity… He was not asking me for anything; all he was asking was for me to remain quiet…

Finally, I saw him blush, lower his head and turn away from me… He was ashamed that he could not cry, perhaps, that he could never cry… I felt my throat tightening with sobs, my eyes were filling with tears.

And so that he would not see my tears, I too turned away.

Prostitution.

As I walked along the boulevards—the congested, busy boulevards—of these quaysides I remembered the port of Antwerp, about thirty years ago, with its winding alleyways, where prostitution, in pink blouses, star-spangled skirts lived just as it did in Le Havre, in Marseille, in Toulon, on the doorstep. Dazed and heavily made-up fat ladies, with a paper flower in their hair, waited for a client, sitting on chairs, or dozed with their chins resting on their bare arms… I remembered how difficult it was to get to the docks, the lack of air and of light in these hovels, their smelly disorder, poverty and filth.

At this time there were no longer the oriental splendours of the Rideck, which I never knew, and of which Antwerp was so proud, of which a few old folks from Antwerp have spoken to me with lyrical enthusiasm…

"It's not what it was, Monsieur… Alas! It's not what it was."

It seems that the council used to do the honours there for distinguished foreigners, as we do for English, Italian,

Norwegian delegations, for students, for lawyers from friend-ly countries, for kings from allied countries, by offering the honours of our Louvre, of our Sorbonne, of our Opera, of our Academies… As soon as a famous person, a more or less crowned prince, landed in Antwerp, it was… quickly off to the Rideck!… It was the obligatory complement to banquets and all festivals. Even on Sundays, after dinner, whole families, fathers, mothers, daughters and sons, nieces and cousins, and their friends, and their maids, came to stroll there, with no shame, in their Sunday best… The children were told: "If you are good all week, if you work hard, on Sunday we will take you to the Rideck!" Mass, vespers, cakes and the Rideck, that's what could be called an excellent Sunday… Nobody thought of taking offence… Quite the opposite…

The Rideck comprised little shops, picturesquely furnished, where they sold exotic products, little cafés where there were negro dances to the tune of banjos… and little cells where yellow, red, coppery, black and even white flesh was sold. And what an array of perfumes!… On days when special visits were planned, it was arranged that everything should be decent and look like some colonial exhibition.

"Let us colonise… There will always be some remnants of that."

I never saw these family scenes. I can only write about them trusting in the memories evoked by dignitaries from Antwerp… But I have seen—and I remember this with great sadness—I have seen at night, in the hot streets, the pantomime of inter-national lust and its unchecked greed which noisily jostled the girls of all races… I have seen sailors from all countries, arm in arm, between the walls of the alleyways, bellowing and run-ning, like large, mad children… But it is not only in Antwerp that I have seen them, I have also seen them in Hamburg, in Le Havre, in Marseille, and on Saturday evenings especially I have seen them in Toulon. All the same no matter where they come from, all identical with their fish heads around their bare necks… And in the hovels, full of noisy smoke, I have seen the brutes stretched out, those who no longer had enough strength to drink… those who no longer had the strength to kiss and to fight… and sleeping, bedraggled giants, their heads lolling on the sympathetic knees of a negress, with a golden comb in her hair, and a thin sash of red gauze on her back.

I do remember, from that time, a negress. She was from Dahomey, from the city of Cotonou. Her long, slender, supple, dark black body had a golden sheen. She was lying on a yellow silk mattress, naked, with violent perfumes that caught in your throat. A large, purple dahlia was flowering in her woolly hair. She had copper rings around her arms. And her smile was of a blinding whiteness. Her narrow bedroom was decorated with cutlasses that had painted wooden handles, with fetishists' masks, with two little idols in blue painted earth, a jug with a long spout, covered with childlike drawings… She spoke only a little French, the only thing in Europe that she had really known being the hovels of Antwerp… When she was young, she had worked as a servant in the household of a ship owner in Bordeaux, then in a brothel in Paris… A trafficker in human flesh had brought her to Antwerp… It was too cold here. It was too grey here. She did not like it here.

Beside her, one evening of sinister melancholy, I tried to raise the topic of her country, the bloody mysteries of jungle, the rough paths sewn with thorns where the horsewomen run barefoot to get used to pain, the houses of pink mud, the palaces and the temples with their flat roofs, paved with human skulls. But it was very difficult. Full of curiosity, indiscreet and talkative she did not have a moment's respite… She told me all sorts of ridiculous stories which, moreover, I struggled to follow and to understand. Memories of Paris, especially, sometimes puerile, sometimes obscene, the arguments, the fights with her comrades in prostitution… Finally, she spoke about her country in order to describe to me, as best she could, the splendours she was missing… It was a stifling summer night… The window was open… I could hear, as she was talking, strangely ululating music coming from a hovel close by…

From all her useless verbiage, without colour, without accent, with no surprises, I have only retained this which I am translating, or rather reporting faithfully:

"You can't imagine what the palace of our great king is like in Cotonou… This palace is of extraordinary beauty and all your monuments are just poor huts in comparison… It has great, thick walls that are completely pink. Almost no windows. The way in is through a low, semi-circular door guarded by frighteningly tattooed female warriors… The most remarkable thing is the roof… a flat roof entirely covered with, or rather paved with, severed heads… It's very difficult, meticulous work… You need skilful artists who know how to arrange the heads like marquetry, like mosaic… The King, who is an artist himself and has marvellous taste, demands that it should be very beautiful, and also very well carried out so that no rain should get into his palace… He wants, under pain of death, that his heads should be as waterproof as tiles in Europe, or the thatch on a Hindu cottage. It is genuinely a fairy-like sight, at sundown, and the smell is delightful… With the winds coming from the north, it spreads over the town, like a rain shower of perfumes. But this type of roof, whatever you do, is not very solid. At least, it does not last very long. Whether the heads come apart because of putrefaction, or vultures succeed in stealing a few of them, fissures quickly appear through which the rain enters and drips into the interior of the palace… Then, our great King sends his most faithful fetishists throughout the kingdom. With their faces covered by their terrifying masks, with red horns, a heavy cutlass in their hands, they shout out, they howl: 'The King's roof is falling apart!… The King's roof is falling apart!' Immediately massacres begin… The chests of the subjects come, by themselves, to offer themselves to the knife… Everywhere the earth of our country, which nevertheless is already red, is made even more red with the flow of blood…

'The King's roof is falling apart!' And the palace quickly has a brand-new appearance, brilliant, truly regal."

She was very sad, now. No doubt, her train of thought had flown away there; her ideal—everybody has an ideal—had retaken and reconquered her... She was walking alongside the ditches which surround her beautiful town of Cotonou... The jackals were yelping around her... Deliciously she was breathing in the natal odour coming from the mass graves.

I lit a cigarette... She had fallen silent and was no longer looking at anything... I remained there looking at this body of precious bronze, stretched out on the yellow silk mattress. The large purple dahlia that flowered in her woolly hair was fading, becoming completely black... I hear the music that was becoming shriller in the hovels... the rushing of drunken sailors, the songs, the shouts, the anger, the savage street battles... For, like royalty, debauchery always needs its murderous gestures and much blood.

Not much of all that still remains today... These filthy districts have been partially demolished. Where once there were these alleyways, now there are business houses with gilded signs... And they have built docks where a different type of merchandise is piled up.

Prosperous Antwerp.

It has continuously prospered, thanks to its powerful economic infrastructure, its practical business sense assisted by all sorts of additional elements, such as the societies of colonial studies and the numerous active banks; thanks to the penetration which gets deeper as each day passes, to its every day more methodical organisation, of the African continent, which opens up, to business, new markets, to military adventures an even vaster field where all individual, administrative violence, is even better tolerated because their accomplices are the ignorance of some and the silence of everybody… It has also prospered because of its more inland location, just as all great ports, sheltered by rivers, prosper to the detriment of bays and useless havens.

Marseille has not lost its importance; Le Havre has not been beaten by Rouen for different reasons. For the same reason, Paris will one day beat Rouen, and Lyon will perhaps be, at some far-off time, the largest French port… I clearly glimpse the wonderful day, the day of scientific enchantment, when Basel, which is already the largest sea fish market, will become the largest port in Europe, when, helped by the Germans, the Swiss will have had rivers and canals cross their mountains in tunnels, in lifts and brought, despite the old jokes from operettas, a huge maritime fleet into their Republic.

Yonder, at the mouth of the River Scheldt, in vain is Flushing exhausting itself wishing to become, even to remain, a port. The Dutch have not spared money. The docks have been enlarged; others have been dug. Everything there is kitted out with the latest inventions of science… You press an electric switch and, one kilometre away, locks immediately open, just to let water pass through and, sometimes, wind… a magnificent breakwater has been built out to sea, tall terraces of white granite, to which one climbs up splendid stairs like those of a Babylonian temple… One always expects to see Semiramis there, with gold armour and a silver veil. But a port is not like opera scenery; the docks and the breakwaters, no matter how redoubtable they are, are not sufficient to create a port. You also need ships. And for there to be ships, you need a financial and commercial infrastructure which is unfortunately lacking in Flushing… Therefore, grass is growing round the docks, grass is growing on the breakwater. The cranes, with their long unemployed arms, are getting rusty… And the docks are empty… In vain do the lighthouses search the sea, and the pilots go out on the hunt… In vain, as soon as a mast appears on the open sea, a twirl of smoke, a grey shape, people get ready… And the hope that has been dashed a thousand times is reborn… The whole city runs to the breakwater… People joyfully climb the stone steps… Spyglasses are focused, handkerchiefs are waved. There is a shout:

"This one is coming to Flushing!"

"Antwerp is finished! It's coming to Flushing!"

"Long live Flushing!"

"Down with Antwerp!"

The ship gets closer, enters the harbour access:

"There it is!… There it is!"

"I told you it was for Flushing."

But no… The ship has passed by… It is still going to Antwerp.

The ships seem to be making fun of the people crowding on the breakwater of this cursed port, where nothing comes except the little boat from Breskens, which brings, twice a week, foreign tourists who are coming to visit Zealand, the Goes Park, the markets of Middelburg and its beautiful laughing girls with their golden hair and their too red arms…

On top of the breakwater, overlooking the sea and guarding the Schelder, a superb bronze statue of Admiral Ruyter, is in command only of his memories… He seems to be saying to himself melancholically:

"Ah! if I still had my fleet, which stood up so well against the French!"

Yes… but there you are, poor Admiral Ruyter no longer has a fleet… All he has now is his glory… and the two little wherries from Breskens and Terneuzen… And moreover, they are Belgian!

It is true that Flushing is a delightful fishing port, with its tightly packed flotilla of boats with red sails and its picturesque shrimp market.

All the wealth of Antwerp does not have the same grace.

IN HOLLAND

Phantoms.

I would be a poor chap, I would feel that I was as deprived of sensibility and imagination as a contemporary playwright, if I said that I entered Holland without trepidation.

It was quite the opposite as my heart was pounding and, for a long time before we got to the border, my eyes were wide open as they stared at the desired horizon. I was very moved, I have no problem in admitting it. However, this is the irony of it all, I had already been driving for about ten kilometres on Dutch soil, and yet I was still waiting for the shock… From the sad wheat fields, the sterile sands, the sickly woods we were driving through, how could I have known? We might have arrived in Dordrecht thinking we were still in Belgium if a peasant we had questioned had not shouted at me, with fierce pride and a violent voice, stamping his heavy clogs on the ground:

"Nidreland!… Nidreland!"

Ah! His homeland really clung to the soles of that chap's clogs!

We had to make a U-turn and go back to the border to conduct the formalities at the customs post that I had so swiftly driven past. You do not mess about with customs officers in Holland.

But I was only even more impatient to get through this characterless area and to see again the bright and unified landscape, conquered from the water, that is to say from the most elusive, the most cruelly pitiless element; impatient to see again those polished and flowery villages, taking refuge on the dikes, like flooded people crowding on the high mounds in the fields, and these glossy towns overflowing with affluence, and the translucid enormity of its moving skies, and this so green springtime, with its pale sun and its brilliant trimmings of tulips.

It was not easy to get the customs officer to understand how I had become distracted. He was a giant, with a flat chest and a prominent stomach. He wore a tall blue cap, mathematically cylindrical. Boosted by his cap, he explained to me that borders were borders and that you did not enter Holland like going into a mill. Showing no respect for the testimonials, for all the official documents in my possession, he searched the car from top to bottom, and obliged me to pay a hefty sum of money. Finally, rolling his large eyes, he declared that he was responsible to the Minister of Dikes.

The Minister of Dikes!… What a delightful country!

I found out that an American, who had arrived at the customs post without papers, was being held in the village inn and kept as a prisoner. His automobile had been put into storage. For six days, getting drunk and sleeping, sleeping and getting drunk, he waited for the Minister of Dikes to send him the authorisation he needed… His driver, a cheeky devil from Paris, came to see us… I urged him to be patient…

"Oh!" he said, "I'm not in a hurry… it isn't a pretty spot… but I'm sleeping with the customs officer's wife… Don't you think he deserved it?"

✳

The first time I had come to Holland was so many years ago… so many years… that I did not dare count them… The years through which we have lived seem, from a distance, increasingly beautiful, as our capacity to hope for happiness gradually weakens with experience and is extinguished by disappointment. At least, now, I will know how countries age… Alas!… They age at the same rate as we age. All beings and all things have no other old age than our own… Neither do they have any other death than our own since, when we die, the whole of humanity and the whole universe disappear and die with us.

If the cruel art of making mirrors had not been taught and if women did not have to spend their lives on riverbanks, each of us would only see other people getting older… Each would always believe himself to be the young man madly chasing after happiness, or even the child, the little child whose sole thought was of playing and whose tears flowed for no reason, and equally for no reason dried up. Each age, only being the adolescence—without bitterness—of a different age, we would remain adolescents in perpetuity… But, so as not to be disabused, you should never return, fifteen years later, to a country where you had lived too happily… That is when there appear, in a bitter melancholy, all our wrinkles, all our white hair and all that has faded above us and all that has withered in us.

There is not a mirror of a purer water, nor one that is more implacable

These doubts were not in my mind—at least I was not thinking about that—when I had the idea of coming back to Holland, and I cheerfully imagined that I was going to see again, as I had before, and admire its blond youth, its quiet luxury and my happiness, in the always identical water of its canals.

It was also in the springtime that we had set off the last time, right at the beginning of spring, an alert, gentle spring, the enchantment of which seemed as though it would last a lifetime. I well remember it, and I now know the origin of my illusion and what excuses it.

All the time of our journey we had always been climbing towards the north before the flowering of the lilac shrubs. Before we left, we had already smelled the last bouquets of them and, as we progressed along the roads, they had begun to flower again… They were flowering, flowering in front of us, and flowering again without becoming tired.

"It is spring!… it is still spring!" they kept on telling us, as we went by, in the little courtyards, in the little gardens, on the window ledges where their cut stems were in water in a blue pot.

And in vain did they fade, we were finding them again further on, younger, fresher, their sprigs scarcely opened.

"It is spring!… It is still spring!"

For young, happy beings, who believe only in miracles—since they are themselves miracles—and who do not wish to listen to any of life's voices, illusion could arise from a lesser wonder.

And now?… I was no longer very reassured.

Before we arrived in Dordrecht—that we called Dordt—was I going to hear again the sounds of the quaysides of the Rhine, crawling with the workshops of the ship owners and where we would hear the hammer blows on both banks? That hotel terrace, from which one sees so well the sun set over the river and the river fall asleep at night, does it still exist? Would I see again a little square in Rotterdam, in which the moonlight would soften so tenderly the tone of the stones? And, in Delft, where the brick gables, the old leaning towers, doors opening onto clear-cut gardens, the waters and the faces, repeat, ceaselessly the magical name of Vermeer… in Delft, on the enclosed canal, the shady canal, scarcely shaded by the pink shoots of a brand-new spring, would I find again those pretty boats, full of flowers, bunches of pansies, round balls of tulips, garlands of daffodils, boats which glided softly, one behind the other, pulled along by a small blond, smiling peasant girl? Would I receive again the thunderbolt which, in The Hague, caused me to kneel before a Rembrandt, just as in Amsterdam I nearly fainted, and had tears in my eyes, the first time that I heard those divine voices which introduced me to the superhuman genius of Beethoven?... Rembrandt and Beethoven... the two passions of my life!

I was asking for all that... And what else was I asking for?

✳

But this time, as I have told you, we did not enter Holland on the river and its meanderings around the nine islands of Zeeland. We no longer had, to sadden us with poetry and memories, the haunting spectres of the water and its softening mirages. We entered by road, by the solid medium of the road. It took no less—so far men are given to weeping—took no less than the car bouncing over a bump in the road or a culvert, to awaken me from these memories and to make their sad images disappear, and also the image—which contained them all—of the old boat which, so slowly, so dreamily, bore us from Antwerp to Rotterdam... in days gone by!

Fortunately, there is no melancholy which cannot be defeated by the keen pleasure of speed.

Now I see the strips of cultivated land turn around... The plain appears to be moving, tumultous, appears to be lifted in enormous surges like the sea. What am I saying?... The plain appears mad with hallucinated terror... It gallops and bounds, suddenly plunges down into abysses, then climbs again and throws itself into the sky... And it turns, turns, dragging in a gyratory dance its long green scarves, and its golden veils... The trees, scarcely caught up in this, flee in all directions like soldiers fleeing in panic.

The André Theuriet Lilac.

When one goes slowly as on foot, even in a car, each tree on the road represents a small event. One accosts it, one recognises its essence, one greets it, one speaks to it… One says:

"It's an oak."

"Ah! there's an elm… a poplar… a plane tree."

"Goodness! A sycamore… what's it doing there?"

And one leaves its shade in order to enter into a new shade…

Amusing anecdotes come back to you…

One day—life does have these sorts of meetings,—I was strolling with M. André Theuriet[1] in the Jardin d'Acclimatation.[2] M. Theuriet—as is well known—is a great lover of nature. He knows woods and undergrowth better than anyone else in the world. That was even by that route that he went into literature, into the Académie, into Immortality[3]… I was proud, as you can imagine, to walk along beside such a man, among all these things that he knew so well… I was going to learn a few of these mysteries!… Suddenly, M. Theuriet stopped in front of a group of shrubs.

"Ah! ah!…" he said.

And he seemed puzzled…

It was only the beginning of spring. These shrubs had scarcely any leaves… M. Theuriet was thus very puzzled as he stood before these shrubs… He said:

"That's curious… I don't know that one…"

He grasped a branch, bent it, for a long time examined its bark, the buds ready to burst out… I admired his botanist's grace…

---

1 A nineteenth-century French poet and novelist.

2 A park and zoo in the Bois de Boulogne, Paris, opened in 1860 by Napoleon III.

3 The forty members of the Académie Française are known as "les Immortels".

"Well! Well!…" he said again…

Then after another and more detailed examination, for which he used a lorgnette which he placed with methodical gestures on his nose… he said:

"That's very strange!… Goodness me… Just think, my friend… No, in truth, I don't know these shrubs… It's very odd."

He let go of the branch, which sprang back amongst the others, and he continued:

"I don't know them… It must be an import… a recent one… I wouldn't be surprised if this import did not come from… from… Ah! it's very strange… it's extraordinary… it's unbelievable!"

Then turning to me:

"No point in my asking you, is there? An import… what would you know about it?"

I was amazed…

"But Monsieur Theuriet," I cried… they are…"

I stopped… for I was ashamed of making this lover of nature ashamed.

"Of course…" sneered M. Theuriet… "They are… they are… You have no idea…"

I plucked up my courage and cried:

"But Monsieur Theuriet, they are lilacs… lilacs, Monsieur Theuriet… lilacs!"

The lover of nature looked at me severely:

"Lilacs?… You are making fun of me…" he said.

Then he shrugged… then he began to laugh:

"Lilacs?… That's stupid!…ah! ah! ah!… And it is I… But, my friend, did you not know that there is a lilac named after me?… There is an André Theuriet lilac, my friend… a lilac with double flowers…"

I think that M. André Theuriet laughed about it for a long time. I still laugh about it, as well, for I have often read that when the Académie is working on the dictionary[1] and is discussing the name of a plant, it says:

"That's Theuriet's field… let Theuriet do it… he is our botanist…"

✳

The hedges also attract one's attention… One smiles at the hawthorns, the dog roses. They remind you of a thousand puerile and charming events, faces that are already far away, names that have been forgotten for ages. One becomes sentimental… Sometimes one picks them to make one's progress more flowery…

From the motorcar one scarcely has the leisure to compare the different foliage. And one does not see the flowers in the hedges… and one does not remember M. André Theuriet's stories… These trees that flee from us, they are just trees, no more than that… and they gallop, gallop… What does it matter if they are called oak, acacia, elm or plane tree? They gallop, that's all… They dash towards us, rush towards us, in a vertigo. One would say—so afraid are they and no longer know what they are doing—that they are going to get into the car and dash across it. They are so afraid that they are no longer material: they have become reflections, shadows, which gallop. The plain also dematerialises, dragged away in a supernatural gallop… And here are valleys, rocky gorges, mountains… forests… At a gallop! At a gallop!… Scarcely glimpsed, immediately passed by. At a gallop!… Does one have the time to think, to dream, to weep? They all gallop by, the little sentimental joys, the little pains that bring tears and in which wallows the childishness of memories!… Besides, are they joys, pains, memories?… One no longer knows…

---

1 The compilation of a Dictionnaire was one of the primary tasks of the Académie Française.

one does not know any more than, of the trees, whether one knows if they are elms, poplars, beech or sophora... One knows nothing... Scarcely is one aware that the air which strikes one's face, and which one swallows, with all sorts of dust, intoxicates one and that one is drunk like the whole universe!...

Vincent van Gogh and Breda.

The road from Antwerp to Breda is neither better nor worse than the majority of Belgian roads. It has the same monotony. That is the explanation—for my reverie could not have been the cause—for my not having recognised Holland in this continuous Belgium... It is nothing but flat, greyish earth in which everything that grows is sickly, where the heavy, opaque light is that of all countries that lack water. Nothing is as sad as passing through these fields without sap and through these unwelcome little woods, of which there are many...

"Quite enough woods..." would say our excellent Belgian friends, about whom, even in Holland, I think with a smile on my face...

Breda—whose name quite comically evokes both an excellent breed of laying hens, and also a breed, if not of cocottes at least of courtesans, Gavarni[1] and Guys,[2] Stevens and Grévin,[3] the *Lances*[4] of Velasquez, the songs of Nadaud,[5] a certain standard of wit, of Second Empire gaiety, "Ah! it was the time

---

1 In Paris Bréda is the name of a district near Notre-Dame de Lorette which was known in the nineteenth century as the district of 'lorettes' or courtesans. It features in the caricatures of Paul Gavarni (1804-1866).
2 Paul Guys (1802-18920) wrote about the life of the 'demi-monde'.
3 Alfred Grévin (1827-1892) was the creator of the waxworks museum that bears his name.
4 A painting by Velasquez of 1635 otherwise known as "The surrender of Breda".
5 Gustave Nadaud (1820-1893) was a well-known singer of comic songs.

when…" and Villemessant[1] and Dinochau[2] and Carjat[3]—Breda is so completely ordinary and so insignificant a town that it maddens me to think that it is not Belgian… I would not mention it if, in its cathedral, the very Italian accent of a Bolognese sculptor had not had the idea of having, above a tomb,[4] the arms of some little prince from Nassau borne by Regulus, Julius Caesar, Hannibal and Philip of Macedonia.

Coming out of Belgian museums and cathedrals, I was rather tired, not only because of the Italian grandiloquence which bubbles up in them, but even more because of the occasionally crushing Flemish magnificence, when all I wanted was to rest amongst Dutch nuances and discretion. I was hoping for this respite as one looks forward to a bath at the end of a long journey. I had most of all to purify myself of all sorts of jests, of all sorts of excesses, before diving into the delight of Vermeer and the splendour of Rembrandt. It was when I was in such a mood that this Italian sycophant—in vain did the guidebooks tell me that it was not Michelangelo—annoyed and shocked me… I should really have laughed about it…

But I excuse Breda, on account of one fact from its history which moves me and of which it seems unaware.

Breda is the town where Vincent van Gogh was born. He lived there for a brief time when he was very young. One dreams for those one admires and who made their mark on life, with a little genius, with a little grace, with a human effort that is different from other men, one dreams about an attractive décor for their birth. I believe in the profound and secret influence of milieu on the direction and destiny of a mind; I believe that details from one's birth leave a lasting imprint on the brain, and that it is very difficult to free oneself from them later, even

1 Villemessant (1812-1879) was the founder of the newspaper *Le Figaro*.
2 Dinochau (1829-1879) was a restaurateur.
3 Carjat (1828-1906) was a photographer and caricaturist.
4 A reference to the mausoleum of Count Engelbrecht II of Nassau and his wife sculpted in about 1505 by Tommaso Vincidor of Bologna.

when they were unpleasant. I was quite surprised to find no affinity between Vincent van Gogh and Breda. It is true that, at the time that he lived there, he did not think for one minute of becoming the original and violent artist that he was. Boring and gloomy, surrounded by landscapes with tight lines, with poor shapes, Breda was not revealing his vocation to him. He was there something of a primary school teacher, a free-thinking teacher. He was talking to the children that he gathered in the street, even the men, and he preached protestant morality to them, spiced up with all that his imaginative and tormented soul already contained of passionate élans towards what is great and beautiful… And then he left, discouraged by his impotence and the futility of his words…

I would have liked to hear details about this time in van Gogh's life, or, if no oral details were available, to see his house, and in his house see the first sights that met his gaze, and which moved him… I asked around… People were amazed at my questions:

"What are you saying?… What's his name?… Vincent van Gogh?… Have you got the right name?… In Breda?… You are not mixing it up with Amsterdam?… Wait a moment…"

Nobody knew.

I explained that he had been a great and sorrowful artist… that, still a young man, he had died in France… not such a long time ago… and coming alive in front of these surprised expressions, I explained that he was famous in France, in Germany… even in Holland… That some of his pictures were in the Rotterdam Museum… And I laboured the point:

"Look here!… In the Rotterdam Museum… ah!"

"That's quite possible," they replied… "Van Gogh, no that doesn't ring a bell. There are so many painters and so many museums in Holland!"

I endeavoured to make them recall his tragic face, his obstinate forehead, his eyes drunk from thinking and looking, his short, blond beard.

"Blond beards… there's no shortage of those round here…"

Stupidly I pressed on:

"But… don't you remember… he was good with children… he used to talk to them…"

But they were no longer listening to me… They were moving away, looking at me suspiciously.

Poor Vincent!… He would not have been humiliated by the ignorance of his compatriots… He did not seek glory… he sought something more impossible: the absolute. It caused his death…

I found out in Rotterdam that a close relative of van Gogh lived in Breda, surrounded by the very finest collection of his works. Only, his name was not van Gogh.

That is why "Van Gogh," "didn't ring a bell".

I have another impression.

Two weeks later, I was coming out of the museum in The Hague where I had spent almost the whole of the day. I was intoxicated with Vermeer, especially intoxicated with Rembrandt… My head was spinning. I could not get *Homer* and, even more, the portrait of Rembrandt's brother out of my mind… That so prodigiously human face, both so hard and so tender, so melancholic and so obstinate, this effigy, with so wide and certain planes, more living than life itself, this forehead still warm from the double thought that animated it, that modelled it, and those eyes in which one sees all that they have seen! The genius of Rembrandt is so great that it makes him sorrowful… One cannot withstand the first shock, without a great upheaval. I needed to get over my emotion… For a time, I walked along the banks of the Vivier. I strolled beneath the trees of that square where everything calms down, becomes gentle, silent, sliding, like those golden waters in which it bathes… And I returned to the town…

As I was strolling across the street, I spotted a little shop in front of which large mobile posters were advertising an exhibition of van Gogh's works… I said to myself:

"No… no… not today… It would be treachery… I'll come back tomorrow…"

But, as I said that, I walked automatically into the shop.

It was early evening… Nobody was there except an employee who was sleeping, with his head resting on a pile of catalogues… On the grey walls, perhaps about twenty pictures. In the middle of the room, a sort of circular divan, of a horrid red, in the middle of which there sprouted a draped column topped in ridiculous fashion by a small palm tree in a ceramic pot.

I sat down, and I looked… I looked for a long time… I looked without tiredness, interested…

I felt that other pictures, even amongst those that are called good pictures, would have made me run away. I would have regarded them as a profanation… Yes, yes, I was sure that I would not have been able to look at them…

I was still looking…

They were spring landscapes, landscapes of the South of France… orchards… golden harvests swaying in the wind… And strangely moving skies, in which vague shapes of large animals, of recumbent women, stretched out, crumbled, took on different shapes… And tormented faces, amongst them the painter's, with so tragic an accent… also the face of good old Father Tanguy,[1] smiling, with his brown jacket, his green apron, his two large working hands… And flowers, adorable flowers, tulips, gladioli, roses, irises, sunflowers, of a life, of an extraordinary radiance, of an extraordinary caress, of an extraordinary radiance…

I was not thinking about these canvases in detail as I am at the moment, but in a very summary way… It was the ensemble of the shapes, the stains of light that they made on the walls, which were retaining me and charming me…

I said to myself:

---

1 Tanguy (1825-1894) sold colours to artists and sometimes received their paintings in exchange for goods. Mirbeau bought two van Gogh paintings from him and organised a sale of paintings to help Tanguy's widow.

"What I have before me... is a different sensibility, different research... it is something different... it is a different art... less precise, less solid, less deep, less sumptuous, than that from which I have just received such a violent emotion... Of course, I sometimes see in these canvases, a painful grimace, sometimes I sense in them a conscious impotence completely to realise, by hand, the work that the brain conceived, sought, desired. And this grimace, I only see it, this impotence I only feel it, perhaps because I have known all the doubts, all the troubles, all the anguishes of Vincent van Gogh, and this cruel faculty of analysis, and this rigour to judge oneself, and this continually vibrant existence, always tense, frazzled, in this maddening, torturing effort in which he consumed himself. Besides, who knows, who will ever know by what is verified complete realisation in a work of art? Is it not in the creations of his later years, in what certain critics coarsely call his sketches, that Rembrandt went further, higher, in science and genius?... But about these canvases which are there, before me, radiant on these grey walls, what I know is that, despite their discordances, their incompleteness, their brutality, it is the only art that my overexcited nerves, that my eyes still full of the most beautiful visions, can stand, today. After Rembrandt, who knocks you over like a phenomenon of nature, one can stop at van Gogh, who disconcerts and who enchants... And the proof is that I am still there, looking, and I am happy.

I did not leave the shop until the evening was well advanced.

About Dutch People.

About ten kilometres beyond Breda, we really are in Holland... the Holland of water and sky, the infinitely green Holland, infinitely pearl-grey, where no longer would dare adventure the smallest memory of Belgium. The roads are smooth, elastic, without dust, with their unified and washed surface of end-laid bricks. They are magnificently planted with gigantic trees, elms, plane trees, Dutch clovers, and one can see that their roots go deep into rich soil where humus was no more lacking than water. Flights of lapwings and starlings travel in the air, flocks of ducks travel on water... And water is everywhere... You see it rising beneath the surfaces of greenery as you see the red glow of embers beneath the covering layer of cinders...

As you drive through the polders, on the dikes, you have to go slowly. They are narrow, frequently lined by low-lying canals, interrupted by little hump-backed bridges and by little drawbridges which you only see at the last moment. Each time you encounter a horse, one of those fine horses with their warlike necks, stop your engine or, even better, get out of your vehicle to assist the carter or the horseman, for everywhere the horse is the same stupid animal, and, here, his danger is increased by his size, and by the small amount of space allowed by the famous minister of Dikes for his gallops.

There is no other rule, about automobile traffic, than what you create for yourself and for your own safety. In Holland, the important thing is to enter the country... Once you are over that difficulty, you do what you like... You may even fall into the canal, if you want... Nobody will see the slightest drawback from it or hold it against you, as long as you get yourself out of it, you and your car, dead or alive, at your own expense. Besides all that is needed is the slightest skid, or that your driver has, in certain spots, a second's distraction. For the roads, at each moment, stop suddenly, steeply, in front of the river or in front of the canal which you have to cross on powerful and rapid steam ferries...

This type of motorcar travel, slow, interrupted by all sorts of stops, is irritating to begin with. Brossette is grumbling all the time, he cries out: "Lousy country!"... And then he gets used to it and then one gets used to it. It quickly becomes a respite, even a pleasure. You mingle much better in the life of things and of people. What is charming and novel, in this country, is that, everywhere, even on the road, you are in continual contact with its inhabitants. You see them live and you live with them… You are at home with them…

Beneath his quiet face, with his measured gestures, the Dutchman is rough and violent. He also likes derision and irony. But if you are not an Englishman and if you dress like everybody else, you adjust to it quite well. If need be, he can be indulgent but without servility, and joyfully welcoming, as long as it does not cost him anything. But avoid walking around dressed in animal skin. Animal skins first of all excite his curiosity and this curiosity can become aggressive and unpleasant. It happened to me in Rotterdam where nevertheless there disembark people from every country and wearing every outfit, and in Leuwarden, where I was followed in the street by a crowd of about fifteen hundred people, men, women and children. They began by laughing and making fun, and soon, exciting one another, ended up throwing balls of paper and orange peel at me. Well, it does not take much to move on from oranges to stones. These were extremely unpleasant moments which reminded me of coming out of public meetings at the time of the Dreyfus affair. It is not that the Dutchman is conservative and mundane, like the Frenchman, and that he is unduly surprised by things that he is not used to. Quite the opposite, he easily accepts progress, especially when it is of general utility. But he has idiosyncrasies, sometimes bizarre customs which he clings on to. You have to know what they are. You have to get to know him, and never frustrate his popular and moreover harmonious aesthetic. And you get to like him, and he likes us in his way, which is not our way, but the roughness of which lacks neither affability nor quaintness.

In Holland there are no coal, wood, stone, metal, fruit. There is just water. The little valleys around Arnhem, that you drive through quickly in top fourth gear, and the forest of Apeldoorn, with its high forest trees, are in fact foreign to it. They are already heralding Germany. There, man is less active; he seemed to me to be less strong, less handsome. It is a different race. The true Dutchman is the Dutchman of the polder and the canal. The war that he ceaselessly wages against the whims, the betrayals, the violence of the water has made him industrious, patient, energetic, crafty. Out of this destructive force he has managed to create an admirable economic tool, an enormous wealth, and moving beauty. An important Amsterdam businessman told me:

"In Italy, in Martinique, they are lucky enough to have volcanoes… And what do they do with them?… Nothing… absolutely nothing… Ruin and death, Monsieur… It's pitiful… Ah! if we had those volcanoes… Our water and those volcanoes, Monsieur!… ah! you would see… you would see!… What pitiful people!…"

"What would you do with the volcanoes?" I asked him.

"I've no idea… that's not the question… But you can be sure that we would do something with them… Look, it's like your wind in the South of France, the Mistral… Yes… Well! What do you do with it?… Nothing, either… However, I have been told that you know perfectly well where its origin is… Nothing could be easier than to capture and make use of it… But no… you let it blow where it will, however it wants to… It's negligence, Sir… pure negligence…"

I think that he was actually making fun of me.

This terrible element that is water, the Dutchman has been able to soften it, tame it, make it quietly carry out all necessities, be useful in all the decors of its existence. Water is not only the ornament of Holland; not only is it the main means of getting around, and, in some way, the vascular system of the country; not only is it the street, the road, the side-road, the highway which, in a thousand derivations, has the major centres communicate with one another, the villages, the hamlets, the farms, the hovels, the barns isolated in the polders, the castles, the gardens, the parks, spaced out along the dikes; it acts as marvellous fertiliser, as barnyard for the ducks of which there are everywhere huge flocks; it acts as demarcation, as cadastral delimitation; it separates and identifies properties. On the picturesque road from Groningen to Zwolle, I went past a whole series of little villages in which each house, each field, is surrounded by water as elsewhere they are by walls, hedges, fences. You suddenly seem to be transported in time to the time of lakeside houses. Nothing is as pretty, and strange, and shimmering, as this succession of dwellings on stilts multiplied by their reflections, in which you see working hard and sailing by, on light boats, large numbers of women, in short, heavy homespun frocks, their corsages enlivened by red needlework, their heads adorned by small flat caps, whose polished metal shines in the sun.

Man's great passion in Holland is work. From Breda to The Helder, Walcheren to The Texel, all, men, women, children, carry out continuous harsh work. They work on water, on land, on the dikes, in the ports, on the ships, with flowers. Nothing is wasted. They make a source of enrichment from the smallest thing. On the day we passed through Leuwarden they had sold on the market one hundred and twenty thousand lapwings' eggs. They know how to organise and develop the laying of eggs of this wild bird as they do with hens.

And there is not a tourist, of whom there are more and more, who is not pressured, emptied, dried out... Because he is pleased with his stay, he pays up without a word.

One day, in Utrecht, as he handed me the bill in which the most fantastical numbers had been added and multiplied, the hotelier smiled as he said to me:

"Sir will notice that we are no longer in Voltaire's time..."

"Why... Voltaire?" I replied... "How is he relevant?"

"Well, Sir... monsieur... de Voltaire... who said, as Sir knows only too well... who said: 'Land of canals, of ducks and of rogues[1].' Ah! we always remember that aphorism..."

"I see... and I see you remember it in your bill, don't you?"

---

1 Translator's note: The translation misses the repetition of the syllable 'can' in the original "Pays de canaux, de canards et de canailles.'

Rogues?... No... Businessmen? Yes... And aren't they a little bit the same thing? They have, as we say, business in their skin. No nation is more talented for business and for banking... They have the same quiet and tenacious ingenuity in draining gold as they have for draining water from polders...

We know that they were the first European navigators to get usefully into China. Before any negotiations, the Chinese, fearing that they were enemies of their religion, forced them to trample and to spit on the crucifix, which they did without hesitation. After that, the Chinese gave them authority to enter the country and to trade to their hearts content.

A strong and hard race, realistic and hard-working, in all things, through self-interest which is unaware of scruples and pushes feeling away. Whatever certain politicians may think, it will never allow itself to be attacked, absorbed by Germany... Holland has not reached the end of its history.

The Dutchman is a good coloniser. He managed to take huge profits from his magnificent establishments in the Indies. But there he gradually met his master in the Chinaman. In Java, the Chinaman is bubbling up everywhere, infiltrating himself and spreading out everywhere... He is a sort of invading, conquering water that that Dutchman cannot stem, and which threatens to submerge him...

A former consul, retired to Arnhem, M. X——, told me this characteristic anecdote:

In Canton—about twenty years ago—M. X—— had a Chinese servant boy working for him, who had extraordinary intelligence, flexibility, fidelity... Valet, secretary, cook, tailor, bootmaker, musician and poet, this boy was everything... everything one wished...

"I liked him a lot," M. X—— told me... and he seemed to be attached to me, for life... A pearl!"

One day the consul was sent to Jakarta, on important government business. Knowing how attached he was to this faithful servant, friends advised him to leave the boy at home...

"As soon as you are there… he will be led astray, taken, then employed by his compatriots… You will never see him again…"

His boy? Fidelity itself… Come on!… Other boys, perhaps… but his?… It was absurd… He took him with him. At Jakarta, as they disembarked, he left his young chap to deal with the luggage and instructed him to bring them to the governor's palace where he was to lodge during his stay and where he went without further delay. Two hours, three hours, four hours went by… No boy… What had happened?… Very worried, M. X—— asked the governor to involve the police when, towards the evening, a black messenger brought the luggage and a letter. The letter was from the boy… In it he explained, with many regrets, that he was obliged to leave his service, given that he had set up as a clock-mender in a fine district in Jakarta… Clock-mender?… Already!… It was no doubt a joke… M. X—— ran to the address on the letter. He went into a little shop and saw, sitting in front of the workbench, with his magnifying glass in his eye, the boy who, with total confidence was examining the mechanism of a watch…

"You are mad!" cried M. X—— "What does this mean?"…

Then the boy told him that, whilst he was waiting for the luggage, he had been approached by an old Chinaman… They had chatted, discussed for a long time…

"What do you want to be?" the old Chinaman had asked… "Do you want to be a tailor… cook… doctor… clock-mender?… What?… Tell me what you want to be."

In short, the boy had chosen clock-mending… And the old Chinaman had installed him in this shop where he was certain he would make his fortune… M. X—— was stupefied. All he could say was:

"But you know all about clock-mending, do you?"

And the boy replied calmly:

"Of course… A real Chinaman has to know about everything."

Gorinchem.

The first delight that I had, in Holland this time, was to see the little town of Gorinchem that I shall never forget, a little town almost unknown by tourists and which from very far away, from the other side of the water,—the Rhine and the Meuse come together there—seemed so dapper and which delighted me even more once we had driven for a time slowly in the narrow streets full of pedestrians… I was as enchanted by it as a child with a toy. It looked like a shiny, brand-new toy,—although it was very old—and its novelty was its cleanliness…

In Holland I am never saddened by old things, old monuments, old houses. You do not see their fissures, their cracks and these wounds that are ceaselessly made worse by the heaps of corrosive dust. They do not present us with the dilapidated sight of ruins. Because of the care that has been taken, they preserve a fine life of youth and health. A little more crammed in than new houses, a little more tilting, and that's about all… They recall those attractive old men, who were polite enough to resist decay, whose faces appear fresher, more laughing, beneath their white hair, and who teach young men forgiveness and how to smile. Coquetry is the great virtue of old folk.

What a delightful small town Gorinchem is!… From the motorcar you could effortlessly touch the painted, washed, varnished house fronts. The streets, where we were driving between these house fronts with their carved gables, were also washed, washed like the tiled floors of interiors painted by Pieter de Hoogh,[1] and paved, it seemed to me, with the same-coloured mosaics that covered the facades of many of the houses. And arrays of exotic fruit, shop windows displaying lace, embroidered material, heavy silver jewellery decorating the shop fronts with special luxury… It was the first town in

---

1 Peter de Hoogh, or Hooch (1629-1684) was a painter of interiors.

the Low Countries which placidly reflected its coquetry in its canals…

We stopped at a patisserie to have tea, but above all to stop so that we could set foot in the town.

People came and went, looked at us and looked at the car, in silence. These debonair but rather heavy faces, I had already seen in old prints of tulip lovers. They were not too sure whether they should admire, despise or be indignant… Once they had looked at the motorcar, they looked at one another, and then they left, without expressing the slightest feeling. And they were replaced by others who repeated their behaviour. There were blonde women with their hair tied back; there were very black women with almond-shaped eyes, and shades where the yellow of the Far East fought with the pink of Europe… Fishermen came in and went out, pushing little carts containing bundles of brown nets, and others with wicker baskets full of salmon. A youngster, at the door, offered us postcards: churches with leaning clocktowers, windmills… canals full of boats… Everything was monotonous and everyday. Life was flowing, before us, just as every day, in front of this shop, it flows gently, peacefully with its little sound of clogs on the flagstones in the street. And yet I felt perfectly, enthusiastically happy. I had in me a violent joy from this gentleness, from this sound of clogs, from this silence of the faces, from this pretty girl with bare arms who served us without haste, from this not very good tea, from these China cups which did not even come from the factories in Delft, from this sickly odour of cocoa which floated in the shop, from these little houses across the road, small childlike houses, like the ones you see, the ones you buy, for Christmas trees in the toy shops in Nuremberg… To me it seemed to be happiness and that I could have spent the rest of my life there. This was not a new feeling for me. Each time I stop somewhere, no matter where, and there is a little water, trees and, between the trees, red roofs, with a large sky above all that, and no memories… I find it difficult to drag myself away.

I had to make an effort to stand up and to leave…

Claude Monet's Discovery.

For the first time I gazed, without seeing in them again the old images of a happiness that had turned so sour, at those canals where the vigour of the Rhine ices up and dies. With delight I admired the little bridges, crossing the thin streams of water, where the arc of their single wooden arch is completed by their reflection; little, round bridges like those in Japanese prints, and which, everywhere in Holland protect and defend each house… And those little, low, decorated gates which open onto little beds of flowers which have a unique brightness, in this damp country, where they are impregnated, caressed and loved by iridescent light. As we drove through villages, sometimes we would see the ladies, ironing at the windows, behind the glass that vaporises them, with their collars embroidered with daffodils, hyacinths, tulips…

Also, for the first time I became aware of this oriental look, indeed extremely oriental look, found in the majority of Dutch towns and villages, without being able to put one's finger precisely on why that is.

It is at one and the same time the art of Japan they evoke and the primordial art of China, but also the art of the Indies, and the whole magic of continents bathed in water, and of the Isles, that the Dutch navy has been frequenting for centuries, as if the navigators had brought back from those countries which are beyond far-off seas, with the commodities that enrich them, a moving reminder of their features.

The development of influences which guide the evolution of thought in time, is only so difficult to understand because the fluctuation of ideas, which is properly intelligible, often deviates because of accidents that are purely mechanical… I have often thought, during this trip, of that magical day when Claude Monet, who had come to Holland, about fifty years ago, to paint, found, as he opened a parcel, the first Japanese print that he had seen. His emotion before this wonderful art, in which all life, all movement, everything depicted are captured in one stroke—art, of which he was moreover unaware, as was everybody at that time, but of which he had in himself the sort of fraternal prescience—well you can guess that emotion.

His turmoil, his delight were such that he could not express what he was feeling in sentences; he could only express himself with cries:

"Ah!… ah!… Bloody hell!" he said… "Bloody hell!"

This expletive contained the complete infiniteness of his admiration.

It was in Zaandam that this miracle occurred. Zaandam, with its canal, its moored ships discharging cargoes of wood from Norway, its packed flotilla of barges, their prows bulging like junks, its alleyways of water, its pink huts, its noisy workshops, its green houses, Zaandam, the most Japanese of all décors in Holland.

You would have to be not only unaware of Claude Monet's paintings, but also of those of his peers amongst his contemporaries and his juniors, and even of the names, unknown at that time of Houkusai, of Utamaro and of Hiroshige,[1] to doubt the excitement with which he ran to the shop where he had acquired the package… A nondescript little grocers, in which the fat fingers of a fat man were wrapping—without being paralysed by them—two pence of pepper, ten pence of coffee, in glorious images that had been brought back from the Far East, in a ship's hold, along with spices!… Although he was not rich at that time, Monet decided to buy all the masterpieces in the shop… He saw a pile of them on the counter. His heart leapt… And then he saw the grocer who was serving an old lady take a leaf from the pile… He rushed over:

---

1 In the nineteenth century the Goncourt brothers helped to make known in France these late eighteenth and early nineteenth-century Japanese artists.

"No... no" he shouted... "I'll buy that... I'll buy everything... everything..."

The grocer was a decent chap. He thought he was dealing with an eccentric... And again, these coloured papers did not cost him anything: they were just a bonus for him... As one gives a picture to a crying child to calm it down, he gave the pile to Monet with a chuckle, and making fun of him a little:

"Take them... take them..." he said... "Ah! you can take them all... They're worthless... It's not strong... as far as I'm concerned, I prefer that paper..."

Turning towards the customer:

"You don't mind, do you?"

"Me?... Oh! Good Lord!"

He took a sheet of yellow paper with which he wrapped the piece of cheese bought by the old woman.

Once he was back home, overjoyed, Monet spread out "his images". Amongst the most beautiful, the rarest proofs, which he did not perhaps know were Houkusais, Utamaros, women washing, women bathing, seas, birds, trees in flower, he saw one that represented a herd of deer, and which seemed to him to be one of the most astonishing marvels of this astonishing art. He later found out that it was a Korin[1]...

It was the beginning of a famous collection, but especially of such an evolution of French painting, at the end of the nineteenth century, that the anecdote has, in addition to its particular flavour, a genuine historical value. Those who wish to make a serious study of that important artistic movement that we call Impressionism cannot neglect it...

Nowadays when so many useless and ridiculous anniversaries are celebrated, could we not celebrate with special pomp the anniversary of that moving and fruitful day on which a great French artist came face to face, for the first time, in Zaandam, with a small Japanese print?

---

1 Ogata Korin (1658-1712) was a Japanese painter, calligrapher and engraver.

The Harbour, Land of the Painter.

I do not think that Claude Monet's emotion would have been stronger anywhere else. It is because you see art from the Far East everywhere in Holland as if it emerges from water. It is true that in the harbours of the West—and the whole of Holland is just one big harbour—ships bring back with them patches, fragments of the East and its creations which are obliged to struggle, in subtlety and in splendour, with light itself.

Venice, dressed in black, was teeming with riches from overseas, and its climate could not perhaps have been enough, on its own, to produce, for the delight of the world, the eyes of Titian.

It was by chance that Rubens[1] was not born in Antwerp where the largest merchant fleet in the world traded throughout Europe every type of overseas merchandise. His parents brought him back there when he was very young and it was there that he spent what was, perhaps, the most fruitful part of his life. With the result that he drew from the famous quaysides of the Escaut, not only the arrangement of lines and the ornamental scale of his compositions, but also at least a share of the magnificence which he gave to the dazzling representations of the sovereigns and beautiful women of his time.

Even Marseille, "Gateway to the East," wrote Puvis de Chavannes,[2] Marseille where Monticelli[3] was born, provided this painter with the strange mixtures of his palette, where red fruits, oriental silks, pearly shellfish, are heaped on one another

---

1 Rubens' father was obliged to leave Antwerp for political reasons. As a result, Rubens was born in Westphalia in 1577.
2 Pierre Puvis de Chavannes (1824-1898) was a French painter.
3 Adolphe Monticelli (1824-1886) was a pre-Impressionist and Expressionist painter. He was an influence on van Gogh.

amongst the blue waters and amongst the powerful blacks, golds, which make the docks, full of ships, tremble…

Is it also possible that nobody has been able to prevent themselves believing that they were setting foot in Japan, amongst those who, early in the morning, entered the fjord of Oslo[1]?

✳

I am convinced that a large port, whatever it is, wherever it may be, is, par excellence, the perfect place for the birth, upbringing, education of an artist's soul. An artist who is born in a port, who lived there in his childhood and youth, amongst the variety, the unexpected, the ceaselessly renewed education brought by its sights is necessarily ahead of the artist born deep in the country, in a quiet, sleepy village, or in the stifling obscurity of a suburb. His imagination, excited by everything that moves and happens around him, awakens earlier. His brain works livelier and quicker and without too many struggles… He is used to seeing, and, in seeing, to understanding. His thought which is not limited by a wall, "the wall of the Meyers' house", or by a hill, is free to wander, through space, like those pretty seagulls that haunt the vast sky, and which have no other limit to their desires than the tiredness in their wings… With one look, he embraces more things here and there, more faces here and there, more of universal life. Unbeknownst to him, and as though mechanically, the motion of the barges on the sea, of the sea against the jetties, the rhythm of the swell, the entry of ships into the docks, the swaying of the crowded masts linked by the soft curve of the ropes, the sails which flee, which dance, which fly, the threads of smoke, all the silhouettes of the teeming quaysides, teach him, better than a professor, elegance, flexibility, the infinite diversity of shapes. Without knowing it, he takes on board many sensations that will never disappear,

---

1 In the text Mirbeau uses the former name of Oslo, Kristiania, which he had visited in 1895.

which he will remember, later, and with which he will bring to life a face, a woman's torso, the ripple of a skirt, the waving of a branch… For there is all that in a port… There is something of everything and there is everything, in a port.

※

And, once more, my reverie ended with Rembrandt.

Rembrandt was not, it is true, born in a large port… But his name is inseparable from that of Amsterdam, where he lived for so many years and found there the outlet for his gifts in all their mighty power… Amsterdam whose inhabitants are dressed in black like those in Venice, with the same pride about and similar taste for brilliant accents and heavy ornaments. In both cities the sun creates the same enchantment with the sky and the water that separates the houses, until the humidity condenses into fog, stealing away the aquatic city and rendering it back to darkness, over which the triumph of the sun will only have a greater splendour. I could not conceive that Rembrandt might have been born in some small, sleepy town tucked away in the country, without ever seeing the sun turn the quaysides golden, turn golden the black waters of the docks, turn gold the deep atmosphere, 'the dark brightness' which teems between the hulls of the ships… Perhaps what he might have been able to find in himself might have been enough to amaze humanity. But I glorify in discovering, in his work, the conception, not only of images, but of the most sumptuous colours, arising from the meeting of his genius with the luxury of a great port, with its infinite variety of miseries, especially in Amsterdam, the most oriental of ports of the West, Amsterdam and its dark Jewish population.

Shutting my eyes to the unbearable brightness of the setting sun, towards which we were travelling, I was thinking about the hero's sad end, of the later years of Rembrandt, trapped in poverty, unhappy, possibly expiating the crime of having, on our behalf, stolen from the sky, the divine fire of its light…

The Dike.

From Gorinchem there is almost as far as Dordrecht a succession of delightful villages, of which I do not know the names but through which it takes perhaps almost three times longer than it does through Paris. From the top of the narrow, elevated dike our gaze looks into the interior of houses below. In front of all the thresholds, washed, polished, the pairs of clogs are arranged, light willow clogs. Before going inside the inhabitants never forget to take their shoes off and it is velvet footsteps which slip, as though to leave behind them no trace, not even a sound, on the wooden floors and the flagstones we see shining as we drive by... A brightly coloured curtain, a copper pan, floral plates, bulbous pewters, a sparkling bonnet animate these houses that are almost all the same... Armed with long sticks with a large pad of wet material women are energetically washing the facades; others are polishing the carefully varnished doors and are rubbing the decorative brasses. The kitchens, in the shape of sentry boxes, are separated from the house so that it may not be sullied by any dirty job... And it makes one think, I am not sure why, of lace, enhanced but only slightly, with metal threads... What is charming is that, behind each house, just as we have stables and a barn, they have a sort of little harbour, which has taken its water from the polder, with one or two wherries tethered which they use when they cut wicker and rushes, and for journeys through the thousand little liquid roads, across the green plain...

I recall, in the bend of an alley where there began a garden, full of fritillaries, seeing squatting a peasant woman with fresh skin, and her gesture which was folding white linen. I had already seen this same peasant woman in a painting...

All the features of the Dutch countryside and people, the houses and the costumes, the inns and the mills, which pump and tame the infinite water of the polder, have, even for those who do not know them, the charm of the déjà vu. Everything about them is familiar to them, thanks to their painters who have presented them, with love, to the whole universe…

A similar fame is owed to Dostoevsky and to Tolstoy by the little folk and peasants of Russia. It is possible that Camille Pissarro, and Cézanne, who never sought the details of customs, the passing anecdote, have created for the villages, the faces, the hillsides, the beautiful undulations of the French countryside, a popularity which will be no less universal than the fame of their painters. Thus, thanks to Watteau and to Renoir, the women as they saw them in the streets of Paris, or sitting on the lawns in their gardens, will endure, less fragile, more living than the Tanagra women,[1] as immortal as the equestrians on Greek friezes…

The sun was already dipping into the horizon when we suddenly found ourselves before Dordrecht which, after so many tiny villages, seemed huge. It owed its majesty particularly to this time of day, which amplifies its shapes, mingling them into one blue mass… The Meuse—or rather the Merwede—was congested, just like the road of a city, before dinner. The ferry was not operating… We had to wait an hour during which we saw the boats gradually lose the brightness of their colours until they became completely black, and stretching towards the sky, where the day was slowly dying, the span of their enormous dark wings… The hulls of the barges emerged from the water which they seemed to weigh down. Tugboats, whistling interminably, were pulling whole trains in their wake… As it lit up everywhere, the town became a brazier the flames whose flames reached the tops of the houses… The wind that had just sprung up began to blow, as if to fan the flames and to prepare the forge needed for the work of some unknown superhuman blacksmith…

---

1 There had been a discovery in 1870 in Tanagra (Boeotia) of terracotta statues mainly of women.

Evening in Dordrecht.

Once or twice on our journey, amongst so many memories, nice ones and irritating ones, if I felt bitter, once or twice there had come back to me the memory of the extraordinary size of the sole into which we had bitten, in Dordt... What good times we had when we were young!...

It was on a hotel terrace, beside the water, where the sun was playing, where the ships were gambolling like pet animals, where the whole apparatus of busy and noisy business seemed to be nothing more than preparations for a festival... no doubt, our festival.

Gorinchem, the prodigy of this town on fire, when the sun goes down, and which had died almost tragically, had made me forget everything, but, until then, I had been impatient only to find once again the vestiges of my former happiness.

Amongst a thousand fleeting images, I had difficulty retaining a few which could be pinned down... I feel on my shoulder the weight and the warmth of a head whose hair and perfume are caught by the strength of the wind, but leaving me my share.... I smile at the hesitation of two bare feet, who need a towel before they dare walk on the filthy carpet of hotel bedrooms. What quality is given to a waltz from *Faust*, quite simply, by moonlight and my contented heart? No cry from Tristan, no lament from Melisande, have provoked in me more emotion than those three poor violins, in which bleated, so pitifully, the music of Monsieur Gounod... I laugh about the lie invented so that I could turn my head away and not see a roll of artificial hair being taken off, and one of those so harsh orders, about decency, which would deprive us, if we obeyed, of the gentlest intimate sight, secret and charming gestures, where all your veins are beating, and which one dares not name... I see the railway stations from which one departs, and also the stations where one returns, and these quaysides, where you miss the terrible handkerchief that no hand, no matter how perfidious, any longer waves… I recall, for a second, the sheen of two polished knees and the tense curve of a breast…a round shoulder, warmly perfumed, the fuzz on her ankle… I wait for tears that will flow on a very pale face, silent with happiness… There come back to my mind, and rush there in floods, my blood, furious caresses, after which you believed yourself strong enough, even if you were tottering, to defy the universe, to triumph over it with all its heroes and its monsters, mixed up together… I am thinking also of trivial things which made one cry with laughter, of insignificant things which unleash tempests… and of those tired afternoons in which you gave yourself up to boredom, which were defined as: "indifference to my life, as to my death".

But in spite of my desire for melancholy, I feel that all that is far off, very far off, that all this past is fading and wearing away… In my core I noticed that, amongst all these memories, which a hypocritical and stupid mania for literature tried to amplify into pain, I still have one that is truly living, and close and so vulgar: the tasty firmness of your flesh, magnificent sole, which were eaten so cheerfully, on the terrace of this hotel, beside the water.

It was, it still is the Hotel Bellevue, a little older, a little more crowded… I recognised the same carpet on the so-narrow steps of the staircase; at the windows, the same curtains; in the dining room which is used, at the same time, as office, as cash desk, as lounge and as restaurant, the same furniture… Followed by the hotelier who detained us—the same hotelier too, I think—I ran to the terrace… Night had completely fallen, without a streak of light and the silent water… Tiny waves came and lapped, and whispered against the bank… Scarcely could I see lights moving in the distance… Thick clouds were hiding the moon, and turning the river quite black, mixed with the black of the land… Not the least violin…No waltz, even from *Faust*, to soften me… So, everything was dead!…

Coming back into the dining room, I surprised the head waiter by shouting:

"Sole... sole, like last time!..."

They did not have any sole...

My companions, whose appetites had been whetted by my enthusiastic descriptions, insisted in vain with the proprietor...

There was no more sole... there was no more anything.

So, we had to make do with smoked salmon and tinned sardines...

But what sardines!... We found them extraordinarily exquisite... Spicy, highly flavoured, we had never eaten such good ones. The sole was forgotten... One of us spoke in ecstasy:

"Only in Holland can you get such great fish... Long live Holland!"

And calling the head waiter:

"Where do they make these admirable, these magnificent, these unique sardines?" he asked. "I wish to order caseloads, wagonloads, boatloads! I want to impress France and embarrass it for its ignorance about sardines... Rotterdam?... Maastricht? The Hague? Batavia?... Where?... Where?"

The head waiter drew himself up and, with dignity:

"We get them from Bordeaux," he said...

As we were finishing dinner, a group of English people came to have tea in an alcove close to our table. Men in dinner jackets, women with plunging necklines... Opposite us, a very young *lady*, a blonde, stood up, walked about and then when she sat down again for five minutes could not sit still. Her fingers were playing with her fan, with a gold-tipped cigarette, with her rings, with her hair. A chain was clinking around her neck, and I discovered that her feet, beneath the armchair, did not stop taking off and putting on the silvery slippers where could be seen the silk of her white stockings... At some words, which caused the men to laugh louder, and their lady friends to look down, it is not sufficient to say that the agitated young woman was blushing; a flush of blood ran all over her, a red wave rose from her shoulder, covered all the skin that could be seen, to finally fade at the roots of her blond hair… My gaze suddenly saw in hers the anguish of not being able to find at the tip of her desperate toe, the slipper which had moved too far away. The lady blushed even more, and her blood seemed so in movement that I imagined more pink, almost red, her white stocking, in which her foot tightened until it disappeared into the silver slipper, which she had finally found again…

That night, I slept, a deep, dreamless sleep…

Dordrecht.

The following morning it was the monotonous music of rain beating against the windows which woke us up.

Attractive Dordt had faded away and with a yawn I gazed at a bored and muddy town in which I remembered—why did I suddenly laugh out loud?—that Ary Scheffer[1] was born…

When one walks through its streets, armed with rubber clothing to ward off the rain, it does not seem however to lack charm, or character, this drenched town, with its feet in its canals, criss-crossed and surrounded by fluvial roads… there you see, but smoothed out, magnificent traditions from an earlier period… In gabled houses which sheltered so much ac-tivity and in which luxury had so much haughtiness, it looks as though there are no longer any inhabitants… In its churches, before the Catholic faith had the time to finish them off, the Reformation had established itself… Its severe, surly simplicity bears better witness to its pride than the pomp of the oriental

---

1 Ary Scheffer (1795-1858) was a Dutch painter, specialising in historical scenes.

rites that it has driven out. But its show of pride does not disdain a little comfort. On the flagstones where pagan piety knelt before its Images, a large number of chairs have been placed in which reason can install itself properly, so that it may freely examine itself. But nothing dies except gradually. The *Grootekerke* is a cathedral from former times… Only, it is completely bare… The stalls, however, are still there which the chisels of the ingenious sixteenth-century artisans devoutly ransacked. The copper railings in front of the choir, the stairs leading up to the pulpit, still seem to be made of divine rays, indeed rays of sunlight, but of rays that had flowered.

These brasses and these arabesques evoke others for me; staircases, banisters, chandeliers, scrolls and all these windings which are present, now, throughout the world, with the name *modern style*, an English name for a mania where the Belgians only succeeded by taking Dutch brasses and then horribly torturing and deforming them…

But where are, in bars and luxury hotels, windows of perfume shops, delicatessens, creameries and sweet shops, in the homes of German financiers, Viennese poets, Flemish aesthetes and Lyonnaise cocottes, red coppers and golden coppers, where are the smiling bonhomie, the harmonious curve, the solid and joyful honesty of charming Dutch brasses?

And here I am once again in the street from which the rain has driven the last passers-by. Groups of housewives, of servant women, have taken refuge in the covered market. In black capes, unstarched caps, stupid, hunchbacked and chattering, they crowd against one another like hens under the canopy of the soaked farmyard. All the houses, on which old wounds are opening up, are weeping; all the bridges, with their deformed arches, which are spaced out before our gaze, are weeping too; everything is weeping. The canal water, beneath the raindrops of the remorseless shower, seems to be giving off bubbles of gas, as though from a putrid pond. Behind the garden fences humiliated, ruffled flowers are leaning morosely, and through the windows which are running with water and steaming up you see, here and there, moving about, as though in a thick mist, vague shapes of human beings… They look like shadows, phantoms from the past.

Luckily everything is not from the past, not everything is dead in Dordrecht, and it is with "a very modern joy" that I saw machines living and steam twisting in the rain. Activity that does not waste time in chatter, like the gossips in the market, but works, animates strangely the new districts and the quaysides. Without seeming to, Dordrecht trades everything with the whole world. It is, at the crossroads of its rivers, one of the most important German water stations. What the arteries of its canals and rivers do not bring to its port, it manufactures, kneads it, forges, tunes itself: smoked and salted fish, cocoas and tobaccos, coals from Belgium, Germany and England, tools which will be used everywhere, machines to make machines, vessels which will—how many times?—go round the world. And all that is got ready, is transported on land, sails, disembarks and embarks, accompanied by whistle and hammer blows, the noise of sheet metal, the creaking of pulleys, and the endless howling of sirens.

It looks as though all this water, in which it bathes, the living town turns into steam and, when it has used its expansive and laborious strength, allows to fall back as rain on the dead town, without stopping working.

The Boer Museum.

We saw only one museum in Dordrecht but one which disturbed me a lot, so much so that it prevented me from going into any other: the Boer museum.

They too, at least as much as the painter of the masterpiece, *The death of the Virgin Mary*, Pourbus or the Brueghels, Jean

Steen or van Ostade, Cuyp or van Goyen,[1] are well and truly from Holland or the Dutch School. Despite the passage of time, the climate, the soil, adapting to new customs, they have kept the same hard and tranquil face, the same robust stature as their metropolitan brothers, with the small addition of the supple loose gait of cowboys. Their work, although very different, is an expression that is just as significant of the physiognomy of a people.

This handful of Dutch families took with them to the depths of Africa all the virtues which made the fortune of their Dutch compatriots, more exactly, which made them rich: sang-froid, tenacity, boldness. But, since they were puritans, the Boers used them only to live worthily, roughly, poorly. They did not, or only scarcely, mix their blood with that of other races, and they kept themselves apart from the fortune hunters, the adventure seekers, who are always attracted by countries which conceal the unknown. In the Cape, they found a desert where they could preach, clear the land as they wished, and which would no doubt have tempted the Solitaries of a Port-Royal.[2] The fact is that French protestants, victims of the revocation of that famous Edict,[3] which is already a gesture of the hatred of tyrants for ideologues, came to take part in the same agricultural life, the same religious austerity. One would like to think that these virtuous pastors were not unaware, at least did not always ignore the fact that they were meditating, labouring on treasures, but that they despised them.

Did they despise them? Or did they simply not know how to exploit them?

---

1 Of these painters of the Dutch Golden Age, Albert Cuyp (1605-1691) was from Dordrecht.

2 Frenchmen who in the seventeenth century chose to live an ascetic and solitary life at Port-Royal-des-Champs.

3 The Edict of Nantes was signed in 1598 by King Henri IV and gave freedom to French protestants. It was revoked by Louis XIV in 1685 and this led to many Huguenots fleeing to Holland.

If the stories I have been told are true, it was the Dutch banks, this time too timid, or not confident enough about success, who are said to have ceded to English brokers and promoters the files concerning these mines, for the conquest of which the financial imperialism of the Greatest Britain would, a few years later, massacre their nationals…

Poor Boers! Scarcely do today a few unlucky speculators complain about their dispossession and their defeat… Truth to tell, nobody talks about them any longer… They are completely forgotten, as forgotten as an unsuccessful melodrama. From this grandiose epic which caused a long shudder of enthusiasm throughout the world, all that is left is this little museum… But already that is better than nothing… However, nobody comes here… I had a great deal of trouble finding the attendant. He was in a courtyard, wearing a gardener's apron and, on his head, a rabbit skin bonnet, and was pulling up hyacinth bulbs. He looked at me in surprise, and even with a little terror, as though I were a supernatural phenomenon…

"You have to understand…" he told me, apologising for his welcome… "for three months now I haven't seen a human face… In summer… from time to time… an Englishman… and that's all… And always an Englishman who's made a mistake… He asks me where the Rembrandts are? Yes, Monsieur, the Rembrandts… Here!"

With an apologetic air he shows me a table of blackened wood on which, amongst the dust, there are piles of postcards and illustrated catalogues that are never sold…

"Good Lord, yes!… There you are!… That's what it's like…"

Finally, he tells me bitterly that, when the museum was first opened, he had been given, in order to attract visitors with a décor full of local colour, a huge Boer hat, a sort of khaki jacket, and leather gaiters… At least it had a bit of style…

"And I had a cartridge belt across my chest… Now," he sighs, "like all my colleagues, I don't even have a trimmed cap…"

He falls silent, and then continues:

"There is, close to here, in a square… a sort of shack, in which they exhibit negroes who swallow swords and who eat sheep's wool… Well, that's always crowded…"

I remembered the gesture which accompanied this complaint, a gesture which said more about the fickleness of crowds and the ingratitude of history than a whole speech.

He said:

"One day President Kruger[1] came through Dordrecht… Well, Monsieur, he didn't even come to the museum. President Kruger!… Indeed!…Oh! Oh! Oh!"

In this solitude, where our footsteps resounded lugubriously, where the dusty daylight covered the objects as though with a funeral veil, I was heavy-hearted. I told myself:

"Nevertheless, the unremitting resistance of those rough farmers, who claimed to draw from the earth only the gold that was wheat and to plunge into it only their ploughshares, was worth providing the keeper of these glorious memories with a cap decorated with a few bits of braid and also worth more than general indifference… This resistance does not only seem worthy of admiration because, as soldiers, they bravely defended their freedom, it seems to me to show an almost superhuman heroism, because, as apostles, they devoted themselves to preserving humanity from that alcoholism, worse than the other, that is propagated by the abuse of gold… They kept the gold buried deep in the earth, as one buries dead bodies deeply, so as not to infect the air one breathes, and not to poison men with deadly contagions… They hid the gold, not to enjoy it as misers do, but to destroy its germs of madness and death… A concealment—however conscious it might have been—no doubt absurd, but sublime!"

That was where my imagination went as I looked at cards, maps, trophies, portraits of old men in long presbyterian

---

1 South-African politician (1825-1904) who founded the Transvaal and led the Boers in the war against Great Britain (1899-1902).

frock-coats, teams of oxen, farms, bibles, stiff faces, and all that evokes the epic grandeur of these armies in civilian dress, of these militia of peasant women, victorious over armies in uniform, laboriously organised for disaster…

But as soon as I found myself drifting into sentimentality, into the ancestral worship of heroes, I began to reflect…

Amongst all the lessons that the history of the Boers suggests, the most reasonable, the most useful, can you not infer it from the folly, the uselessness of their resistance?… In the Cape, no militia, even one with angels with trumpets and miraculous saints, could have succeeded in diverting the avarice, the greed, the frenzy of human beings, from these lands of crime and madness where gold is hidden… They have to have their poison, which sustains them until it kills them. How many millions upon millions will always massacre one another, to possess gold, rob others of it, and get drunk on it, leading to the daze of madness and the fury of serious crime! How many poor, kind dreamers will be sentenced to death, will be treated as bandits, because they wanted to cure incurable humanity of its greatest delirium!… No policy, no law, not even a book has the power to transform men in one go. Not even any martyr—no matter how sorrowful—is fertile. And when he elevates himself to become a splendid example who endures through the centuries, then it is even worse, he becomes criminal… It needed the terrible Jew Paul, to brandish and raise up to the world the bloody cross of the gentle Jew Jesus, and the only true pieces that the faithful and Jews have retained of this emblem of love, were gallows and pyres: "Accursed race," cries Schopenhauer, "it has entangled humanity with a God!"

If we ever free ourselves from gold and the evils it causes; if one day we renounce gold—and I mean individual wealth,—it will not be through disgust with the power gold has to change men into animals (an alchemy already expressed in the fable of Circe), it will not be through wisdom, virtue, dignity, it will be by force. We may imagine that, in the economic evolution in our times, this metal may lose its exchange value, representative of our passions, of our ambitions, of our interests, of our energies, of our laziness, and that we may finally find the method of living differently—a more rational, less complicated, method such as drawing, for our needs and our pleasures, from the inexhaustible reserves of the common treasure… Alas! that will not happen tomorrow…

And here we have a portrait of good old Kruger, who did not even come to the museum in Dordrecht, and that the little Queen of Holland,[1] who knows what it means to suffer, received like an unhappy granddad, here this portrait makes me think again, with his placid, crafty face, and his chinstrap beard of a planter of tulips, of these Dutchmen, nation of hoarders, of speculators, of bons vivants as well, who produced these ascetics and these despisers of gold, over there, in the depths of Africa which is awash with gold and diamonds…

But is there not a race or a people, or at least a disparate minority, reduced entirely to trading, in whom a similar perpetual injustice cements solidarity—once again the Jews, quite simply—who gave birth to a Karl Marx, himself a speculator and also, amongst the more audacious, a purchaser—to what deficit? In how many centuries? and against the total of coalesced capital—of the happiness dreamed of by the universal proletariat?

As I left the Boer museum from which, to the great joy of the assistant who had regained his optimism, I carried pocketfuls of souvenirs, coloured postcards: round dances of pretty girls from Marken, fishermen from Volendam, with their sheepskin bonnets, windmills in Vormerveer (for, as far as Boers are concerned, of landscapes of the Transvaal, of battles, of mines, of

---

1 Queen Wilhelmina (1880-1962), Queen of Holland, sent a warship in 1900 to bring Kruger back to Europe.

Kruger and de Wet,[1] there are not any, as they are unsaleable), I start to go back down to the town. One moment I stop before a bronze of Ary Scheffer, on the Scheffersplein, and it seems to me to be neither cold, nor boring. As far as you may see, in molten metal, the expression of a human face, I felt that there was there, under this skull, a lively intelligence, an attractive, elegant taste for shape, and I blushed that I had burst out laughing a few moments ago… Maybe very little would have been necessary,—genius, perhaps—for Ary Scheffer to become a great painter… In any case, I better enjoyed the charm of his seriousness, and I think of what remains, in the charming smile that Renan's[2] granddaughter inherited…

The rain, its reserves seeming to decorate the depths of the sky, had stopped falling. Even some sunlight showed itself between the clouds. The sky became vast and light again. Then we saw a dashing, coquettish Dordt. The new light mitigates the dark and severe aspect that the streets of the old town have retained from the Middle Ages. You finally see the Dutch grace, the freshness they have in places, and to which the abundance of flowers contributes. The canals become animated, the streets full of people, and the houses from which the ghosts of the past seem to have departed… This contrast has a sudden, sharp pleasure, where you linger with a new desire to wander… In front of the houses, with their stepped-up roofs, of which time has clothed the walls with layers of dust, on which it has left a patina for centuries, the small gardens are imprisoned. Behind the wrought-iron railings, with heraldic lances, the flowers of today seem to be guarded by halberdiers of yore… From the top of the raised bridges, the canal water no longer looks liquid, because of its stillness, apart from its semi-transparency. And, when you look at its depth, you begin to imagine that it plunges, to infinity, not in space but in time…

---

1 A Boer general.
2 Ernest Renan (1823-1892) had married the niece of Ary Scheffer.

In vain does the spring sunlight use its coquettishness attempting to dry so slowly the attractive town, so attractively soaked, we must leave... A girl offers us lapwings' eggs which we buy and will eat en route.

And the 628-E8 starts in the slippery mud, skids more than once... But the soil dries out in the countryside. We would forget the shower, if it were not for the number of puddles in which celestial blue and scraps of mother-of-pearl clouds are reflected, rather like many fragments of a large mirror, which, as it fell from the sky, had shattered on the road...

Rotterdam.

I do not remember anything about the short journey from Dordrecht to Rotterdam except that the motorcar went, slid, with no shocks, no jolts, and as though freed from the servitude of gravity. She was providing me with a joy that is neither the joy of leaping nor the joy of skating, but which is like both of them. She carried me along with extraordinary speed, and, truly, I felt myself endowed with her elasticity. You could have said that, to make herself gentler and to go more quickly, she was running with all her energy, barefoot, along the road.

And now, suddenly, at the top of a little hill which, in this country, seemed to us like a Himalayan mountain, beyond an enormous bridge, we found ourselves in front of a sort of cliff, or rather a section of dream-like wall, created by some pile of multi-coloured bricks, fragments of coloured glass, splashes of sunlight, at the foot of which there broke, like an untamed sea, the furious tumult of a city at work and a feverish port. Cliff or section of dream-like wall, it took us a few minutes to recognise that we were opposite the new city of Rotterdam.

Scarcely had we entered Rotterdam than we were enveloped by a movement, an agitation, that the sirens on the canal, the whistles of the locomotives on the railways, the rolling of trucks on the cobbles, made resound into infinity… But we were even more enveloped by the population who surrounded us with open-mouthed faces, with gestures which were childishly trying to learn through the very brief touch of a brass, the touch, quickly ended, of the radiator, testing the tyres, leaning on the mudguards. The amazement of this crowd, which either smiled or scowled, but which remained silent, surrounded us so tightly that we had to stop.

No matter how noisy and restless it might be, Rotterdam struck me more as a wild and far-off town. In the most agreeable, the richest centre of Europe, its inhabitants looked like startled Laplanders. At the very least, they had never seen, or very rarely seen, motorcars… This population, which was used to all the din, to all the quirks of cosmopolitan life, to the sight of trade on a global scale, to superhuman efforts, panicked at the sight of our motorcar without uttering a word.

In no circumstance do ladies forget to prepare themselves to be looked at, and indeed like being looked at, except when they see the gaze going on for too long. Ours were wriggling on their cushions, rather ill at ease, as they noticed—vision of terror—rough hands touch the windows and wander about on them. My neighbour shut her eyes… Her gloves were trembling.

This silent crowd, in this feverish city full of noise, it was the working population that is not heard in a deafening factory. Civilisation loosens, polishes the instincts and the energy of which it only uses living force for its obscure ends… But does it not artificially collect the elements that it deforms as it compresses them, and from which the explosion will multiply, in a certain circumstance, the redoubtable inert power?

Using the horn, Brossette managed with difficulty to make a way in the crowd that was gently parted by the bonnet… As we passed by, we saw, noiselessly, behind the windows, a crowd of raised heads, open-mouthed, which, even when the flow had reformed, did not lower, did not close their mouths…

No motorcars, therefore, no garage. I had great difficulty finding one... It was a dirty district on the outskirts, a sort of storage shed in which there were empty chests, an old broken-down cart, barge sails wrapped around rotten masts.

Brossette was worried.

"What sort of a country is this?" he said, scratching his head... "Oh! Dear me!"

We had only got there slowly, painfully... Children were sticking to the running-boards, huddling on the bonnet, and we had to get them off by shaking them, like the clusters of roasted insects that you get off the radiator at night...

A Speculator.

If I only managed to get a poor view of Rotterdam, if I only just glimpsed its harbour, it was because in the foyer of the hotel, just as I had finished eating, I met my old friend Weil-Sée[1], my best friend, my dear Weil-Sée that I had not seen for years...

We embraced several times... My friend Weil-Sée is one of the rare men that I embrace and who embraces me, and we have been embracing, for about forty years, every time we separate and meet again, that is every five or six years.

"You here!... Fancy you being here!"

And secretly I wiped the wetter of my cheeks...

He looked at me with a smile but without responding...

"Are you no longer in Grenoble? I thought that you were in Grenoble... rich... happy!... And your factory for producing electrical energy?... Do you not sell energy anymore?"

To all my questions he shook his head with a smile.

"What are you doing here?"

---

1 Not a real but a fictional character loosely based on Mirbeau's friend Natanson (1868-1951) who was an unsuccessful speculator. The name is based on the names of two other of Mirbeau's friends, both dramatists. René Weil (1868-1952) who travelled with Mirbeau to Holland and Edmond Sée (1875-1958). Natanson, Weil and Sée were all Jews.

I know my friend Weil-Sée too well to imagine that he could live in Holland, or anywhere else for that matter, without serious motives… I was aware of his wisdom in finding pleasure in everything, but in finding it, principally, in a frenzy of always renewed activity. If he were in Holland, it could only be for some fabulous discovery, for some colossal enterprise.

"What… what are you doing here?"

And I repeated:

"Are you no longer selling energy in Grenoble?"

"No…" he finally decided to reply… "I am not selling energy anymore; I invest in risks… I invest in risks… here… in Rotterdam… risks, my dear friend."

From anybody else I would have thought it was a joke and even—looking at his staring eyes and the fixed nature of his smile that the poor quality of his teeth did not entirely spoil—possibly madness. But where my friend Weil-Sée is concerned, I have never doubted the soundness of his intelligence. I listened to him eagerly and let myself be led towards his table, at the back of the room, or rather, I followed him without even being asked to do so, for Weil-Sée has such a horror of violence that he would not dare to take his best friend by the arm, even if it were towards a treasure.

These "risks" he was talking about, these "risks" that he was investing in, I quickly understood that they were houses, harvests, motorcars, racehorses, masterpieces, boats, furniture, workers, that he was insuring against accidents and even against insurances… An insurance agent… there you are… he was just an insurance agent… but nothing is ever simple with my friend Weil-Sée. I straight away glimpsed ingenious, large speculation.

Animatedly he explained to me…

"Insurance against fire, accidents, theft, shipwrecks, rain, hail, locusts… no doubt… but, so what… one has to live… But the new thing, the important thing, my dear friend, are insurances and reinsurances that I contract against lies, truth,

230

sterility and fertility, against sickness—all sicknesses,—against debauchery and against virtue, against war and against peace, against monarchies and against republics, against boredom… the stupidity of functionaries and the tyranny of laws, against treachery, love, literature…"

I think that he even spoke about reinsurance against doubt, disappointments, then even about a stock exchange of insurances, of risks of risks, of individual mutuality, of collectivist individualism and, always at every turn, of statistics…

In every conversation with this philosopher, the past of humanity, the future of the world, evolve easily. I thought that I heard being spouted the prospectus of an International Bank of Universal Ataxia. But what I remember best is that his lucid gaze was edged with blood-red eyelids, as are to be found in certain faces painted by Poussin; that his nose had got longer, since our last encounter; that his beard which had been chestnut when I was blond, was losing its silver and was turning yellow around thin lips, on which I was seeing, with volleys of words and spurts of spittle, the happiness of humanity being confidently constructed… What did it matter if some figures, particularly the billions, had such a bad odour?

Taking small steps, we had arrived at his table, close to one of those glasses, from which for about forty years, I have seen him drink the same blond tea, a river of which has passed through his body.

Once more, Weil-Sée proved to me that he was incessantly going to make this world-wide fortune, that he…

"Quite simply, my dear friend, to end up, amongst other things, at multiplying the power of the microscope and making one which can enlarge the object sixty thousand times… sixty thousand times, that's absolutely indispensable. But that's not all… I would also need high temperatures… ah! temperatures that could cook, lock, stock and barrel, and in half a day, the universe like a ceramic panel…"

I trust, without restriction, the intelligence of my friend Weil-Sée… I was following him with admiration, and I was convinced to the point of swearing on oath, that nothing that he was saying was not both true and important… But now that I can no longer hear him, I am incapable of explaining what he told me, and what his plans and business consisted of…

"You can feel it, can't you? It's just a few months of being patient… shhh!… a few months…"

At this point, he pushed aside piles of catalogues—nobody reads so many catalogues as he does—of books, goods, grains, plants, instruments, machines, he picked up some graph paper, and began to draw, in order finally to convince me, diagrams and graphs…

In his battered, lined face I was looking for something, but what?… something that still remained from the features of the child that I had seen arrive in the school, in the depths of Dalmatia… something of his aquiline nose, the expression of his so-gentle eyes, the youthful arc of his top lip and even the curls around an enormous, prominent forehead… But it was now so faded, so hard! I remembered how his intelligence had immediately stunned us all… He had shown himself straight away to be a prodigy of a student… Our teachers were predicting the most successful future for him… And this is what it had come to, his future!…

"Do you understand?" I heard as I was recalling these memories… "what would be really important, would be to dig down into the earth a little… I don't think that one has ever been beyond about two thousand metres… And further down… down… Just think!…"

He stopped.

"Down there… there are clearly… there just have to be unknown metals… fantastic metals…"

His eyes were shining:

"And with special properties, my dear friend!"

As he spoke, his fortune prospered, and he was snatching yet another secret from nature...

As he aged, poor old Weil-Sée, he did not change...

When I was very young, I had met him in Manchester. He was passionate about geology but seeking, at the same time, capital investment for a factory making arms that were so terrible that it would mean the very end of warfare... However, it had been he who had helped me endure the hardest days of that winter in 70-71,[1] during which, at Chanzy's[2] orders, vagrants like us were fleeing from everywhere in the Loire...

Ah! his tenderness and his jollity, during those horrible weeks!... I did not see him again until I met him at the Stock Market, on his return from Paraguay, full of enthusiasm for rubber... at the Stock Exchange, of which, later, he was one of the countless victims of Bontoux's financial crash.[3]

"You must understand... my friend... that what I need... is a fortune... but such a crazy fortune, that it makes all other fortunes impossible... like the cartels that were needed to bring private industry to an end..."

Since the crash, he had sought and discovered graphite in Siberia, tin in Spain, iron in Australia, manganese in Transylvania, copper in Romania, and even oil in Galicia, but always too soon... No bank wished to believe in him... His imagination, his general culture, the enormity of his ideological lyricism also terrified businesspeople...

"It's perhaps a good thing that I did not succeed too young... For, now that I know..."

And his gesture was so wide that he seemed to be stealing the universe...

---

1 The years of the Franco-Prussian war and its aftermath.

2 Antoine Chanzy (1823-1883) commanded the Army of the Loire in the Franco-Prussian war.

3 A reference to the crash of the Union Générale in 1882 in which thousands of small investors lost their savings. Bontoux was initially sentenced to five years in prison.

I happen to know, tired of not succeeding in exploiting a mountain of gold there, that he had, in the 1890s, left the Cape on the very ship that had brought to the colony a dying Cecil Rhodes[1]… Then, seeking a source of energy that would allow him to carry out experiments in thermochemistry in which, I think, he was deeply interested, he had looked for coal in America, had been obliged to sell at a rock-bottom price an extraordinary coalfield, that he did not have the means to exploit, and that he had come to the South-East of France to engage in the nascent industry of hydro-electric power stations, the last one of which I had seen him involved with in Grenoble…

He was glad that circumstances had made him give up…

"All these businesses… second-rate… really second-rate."

I protested.

"No… no… I can assure you… very, very second-rate."

Above all he was appreciating that the same circumstances had brought him to choose the rich, hard-working, thrifty and fertile Holland in order to found…

"Ah! this will be worth it… something like the Stock Exchange of Stock Exchanges where there will be no more speculation… what childishness!… about the chances of contemporary activity and production—that's of no interest!—but truly, about pure probabilities… about future paths… and in Rotterdam… Rotterdam… exciting!… Rotterdam, my dear friend, which is not only the first place for business in Holland… Rotterdam to which I assign…"

He was vigorously rubbing his nose with a bent forefinger…

"To which I assign, between all ports in the world, the most powerful specific virtuality of speculation."

And he sneezed seven times in a row, for it was one of his special talents that he could sneeze a lot without losing the thread of what he was saying…

"It will no longer be a question," he said between the last sneezes, "of the rise and fall… atishoo!… of stocks of mer-

____

1 Rhodes died in the Cape in 1892.

chandise in the world… or of the price of several billions of public funds… that's nothing… But no,… it's a question, do you understand… of a sort… think about it, if you will… of a Stock Exchange… of Agency, of Tribunal, in which human misfortune will be determined and compensated for… which will balance all the bad luck of the calculation of probabilities and in which the inevitable crises of future evolutions will successively amortise themselves…"

Well, I never wondered as I listened to him whether he would ever succeed in possessing this fortune he had been seeking for so long, in vain, but only—as I looked at his poor stooping back—I was feeling secretly sorry that he would have so few years to enjoy it.

"Listen," he said to me finally, very late in the evening, when the last waiter who had stayed to serve us was dozing heavily on a chair, his napkin between his legs… "listen… For many years I haven't been able to say as much about it to anyone… With my Dutchmen… I also know…"

He smiled thinly:

"I can be quiet, for Heaven's sake!… or just talk figures… But I want to confide in you, just you, a secret… There have been people who doubted my future… In general, scarcely anyone has believed in me… You… But yes… Oh leave it! It doesn't matter!… Do you remember?"

He burst out laughing, with a laugh that sounded like a sneeze…

"Do you remember Charlotte who claimed that I was a poor boy… who would never succeed at anything? Ha! Ha!… Yes… and Noémi?…"

He laughed even louder.

"Noémi, who left me because I was penniless?… Amusing, isn't it? Penniless. With that forehead…"

He smacked his forehead, felt inside his pocket, brought out a few poor florins which he threw on the table:

"Penniless? Funny!… Funny…"

Then:

"There are even some who tell me off for dreaming... for being carefree... light-weight... not practical enough... of, how do they put it?... of exaggerating everything... yes, my dear friend, exaggerating!..."

He confessed, in a new burst of laughter, that he had, sometimes, been one of them...

"Everyone was saying: 'He's dreaming... he's dreaming!...' For nothing... about everything... I reproached myself for dreaming... I criticised myself for dreaming... I held it against myself for letting myself be absorbed for so long in watching a river flow by, a woman passing, a fireplace flaming... whilst plans were beating at my temples... or simply gazing for a whole evening at my piece of paper without touching it... And my days... my nights, spent building prodigious impossibilities, whilst singing as loud as I could... I ended up renouncing the pleasure of dreaming... as I gave up ether, hashish, women and even tobacco... I ended up—this is horrible—I ended up accusing, for this hateful and delicious penchant for dreaming, the worst and most exquisite of drugs... my mother of passing on this feature to me..."

It seemed to me that this phrase made his old lips tremble.

"I inherited so much from her!... Yes... this gesture in which I saw her so often lose herself, for hours, opening and closing, with a wandering gaze, opening and closing, poor mother!... possibly two hundred times, the clasp of a gold bracelet, on her arm... Idiots!... What an idiot I was!"

He howled and he spat... I can even say that he spat in my ear:

"Well! Whatever good fortune... no matter what good fortune... may bring... I've got it already because I've imagined it. And my brain still gives me an advance, not calculable in figures, over all the billionaires in both Americas... Everything... I've already had it... listen to me... had it!"

He stressed this word... and, pulling me to him—definitely too much tea was finally intoxicating him,—he added, even more confidentially:

"What does possess mean?… Possess, is to understand… or, if you prefer… to imagine. Our miserable plutocracy is giving way to a *gnosticracy*![1]…"

"What?"

A *gnosticracy*… don't you understand?… *gnosticracy*."

Did I understand?… Not really!

"A *gnosticracy* that will finally no doubt lead thought to the perfect nihilism of absolute indifference, in which the great-nephews of our great-nephews… But it's obvious… I will have understood everything…"

He smiled at me:

"Or I will have thought that I'd understood everything."

He burst out laughing.

"It's all the same thing…"

It was not without some anxiety that I saw him get up, and shout:

"Who could prevail against me?… I disqualify all judges… all… even the oldest Jew… up there…"

His forefinger pointed towards the ceiling.

"Even the oldest Jew… I forbid him to prevail against me… Him!"

He shrugged, with an expression of complete disdain…

"Look!… he might continue to think, to dream the world, during an eternity of eternities… And did he create it?… The imbecile!… And did he create it as it still is?… And for the misery of some billions of centuries?… Unimaginable!… And what's he now got, with his responsibility for this universe?… Nothing… Nothing… Nothing… Serves him right!…"

He banged his fist on the table, and the waiter, who had woken up with a start, ran over:

"Tea!…" ordered my friend Weil-Sée, suddenly mellowed…

❋

---

1 Mirbeau's neologism, from its etymology, no doubt refers to 'an aristocracy of knowledge'.

My companions wanted to see some friends who lived in a property nearby. I took the opportunity to spend a few days with my friend Weil-Sée. He was keen to show me Rotterdam, to explain how it worked down to the most elaborate details... Naturally it ended with Weil-Sée taking me everywhere, except Rotterdam. He thought that, since I had not seen enough sky and water in Holland, and since, not having seen Holland, I would not be able to understand Rotterdam at all... By ferry, boat, car, railway, he took me on all the branches of the Meuse, on all the canals which lead from the Meuse to the Rhine, on all the branches of the Rhine, out to sea, between sky and water, and alas, especially, on bridges... I spent days without seeing the sky, without daring to look at the water, on all the bridges on the roads, in the towns, and on those which dare to span the sea... Of Rotterdam, all we saw was the huge bridge which seems to span the whole width of the city.

Of these few days, all that remains are intolerable sensations of vertigo. Vertigo, in Holland? Well, yes! Did I dream? Am I still dreaming?

Today I wonder whether just the presence of Weil-Sée, his distant voice, his jerky gestures, his extra-human grimaces, the immensity of his illusions, which amplified, deformed, things around him... I believe, in truth, he had the extraordinary power of communicating to the most inert matter his unease, his pain, his vertigo, his torture... In contact with him, nature itself panicked...

There, looking up at railway viaducts we saw wagons passing by up there, above our heads, and we had to sense the noise as they disappeared... Elsewhere, we were looking down—I feel sick thinking about it—trains of boats that looked like barges, barges that looked like flies... I closed my eyes... Here it was the terror that the wherry on which we were bobbing about would be destroyed by a catastrophe of broken arches and pillars; there, the anguish that the metal deck, whose curves looked like ducks and drakes, would give way, this so fragile deck that it moved about in the wind, and resounded, in all its assemblies, beneath our weight… I remember bridges on which I would have swapped millions of hectares of Dutch sky for a good, solid kilometre of main road in the Beauce. And to add to the horror of this impression, we had the bursts of whistles above us, like the presage of some misfortune, and we heard, below, alternating and replying to one another the lamentations of sirens. I tried to persuade myself that I was resisting the forces that were tugging my entrails, my heart, as though with ropes, which were tickling my ankles, irritating the marrow of my tibias, and a shiver ran through me as I felt that 'I was weightless'… A disgust with living, worse than the fear of dying, kept me suspended in the air… No, truly, I was weightless… When on embankments, on dikes, and then driving on solid bricks, I had gradually regained my weight and my reason, I tasted as it were the delight of a convalescence, following the rolling clouds, in the sky, plunging my gaze into the transparency of the waters, at ground level… And I was talking lightly about vertigo as one speaks ill of a friend…

"I am envious," my friend Weil-Sée said to me, "of those who are unaware of vertigo, but I feel sorry for them as well… What idea can they have of hell and how do they think that it could have been imagined?"

This idea made him giggle for some time… Then he continued:

"It's certain that damnation means, eternally, heels searching for a wall which is moving away, to the point where one feels invincibly drawn… to feeling oneself falling into a chasm, of which one knows that one will never reach the bottom."

In my turn, I was conjuring up vertigo, on board a tethered balloon whose basket is resisting the rope and the wind and comes to earth; on the cliffs of the Breton coasts which you can feel slipping under the soles of your shoes, when you lean out towards the sea; on a balcony where you climbed, laughing, and where the parapet is too low by five centimetres; on the ladders of scaffolding of which you hold the jambs tight for an eternity, and whose bars I have sometimes bitten… yes, bitten, hard enough to break my teeth.

"My dear Weil-Sée, one day, on the Mont Valier[1], I was mad enough to follow a friend on a pathway which after ten minutes I felt—I would not have lowered my gaze for the world—was getting narrower to the point that it was narrower than the soles of my shoes… I finally stopped and took easily half an hour—like a little Japanese acrobat on top of a pyramid of barrels—to turn round, and double the time to lie down flat on the ground. My friend, my executioner, had the courage to make fun of me… I did not even have the strength to wish for his death… And face down, tearing my cheek that was stuck to the mountain, so that I could not see the precipice, it took me the time of another life to retrace our footsteps…

"That's nothing," said Weil-Sée, showing his blackened teeth… "The Mont Valier is nothing… You haven't followed, as I have, torrents in the Alps, on the mountain sides, along faces which seem to be made of polished marble or of schist mud, in chasms so deep that the sky only appears as a little blue stream… That is real vertigo…"

And he went on, after a moment's silence, with a chuckle:

"It's because I know what vertigo really is… that I understand what trembling poor Jesus must have felt in his knee joints and his pelvis, when he was tempted by Satan."

Jews are very preoccupied with Jesus… Weil-Sée liked to talk about him; he talked about him no matter what the topic… Deep down, he was proud to have a God in his family. He went on:

"The Evil One—he deserves that nickname—had led Jesus to the mountain and, on the pretext of offering him the world, was showing him a chasm… Now, what was truly divine in his refusal, it wasn't to have refused the derisory offer of a world—

------

1 A mountain in the Ariège in the south of France.

what world, which doesn't already belong to him, can one offer to a Jesus or to a Spinoza?—No… the truly divine… listen to me… was to have, on the mountain, at the edge of a chasm, turned down the tempting arm, the support…"

He took on a casual look—we were now on terra firma—and he added the quite quite cheerfully:

"As far as I'm concerned, I'm convinced that I won't go to Hell… Oh! It's not that I believe in Hell all that much… Nor is it the confidence I have in the virtue of my actions… nor in the justice of the God who, having created the world in six days, any old how, then had announced everywhere—what boast-fulness!—that he would judge it in one single day, as one dis-patches minor crimes at the beginning of criminal hearings… At least God knows that since I have experienced all sorts of vertigo, this infernal vertigo could have no further novelty for me, and, as a result, would not be a torture… Then… What's the good?… Ho! Ho! Ho!…"

And without further ado, he talked to me about the Reformation in the Low Countries, of the Reformation in Germany, of the Reformation itself, and of the role that the Iconoclasts played in it, that admirable sect, that he missed every time that he visited an exhibition of paintings.

It was because I had listened too long to my friend Weil-Sée that I saw nothing of the port of Rotterdam. However, I had promised myself that I would make a long visit, and Weil-Sée had promised to explain it to me. All that I know about it, no doubt all that I will ever know about it is that 'you see the trading of the produce of colonies of the whole world'. The power of evocation that some of the sentences he utters always has!… All the other ports I have seen since seem to me to be small, narrow, inanimate. The only port that can impress me henceforth is the port of Rotterdam, that I have not seen, that

I do not need to see, that I shall never see nor dare to go to see, this port of Rotterdam, about which I only know what Weil-Sée told me briefly en passant: "that produce of colonies of the whole world is traded there…"

❋

There are men like this that I do not have the strength to resist, I would not even have the idea of doing so… My friend Weil-Sée is one of these. You may laugh, if you wish, at my enslavement; for me it is the only feature of happiness. But it is an understatement to say that I do not resist those that I like; neither do I know how to speak to them, nor speak in front of them… This is why, perhaps, no character moves me more than Cordelia.[1] Only I admire the fact that this unfortunate girl can say as much as she does… It is true, of course, that this is theatre.

On the other hand, if a man makes me impatient, or a pretentious or literary woman begins to formulate her sentences, I am immediately seized by a furious desire to contradict them, even to insult them. They can support opinions which are very dear to me, I immediately notice that they are no longer mine, and my most burning convictions, spoken by them, become detestable to me. I do not contradict myself; I contradict them. I do not lie to them; I struggle to make them lie… I feel happy. And in order to convince myself that the friendly mouth is deciding, at that very moment, what I am thinking and what I am, all I have to do is to listen to it… I listen, I no longer speak… How many expectations I must have disappointed! How often must I have appeared stupid!… These are, however, without any doubt, the moments when I have best understood what I could understand, and my silence was only the inattention of satisfied intelligence…

---

1 The third daughter of Shakespeare's King Lear, who remains loyal to him even though she has been unjustly disinherited by him.

My dear friends… my dear lady friends… all my loved
ones, all you who are, alas, detached from me, especially you
from whom I have detached myself, for how many denials,
little acts of cowardice, you are responsible… and I may also
tell you, how many tears! For, poor imbeciles that you are, you
have always been unaware of the fine source of tenderness there
was in me.

✳

One evening my friend Weil-Sée took me along a deserted
quayside to a club in the city, where I was welcomed with much
cordiality; at least, Weil-Sée assured that for me.

The members of the club—ship owners, bankers, merchants—were gathered in a hall around which only the pe-
riphery had benches, in front of which, at regular intervals,
pedestal tables were fixed. The whole central part remained
empty, and copper chandeliers were reflected in the shininess
of the parquet floor. Each place was occupied, moreover, silently, by a drinker in front of whom stood a pot of beer. Above
each drinker, a small cloud of smoke became thicker, all these
clouds feeding into the central cloud, of which the pale edges
were rolling and turning blue above the lights. Each drinker
had, between his teeth, a similar, short pipe. The pipes were
not all smoking absolutely at the same time, but there were
always a certain number which left the mouths together at the
same time, and came back at the same time to take up again,
between the teeth, the place that had been occupied by the pot
of beer… At certain moments, shocks of stoneware on marble,
smacking of lips, spitting, shuffling of feet, bouts of coughing,
were replaced by the guttural speech of one or other of the club
members, listened to for a sufficiently long time until his final
words ended up melting into a tutti of laughter. And Weil-Sée
went from one to the other, amenable, craftily, with complai-
sance, humility, servility that rather saddened me.

243

From time to time my two neighbours spoke to me in quiet voices. One had a face cooked in the wind and the sun, tints of old earthenware; a thick yellowish chinstrap beard was like a scarf around his neck. The other was a small, old man, mainly busy raising his small person and his tiny chin above the edge of the table. All the time he was straightening up so as to avoid both the bowl of his pipe resting on the table and his bald but fluffy skull showing… When he smiled, he took the precaution of taking his pipe out of his mouth and his smile looked like the toothless smile of a tiny child. All he really did was smile… Weil-Sée told me that he was one of the richest men, one of the boldest, most implacable speculators, one of the luckiest men in that place, the man who had ruined the greatest number of families in Holland.

The evening continued like that, tediously, with no notable incidents. I found it hard to believe that the desire for filthy lucre, the passion for money, could be hidden beneath these calm faces…

As the hour advanced, we saw, with satisfaction, coming towards us, carried by a lackey in livery, but with a moustache, an elegant tray on which was a pyramid of lapwings' eggs

In an instant the pyramid was flattened… Hurried, small gestures were removing the shells from the eggs, with the same noise that might have been made by the teeth of a colony of rats.

The pleasure that I might have had of tasting, on my own, the opaline whites and the slightly muddy yellows, was ruined by the quiet but indiscreet curiosity with which the chorus of eaters was watching me.

It was after this meal consisting of one single dish, that a long, white beard yelled at me… It was a speech. It was spoken in French, but a French mingled with expressions that must have been left by the armies of Louis XIV, in the delta of the Meuse and the Rhine… Everything I said in reply was received in a friendly manner. My neighbour on the right grasped my hand with emotion; my neighbour on the left, the small, old man smiled. But I only found out when we left, thanks to my friend Weil-Sée, that I had spoken far too quickly... and that the Dutch—even those who are most familiar with our language—had not understood a thing that I had said.

"So much the better!" he added... "So much the better!... That often happens... in all things... everywhere... But yes... The words that we understand, are only signs... Look!... ah! it's funny... One day, in Africa, I was invited by a negro King to a sort of banquet... Not knowing his language and not wishing to tire my imagination uselessly with an improvised toast, I recited, with fine gestures... and with a musical voice... a page of *Salammbô*[1]... That's all... There was enthusiasm... delight... They were weeping tears of emotion, of joy... They kissed me. The King offered me all the land I asked for... and even those I did not ask for... he sang, he danced... Don't you see, my dear friend, when you understand, that makes you sad... and you are wicked."

Never would I have dared to admit to myself that I might miss my companions, even less that I was becoming tired of the eloquence of Weil-Sée, or of the trouble that he was taking over my entertainment, this excellent, this perfect friend... However, what a sigh of relief escaped me... what a cry of deliverance when the Charron brought them back to me! Never did I see with greater ease our ladies get out of the motorcar, veils wrapped round their heads, or dragging behind them scarves of tulle, an allusion to the dust on the roads... I was impatient to set off again; I was mainly anxious to tell them all about my friend Weil-Sée, to amaze them with his plans, with his insights, with his vagrant life... And if they did not

____

1 A historical novel by Gustave Flaubert, set in Carthage, published in 1862.

understand the sublime nature of it, did I not have—why not admit it?—enough material to make them laugh about it.

That is how our enthusiasms finish, most of our friendships, as well as the dreams from our youth. That is how it is with many great men, and many masterpieces… And it is just the same with fashions which, praised to the skies yesterday, to-morrow fall into ridicule and caricature.

Philosophical systems, in men's heads, and birds' feathers on women's heads, suffer the same fate…

✳

My very last day there was entirely devoted to my friend Weil-Sée.

He was bitter and sad, possibly sad because, the following morning, I would leave him, for how many years?

He talked to me in vague, offended, sad terms of all the friendships lacking courage that he had been obliged to leave behind along the way… of the irony, of the egotism, of the best friendships, of the insulting pity of the worst. And now… he was tired of feeling himself always so alone… tired of feeling sometimes, often, that he was not even a 'companion' to himself… And what would happen when old age came completely?…

"There are moments when I don't like myself anymore… I'm not interested in myself any more, moments when I don't understand myself any better than others do… Perhaps I'm a failure?…"

He looked at me for a long time, anxiously, waiting for a reply… I gave a shrug to reassure him.

In the Museum where he took me, he remained completely silent and worried. He let me admire, without any commentary, the two great paintings by van Gogh, *The Mill in the Polder*, and *The Path in the Woods*, which already have the smiling majesty, the tranquil eternity of old masterpieces.

Whilst I was looking at them and comparing them to Mauve's[1] boring animals, Weil-Sée remained thin-lipped and had a sort of grimace of a sadness which refused to speak, and which had nothing to say. At one moment, this crease at the corner of his mouth twisted itself in such a way that I thought that the poor devil was going to burst into tears… I thought that I had been for him a moment of exaltation, of oblivion, of respite, in his life and that, once I had left, he would fall back deeper into the torments of solitude and… who knows?… of desperation.

"But no… but no…" I was telling myself so as not to make myself sad… "I'm wrong… He's jumpy, this morning, perhaps it's the weather… Weil-Sée? Come on! His imagination replaces everything… wife, family, friends, fortune, success, happiness… Yes… yes… he's happy…"

And suddenly, shaking him joyfully:

"Ah! My old friend, Weil-Sée!… old Weil-Sée!"

Without a word, my poor dear Weil-Sée continued to walk through the rooms, seeing nothing, not looking at anything, visitors, or pictures, only seeing and looking at himself, I suppose…

He only stopped in front of Rodin's *The Age of Bronze*; he stopped there for some time… He sat near it, walked around it, his hands behind his back, leaned back against a wall, winked, and from time to time with a preoccupied smile passed the palm of his hand, slowly, gently, over the patina of the bronze. He did not convey any impression to me. My heart sank.

Late in the evening I accompanied him home… He lived in a little deserted street, a little street near the Zoo…

He had always used a different array of pretexts to avoid showing me his room. I imagined the untidiness, the filth, all the strange things lying around there, samples of minerals, mathematical instruments, maps, photos of Cranach and of Rembrandt pinned to the walls and the Cézanne, the only

---

1 Anton Mauve (1838-1888) was a Dutch impressionist painter who may have influenced van Gogh.

painting he had kept from his collection,[1] which had been broken up a long time ago, and which went with him everywhere…

We were at his door, and he would not make his mind up to ring the bell.

"Look…" he said to me suddenly, "… we'll never get anywhere… Ours is a doomed century… a dead century… if men like you… indeed… Leave literature alone… its uselessness… its frivolity… its crushing stupidity… Make your mind up and join…"

On the opposite pavement, near to a lamppost, whose low, trembling light made the street look like a slum, a woman was walking up and down. Weil-Sée did not see her but she was troubling me… How could he have guessed that our presence in this deserted, gloomy street, at such a late hour, could bother anybody?… However, it did probably bother the couple which, after two fruitless attempts, the lady of the night had managed to form with a passer-by, roundish, stumpy, whose top hat I saw gleaming in the shadow.

Weil-Sée went on:

"Believe me… get involved in superior speculations… tackle the vast field of futures. The past is dead… the present is dying… and tomorrow it will be dead too… The future… always the future… nothing but the future… hypotheses… probabilities… what they call the impossible… Thank Goodness!… Work… the world… the world…"

The woman had taken her companion off into invisibility, at the end of the street.

And Weil-Sée carried on talking, talking… talking… But his speech was no longer the same… It would swell for a moment, only to drop down again, flaccid and soft, like a balloon deflating…

---

1 Nathanson, the real-life character on whom Weil-Sée is based, had an impressive art collection.

For ten minutes I had heard enormous words rising up, the bursting, fainting, when the roundish man from a few minutes ago passed by again, but this time on his own, on the other side of the street... He was walking quickly, his face hidden in the raised collar of his overcoat... A reflection on the front, then a reflection on the back of his hat... and he disappeared without once having looked back...

"Gnosticracy... my dear friend... do you know that gnosticracy..."

It was at that moment that there passed, opposite us, always under the same gas lamp, the active lady of the night who waddled by... She did not suspect that, at that very moment, we were deciding the fate of humanity... In the full light, all I saw was that she wiped her fingers on her handkerchief... And then, gradually, gently, she was absorbed by the night...

Amsterdam's Canals.

I will not tell you that Amsterdam is the Venice of the North. First, because I have a natural horror of such phrases and second, because I have no idea since I have never been to Venice.

"Really, Sir?..." a lady said to me offended by such a cynical declaration... "Is that possible?"

And, disappointed, sad, languid, she added:

"So, you have never loved?"

"Not in Venice... no Madame... not in Venice..."

"Well, Sir... I pity you... it is only in Venice that one may love properly."

Did she pity me?... I rather feel that she despised me...

Should I say—perhaps it is the right moment—that I was resting?[1]

---

1 Mirbeau uses the verb "se gondoler" but the translation unfortunately misses the pun.

It was reasons of this type that have always prevented me from going to Venice.

Manet, out of hatred for the School of 1830,[1] never agreed to set foot in the Forest of Fontainebleau. He was put into a furious temper at the very names of Barbizon, of Marlotte. What is scarcely credible is that he refused on several occasions Mallarmé's invitation to come and see him at Pont de Valvins.[2] But he went to Venice. Not only did he go there; he painted there. Where I am concerned, if I have never been to Venice where, however, I would have liked to visit Titian and Tintoretto, where they lived, I am on the receiving end of conversations like the one I have just recounted, a whole heinous iconography and a no less heinous musical and poetic library. Perhaps there was only one way to wash myself free of these words, of all these melodies, and of so many topics for fashionable newspapers, illustrated by M. Pierre Laffite[3] and Company, and that would be to go to Venice. But every time that I was on the point of planning to go, I was so afraid of only meeting, on the lagoon, lovers of the output of M. Donnay,[4] or the landscapes of M. Ziem,[5] or the jingles of M. Gounod, that I always preferred, once again, to return to the Dam.

When you do not know them very well, and if you do not have an acute sense of the varieties and differences, all the quaysides and all the canals of Amsterdam look like one another.

"It's terribly monotonous…" cried the lady quoted above.

Now, I have been to Amsterdam often enough to understand, to my great joy, that nothing is more diverse, and live-

---

1 The Barbizon School, active from 1830 to 1870.

2 Mallarmé lived on the edge of the Forest of Fontainebleau.

3 Pierre Laffite (1872-1938) was a journalist and later publisher of illustrated magazines.

4 Maurice Donnay (1859-1949), a popular dramatist.

5 Félix Ziem (1821-1911), a pre-Impressionist painter.

250

lier than Amsterdam; that no reflection of the houses in the identical canals, that none of the identical houses look like one another. Each portion of canal is a different landscape of walls, of gables, of barges, of windows with flowers; each house has its own face, its individual structure, depending on the degree of subsidence of the piles that support them… And it is, especially, a different landscape of sky, of which it looks as though the Dutch have, each time, put the prodigious patina under glass.

✳

At the edge of the Amsterdam canals, and on their bridges, since I have been lingering imagining the silvering of deep mud of these dying mirrors, I feel that there is coming up to me an odour which becomes, each year, stronger and more fetid. On my last trip, at the height of summer, there was, in the evening, a stink whose memory remains with me.

I am aware of the power of imagination over the senses, over nerves. It was on the last trip that I discovered this terrifying thing: the Amsterdam canals had not been dredged for three hundred years. And simply by having learned this fact, it suddenly seemed to me that a horrible odour was making me feel sick, and I trembled with fever, for a whole week, in my hotel room where I saw passing by, on the canal, the black barges, floating above the waters, close to the waters of the canal, long, grimacing images, long, green spectres.

The lady of the sea[1] finds the water in the fjords heavy… If she had come to Amsterdam, what would she have said about the water in the canals? It is made of lead… A sort of purulent grease, a sort of mucus that it has secreted, that froths, twists, ripples on the surface.

Still, one can stir water, even muddy water; the hulls of the barges make it move all the time, strip its surface for a moment; the sea currents that they manage to force in renew it a little,

---

1 A reference to Ellida, the heroin of Ibsen's *The Lady of the Sea*, 1888.

251

refresh it… But the mud? But these centuries-old muds, these slow and continual outpourings from sewers, these deposits of so many millions of human lives which are stratifying at the bottom?… How to get rid of them? Already, the miasmas are passing through the muds and the water and are sending their bubbles of infection to pierce through the surface. If you were to stir this deep bed of rot, where the tiniest pebble that falls frees the captive fevers, if you were to dredge it, to expose it to the air, it would be the city, the whole country, neighbouring countries, the whole of Europe that would be poisoned… It is the plague, cholera, perhaps unknown fevers, it is death throughout the world!

The Dutch have thought of everything except that. They think they are sheltered from all surprises behind their ramparts of water. They only have to smash a dike in order immediately to drown their invaders. But if the water uncovers its bed of mud, then they will have had it. Water takes its vengeance for having been tamed, immobilised, crushed between stone walls. It is made to run, to spread out and to sing on golden pebbles. Every time that it crouches somewhere, it becomes deadly… It does not matter what you do, there is always a moment when nature superbly shakes off man's yoke…

Let us also get used to the idea that our fate, even the fate of the man of genius who carries thought beyond the confines of significant horizons, means that his excrement, his vital organs are an infection and a shame. The myth which tells us that the bodies of the saints smelt nice is worthy of the Immaculate Conception. Miserable inventions! All dead bodies stink; all human bodies stink.

Reader, divine Plato defecated every day, ignominiously, just as so must every day your beloved. If she does not, the dear heart, she will not love you any more… When he was constipated, divine Plato became straight away a refractory and stupid brute. The intestines give orders to the brain... Where the putrefaction that cities have under them is concerned, it threatens all the agglomerations in the same way, just think about it, as the social garbage and outcrops of the pleasure of the wealthy threaten societies with an unrelievable fermentation of poverty.

Here, this filth remains, pullulates in the streets, beneath a water surface that it repels and slims, each day, each hour, increasingly. The longer one waits to do something about it, the greater the danger. But what is to be done?... One is impotent. Commissions are formed and set to work, reports pile upon reports, fanciful projects are piled upon unrealisable projects; parliaments pass laws. From which of these systems, from which of these suggested utopias, will salvation come?... No one knows... What is known is that the workers in this redoubtable enterprise will all perish, just as all the soldiers perished who, at the beginning of colonisation disturbed the deadly lands of French Guyana.

Meanwhile Amsterdam is blossoming in the spring sunshine. The delicate tones of its streets play with the black waters of the canals, with the rare skies which put the finishing touches to its delight. Its inhabitants are prospering; they are providing us with the example of activity and the judicious use of wealth; they ask about a hundred religious sects to teach them the way that will most certainly lead to God... They are growing tulips, daffodils, and fine lilies from the Far East, are cutting diamonds, speculating on far-off goods, piling up gold, dreaming of a huge polder to replace the dried-up Zuiderzee... And, minute by minute, the lethal muds are being dropped, are piling up one above the other, are increasing...

And when they come to the surface?

Cheese Fair.

As we came into the town of Purmerend, on a cheerful, busy square, beside the canal, we are stopped by the preparations for a cheese fair... A long line of barges, full of those red or purplish balls that are called 'negroes' heads', are tied up along the quays where, from place to place, using this cargo, they construct little hillocks, similar to these pyramids of Louis XIV cannon balls that we still see in maritime arsenals. It is quite strange, and very colourful. The morning light makes the foliage vibrate joyfully. The air in which a sour smell pervades is very transparent. The contours of the objects, of the cheeses as of the faces, of the varnished houses, the trees, the boats, have the same clarity, the same pretty dryness...

From these boats, which look as though they are filled with new toys, the dockers throw, just as one juggles, the coloured spheres to guys, to girls who, still juggling, throw them again, some to tradesmen who set up piles of them in front of their tents, others to the carters who fill their carts with them up to the brim.

Peasant women,—almost all of whom have their temples decorated with golden shells, or are wearing golden headgear beneath the lace bonnet,—peasants, in short pants, with light-coloured clogs, as they throw these round, red balls to one another, have round, red faces with the result that sometimes we could believe that they are playing ball with their own heads, and that we are present at the last act of a fairy-like operetta, or a ballet of jugglers beside the water.

The 628-E8 had to manoeuvre carefully between these obstacles and these games. Fortunately, we were surprising the crowd at least as much as it was amusing us. There was no demonstration against us. Even when, suddenly, following a slight explosion from the carburettor, on the boats, on the piles, in the carts, at arm's length and, I even think, in the air a thousand coloured spheres became motionless…

When we braked, the circumference of a wheel was for an instant tangent with that of one of these balls which had rolled towards us… A second later, one bound of the motor destroyed this geometric concept, of which there only remained on the ground a little bit of flattened, red paste.

And, from a distance, looking back, we saw all the balls and, I also think, all the heads as well, regain their flight and their parabolas…

"Cheeses, mirages…" Jean Dolent[1] would say.

The Half-Open Door.

From the very start of our trip,—and this is a painful confession for a Frenchman to make,—we had not had a single adventure in a hotel, by that I mean an amorous adventure. Gérald B——, the man amongst us who has travelled the most and who is, moreover, English, claims that nothing ever happens in hotels.

"I can assure you," he repeats… "nothing, nothing, never anything… except of course what may happen to anyone on a pavement or in a nightclub… German women, English women travelling on their own, when the sentimental novel or the bottle of gin, the memory of an opera, of an officer, or quite simply of a shop assistant, stirs their imagination, and they need assistance, they ring down for the bellboy… Do you regard as an amorous adventure the offer of the hotel servant woman in the little towns of Serbia or Romania?…

"What do you mean, in Serbia?"

---

1 Jean Dolent (1835-1909) was a novelist of whom Mirbeau did not have a high opinion and this passage may be a pastiche.

"Yes... in Bulgaria and Hungary as well... But that's part of their service as polishing shoes is a job for the sleeping car attendant... There is just one thing... one thing I remember and worth telling you about... And even so!... It was in Transylvania, in the land of gold. In summer, early in the morning, after we had spent the night in the train and before we set off again in a motorcar, we had stopped in a hotel for a wash and brush up... Two girls were serving us... One of them, complaining, begged us, in bad German, to accept her offers, cried out that she was poor, that she had absolutely nothing... No doubt to prove to us her penury, she suddenly and boldly lifted up her skirt which she had hastily put on as she jumped out of bed upon our arrival to disguise her nakedness... her daring was not without grace... She was tall, good looking... fine curves... a refined skin... But there were too many of us... I pointed this out to her: "So what?" she replied. "All of you... all of you... I'm so poor!" During all this the others did not say anything but smiled as she continued her work. Having scarcely washed our faces, poorly brushed... we took flight... I have never had another adventure..."

However, one evening, in The Hague, after dinner, Gérald B——, who, during the meal, had seemed a little dreamy, troubled, confessed to us, once the ladies had left, that he was wrong, that it could happen, that amorous adventures could happen to a traveller in hotels... He had certain scruples about talking, but we found ways of helping him get over them.

"Well, here you are! Actually, it's quite funny..."

He had come back to the hotel at about five o'clock. Trying to open the door to his bedroom, he was surprised to find that it was ajar. And, after he had pushed the door open, he was even more surprised to see, in front of the mirrored wardrobe, a chemise being slowly raised, rippling over a female backside, displaying the back, the shoulder blades and finally, rising very carefully without disturbing the blond arrangement, above the undulations of the coiffure. Nothing could have been redder than the face of the lady, without her chemise, after she had turned round when she heard the slight creaking of the door.

"Monsieur! Oh! Me… Monsieur!" she cried, but not too loudly and without too much anger, whilst her fingers became entangled then disentangled from the lace…

But the best thing was that, in the depths of her embarrassment, she did not even manage to clothe, with this cloud of batiste wrapped around her arm, her naked breasts… Her whole body was of a golden whiteness, dazzling, apart from her waist where her corset had made as it were bite or pinch marks, and her legs where her skin shone through the mesh of two black silk stockings…

Our friend had closed, bolted the door.

"Monsieur!… Oh! Me… Monsieur!"

Without replying to the trembling voice—was it really trembling?—he crept silently across the room towards the mirror which, far from offering a veil to the lady's modesty, only undressed her even more…

"Me… Monsieur!… No… no… be gentle… no… I… I… Please go away!"

Pleading arms are weak. Our friend's arms had taken her, wrapped themselves round her, pulled her to the bed, which was covered with dresses, corsages, gloves, pieces of material, perfumed lingerie that, one after the other, he sent flying across the room, without a word… And the lady could only cry out, but scarcely, and more and more softly:

"Me… Monsieur!… Ah!… Ah!… Me… Me…"

Then he felt that an embrace was responding to his embraces and caresses were responding to his caresses… And her voice, gradually throaty, then husky, finally panting and close to fainting, whispered:

"Oh! My darling!… my darling."

Gérald was still laughing about it when he got back to his room, next to that of the lady, and had slumped into an armchair where he slept until dinner.

When he had finished his story, he said to us:

"I can understand that I got the wrong room. But what about her? Why was her door, at this crucial moment, half open?...

We were on the point of joyfully offering up a range of hypotheses, when we saw Gérald suddenly blush... oh! Blush as the lady in the chemise, or rather without the chemise, must have blushed. But he was not the only one to blush. A couple was coming into the restaurant where we had lingered to smoke. A woman, scarcely twenty-five years old, blonde, her cheeks on fire, glistening with jet, and with composure pulling around her the green gauze which puffed up on her shoulder, was advancing, uncertainly, hesitatingly. An enormous man, much older, tall, bulky, fat, hairless, with an unhealthy look, a coarse look, a cunning look too, was following her, striding, prancing in a stupid manner, on overly large hips like those of an old woman... A dark-purple carnation was decorating the buttonhole of his dinner jacket...

"Move forward, my darling!" he said in Russian, in a harsh voice.

There was a basket of red roses on the table next to ours, and a head waiter was busying himself to bring them to the new arrivals. It was obvious that the lady did not want them... She turned her head towards the other end of the room where, though an open bay window, one could see a sort of little garden of palm trees illuminated with candle holders; a fountain was coming out of a pile of small cardboard rocks, covered with dried ferns.

"No, not here..." the husband said... "There is a draught... move forward a bit."

It was he who insisted that she should sit down in the place which was exactly opposite us... A sharp word, spoken in a cutting voice, forced the giant to be quiet, to lower his dyed head... He stood back, finally allowing his wife to take the other chair and to hide her blushes from us...

In these circumstances I am especially interested in the husbands; for it is the best means I have discovered for finding excuses for their wives. In this husband's enormous, flabby face, the chin jutted forward. He was either absolutely deaf or at least hard of hearing, which forced him often to lean towards his wife, his clean-shaven face, with two bands that were too black, and only the monocle destroyed his similarity to the coachman of a wealthy household. His fat fingers, short and stubby, very white, dripped with sparkling rings. As he looked over the menu, he shrugged, spoke loudly, grumbled, seemed to be chewing his words as though they were made of tough meat.

Of her, who had her back to us, the only thing I noticed beneath her wavy hair which crowned her like a lightweight tiara, was a dimple running from the nape of her neck, a detail which Gérald, in his intimate description of the unknown lady, had just given us.

Our friend, who was very embarrassed, suddenly pointed out softly that our cigars were creating a lot of smoke… There was in his words a pleading urgency. From time to time, the fat gentleman, without looking at us, would waft the air with the flat of his hands decorated with gold and jewels and would puff noisily:

"Pfouou!… Pfouou!…"

Ah! If there had only been the fat gentleman!… We got up without another word… The others walked in front of me before the table laden with roses… Not one of us, I have to admit to our shame, had the good taste or the strength to look back. And I, more of a cad than the others, without even excusing myself that we were on holiday, braving the woman's looks and the furious monocle of the husband, I looked back too, quickly, stopped for a few seconds, pretending to brush off the lapel of my dinner jacket, on which a little cigar ash had fallen, and I saw with a sort of jealous and low pleasure, the pretty blonde face blush deeply… I just about managed not to say, as I passed by:

"Me… Monsieur…"

Outside I complimented Gérald who had totally regained his self-assurance. After he had called us "pigs" as a matter of form, he confessed:

"It's curious… Do you know that if she hadn't blushed when she saw me in the restaurant… I think, good gracious, that I wouldn't have recognised her!… Lady, with her clothes on, isn't that what they say?… But who on earth can those people be?… I'll have to ask the hall porter…"

Hymn to Peace and to The Hague.

I can understand why Holland was chosen, and, in Holland, The Hague, to set up the court[1] which, one day, despite the jokes and the pessimistic denials, will replace the pleasure of Emperors, of Kings, of Parliaments, to take account of international disputes and find solutions to them which will no longer be massacres, and finally establish peace, not between men but between peoples.

It is certain that Holland, and amongst all the cities in Holland, The Hague has a charm, a virtue—perhaps not yet pacifist—but strangely pacifying. There one may dream of marvellous things, one may dream of universal happiness, as one does in a beautiful garden, in the evening, after dinner…

This virtue of Holland, this charm of The Hague, I have felt many times their sedative influences, and others, like me, but who were more troubled, sicker than I, have felt them as well. It is delightful. The smoothness of the even ground, its light and profound monotony that is broken and diversified, to infinity, by the immense light in the sky mixed with the reflections of the water, the absence of all warlike apparatus, the

---

1 A reference to the Permanent Court of Arbitration (PCA) created by the Hague Peace Conference of 1899.

sight of a life that is both active and very calm, from which all painful effort seems to have been banished, the tranquil energy of the faces, the silence of the polders and the canals, it all grabs you, tames you, conquers you. There is never anything which rasps, and which threatens… And the land, so bitter elsewhere, the water, so terrible everywhere, become docile in the hands of the man who seeks in them his daily bread and his joys.

As good egoists, as wise people fortunate to have good luck, do not try too hard to break this happy surface which perhaps covers, as it does everywhere, fierce hatreds, many fratricidal struggles, a social fermentation which, in Amsterdam, in Rotterdam, mainly, heats up and boils in the lower depths of poverty and work. Be happy, as always, with reassuring appearances, and, as always, turn them into realities. So, what if they are lying?… There will always be time for you to awaken from your ostrich-like dreams.

How often have I come here, depressed, overwrought, my nerves stretched and twanging, as a result predisposed to all sorts of bad impulses! And, after two days passed in The Hague, where what remains of the slightly savage, of what is mildly disconcerting in the Dutch character disappears, after two days of wandering in front of the Vivier, the Palace of Rembrandt, guarded by the swans, the Palace of the sad Little Queen guarded by not a single soldier, after two days of walking along these attractive streets, past these pretty gardens, so full of flowers, across this beautiful green countryside which spreads around the city, like a soft and sumptuous carpet, that is when the miraculous relaxation happens… Everything calms down, soul, muscles, nerves and brain. I am happy just to be alive, with no feverish haste, without sudden and jerky desires. With complete tranquillity, I enjoy the melancholy which surrounds and penetrates me, not a melancholy as bitter as the bile in which it sought its name, but this radiant melancholy which, when I was young, I had so often at the approach of love, and which is also given by the few moments of perfect happiness, which each man, even the most impoverished, keeps in the depth of himself, without knowing where it came from, the compassionate and far-off memory; perhaps a glimpsed landscape, in the evening, after a day's tiring walk; perhaps the look of hope in a sick person one loves, perhaps even less…

How can you not believe in love, in future fraternity, when, on all the roads, on all the dikes, from The Hague to Harlem, all you encounter are happy faces, hats, corsages, hands, bicycles, carriages, decorated with tulips, daffodils and hyacinths; only pathways of silvery water where, between red banks, dark red banks, golden banks, the barges slide silently, laden with their red harvests, their dark red harvests, their golden harvests?… One day our paths crossed those of a small detachment of infantrymen… They were singing, in delightful harmony, idyllic songs, sort of lieder of love… And tulips, as in the vases in the houses, were dipping their stems in the mouthpieces of the rifle barrels.

Peace radiates everywhere, it inhabits so appropriately these glossy and smiling abodes, which are spaced out in the greenness of this continual garden that is Holland… and I feel it so strongly in me that I do not even wonder to whom all this abundance and all this richness of the soil belongs, the water and the sea so abundant in Holland… Nor do I wish to know what is hidden, in Amsterdam for example, by this very red Stock Exchange, of which the high walls, the battlements, the spyholes evoke warlike citadels, and castles of plunder of yesteryear.

✳

We saw again the husband of the lady with the chemise… Questioned by Gérald, the hall porter tells us that his name is Count K——, that he is Russian…, a delegate to the Peace Congress…, or something like that… And he tells us:

"He's not a very agreeable gentleman… He grumbles all the time… and he's violent!… Each time he goes out into the city, he always has problems with someone. The other evening, in the theatre he slapped the doorman. Yesterday he grabbed a shop-owner by the throat in his own shop. This very morning… is Monsieur not aware of this?… we had huge difficulty in preventing him from throwing the bellboy out of the window… Finally, he threw a carafe of wine at the head of the maître d'… the poor devil is badly injured… He can't utter a word that's not an insult, make a gesture that isn't a punch… The boss would like to get rid of him… But! He spends a lot of money… And then there might be questions… international complications."

"War, Good lord!"

"Well!… who knows…"

After a short silence, Gérald asks again:

"What about his wife?"

The hall porter, who was a superb man, muscular and stocky like an athlete, smiles. He twists his moustache, clicks his tongue, pulls back his bull's neck in which I see tendons tightening like cords. He does not reply immediately. For a moment I admire his strength and the gold decorating his cap, the collar of his frock-coat, the back of his sleeves…

Then, in a low, dreamy voice, he murmurs:

"The lady!… with a man like that… well you can imagine!…"

THE FAUNA SEEN ON THE ROADS

Last spring, travelling to Grenoble, via Grand-Goulets, we were stopped a few kilometres away, beyond Pont-en-Royans, by a flock of two thousand sheep, that was being brought up into the high pastures, and that we had to follow, very slowly, as far as Villard de Lans. In these difficult regions, where the roads, that are often dangerous, always narrow, not very frequent, never cross one another and where a crossroads is unthought of, it is impossible to get through such a mass. The shepherds, let us be frank, did not trouble themselves to help us to get past. They even seemed to be very amused by our discomfiture. They would have been even more amused had they known that friends were expecting us in Grenoble and that, because we had stopped too long in Valence, before the Duchesse d'Uzès's statue of the unfortunate Émile Augier,[1] we were very late. Perhaps they already knew, for shepherds know everything, since they are magicians.

Following the example of their masters, the dogs, were clearly encouraging the flock not to move aside and, showing their truly human ill-will, they added to their almost human enjoyment by turning their heads round towards us from time to time to insult us with their barking. Rather like the carter, the gentle carter of the fine roads of France, who, having parked his

---

1 The Duchesse d'Uzès was responsible for commissioning a statue of Émile Augier (1820-1889), a dramatist born in Valence, inaugurated in 1897.

cart like a barricade across the road, only allows you through so that he can give himself the pleasure of insulting you with an obscenity, almost always accompanied by a loud crack of the whip; a stupid, purely animal gesture thanks to which he hopes to terrify the motorcar, to make it bolt and tumble over like a horse; thanks to which also, or so he imagines—and this relieves his hatred—he has given us what for.

Never have I sworn as much as I did on that day.

Because it was going so slowly the motorcar was not happy, was overheating, was smoking horribly, and in spite of the fact that they had been copiously greased, I was not without anxiety where the cylinders were concerned.

I have for animals the tenderness of a neurasthenic and of a misanthrope. I hate their suffering. But I am certain that I would have plunged with all the force of our forty horsepower into the flock, and made a bloody mash of those sheep, if I had not wisely reflected that such an operation would cause, for the motorcar and for us, serious damage. All I did was to sound the horn wildly. Criminally, I was telling myself that the animals would be panicked and that, distraught, bounding, jumping, together, over the parapets, they would roll down to the bottom of the precipices where the torrent would carry them away… Adieu! Adieu!

But that did not happen.

The horn and its most noisy, heart-breaking calls, multiplied by the mountain's echoes, had no effect on the animals who were no doubt used to the more terrible noises of avalanches.

So, I took the wisest course of just looking at them.

It looked as though these two thousand sheep were carrying one another along and that their mass, bleating terribly, was floating. It was only moving at the edges, and it seemed as though its thousands of fragile feet were scarcely touching the ground… However, the noise of their hooves was making, on the ground, the sound of a continuous peal of thunder. I also noticed that this din was like, from a distance, the backfiring of a not very well-maintained motorcar.

Flocks of sheep have another similarity with motorcars; they create just as much dust and damage the roads just as much.

The sheep defend themselves by their mass which is an impassable obstacle, like a flood, flowing lava… a falling surge of stones…

In certain regions, the Nivernais, the Bourbonnais, the Morvan, the Auvergne, Brittany, the roads are stables, sheep pens, pig styes, cowsheds, poultry yards, hutches, anything you like except roads. Sometimes they also replace the land in front of barns. Not content to let their animals camp and frolic, the farmers park their machines there. One day, in the Auvergne, we were held up by a mechanical thresher and its accessories which blocked the whole width of the road. The farmers refused to let us through. And they stopped working in order to look at us with a snigger.

"You are not entitled to hold up traffic," I said…

"We's entitled to thresh the wheat… where us wants…"

"Thresh it at your farm, in the courtyard."

"That gets in us way… And then we's at home here… And you, where's you from?"

Another, resting his arms between the prongs of his pitchfork, sniggered:

"He's probably not from round here…"

A third one said:

"Come on… pass us the sheaf…"

And they started working again… Had they read Barrès?[1]

I spotted an old man who, from his military goatee beard and the badge he wore on his arm, I took to be the village policeman… He had heard this dialogue, without a word, gently nodding his head… I summoned him to do his duty.

---

1 Maurice Barrès (1862-1963) became famous with the publication in 1888 of *Le Culte du Moi*, [*The Cult of the Self*].

"Of course… of course!" he said… "I's to tell you, Sir, they's right… They's got to thresh the wheat, those folk… ha!… ha!… wheat is food of t'poor folk…"

He refused to listen to our protests.

"Listen, Sir… Go back towards the open countryside… Turn right… then right again… at the corner of a small café… it's called Rémongeat…, the Café Rémongeat… yes… and then you go straight on… In two kilometres, p'rhaps three… you'll see an outdoor washhouse on yer left… Go to the right of the washhouse… And then straight on until you reach the road… The path isn't too great, but it's not too bad, either… Well, that's how it is!"

We were obliged to go that way…

"Always towards yer right!" the policeman repeated as we reversed… "Yer can't go wrong…"

The path was terrible, bristling with bottle bottoms and full of sharp stones… it did for two tyres.

The farmer has not yet understood, will probably never understand that the roads have been built so that one may get from one place to another. He imagines, perhaps in good faith, that they are exclusively made for him, for the unique needs of his operation and the services of his husbandry. The gendarmes, the village policemen, the land agents, the mayors, the prefects and the ministers imagine it as well. It is therefore agreed that one must meet on them, as in Noah's Ark, all the beasts of creation, and their dung.

An excellent field of observation for a driver who has time on his hands and who wants to study what I shall call: the fauna seen on the roads.

✳

Nothing could be more different than the way animals behave when motorcars pass by. It says a lot about their character and their degree of intelligence. Well, the resulting classification scarcely corresponds to current thinking, and even less to old sayings and popular metaphors.

The horse, about which I have to repeat for the hundred millionth time, the annoying phrase of Buffon,[1] the horse, 'man's most noble conquest', who sees with no emotion, his harness companion collapse and die alongside him, the horse is stupid. However, if he comes across a knacker's cart in which the four hooves of a dead friend are sticking up in the air, he immediately begins to tremble, to shudder, to get excited. According to the most knowledgeable experts, one should not see in this concern the manifestation of an altruistic sensibility, nor the selfish fear of death, but simply an olfactive protest, the unconscious revolt of the sense of smell. The horse is afraid of smell, afraid of colour, of light, of shadow, of his own shadow, of the shadow of the person leading him; he is afraid of a piece of paper, of a sack of oats that has fallen, of a shiny piece of glass, of the glimmer of the moon in a puddle of water, of the reflection of a moving leaf, or of a cloud making its way over the road. The horse has every possible phobia. He has even every motorphobia and to a degree of morbidity perhaps not reached by M. Émile Loubet,[2] who, with such fine relevance and as much prophetic fury, fulminated against motorcars with the same baleful predictions as M. Thiers[3] did against the railways… Ah! These great men!

It is only when the machine that he has neither predicted nor foreseen,—I am talking of the horse here,—brushes past him that he swerves, rears, breaks his harness, and sends things, people, cart and himself flying into the ditch. Rather like the hare, who is only dangerous to himself but who does not frequent the roads, the horse has this physiological inferiority of

---

1 Buffon was a famous eighteenth-century French naturalist.
2 Émile Loubet (1838-1929) was a Prime Minister, later President, of France.
3 Adolphe Thiers (1797-1877) was the first President of the Third French Republic.

seeing nothing in front of him. He only sees what is to the right or to the left, like a politician in the Chambre des Députés. In order to walk without snags and damage, he must see nothing at all… Cover his eyes completely, and with a regular tread, with a somnolent gait, this four-legged *Love* will go on for ever, and will, for example, turn for hour upon hour upon hour, the wheel of a carrousel without ever stopping, without ever rebelling.

When you drive you do not meet any animal—I include man and the cyclist—who is more dangerous and who you should mistrust more. Each time I see on the road this dangerous imbecile, I always slow down and sometimes stop, for you do not know what antics, what murderous eccentricities might pass through his head. His stupidity recalls that of a caste, formerly omnipotent and which, in its current decay, only retains, to give itself the illusion of power and vitality, the faculty of galloping. You applaud at the thought that it will soon be dispossessed.

The horse is only a mechanism—an old mechanism—put together to prance and be the animal… the animal of luxury and of the circus, if its outlines are beautiful… or the beast of burden, for he is strong… strong as a horse.

Near Grenoble, in the hill down to Sassenage, we saw coming towards us from far off a heavy cart. Since the horse seemed to be terrified,—although he had great difficulty bracing his hooves on the dusty ground and pulling fully on the harness, for the slope is steep,—I put the motorcar alongside the verge on the right and stopped the engine. There was a load of tiles on the cart. Completely stretched out, the carter was sleeping, his belly on the tiles and his chin resting on a sack of oats. He did not wake up on the repeated sounds of the motorcar horn. His hands were not close to the reins or to the whip. He only raised his head a little and revealed one of the heaviest faces of a brute that I have ever encountered.

"Whoah!" he said, in a voice hoarse from alcohol and sleep…

The carter sought vainly for the reins, waving his right hand about and, getting up a bit more, he leaned on his elbows… I heard him grunt something. Left to his simple horse's instinct, the horse naturally led the cart to the verge on the left.

"Whoah then!" the carter said again, without any further movement…

The wheels went into the bank, behind which the land went down steeply to the bottom of the valley… I saw the cart lean, lean further, then slowly tip over. The man had manged to jump off… But the tiles lay on the ground, smashed to pieces…

"Bloody Hell!" the man swore. "Bloody, bloody Hell!"

He began by throwing his cap on the pile of tiles with a furious gesture. Then he started on his horse which he beat, and on us to whom he would have liked to do the same thing.

"Ah! bastards!… bastards!"

He cracked his whip:

"Wait a moment!… You bastards!"

We had to hold him at bay, get the horse up, clear the road a little… Seeing his impotence he had decided to sit on the bank and, whilst each word shot specks of dust from his beard and his eyelashes, he groaned:

"I'm shattered… I'm going to die… bloody well give me compensation!"

He was completely drunk.

I remember that one night, we were driving from Dordrecht to Rotterdam… A moving night!… we were driving slowly, quietly. We were listening to the water, the infinite water of Holland, trickling and singing everywhere around us. Our headlights which were magically illuminating the mist in which golden, silver, emerald and ruby dust was twirling, in which nocturnal insects were passing, fiery moths; our headlights which sometimes were illuminating a small stretch of canal, and silhouettes of shadows slipping along the canal, suddenly lit up the effort of a white horse that was bringing towards us, from Rotterdam to Dordrecht doubtless, a very large furniture wagon. Scarcely had we spotted the carter deeply asleep on his seat, than the horse, frightened by the lights,—for light frightens them as much as darkness,—turned sharply round and doing a U-turn on the dike which fortunately was very wide at that point, following us took the furniture back to Rotterdam from where he had just come… His master had not woken up. The shock of the U-turn had wedged his head even further on a mass of pillows, and his back on a mass of mattresses. He was sleeping as comfortably as he would in bed, open-mouthed, his stomach dangling, his legs wide open… and the reins were wrapped around his wrist that was hanging down.

We could not help ourselves from bursting out laughing, thinking of his astonished face, having woken up, perhaps once or twice, on the dark main road, identical everywhere, when he found himself, in the morning, with his cart, his furniture and his horse, in Rotterdam from where he had set off the previous day.

It is just like that with social reforms which are poor horses frightened by everything and whose drivers are always asleep… They set off, one fine evening, enthusiastic, lively… The slightest incident on the way makes them turn back… they come back, in the morning, to the place from where they set off.

The Breton farmer, or the one from the Morbihan or the Gallo, has a special fear of the motorcar. He certainly regards it as a work of the devil, if not the devil incarnate. As soon as he sees one, he immediately mumbles prayers. If he is on foot, he kneels and clasps together his trembling hands. He prays to Saint Yves, who brings wealth, and Saint Tugen, who cures rabies, for there are not yet saints, in Brittany, that protect you from the motorcar. If he is on horseback, he hurriedly gets off, and with a pale face and chattering teeth, but always praying, he takes refuge behind his mount, which he uses, depending on circumstances, as a shield or a rampart.

Once, not very far from Vannes, on the road to Larmor, a farmer was hidden like that, almost crouching down, behind his horse… It was a very small moorland horse, with long red hair, and a beard like a goat. He scrambled, stampeded, neighed. The man who was clinging to him cried out, beseeched, implored:

"Dear Jesus!… Ah! dear Jesus!… What's going on?"

But as terrified by the noise of his master as by the engine noise of the motorcar, the little horse ended up kicking out more violently, striking the farmer and sending him rolling in the ditch…

We had a lot of trouble seizing the injured man to take him to the hospital in Vannes. Despite his broken leg, he struggled with us, desperately, imagining that we wanted to take him to hell… and to frighten off the demon, he was howling very quickly:

"Oh! Holy Virgin!… Oh! Good mother Saint Anne… Oh! Lord Jesus!"

As for the little horse, with one bound he had jumped over the stone wall alongside the road… And he was galloping noisily across the moorland, followed by four mad cows and two lost black sheep…

Cows, bulls can go together with horses. However, it seems as though there is, between the proletariat of towns and that of the fields, a sort of intellectual advantage, in favour of the heavier, less cheeky, but wiser peasant.

One or two cows, surprised, a herd of bulls going to pasture or to the slaughterhouse, will have the awkward, comic look of scurrying heavily, of their great backsides rearing, wiggling, and their ridiculous tails swishing in the air, before the motorcar which is pushing them along. They will perhaps take you far like that. But even a herd of calves, followed for a very long time, will always turn into a pathway, into a gap in the hedge, into a field, where they will rapidly recover from their excitement, and will watch you drive past with a slightly trembling curiosity, a surprised kindness… I have noticed that cows have, as a rule, a certain wisdom. They only lose their heads when, in their midst, a horse passes on his stupid fear to them.

Goats are nervous, to the extent that their milk sometimes gives convulsions to small children. Goats only get frightened if they are tethered, with their kid beside them. Then, helpless, they pull on their shackles, scamper round their stake, with the full length of their chain, jumping, shaking their horns, rushing, falling down, capering, and collapsing… If they are untethered, with an agile, precise bound, without too much terror, they climb to the top of the mound where, feeling themselves safe, they straight away begin to nibble the tender shoots of the undergrowth…

A fine topic for an academic lecture on the educational virtues of freedom.

One knows all about the profound meditations of cats, the Baudelairean magnetism of their pupils, and their agility to get out of the trickiest situations… From the very first day they recognised a new danger in the motorcar and immediately, noiselessly, with no fuss, they avoided it… You do not encounter many of them on the roads, which are not a good terrain for their always rather mysterious business… They prefer leafy, dark places. Sometimes, from far off, they come prudently out of the hedge and cross the road, on their belly, with a live field mouse between their teeth. Most often, in villages, sitting on their backsides in doorways, they follow the passing motorcar with a dreamy look, artificially absent-minded, as though they are following the flight of a butterfly in the air…

Very rare are the drivers who can catch them out…

Piglets, so pink, so gay, so pretty, accompany the motorcar, galloping happily along the verges. They never cross… It is one of the pleasures of the road to see these small, charming beings follow one another and follow us,—a deliciously charming line,—snouts forwards, ears flapping, tails twitching… Just as fat and chubby as, and pinker than, those Cupids who, on ceilings, on tapestry, on boxes of chocolates, emerge from rolls of streamers, from flowery shells, from baskets with ribbons. Ah!… piglets… piglets!… It is very sad to tell oneself that all this youth, all this pulchritude, all this prancing gaiety will soon end up as black pudding…

These animals, thought of as inferior, give excellent examples to the horse but he does not benefit from them. Perhaps it is the narrow slavery in which he is kept, perhaps the absurd education given to him by man, which diminishes him to this point? I am very afraid that, even if he were free, in the meadowlands he came from, he could defend himself no better than this, and that he would use his strength for even more coarse, stupid acts… His mass of meat, his enormous size, are they not at the mercy of a wolf, of a little panther, of a tiny rat?

The donkey and the mule are fairly similar… But what a difference! As the donkey and the mule know how to assess the stupidity of their masters, their pitiful ignorance, their inexplicable fantasies, their contradictory demands! And, above all, because they can put up with them with admirable courage… the courage of reason!

They hate incoherence. Both of them are smitten with logic and reality, giving the impression that they are ineducable… Instead of all the horses' manifestations of terror, their sudden changes of direction, their sudden hallucinations, their spinning round, rounding their backs, kicks, gallops, backward steps, the whole vain and noisy pantomime, donkeys pass by quietly, at their reasonable little trot, look without fear at the motorcar, and without ecstasy, infinitely less puerile, much more dignified… and, deep down, jokesters!… They are not impressed!… Better than horses, which have feminine nerves, annoyed and put out by the slightest thing, they are fully capable of resisting the confusion of the men or particularly the women guiding them, when they jump down, so inappropriately, and quite simply, they turn their heads to look, smiling maliciously, at the terrified flight of skirts.

Beasts with admirable wisdom, of which the head is solid, the foot certain, the character worthy and good, who recognise the weakness of children and who respect it, as far as allowing themselves to be tortured by their cruel little hands, with no other rebellion than a slight movement of their ears…

Of all the quadrupeds,—I am speaking of those frequently found on the roads, for I have not yet met elephants or lions on them,—donkeys and mules are the only ones to deserve a too often dishonoured appellation: they are human beings.

They would be human beings if human beings were not, alas, horses…

What dogs have against them is their faithfulness and the stupidity of their masters, and I do not know which is the more disastrous for them. They have no fear of their dear master right up to the moment when he puts them down. And even at that supreme moment, before giving up the ghost, they prove to him one last time their stupid love, thanking him with a dying look and licking his hands… They rush out in front of motorcars because they want to defend their masters, and the possessions of their masters, against imaginary dangers, for this famous love that a dog has is only used to invent a thousand dangers, and to find in them the opportunity to bark, to bark endlessly, at anyone, at anything, at nothing at all. I cannot imagine that their so impeccable nose fools them to the point of mistaking a car's radiator for a friend's backside… No… It is the case that dogs think less of avoiding the motorcar than of charging at it, so as to bark, and that this regrettable habit always makes them swerve just in time to fall under the wheels…

"Shtupid animal," says Brossette.

Few of them have noticed that motorcars go faster than horses and even that they are not horses… However, I think I have observed that, nowadays, around big cities, and on particularly busy roads, they are beginning to acquire a semblance of education. They are becoming careful; they think. I see some in whom, even if obscurely it is true, the meaning of life, of their dog's life, and a clearer sense of realities is showing itself… Perhaps they would end up being completely sensible and practical, getting completely rid of their phantasms, if it were not for the master, if there were not the fidelity paid to the master. That is their great misfortune…

It is quite clear, nine times out of ten, that man is entirely responsible when a dog gets run over. The dog has just put himself safely on one side of the road when, quickly, the master calls him, as if all that a dog requires is to be next to his master… The master calls him with an imperious, yelping authority just like the way mothers call their children in the streets just so that they can rush under the wheels of vehicles. Wonderful instinct of mothers' maternal love, mixed with their stupidity! The dog who enjoys caresses more than a man and enjoys blows more than a woman runs towards the call. Did he perhaps see the danger? No matter. He runs because he is faithful and as he runs, he is run over. Of course. Besides, what else may happen, when one devotes oneself to a man, to a woman, to a principle, instead of following one's life to the extent of sacrificing to them, like the dog, his ideas, his tastes, his personality?

So, the dog is run over. And, in front of the little bleeding heap, whilst the motorcar continues to drive, far away, already lost in a cloud of dust, the man, instead of accusing his own pride, his own clumsiness, curses progress, science, the whole world.

"Ah! Motorcars! What a disaster!… What madness!… What a crime!"

He swears that he is going to get a rifle and, henceforth, to hunt "these tools" of misfortune.

"Two men… ten men… twenty men for my dog!"

Richard III had already said in a fit of madness: "My Kingdom for a horse!"

Poor Brossette pays careful attention. As soon as he sees a dog in the distance, invariably, whichever region he is driving through, he calls out to him in the patois from the banks of the Loire:

"Shir!… Shir!"

He never insults it before he has either avoided it or run it over. After which, he grumbles through gritted teeth:

"Ah! Shtupid animal!"

Which gives this man wholly from the Touraine—and only at these tragic moments—a pronunciation which surprisingly seems to come from the Auvergne.

But it is the price of the effort he has just made, the expression of his joy and of his spite.

Unfortunately, too often the phrase "Shir, Shir!" is as useless as the precaution of a charming woman who, with a maternal instinct where hens are concerned, cannot stop herself as soon as she spots some of them, from clapping her hands in the back of the motorcar, imagining that in addition to the noises of the engine and the tooting of the horn, this muffled noise will alert, twenty metres away, the animals about the danger which threatens them.

"Shir, Shir!" Brossette shouts at the dog.

But, on the one hand, it is unlikely that the dog hears and moreover impossible that, except on the banks of the Loire, he understands.

"Clap! Clap! Clap!" goes the lady.

But it is gone with the wind…

Sterile efforts! Brossette does not stick to them again and again. He slows down and, if necessary, stops. Thanks to this method we have very few murders to reproach ourselves for. Unfortunately, it is not infallible. No matter how small, it does need the collaboration of the dog. Above all it would be necessary that this collaboration were not, in the majority of cases, annihilated by the stupidity of the master.

Fortunately, as a careful driver, I am still able to count my victims.

As we were coming out of Moerbeke, an old man was walking very slowly on one side of the road. His dog, a tiny dog, made comic by having at fourteen centimetres above the ground, a small lion's mane and something like a powder puff at the end of its tail, was trotting along on the other side. Very hard of hearing, no doubt, the old man only heard the car's horn very late. Immediately he whistled to his dog. The dog, seeing the car coming, hesitated to begin with, and in order to demonstrate the danger of crossing the road, barked weakly. But old men, who are so perfectly cowardly in front of their wives or their maids, avenge themselves fearlessly on their dogs, from whom they demand passive obedience. Thus, the old man whistled for his dog a second time, and this time more energetically. Then, without any further hesitation, the poor corporal in disguise[1] leaps forward at the call of his donkey, excuse me! of his horse of a master.

---

1 Mirbeau is playing with words here. The French word "cabot" he uses is both a familiar term for a "corporal" and for a "dog."

"Shir! Shir!" shouted Brossette.

"Clap! Clap! Clap!" went the lady.

Brossette had not finished his shout, the lady clapping her hands, when the tyre had turned the dog, his mane and his powder puff into a terrine.

"Ah! Shtupid animal!"

I got out to offer my condolences to the gentleman's grief. He would not hear of it. He scarcely looked at me. In terror and despair at the sight of this pancake of black fur, made red by a little blood, he continually repeated:

"Oh, thank you so much… Thank you so much!… He's dead… Yes… Yes… He's really dead!… What's Rebecca going to say? What's to be done? Good grief! What's to be done?…"

And when I offered to drive him home with the remains of his dog:

"No… no!… Home?… No… no… It's terrible!… I can't go home… I can't go home. Ah! Thank you so much!…"

With his head down, his hands at his side, he was walking around this black circle that had been a dog, his dog… Rebecca's dog… and he was wailing:

"Oh! Oh! Oh!… what's to become of me?… Where can I go?… Where can I go?… I can't go home…"

✳

And now we have the murder of another one, the large dog of a small shepherdess.

I was cruelly haunted by this memory for several days… And today as it comes back to me, I cannot help feeling a sadness which is almost painful.

Poor dog, with long silvery hairs, rather like those of our Briards, and the eyes of which reflect a touching stupidity… how handsome he was!

It was on the road from Leyden to Harlem.

280

We had set off at dawn and wanted first to go and see, in Endegeest, which is between Leyden and the sea, the house where Descartes may have lived. The reputation of Endegeest is limited; we got lost. Not bothering at all about the prodigy that this philosopher is, the peasants looked at us, laughing, without a word of reply. Perhaps, quite simply, because we were mis-pronouncing the name of Endegeest... But even in Endegeest, nobody could point out Descartes' house to us... And as far as Descartes himself was concerned it was even worse... His name had disappeared for ever from the memories of this little region... Several directed us to the lunatic asylum of which the brand-new architecture is one of the curiosities of the town.

"Perhaps it's there... Yes, that's possible."

Others sent us to the best hotel...

"It's very busy at the moment!"

They asked one another:

"Descartes?... Have you heard of this Descartes?"

"Wait a moment... Descartes?... No... heavens, no... What does he do?"

"He's dead," I replied.

"Well then... try the cemetery..."

And they all laughed...

A fine gentleman, definitely with a better education, who was totally silent about Descartes, nevertheless strongly sug-gested that we should travel a few kilometres to visit the house where Spinoza lived:

He explained:

"Spinoza... my God!... he was a philosopher... a famous philosopher. He is dead... Of course, he died... like every-body... But that doesn't matter... they have turned his house into a museum... a very curious museum... There you'll see old, felt slippers... slippers that he wore... and spectacle lenses... for he was an optician too... lenses polished by him... it's amus-ing... it's even very interesting... And much more besides... Spinoza... the Spinoza house... You won't forget, will you?..."

Fearful of adventures, knowing the type of emotion produced by the old slippers of great men, rather tired of museums and anxious to arrive in Harlem where Franz Hals[1] was waiting for us, and where we were supposed to visit a horticultural establishment, we took to the road again...

I was thinking about Descartes, about the trajectory of his thought that no importunate person could disturb in this peaceful countryside. I was thinking about his meditations on animals and about the difficulty La Fontaine had in accepting his theory of animal mechanism... Which one of them was harshest on the animals? The scientist who rigorously refused to accept that animals had intelligence, even sensibility, or the most delightful of our poets who marvelled at the sight of them, but who only made them talk the language of our vices and of our stupidity?

My reverie was disappearing, far off, in the polder, above which lapwings were circling. It stretched away into infinity, with its rare poplars, tall and slender, its flocks, the sparkling roads of its criss-crossing canals, and its valve gates operated by small windmills... Then the polder ends, the dike becomes a highway; then there appeared coppices and sandy fields, speckled with tulips and daffodils, the magnificence of which—it does not hurt me to concede—puts in the shade our poppies and our wild mustard plants.

Suddenly, to our left, I spotted the small herd—two cows and three sheep—looked after by a small, blonde shepherdess, attractive despite her square shape and her short skirt, with heavy pleats... A large dog, out of all proportion, was lying peacefully on the other side of the road... He seemed to be asleep... His bearded head was resting between his stretched-out paws...

By misfortune the girl noticed the motorcar, stood up, got her little group around her, turned round to look for the dog

---

1 Franz Hals came to Harlem in about 1591 and the local museum has a number of his paintings.

and just as we were about to pass by—not particularly quickly, however—called him.

"Clap! Clap! Clap!!" went the lady.

"Shir! Shir!" shouted Brossette.

But nothing could prevent this stupid hero of fidelity from crossing the road, so close to us that, despite the most violent pull on the steering wheel, he disappeared under the engine casing.

I felt a strong shock… I heard something like a cracking of bones under the wheels… then the lugubrious voice of Brossette:

"Oh! Shtupid animal!"

I still see—and shall see for a long time—this fine dog, his large, hairy body get back to his feet, angular, disjointed, and start to turn round and round, like those used in vivisection experiments. Then he found the strength to round his back, to block out just for a moment the whole horizon, before falling down without a sound. And on the road he was nothing but a tiny, flat, inert thing, a thing without height, without any more height than a shadow.

Immobilised by terror the small blonde shepherdess had not moved… She had enormous eyes and her teeth were clenched… Overcome by shock she did not even see that the two cows and the three sheep were galloping, terrified, through a patch of withered hyacinths…

After that, we did not run any more over… or rather no more went under our wheels, or else their masters spared them…

✻

Hens are absurd.

They are, on their own, the very epitome of the absurd. In the animal world one could not find a worse example of mental imbalance.

The only excuse that hens have is their voracity, for it is the only passion that preoccupies them, even more than their licentiousness. In comparison with them, pigs—brave anchorites in their styes—are sober and chaste. No other carnivore is as bloodthirsty. They are bloodthirsty to the extent that, amongst themselves they pull out their feathers to drink the blood of which these tubes are full; bloodthirsty to the point that, as soon as there is a red drop of blood on a crest, on a foot, they make the wound wider and devour one another... No sparrowhawk is more rapacious than these monsters whose head is no more than a beak, whose round eyes are more cruel than those of a bird of prey and who wear, without having made them, the prettiest dresses that one can imagine. They allow themselves to be run over for the sheer pleasure of pecking, for a moment longer, on the bare soil of the road, something or other, some manure left from place to place by horses, cows' dung, most frequently just pebbles.

It looks as though they only cross, for nothing is calling them from the other side of the road, for the simple pleasure of hitting the radiator. If, by chance, they have avoided the latter it is only the better to smash into a telegraph pole, a tree trunk, a wall, get tangled up in the undergrowth of a hedge, in which I have seen some of them lose all their feathers and mangle their feet. To escape, they lean forward to such an extent, their beak open, their feathers bristling, bend forward to such an extent on their wing tips, that it looks as though they will continue on all fours, when the peril awakens, at the crucial moment, the instinct of the race, and, just for a second, transforms a fowl into a bird... but, no sooner have they dragged themselves to safety, than a single speck of grain, or a midge seen on a blade of grass, makes them forget the entire drama. They will not remember tomorrow nor in a few minutes... They are like that woman in the Scriptures who, after a meal, wiped her lips and then said: "I haven't eaten."[1]

---

1 This appears to be a reference to the adulterous woman in Proverbs

There are fat hens that have fed, have raised generations, who ought to know about life, having experienced every danger, and yet who have learned nothing, and who are more obtuse than their last brood, and as they get older become more voracious and more obscene. Fat, heavy, they walk with effort, waddling, their feet apart, like women do whose stomach is too heavy. Next to their henhouses they give me the impression of those old female pimps you see hanging around at the exits to studios, shops. I run them over without the slightest pity, and Brossette who has a very keen sense for analogies—I hope English women will excuse him!—shouts out to them: "Chucky!" which is still an affable expression in comparison with the terrible expression: "Kept woman!"[1]

Where the males are concerned, they live for nothing other than love and warfare. They are roughnecks, noisy, ridiculous, pretentious, disgusting as all animals are... who are only interested in women. Fighting when they are not making love, making love when they are not fighting, how many have we run over in this double position!...

Like Wallenstein, "who had this in common with lions," said Schiller,[2] I detest the cockerel's crow. From morning on he trumpets a monotonous, stupid song which wakes me up and irritates me... If they were not so well got up—however, a trifle over the top—oh! How we would detest them.

The Gauls, talkative, boastful, bawdy, looters, loudmouthed, warlike and militaristic, could not have chosen a better mascot.

20:30. But in the English Standard Version the text is: "...she eats and wipes her mouth and says, 'I have done no wrong'."
1 Mirbeau is playing with the French word 'cocotte', which is used in children's language meaning 'a hen' and was used in adult language meaning 'a kept woman'.
2 Schiller wrote a trilogy of plays about Wallenstein performed in 1798-1799.

Ducks are much better endowed. I am happy to pay homage to their virtues. Although they have had all means of defence taken away, by keeping them far away from rivers and ponds where they sail with a marvellous ease and grace, they get by... Their humiliated little troupes always slink along at the side. They never monopolise the middle of the road knowing full well that they have nothing to fear at the edges... Ducks know lots of things... Rarely do we run over them...

Nor turkeys.

Turkeys are well protected.

Moreover, they hate mixing with *hoi polloi* on the roads... It is in enclosures, sorts of Academies, that they swell with pride, like poets, artists, at their ease.

But it is geese that I wish to rehabilitate.

Never have I regretted so much not being Plutarch, to narrate properly the life of these illustrious animals. I am now no longer astonished that the defence of the Capitol was entrusted to them... They deserved that honour.

The finest geese come from Toulouse, like M. Pedro Gaillard,[1] like the majority of the great tenors and great politicians of our Republic. They inspired the most admirable masterpieces from Japanese designers; and bath-taps, sinks, washbasins, the arms of Empire chairs, have popularised their decorative forms. They have only one inferiority which they bear with fine irony, that of providing men with the quills with which they write so many lies and nonsense. On the other hand, we owe them their down and Strasbourg pâté.

---

1 Pedro Gaillard (1848-1918) was born in Toulouse. He was initially a bass but was in charge of the Paris Opera from 1884 to 1907.

Geese have a strong, tenacious, tranquil wisdom. Their prudence consists of imagination, boldness and cunning. Their incorruptible vigilance saved Rome. Perhaps the Pope, instead of entrusting to French bandits and Spanish cardinals the task of keeping watch over the Roman Catholic Church, which is under threat, could have acted wisely in appealing to the prudent wisdom of a simple council of geese. Having saved the Capitol, they could easily have saved the Vatican.

With their heads perched on very long necks, they became accustomed early in life to looking at things from on high and from afar. If they like general ideas, vast ensembles, they do not however disdain the particular detail, but they never tarry over the thousand puerilities, the thousand stupidities, in which bask the lives of other poultry. Nothing surprises them and nothing frightens them; nothing eludes them. Knowing how to keep their nerves under control, they are, in all circumstances, harmonious and logical. Better than all animals and, as a result, better than all men, they recognise the social value of discipline. Well before M. Jules Guesde,[1] they managed, without a congress, without scandals, without battles, to unify their socialism. For geese are socialists... It seems that only geese are socialists lock, stock and barrel. Until now not the slightest dissidence has been detected in their so perfectly organised ranks, in which they maintain close contact, happy in an absolute equality.

One of my friends has on his land a small lake, that he has populated with all sorts of water birds. You will see two very majestic Siamese geese. Their whiteness is dazzling, and their heads decorated with strange orange-coloured carancula. This little world lives divided by species, who never mingle. They do not fight, but they energetically refuse to recognise or to help one another. One day my friend introduced into the lake two

---

1 Jules Guesde (1845-1922) represented the Marxist wing of the French Socialist party. Mirbeau saw Guesde as too dogmatic and also fell out with him for his late entry into the Dreyfus affair.

couples of barnacle geese, that naturalists call 'Cravant geese'. Nothing, in their size, their shape, their plumage, indicates to the uninitiated that barnacle geese are geese. The two Siamese geese, who had never seen one, made no mistake. They hastily welcomed them as though they were people that they recognised as part of the same family, got them settled in, brought them up to date with everything. And, since then, they have never been apart.

On the road—I call upon all drivers to testify—when a motorcar passes by, invariably the geese move to the side in an orderly way, without the slightest sign of terror. They line up, one next to the other, on the side of the verge, and a trifle annoyed, very proud although lame, they let rip at these intruders who are disturbing them but who have not 'impressed'[1] them.

I have never been able, in a car, to drive in front of a flock of geese, without feeling awkward, humiliated, by their mockery. They intimidate me, for, from their whistling voices, I understand only too well that it is with mockery and not coarseness that they are addressing me. Geese are never coarse. You can get over coarseness; only irony is painful.

But what are the geese saying when I drive by?...

I have spoken with compassion about attractive little piglets... To be fair, a few words about old pigs...

Not much is known about old pigs. These animals, contrary to what is generally thought, have a very strong sense of cleanliness and only wallow in muddy puddles because they are tormented by the need to bathe, and they are rarely seen on the roads except when they are coming back from fairs. You rarely see them except beside ponds and ditches, in which they

---

1 Unfortunately, the translation misses the double connotation of Mirbeau's use of the verb "épater." He is here using it with the sense of "impress," but he is playing the idea of "é-patte-er" [to remove the birds' feet].

paddle voluptuously and enjoy their muddy wetness. But are they enjoying it as much as one thinks?…

I have always admired their small, malicious, intelligent and so lively eyes…They seem to be saying, for they possess bonhomie and indulgence, like all those who are fat:

"Good Lord! We just adore cleanliness, don't you think we would prefer a nice bathtub, with fine clear water perfumed with benzoin… We old pigs dream of nothing but soapy lather, almond paste, massages with horsehair gloves, pedicures… But you see… we don't get that!… We have to put up with it…"

They seem to be adding:

"It's a pity that men, in France, are so dirty… that they really have a taste for filth… They don't even imagine that, if we are as clean as the pigs in Alsace or in England, we are much better to eat and are worth much more money."

If, exceptionally, crossing the road, they get run over, you can believe that they get their own back. There is not one example of a motorcar crashing into their mass of fat and of meat that did not instantly create a horrible pulp of man and of pig…

Completely by chance I have seen camels on our roads… Camels are very rare in France—I mean that literally, of course. If I can judge from the one I met a few times in the Forest of Saint-Germain, motorcars seem to leave them completely indifferent. Led by a camel driver from Le Pecq, peeling, mangy and sad like all fatalists, he was walking with his rangy, gentle gait. One day, he was transporting to Poissy a bed, a wardrobe, mattresses; on another day, in Maisons-Laffitte which is a less prison-like colony, a piano and two Louis XVI armchairs… It was, if you will pardon the expression, a removal camel… When he encountered a motorcar, he did not even look at it… But what was odd was that the shaken piano resonated, and it seemed to me that it was playing, all by itself, a waltz by M. Gounod…

However, I did not infer from this anything about the aesthetic inferiority of the camel…

It seems—it is our charming friend Capus[1] who asserts this—that one can drive hares from a motorcar, but only at night. Once they are caught in the beam of the headlights, it does not even occur to them that they can escape. They run, in a straight line, in front of the car until they are caught without trying, for a second, to go back into the darkness of the fields or the woods. Another attractive theme to develop about how writers may be dazzled by fleeting successes leading to their downfall…

But I imagine that Capus must have hunted in the South of France, which is on the road to the Blésois,[2] or in the Blésois which is on the road to the South…

In Germany, at night, driving through woods, I have often encountered rabbits, enormous colonies of rabbits, and I have never either caught them or run them over. They were charming—even though they were German rabbits—charming to play with, all white on the road, white in the light from the headlamp. They came and went, jumped, frolicked, held curious confabulations and only decided to run away, showing the white powder puff of their backsides, at the moment when the motorcar was upon them.

Yes, but—I hope that French rabbits will forgive me—in Germany these are famous rabbits.

---

1 Alfred Capus (1858-1922) was a close friend of Mirbeau and for a time was the director of *Le Figaro*.
2 The area around Blois in the centre of France.

Martians…

It is the dead of night. Not a soul on the road, not even the ghost of a motorcar. Not an illuminated village, not a living house. The barking of dogs has died down. Those of us who are not sleeping in the car are dragging ourselves sadly along the embankment, trying to warm ourselves up. The headlamps pierce the ground with black holes, transform simple undulations into precipices, and enlarge our shadows disproportionately. Brossette is working, slaving away. A tyre with a hole in it, a burst inner tube, both are lying in the ditch… We feel as though we are victims, and we remember that we have been very hungry…

Finally, with the fourth tyre mended, we set off again and are climbing a steep hill.

Soon a glow, a sort of dawn, but cold, appears on the horizon, spreads and gradually occupies all the sky. It is certainly not daylight but no doubt the birth of a heavenly body rising to disperse the night… Indeed, a star, a prodigious star!… Suddenly it surges over the crest of the hill, enormous, blinding, dazzling, splashing, and rolls towards us at ground level. It roars, spits thunder and in a cloud of dust drags away with groans of sirens, cries, women's laughter, the only visible things being splinters of copper and bits of moon-coloured sails… And, like a bolt of lightning, it passes by bringing back with it the darkness that it briefly ripped apart… Then a new glow in the sky, and on the road a similar whirlwind of light which only leaves behind darkness in its progress… Then another… then others…

We have gone over the top of the hill… Now we are on, as far as we can guess, in the less dense darkness, through more vague silhouettes and more sky, a wide plateau. Muffled noises, far-off groans, stifled roars, scarcely distinct metallic voices: closer, explosions, crackles! And everywhere stars, stars which run, gallop, roll, bound, criss-cross, seem to be riding waves… suddenly burst into light on top of a hill and, behind a fold in the terrain, are suddenly extinguished… It looks as though the stars have fallen from the sky onto the earth…

Stopped once more we hear a sort of panting, then rattling of something which we guess to be more of an animal than a machine… It cannot be a motorcar, this time… for this noise is accompanied by no light. Nothing lights up around this noise that is approaching… However, yes… there is a small point of pale light, like a firefly travelling in the shadow of an orange tree… And suddenly we see jolting along the road, like a giant beetle, farting, backfiring, a motorcycle bearing, gripping the saddle tightly, a being lying flat, about whom there is nothing human, a fat larva, dressed in a black, smooth, reptilian skin…

And now our headlamps have suddenly brought from the darkness, before us, leaning over an enormous, broken-down, dead motorcar, two men the same colour as the trees and the horizon… I say two men: possibly two Martians… They are shapeless, wearing long sack-shaped jumpers, which cover them from head to foot and from fingers to shoulders. The only bit of their faces showing is a small triangle of wolf-like skin, above which shimmer the metal antenna of their goggles… Two arms are waving about. The 628-E8 stops.

One of them is small… He has his head buried in the enormous bonnet of the motorcar. He takes no account of our arrival… The other, very tall, very thin has straightened up… He is holding a steel rod and the movement of his hands sometimes makes it sparkle. He asks me, in a Russian accent, whether I could lend him a pin, a tie pin, and what he would really like would be a gold one… Once over my surprise I re-alised that he needed to unblock a headlamp… But why did he need a gold pin?… At that moment, a motorcycle, like a demented insect, brushes past him, so close, that I thought that his jumper must have been ripped off… But he shakes it slowly and, laughing, he watches the motorcycle disappear into the night, with regret, possibly because he has not had time to ask him for a gold tiepin.

We leave them on the road, without them having tried to retain us, saluted by the larger one, and always without the smaller one having said a single word or turned his head from the machine, in which he continued to busy his fingers, grave, serious, with the stubbornness of a drunk, whose hands cannot be distracted from the apron of a servant woman…

※

I have left the cyclist to the last.

As soon as a man—even the most charming man in the world—gets his leg over a bicycle, one may say that from that simple act, he becomes a horse, with all its whims, all its stupidity, all the troublesome and mad movements, all the mortal dangers of the horse… but even more dangerous! To the dangers of the horse that he makes his own, the cyclist adds his own personal ones which are consecrated, legalised, intangible, for the very reason that in addition to the horse that he has become, he is also, for most of the time, a voter… Bolstered by this honour, he never moves to the side of the road… Is he not sovereign, this animal? Does everything not belong to him?… The road, the political fortune of the parliamentarian he nominates, the majority of the government that he supports…. Just like the innkeeper who pours out illness and death, in small glasses, and on whom the whole social system is based, you must not annoy the cyclist. His annoying importance, his aggressive dignity picks on everybody, pedestrians, carriages, cars, animals… He is the master, the sole master of the road… You see him, in front of the motorcar with his hands in his pockets, his cap back to front, working his body and his legs, amusing himself making curves, spirals, zigzags, useless and annoying exercises, during which, like a dog, he falls under the wheels… Then it is a whole business involving months in prison and huge fines.

Not so long ago, the cyclist was on the receiving end of all the curses aimed at the motorcar driver today… There ought to be, between them, a sort of fraternity, a solidarity of the road. Now the cyclist has become the worst enemy of the driver. He associated himself with the hatred of the farmer and, if necessary, provokes it. I have seen some who, in front of a motorcar, carelessly threw down large nails and burst out laughing if they hear a tyre burst…

The older I get the more I see clearly that everyone is the enemy of everyone. A similar mad desire gleams in the eyes of two people who meet: the desire to eliminate one another. In vain will our optimism invent laws of social justice and human love, in vain will republics replace monarchies, as long as there are human beings, as long as there are men on earth, the law of murder will predominate in their societies, as it does in nature. It is the only law that can satisfy lusts, distinguish between different interests…

But a solitary cyclist on his own—no matter how evil—is nothing compared with a group of cyclists… When they are occupying the road, goodbye pedestrians, carriages, motorcars… You may as well go home.

I prefer the threshing machine blocking the roads in the Auvergne; I prefer the two thousand sheep in the gorges of the Grands-Goulets…

✳

In Karlsruhe I was told this saying of German cavalry officers:

"First of all, there is God the Father… then there is the cavalry officer… then there is the mount of the cavalry officer. Then there is nothing…"

Here there is a long sequence of full stops. Then the saying goes on:

"And then there is nothing… then there is nothing… then there is the infantry officer…"

To classify the animals you meet on the road, by order of merit, I propose the following saying:

"First of all, the goose, the Mother Goose... Then the duck... Then the donkey and the mule... and then the pig... and then nothing. And then nothing..."

Here a long sequence of full stops...

"And then the cow... and then the dog. And then the dog's owner..."

More full stops...

"And then there is the hen... And then there is the horse... And then there is the carter... And then there is nothing..."

Again, a long sequence of full stops...

"And then, there is the cyclist!"

✳

Of course... there is the cyclist...

But there is also the motorcar driver...

Let us be courageous enough to own up to the fact... Perhaps he is the worst of all the animals on the road?

I feel it myself. When I have my feet on the ground and a calm head, and when I occasionally examine my conscience, I am sometimes horrified to be that animal...

And yet, dear Monsieur Bourget, in the general conduct of my existence, I am not a snob excited by the spectacle of wealth, nor a bad man offended by the sight of poverty. Without pretention, without literature, with no thought of ambition, since I am expecting no position, no term of office, no decoration,—I have great pity for human misfortune. Every day, more and more, I am indignant that,—whatever its label, even the deepest red, with which they arrive in power,—powerful men, for the simple love of power, make social inequality, carefully cultivated, an always similar method of government, and maintain fiercely, in the hardest conditions, in the most unjust slavery, a sorrowful proletariat who work to create the wealth of the country, without ever being allowed to share in that wealth. And since the rich man—that is the person who governs—is always blindly against the poor man, where I am concerned, I am just as blindly, and always, with the poor man against the rich man, with the stunned man against him who stuns him, with the sick man against sickness, with life against death. It is perhaps a little simplistic, with an easy bias, against which there is probably a lot to say... But I understand nothing about the niceties of politics. And they hurt me as would an injustice.

Well, when I am in a motorcar, carried along by speed, captured by dizziness, all these humanitarian feelings are obliterated. Gradually I sense stirring in me obscure ferments of hatred, I feel stirring, turning sour and rising in me the heavy yeasts of stupid pride... It is as though a hateful intoxication overtakes me... the puny human unit that I am disappears and gives way to a sort of prodigious being in whom is incarnated—oh! Please do not laugh, I beg you—Splendour and the Force of the Element. Several times, in these pages, I have referred to the manifestations of this cosmogonic megalomania.

Therefore, since I am the Element, since I am the Wind, the Tempest, since I am Thunder and Lightning, you must realise with what scorn, from the height of my motorcar, I look down on humanity... What am I saying?... the Universe subservient to my Mighty Power? But a poor Element for whom all that is needed is a little cart across the path for it to be brought to a halt, disarmed and sheepish... Poor Mighty Power thrown into the ditch by a stone on the road!

No matter... No matter.

Because I am the Element, I do not admit, I cannot admit that the slightest obstacle stands before the whim of my evolutions. Not only is it undignified for an Element to stop if he does not want to, but it is absolutely laughable and unseemly that a cow, a farmer going to market, a carter delivering sacks of flour or coal to town, that all these people conducting their daily menial tasks, force him to slow down his invincible, dominant progress.

"Get out of the way... Get out of the way... It is the Element passing by!"

And not only am I the Element, affirms the Automobile-Club, in other words the fine, brutal, blind Force which ravages and destroys, but also, I am Progress, the Touring-Club suggests to me, in other words the organising and conquering Force which, amongst other civilising benefits, which adds gloss paint to boarding houses tucked away in the mountains and distributes English-style toilets, and how to use them, in the most remote small provincial hotels...

"Make way for Progress!... Make way! Make way!"

"Well, yes indeed!"

At the sound of the horn people come from their houses, leave the fields, gather, curse at me, shake their fists at me, brandish their scythes and their pitchforks, throw stones at me. Since the time of Jesus, it has always been the same. You devote yourself to men... They throw stones at you, the spinelessness of the age no longer allowing them to crucify you!

Is it not the most disconcerting, the most discouraging, the most irritating thing that this retrograde stubbornness of the villagers, whose hens, whose dogs, and sometimes whose children I run over, means that they do not understand that I am Progress and that I am working for universal happiness? Disgusted by this welcome, furious at this incomprehension, I could easily leave them to their ridiculous fate, respect their gloomy peace, go through their villages and on their roads with a regressive slowness, at the pace of an old stagecoach... But no... I must not let their stupidity prevent me from accomplishing my mission of Progress... I will give them happiness, despite themselves; I will give it to them even if they are no longer of this world!...

"Make way! Make way for Progress! Make way for Happiness!"

And so that I can prove to them that it is Happiness passing by, and so that I can leave a grandiose and lasting image of Happiness, I mangle, I crush, I kill… I terrify! Everything flees in a distraught manner before me… Even the telegraph poles are in a panic; the trees have vertigo… epilepsy seems to convulse the houses… In the fields I see ploughing horses rear up as madly as the stone horses of Coustou,[1] snap their harness, gallop as they shake their terrified manes. Cows collapse into ditches… And behind this Jupiter, gatherer of dusts that I am, the road is strewn with broken carts and dead animals…

"Faster! Even faster… it is Happiness!"

The day when I finally returned from my trip, through the sad Forest of Argonne and the lugubrious deserts of chalky Champagne, between La Ferté-sous-Jouarre and Meaux, I saw, from far off, a group of people who were fussing about in a strange manner… Someone detached himself from the group and gestured to me that I should stop…

A motorcar, smashed in, twisted was lying on its side in the middle of the road… A few paces away, on the verge, a little peasant girl scarcely twelve years old was also lying, her chest smashed in, her face covered in blood… Leaning over her, a woman was trying to revive her… She was crying out:

"Madeleine!… My darling little Madeleine!"

I approached, examined the child, injected her chest with ether and caffeine, but alas, to no avail!

"She is dead," I told the mother.

Her cries became harrowing. Then the owner of the motorcar on its side approached too. He did not have a scratch on him… He was bare headed, having lost his cap in the commotion. There were a few specks of white dust on his black beard… He said:

"Don't be upset, dear woman. Of course, what has happened is a nuisance and it would have been better if I hadn't killed your

____

1 A reference to the *Chevaux de Marly,* [*Horses of Marly*], by Pierre Coustou (1677-1746).

child… I sympathise with your grief… But there is some merit in it, for, since I am insured, where I am concerned the affair is unimportant and without loss… Just think about it, my dear woman. There is never progress in the world if it does not cost a few human lives… Just think about the railways, submarines… I could cite you even more persuasive examples… But let's talk about the matter in hand… It's obvious, isn't it?… that motoring is progress, perhaps the greatest progress of these admirable times?… So, raise your soul above vulgar contingencies. If it has killed your daughter, tell yourself that motoring provides work, in France alone, for two hundred thousand workers… two hundred thousand workers, think about that… And the future… Think about that, my dear woman! Soon we will have public transport everywhere. You will see little regions, that are today isolated, with no communications, tomorrow linked to major centres of activity… You will see arise new commerce, new sources of wealth, a whole unknown, unhoped for life bring back to life dead regions… Tell yourself that your daughter sacrificed herself for that… that it's a martyrdom… a martyrdom for progress… And you will be immediately consoled… Now, I'm going to take your name and address… This very evening I'll write to my insurance company. It's an excellent company… It will offer you a small indemnity… of course, an indemnity appropriate to your social status which seems to me to be rather modest… Rest assured, it will do things properly… I'm the one who should be pitied… Look at my car… I'm going to have to take the train to return to Paris, which is always tough for a real motorcar driver, like me… But I'll console myself about it by telling myself that I'm working for progress, for universal happiness… Farewell!"

I did not want to inflict on such a perfect driver the humiliation of returning to Paris by train. I offered him a place in my motorcar.

And, since the mother was still sobbing, as she leaned over the dead body of her child:

"Oh!" this eminent colleague said to me sadly as he installed himself next to me, with the maximum amount of comfort… "It's going to be very difficult to teach these poor people the notion of progress… Their h…"

He did not finish his sentence which was supposed to end as follows: "Their head is too thick!" Perhaps he was afraid that the little peasant girl stretched out on the road gave too easily the lie to his words…

It was time for me to leave… As soon as I felt the ground, under my feet, my ideas about driving were becoming mixed up… And already I was beginning to wonder, not without some terror, whether I really was Progress or Happiness?

One moment more… and I would certainly have added to the saying about animals on the road:

"And there is nothing… And then there is nothing… And there is the motorist!…"

THE BANKS OF THE RHINE

Readers will possibly remember the unexpected way that we crossed the German frontier, at Elten[1], and the welcome from the fatherly customs officer who waved *bon voyage* to us with his cap.

If you remember, we were going to Dusseldorf.

We had left behind the brick-paved roads of Holland. The landscape was still very flat, very green, half polders, half cultivated fields with, here and there, quiet little villages, attractively surrounded by woods, and small, low houses—farms and dairies—with whitewashed facades, tiled roofs, on which the red played discreetly, beneath a pearl-grey sky, very deep and very gentle.

We were no longer in Holland, but we were not yet in Germany. It was a residue of Holland in a small amount Germany, something between the two which gave the landscape a sort of kind melancholy, a charm of something very young or very old—and I am not quite certain—quite moving.

And the straight road, without a bend, without a bump, simply invited speed.

Not a single object anywhere. Not a culvert, not a bump: a well-maintained velodrome track. Scrupulously, the carts that we overtook kept to the right and the carters, careful about their horses, saluted us as we went by, without servility, almost as friends.

---

1 Referred to earlier in the section *The German Frontier Post.*

Brossette said to me:

"What a pity, Monsieur, that we are in Germany!"

"Why, Brossette?"

"Because I don't like these people… and then, Monsieur, the road's so good that we could easily do ninety… perhaps more…"

And, after a silence:

"It's curious!… Is Monsieur really sure that we are in Germany?"

"Look here!… and the frontier?… Not long ago?"

He gave a shrug.

"That? A frontier?… Goodness!… Givet, yes… that's a frontier… But if Monsieur is certain?"

And he growled:

"Nasty country, nevertheless!"

We were going slowly, as though in an enchanted forest, a forest full of pitfalls, of snares, of dangers, a forest full of bears, of tigers and of lions… Anxiously we were scanning the horizon… We were examining the countryside to the right and to the left, fearful of seeing suddenly the pointed helmet of the Prussian army, with the terror of all that this insidious calm must be hiding of the unknown and the savage.

And the 628-E8 was impatient. You could feel that it was trembling with restrained energy… It seemed to be holding in its bonnet, as a lively stallion does with his neck, under the bit on which he is chewing, and which tames him. It looked as though it was pulling on the steering wheel, like a horse on his reins… From the village clock I saw that it was half past four. We still had two hundred kilometres to go before reaching Dusseldorf, where we would have liked to be before nightfall.

Why, at that moment, was I thinking about the war of 1870? And why, in fact, instead of its horrors, was I remembering an intimate, a consoling episode that my father had told me about when he returned from it?

He had been obliged to house, for a month, a Prussian general, his staff and his retinue. Very discreet, with a perfect education, and a very delicate good grace, this general had taken from our estate only what was absolutely necessary for himself and his services. In every way he had tried to make this occupation less humiliating and less painful, and he took great care to ensure—as far as was possible—that as little as possible was changed in the routine of the house. He behaved like a well-educated guest, not as a conqueror.

One morning, he went to see my father:

"I have just learned, Monsieur, that you have a son in the Army of the Loire… Is that true?"

"Yes."

"Have you had any news of him?"

"I have not had any for quite a long time."

"Since when, exactly?"

"Since Patay[1]…" my father sighed.

"Oh!…"

Then:

"Will you allow me to find out?… I too, Monsieur, have children… I know… I know… I hope that you won't mind if…"

"Absolutely not, I'd be very grateful to you… I confess that I am very anxious…"

The general asked for a few additional details… and saluting:

"Soon, I hope…"

A few days later he came again… He was all smiles:

"I have news of your son, Monsieur… He is in Le Mans… He is very well… I am happy to have been able to…"

Then:

"I think that we're getting to the end of this terrible business…"

Then, again:

"Will you allow me to shake your hand?"

I can still hear my father telling me that he had never been more touched by the kindness of a man and that never had he

---

1 Mirbeau is here getting his father to make a joke. The battle of Patay took place on 18 June 1429 and ended the Loire campaign of the Hundred Years War.

shaken a French hand with as much joy as he embraced this German hand… My father was also a decent man… Thank the Lord, he had nothing of a theatrical hero about him.

Stimulated by this memory, I became excited:

"Sod it!" I shouted suddenly… "No matter what… Let's get going Brossette, let's get going!"

The air was cool, the carburation excellent. The fine C.-G.-V., released, bounded and raced along the road.

"Put your foot down, Brossette!… We'll soon see…"

"Nasty country!" repeated Brossette, adjusting his carburation and methodically advancing the ignition.

In a few minutes we were in Emmerich, where we crossed the Rhine on a very powerful steam ferry; and in a few more we were in Kleve, where we climbed the winding, steep streets to the great joy of the pedestrians—it was a Sunday—and being guided by a small pastry cook, very proud of having climbed onto the running board, and who sent us kindly on our way on the other side of the town.

Oh! What a road!

What a road was this road to which the little pastry cook of Kleve had brought us, the finest of those fine Rhineland roads, built by Napoleon, for the appalling marches of war and on which pass by now what motoring brings with it of less coarse civilisation, of universal sociability and peaceful future.

This road was lined with a double row of magnificent elms, with very tender, very young spring between their branches, a dusting of spring, scarcely pink, scarcely green, at the tips of their branches; it was wide, spread-out, like our Avenue des Champs-Elysées, gentle and without blemish as if it were made of stretched silk and straight, so straight, that the end was not in sight, unless, over there, completely over there, touching the sky, a very thin yellow ribbon, a little daub of yellow pastel that we can never reach… And the sun, at this end of the day, was making, with the tracery of the shade, a sort of carpet never woven even by the most skilful artisans in Persia.

On this marvellous ground, the car, carried along on the rhythm of a light, regular, infinitely gentle roaring—noise of wings or breath of far-off wind—was gliding, flying, like a speeding bird skimming the motionless surface of a lake.

Brossette was no longer talking, nor was he replying to my questions. He was serious, was looking at the road with a slightly screwed up gaze, and he was listening to the fine song of the cylinders.

I was struck by the fertile soil of the fields, how plush they looked, their fine crops, the abundance of their herds and flocks. The villages, very clean, their thresholds scrubbed, their bright windows, their doors with gleaming brasses had an aspect of tranquil riches. Everywhere it smelled of work, security, wealth, I will not say happiness for happiness is something else. It does not show itself immediately to our gaze as wellbeing does in the windows of houses. It only reveals itself with time, it does not reveal itself often, it sometimes never reveals itself.

We took on 'benzine' in a small town whose name I have forgotten, a town of about five thousand inhabitants, rebuilt, almost brand new, with wide streets, interrupted by shady squares, and houses in which solid comfort seemed to prevail. Two bridges, one brand new, the other very old, spanned, the first with one single arch, the second with two Gothic arches, the two arms of a river flanked by small industries which, from their busy, attractive appearance, seemed to be prospering.

As, in the whole of Germany, the administrative buildings imposed themselves on the taxpayers by their rather terrifying hugeness, often with awful taste, of proud opulence, and always well located. I was surprised to see, in such an unimportant place, so many shops of all kinds, luxury shops, draped silks, velvets, sparkling leatherwork, jewels, displays of victuals tied with ribbons, architectural displays of charcuterie, looking like churches, on feast days. Everywhere abundance, sensuality, wealth.

I told myself:

"These objects are not there just for display. Therefore, there are, in this little region, people who want them and who buy them."

Not without melancholy I said to myself:

"How far away I am from France, from small French towns, from their dead streets, from their cracked houses, from their dirty, faded shops!… In France the only work is in Paris, in a few major cities, a few towns in the North, and in the South-East… The rest is petering out and dying each day. Everywhere, enormous riches lie unexploited. Who, for example, is thinking of obtaining from the Pyrenees the secret of their metals? Who, for example, would dare to invest unproductive capital in this bold youth who, for want of finding use in France for their activity and strength, is forced to go abroad and work for the enrichment of other countries?… How far away I am, here, from those stupid Frenchmen, annuitants and suckers, who speak of themselves as the light and the conscience of the world, and that I see perpetually sitting on the doorsteps of their shops, in front of the door of their houses, befuddled and bitter, dying from their laziness, impoverishing themselves with their savings, spending hard days envying and defaming one another! No individual effort, no collective energy… When I return to regions I have been to a few years before, I find them a little dirtier, a little older, a little more reduced; and everyone has plunged, a little more deeply, into their routine and their filth. If it falls, it is not picked up. They add patches to their houses as housewives do to their husbands' pants. Nothing is created. Scarcely do they straighten up what has become too warped, do they replace missing tiles on the roofs, rotten doors, rickety windows… Since they have nothing to do, nothing to imagine, nothing to sell, nothing to buy, they are making economies… Good Lord, on what… But on their needs, their

pleasures, their human dignity, their education, their health…
Dreadful little souls, that this great antisocial lie, savings, has
led to avarice which is, for a nation, what arteriosclerosis is for
a person. France does not need their woollen stockings, rather
it needs their arms, their brains, their work and their joy…
And, after all, it's not their fault… Nobody has ever said to
them: 'Live! Work!' They have always been told 'Save!' and so
they save…"

I conjured up the small town where I was born and which I
had seen again a few months ago… Oh! How heavily it weighed
on my childhood! What memories I retain of mortal boredom!
And how much it still wearies my nights with the persistent
nightmares it brings me! What long and painful treatment I
had to follow to wash away all the bad seeds it had planted in
me! Well, I have seen it again… Nothing has changed in fifty
years. Neither the people, nor the things. Not a new house has
been built; not a single industry—no matter how small—has
been established there. On the river, the same mill pounds the
same flour… There are the same shops, with the same shop
signs and, I think, the same merchandise. You cannot say that
the people there are dead… for the sons have become fathers…
And I met again the same sad faces, the same tics as before, the
same sleepy heaviness, the same gloomy stupidity… I was told:
"Did you know… old so-and-so left fifteen years ago… He has
some sort of factory in Madagascar!… It was clear that he'd go
wrong!…"

Only the cafés give the impression of life. And yet it is death!
Oh yes! What pleasant remembrance I have!…

We set off again.

Full of new petrol, that machine had gained in energy and
speed. It was no longer a machine, it was the Element itself,
not the blind and brutal Element which howls, shatters and

destroys everything it touches, but the submissive, disciplined Element which conquers time, space, human happiness, the future; the Element which, like a little child, obeys the expert hands and the superior will of man.

Brossette says to me:

"Well, Monsieur, are we really in Germany now?..."

"Actually, in Prussia... in Rhineland Prussia, my fine Brossette..."

I showed him a signpost, on which was written in large black letters, after an arrow, these words: *Krefeld... 50 kilometres...*

"Terrific!" he said... "But it's a terrific country! And if we continue at this speed... Monsieur... of course we'll be in Berlin... before the French army!"

I had indeed promised myself to stop in Krefeld. That was where I wanted to visit a few of those fine factories making cotton velour for the whole world... However! Dusseldorf was only forty kilometres away... I was under no obligation that evening, in fact quite the opposite, everything was advising me not to push on to Dusseldorf, apart from the imperious need, the imperious and stupid need to cover more kilometres... I drove quickly through Krefeld, whose economic development, its movement and its life, seemed to me to be a fabulous thing... Business and pleasure, it was all there... A charming, clean, colourful town. The streets were full of people... And the people seemed joyful... A happy crowd, now that is a rare sight.

I hope that you will excuse a personal memory... I could not but be amused to see that *Business is Business* was on, that evening, in the municipal theatre...

A few kilometres beyond Krefeld, a small traffic accident which I am noting because it is characteristic of German mores, left in my mind, at the same time, a slight impression of remorse, also an impression of very gentle and attractive gentleness.

Before us a little horse was trotting, pulling a small cart being driven by a peasant girl. The horse took fright—everywhere horses are the same—and, with his ears pricked, he suddenly began to gallop. I stopped the engine, but this did not calm down the terrified horse. He was off, as the coachmen say. At the risk of killing herself, the girl jumped clumsily from the carriage and rolled on the road… I ran to her assistance, helped her to get up… She was blonde, very fresh, almost expensively dressed…

As soon as she was standing up, she tried to smile… apologised:

"It's this naughty little horse… Good Lord, how stupid he is… He's afraid of everything… Please excuse me."

I asked her if she was injured, if she was hurt:

"No… no…" she said, gently… "oh no! it's nothing… please excuse me."

She had modestly raised her skirt and revealed a slight graze on one of her knees. I ran to fetch, in my medical kit, some peroxide with which I washed the wound that was scarcely bleeding… She was protesting and laughing as if she were being tickled:

"It's nothing… it's nothing… Oh, that stings a bit…"

And then, laughing more and more:

"It's that blasted horse," she said again… "And how embarrassed I am to have caused you so much trouble!"

Brossette had brought the horse back and was calming him down by talking quietly to him… As we were helping the peasant girl back into her cart:

"I am very grateful… really grateful…" she said.

And with a pleading look:

"Oh, Monsieur, do not mention this… Don't tell anybody… Because, if they knew, where I live… well, never again would I be able to go to Krefeld on my own with my little horse…"

She had taken the reins:

"There! There!… Please be quiet now… Little imbecile!… Please excuse me again… Excuse me…"

Half an hour later we were crossing the Rhine on the huge bridge at Dusseldorf.

Dusseldorf.

And so, the first city in Germany where we stayed for a while was—and I am not proud of the fact—Dusseldorf. And, as soon as I arrived, I was sorry that we had not stopped in Krefeld.

We stayed, as one should, at the Bradenbrager-Hof.

All that I will say about this hotel also applies in every way to the city, to the whole new part of the city at least, which is, as is well known, the city *par excellence* of *Art Nouveau*. Once I have described the hotel, I will have described the city, its streets, its colourful houses, its luxury shops… apart from the Rhine, the wide and beautiful Rhine, which persists in repelling M. van de Velde,[1] and in preserving a very ancient style.[2] By simplifying my task in this way, this will then allow me not to prolong any longer in me and in you, dear readers, the sort of frightening nightmare inflicted on our imagination, passionate about beautiful lines and beautiful shapes, by so many infuriated and pioneering Belgians… For, what is the point of hiding it from you?—everywhere we collide with the decorative lyricism of M. van de Velde. Having disrupted the houses and furniture of poor old Belgium, he came to live in Weimar… It is from there that he is discharging over the whole of Germany the products of his carnival fantasies which led him finally to discover the squaring of the circle and the circumference of the square.

---

1 Henry van de Velde (1863-1957) was a Belgian painter, architect and interior designer and one of the founders of the *Art Nouveau* movement.
2 Mirbeau is here contrasting *le modern style*, a French term for *art nouveau*, with older styles.

310

✳

Among other curiosities Maupassant had a valet who served him faithfully. Moreover, he was a very knowledgeable servant. He knew about literature. One day he said to his master, in a serious and reserved tone:

"This morning I read Monsieur's article… It's good…"

"Oh! I see that you don't like it…"

"Good Lord!"

"What's wrong with it?"

"I have to tell you, Monsieur… that Monsieur sometimes lacks sophistication where his adjectives are concerned… They are too simple… They don't paint objects sufficiently closely… And so, in this morning's article, Monsieur says that an orchid is beautiful. Obviously, an orchid is beautiful… but it's not beauty… vague beauty which gives the orchid its character… the orchid, Monsieur, is strange, sickly, perverse, fallacious, disconcerting… I would have written: 'The disconcerting orchid'… That's all I wanted to say, Monsieur…"

"But you are right…" confessed Maupassant who was always amused by his valet's remarks. "You really are wonderful…"

"Oh Monsieur!"

"Yes, you are… where did you learn all that?"

Then the valet preened himself and in a very serious voice:

"Monsieur," he replied… "Monsieur knows that before serving him, I spent three years serving a Belgian poet!…"

And then, after short silence, casually:

"Monsieur will not forget again my palms[1] for the first of January, will he…?"

---

1 This is a reference to the order of the *palmes académiques*, a distinction given in France for outstanding academic service.

Art Nouveau.

The Bradenbrager-Hof which, I know not why, reminded me of Maupassant's valet, is one of the grand hotels to be found in the smallest towns in Germany, and such as we have only in Paris and a few spa towns, one of those new caravanserais and new art of the West, built by Belgians and the Swiss for the habits of comfort of Americans and the English… In them salons, more or less in the Louis XV or Louis XVI style, alternate with smoking-rooms in the styles of those on an ocean liner. In them nothing is straight, nothing is square, nothing is upright. Everything that is round becomes square, everything that is square becomes round. I mean that in them nothing is round, or square, or oval, or oblong, or triangular, or vertical, or horizontal. Everything turns, warps, scrolls, goes wrong;[1] everything rolls, rolls up, unrolls and suddenly collapses,[2] one knows not why nor how. We have nothing but festoons of varnished copper, astragals of painted wood, ellipses of multi-coloured pottery, scrolls of *flambé* stone, trumeaux of embossed leather, friezes of bushy waterlilies, angry poppies and sunflowers on the mouldings of stylobates like parrots on their perches… Flat, thin grubs are asleep at the entrances to locks; embryos, tadpoles climb, slip in viscous undulations along doors, windows, drawers, chamfers. The fireplaces are libraries; libraries are screens; screens are wardrobes and wardrobes are sofas. Electricity bursts forth just as much from the floors as from the ceilings, crystal bulbs shaped as dream-like flowers or nightmarish animals; it runs, catcalls, dances the Boston, spins round, dances the cakewalk, in the sconces and chandeliers, which are dancing the fidgety dance of Saint-Guy. The furniture looks as though it has drunk and seems to be inviting the

---

1 Mirbeau is playing with a series of verbs based on *tourner*: *bistourner, chantourner, maltourner.*

2 Here he is playing with series of verbs based on *rouler*: *enrouler, dérouler, s'écrouler.*

livery to the worst acrobatic excesses. And so that there might
be no mistake, on the asymmetric facades, with deep holes and
enormous protuberances in which all known materials, jux-
taposed with one another, neutralise and cancel one another
out, the balustrades of the balconies are supported by frenetic
sarabands in the shape of question marks.

These types of hotels, so unpleasant in all their aesthetic
details, have at least one precious advantage, in that they offer
the most delicate and refined traveller the most complete re-
sources of grooming and hygiene. As I carried out a meticulous
wash, in a bathroom equipped with all desirable apparatus of
hydrotherapy, I could not help thinking, in this respect too,
how far away I was from our beautiful France, where, almost
everywhere, even in the large cities, the hotels jealously preserve the habits of the race, the hereditary flaw in which may be
recognised, better than by his wit, a genuine Frenchman from
France: uncleanliness. A monarchical and Catholic uncleanliness which Louis XIV endowed with the character of a virtue
and turned into a competition. Does Chamfort[1] not recount
that a gentleman, noticing that the approaches to the Palace
of Versailles stank of urine, ordered his servants and vassals to
"piss" copiously around his castle?

How often, arriving in a hotel in Normandy for example,
have I had to flee from the filth in the bedroom, the question-
able sheets, the accumulated dust in the curtains, the abundant
dirt in the carpets and, above all, the ammoniacal smells which,
in the corridors, through cracks in the doors, infiltrates, enters,
impregnates all objects!... How many times have I resigned
myself to sleeping in my motorcar, like a showman in his caravan, on the outskirts of towns, under the trees of the avenues,
and, even better, out in the fields, where you breathe an air that
is less mortally human!...

----

1 Nicolas Chamfort (1741-1794) was a writer of aphorisms and epigrams.
He was secretary to the sister of Louis XVI.

I was remembering that one day, in a town in the Morvan, having stopped off in a hotel, a pretty little hotel, recently renovated, said the Scripture according to the Touring Club, I was surprised to see how ignominiously were maintained the intimate places, with earthenware walls, which, however, if the brand of the factory were to be believed, came directly from England. Strongly I complained to the owner who replied with a discouraged air:

"Oh! Please do not speak about it, Monsieur…"

"But yes… on the contrary, I do want to talk to you about it…"

"I know! It's not my fault, I can assure you… I take care, I really do take care… But the French who know so much, don't know how to sh**… They don't know!… They are pigs, Monsieur…"

He lost his temper:

"You must have seen… I have put up notices… notices which show how to use this equipment… Well, no… They don't want to… They always climb on them… It's disgusting!…"

And he added, for this man from the Morvan was, in spite of everything, an optimist:

"Perhaps with all this sport… yes, indeed… with the motorcar, perhaps they'll learn how to sh** like everybody else. I have confidence in sport, Monsieur… but damn it… there's a lot to do… there's a lot to do…"

"To do differently," I grumbled.

My Friend von B——

Although our C.-G.-V. was as soft as it is possible to be and carried us along as though on a pile of cushions, you look forward to rest after ten hours on the road. It seems, however, as though you only feel your fatigue when you plunge into the cream and the pink carpets of these halls in which everything turns, and which throw out blinding lights.

As I was staggering about on wine-lees-coloured rose motifs, and trying to hold myself up on belligerent chair backs, I was surprised to recognise my friend von B———, a German I had often met in Germany but even more often in Paris.

"I have just arrived from Essen, by motorcar," von B——— told me . . . "Let's have dinner together."

I could not have had a better dinner companion, nor anyone better informed about what was happening in Germany, and who, even better, could express them in excellent French.

I accepted with pleasure.

My friend, Baron von B———, as a genuine German, is a philosopher, a great lover of music, if he is not actually a musician, a great lover of philosophy. You never know with the Germans. However, he is not only a lover of philosophy; he was formerly a successful professor of the subject, in a famous university and, when he was still young, he retired to live out his philosophy in the world. He is a strange character, very delicate, and he well deserved his reputation as a brilliant conversationalist. Perhaps you could reproach him for being a little too talkative... I do not know whether it was his studies or his work, some position of which I am unaware, or quite simply his birth which give him access to the Emperor. I think I heard him say that he was a student at the same time at the University of Bonn... But so many Germans, and even Frenchmen, boast of having been fellow students with the Emperor at the University of Bonn, that this could not explain the close friendship that exists between Wilhelm and my friend von B———. Von B——— likes the Emperor or the Emperor as a private man; at least, he says that he does. But he is very free with his judgments about the Emperor, and sometimes judges him very severely. It is therefore worth listening to him.

Need I add—and he will immediately have your sympathy—that he is a fervent motorist, a motorist from the very beginning?

Twenty minutes after our meeting we were dining together.

❋

I ordered German cuisine. The Swiss-Italian head waiter who, in this appallingly Belgian dining room, came to give us a menu, decorated with women crowned with laurels in the Boecklin[1] style, and printed in a surly Gothic script, seemed very scandalised. Von B—— came to his aid, explaining to me that German cuisine does not exist, except in a few very old Pomeranian families, and that in no hotel, in no German restaurant, may you be served anything other than poor French cuisine.

With a laugh he said to me:

"But, my dear friend, don't you know that Germany is perhaps the only country in the world where it is impossible to eat… for example… sauerkraut?"

That evening, where German produce is concerned, Germany only provided two of those tall bottles of Rhine wine leaning in buckets of ice, and whose dark golden bottlenecks added to the colour of the tablecloth.

I began by extolling the welcome motorists get here; then I raved about the fine roads, those admirable roads about which I have been made so afraid in France. Von B—— replied:

"It's only in France, from where we get relatively few tourists, most of whom are Belgians, English, Americans, that they do not know these things… It is perfectly true that, here, we do not annoy tourists with prohibitive rules. I am told that there are some terrible ones… But we make sure not to apply them. Traffic is absolutely free, even better, it is protected… We have orders to be extremely friendly and because this order comes from on high, always and everywhere it is obeyed. I also know—for he has sometimes talked to me about it—that the Emperor dreams of endowing the whole of Germany with

---

1 Arnold Boecklin (1827-1901) was a Swiss artist who painted in a late Romantic style.

roads similar to those in the Rhineland, to turn Germany, as it were, into the finest motoring track in the world... Oh! In this respect, his ideas are very different from those of M. Loubet. Your excellent M. Loubet has ended up finding that even the horse is too bold, too modern a vehicle of progress; he prefers to stick from now on with the mules of Castilian songs. As he ages, perhaps we will see him in a little donkey-drawn cart. His aggressive attitude towards motoring is that of a limited, fearful, conservative *petit bourgeois*. As far as Wilhelm is concerned, he has understood perfectly well that there is here an enormous industry, of which the profits are incalculable and that, as Head of State, it is his job to encourage it, to protect it, and, if he is able, to corner it for the good of his country. That is not in doubt. But there is something else. In spite of our workers' allowances which are, I think, the most liberal in the world—and that's not putting it too high—in spite of our economic transformation, we have remained, in many respects, a feudal country, a country of castes. The nobility always has the upper hand, and also wealth, which is a sort of nobility that is as powerful and more active than the other. It is not only officers who insolently clanged their spurs and their sabres on our subservient soil. In villages the squire is master; in factories, the bosses treat their workers like slaves... We have—you would only think that this is possible in operettas—we have a law of *lèse-majesté*."

At this point von B——— burst out laughing:

"I tell you that magistrates apply this law strictly, more by conviction than servility... And this is why, apart from the ideas of commercial conquests held dear by the Emperor, motorists hold sway in Germany... They hold sway as the master's carriage holds sway over the cab, as the military vehicle holds sway over the civilian one... They are the barons of the road. The road belongs to them by a feudal right, just as in France it belongs to carters, by electoral right. And then the German, who is mostly a very decent chap, has no sympathy for the person who is run over. The person run over is always in the wrong, being in the majority of cases only a cripple, a poor devil, indeed nothing at all. Also, I have to tell you that road accidents are much rarer here, where there are no rules, than in France where there are so many and such vexatious ones."

He recounted:

"Imagine, my dear friend… last year, in Paris, at the top of the Avenue Friedland, a girl crossing the road slipped on the cobbles and fell under the wheels of my motorcar. I rushed; I picked her up. She was very pale, covered in mud. Fortunately, she was unhurt… not a single injury… Completely reassured I was getting back into the car when her mother, who was scrambling on the pavement, shouted: 'No… no… stop him!… Call a policeman!… A policeman!' The girl declared gallantly that it was her fault… that she had been careless… that she had slipped… that she was not hurt, etc.… The mother was pulling her daughter by the arm; she was yelling, furiously: 'Just shut up!… Shut up! Who's asking your opinion?' And she addressed the crowd that had suddenly gathered around us and who had seen nothing: 'Yes! Yes!' said the crowd, instinctively believing the mother… A policeman arrived. Despite the repeated declarations of the girl, smitten with justice, a ticket was immediately written and handed to me… A fortnight later I was fined twelve hundred francs damages… But I don't regret anything for it gave me the chance to see an aspect of your story-book imagination which has always amused me. As I left the hearing, a barrister behind me was saying completely seriously… 'The girl's evidence is dodgy… There must be something behind it… It must be the lover!' All the same, in Germany, such a fine would be impossible…"

The conversation moved on to a different topic. We started to talk about motorcar makers, about the automobile industry. He said:

"When you see the rise this industry has had in Germany,— you created it, but it will slip away from you one of these days because you are a strange people, as charming as possible, but inconsistent and flighty,—the Emperor has done all he can to develop it in Germany as well. There is nothing that does not interest him, and he wants Germany to be first in everything, everywhere and always. This sometimes pushes him into un-coordinated and really comic actions. He is like those parents who want their children to have all the school prizes, even if they ruin them for the rest of their lives... No matter what one says, it's not that we have no money, and you are probably the first, without knowing it, to give our banks all the money they wish to have from yours; it's not the driving force that is cheaper here than in France; nor is it the perseverance nor even the familiar stubbornness in our square heads... No, it's something special, inimitable and rather fluid, as your Rostand would say: imaginative spontaneity, good taste, wit... Your workers are witty and, because they are witty, they are skilful... In France it is one of my pleasures to chat with them... Listen... our drivers... they are sometimes, rarely, vain and stiff, the most often just servants... Whereas your drivers are genuine fellow travellers, alert and happy... Oh! If we had workers, like yours in France, you would be way behind us."

In order to reply to these flattering compliments which, in my modesty, I judged to be exaggerated, I would have liked to mention Wagner, Bismarck and Nietzsche. The moment could have been propitious for an apologia about Goethe, Heine, Beethoven of Schiller... But I was not on form. All I could do was praise, rather clumsily, Piesporter wine and German motorcars.

"No doubt," agreed von B— — we do not have good motorcars, but we have one good motorcar... we have the Mercedes... I have a Mercedes... one just has to!..."

After a moment:

"One just has to!" he repeated, not without melancholy... "The Mercedes is quick, solid, its works are a bit crude, too complicated... It's terribly prone to break down... After six

months it goes wrong and makes a noise like scrap metal…
and as well—it's possibly the Spanish name that suggests it—a
very disagreeable castanet-like noise… But it's a good motorcar… we owe to it a degree of progress, ingenious apparatus,
which French motorcar makers have used to their advantage.
For example, the ignition is excellent; its motor bearings are
famous… On balance it is certainly not up to your great
makes which is what, allied to its high price, explains its lack
of success in France… It does not compare with the massive
and robust Panhard, the Renault, the Dietrich, nor the admirable C.-G.-V., so supple, so long-lasting and so simple, with
its attractive, healthy mechanism, the marvellous finish of its
workmanship, its so tenacious and smooth operation, its always
fresh and ardent organs even after the fastest of journeys… Oh!
I know that car well!… I have the honour to be a great friend
of the Princess of Hohenlohe, who owns two C.-G.-V.s. She
sometimes takes me for a drive. It's enchanting…Last winter we
went from the depths of Silesia—and by what awful roads!—to
Cannes, without a mishap… I dream about that car which also
happens to be as beautiful as an *objet d'art.*"

"But" I said, "you can easily transform this dream into a
fifty-horsepower reality…"

"No… it's not that easy…" replied von B———. "Damn
it, the Princess is sufficiently important to be allowed to buy
where she wants… But, as for me… in my Château, my dear
friend, they are quite against produce coming from France…
Listen… the young wife of the Kronprinz caused a scandal in
Berlin. You know that she was brought up by her mother, the
Grand-Duchess Anastasia of Russia, almost entirely in France.
Four months of the year in Cannes, where the Mecklenburg
family possesses a magnificent property… three months
in Paris, the rest in Russia and Germany… in Germany the
smallest possible amount of time. The Grand Duchess, who is
stubborn and knows what she wants, absolutely loves the rue
de la Paix. In vain were representations made to her, it was in

Paris that she ordered the bridal trousseau for her daughter... the Emperor was outraged... In no way did he hide his anger and displeasure, so much so that the young Princess, who was originally joyfully welcomed, thought her popularity was waning. After some rather humiliating family arguments, so it is said, she had to promise henceforth to dress herself, from top to toe, in Berlin. I feel sorry for the charming child. She has infinite grace. She's going to be badly dressed."

"Bah!" I cried, "if Paris is worth a Mass,[1] the Imperial Crown of Germany..."

"It is not worth," von B interrupted quickly, "...being forced to buy from a German shoemaker when one has pretty feet..."

One evening, when dining, a fat German financier was boasting, before his French guests, about the moral, commercial, military and scientific superiority of his country. Did he become aware of his lack of taste before all these icy faces?... Did he try to excuse himself? He suddenly took, with the point of his knife, the tiniest portion of an exquisite Camembert and said, with a smile:

"For example... we don't have such cheeses in Germany. Where cheeses are concerned, I concede that you are superior..."

Von B—— is a little, but with more grace, like that German, and like so many foreigners who, deep down, despise France for its aggressive and boastful frivolity and who only admire it—whilst still despising it—for the elegance of its women, of its fashions, for the unique quality of its pleasures and its corruption. As a patriot, whatever anyone might say about me, I would have made sure not to take away this last illusion.

The restaurant was emptying... and as we were being brought a third bottle of a sparkling Moselle wine, I saw, at a table close to ours, in front of a superb general, stiff, with a

---

1 The future Henri IV of France was supposed to have said "Paris vaut bien une messe" ["Paris is worth a Mass"] when he converted to Catholicism so that he could become King.

monocle, shining bright, very red from his tight belt, very red from having drunk copiously, I saw two officers, two cavalry captains who, as they bowed, had just clicked their heels. I watched him, this old chap, who, impassively, left them for more than a minute in humiliating immobility, their elbows raised to the level of their temples, their buttocks indecently stretched against the edges of their sky-blue uniforms. After which, with a swift gesture, he dismissed them.

Then I said to von B———:

"My friend… tell me about the German Emperor."

The Superemperor.

"The Emperor," von B——— said to me after a pause and with a slight grimace… "Indeed! I am very embarrassed to discuss him with you… No matter how well one thinks one knows someone,—especially someone of that calibre,—you never know him completely, and you risk being unfair to him… And then… Good Lord!"

He pulled the misted-up bottle from the ice-bucket, filled our glasses with this sparkling wine which, in our mouths, makes as it were a pretty little sound of the sea over pebbles, and he went on:

"Look here, my dear friend, to understand our Emperor, you must remember, you must never forget that he dates from the *Gründerzeit*… and that we do not… at least not all of us."

"From the…? Sorry, what was that? The…?" I said having emptied my glass.

"*Gründerzeit*… the *Gründerzeit*… the time of the founders, of the victors—pardon me for this—of 1871. The founders of '71 were, perhaps, colossi, but they were certainly *parvenus*. They had set off for the frontier as Prussians and poor; they returned from Paris as Germans and billionaires… Nothing increases bad instincts more than triumph. It makes us pleased

322

with ourselves and stops us thinking… Victory only has brutes for sons. Think about Napoléon's armies, especially so many thirty-year-old colonels, at the end of the Empire, on suspect pensions, who, because they did not have the time to be promoted to the rank of marshal, died as adventurers… We are created in order to reflect… The habit of misfortune forces man to turn in on himself… It's in this sense that he is a school of intelligence and generosity… Someone who succeeds—even a philosopher—stops thinking… in '71, it was a whole people, used to being on the receiving end of blows, who came home drunk from having dished them out… I admire men who resist bad luck; I admire even more those who resist success… they are heroes. Don't forget that these victors came home from France, not only covered in glory, but billionaires. The era of billionaires dates from '71… It's a word that wasn't in use… The billion of the emigrants?… Yes, all right… But this billion of the emigrants, wasn't a real billion, it was just lots of millions… the billion only really came into everyday language at the Treaty of Frankfurt.[1] What a business!… Just think! You could easily lose your head… Then they began to create Germany, to build it… Here we are not thrifty… we like eating noisily, drinking copiously… and building a great deal. We ate, we drank, God knows we did!… And then we built!… We built forts and cannons; ports, ships and cannons; roads, canals and cannons… and then barracks, then factories, then palaces, and always cannons. We rebuilt Berlin from North to South. We needed a proper capital city for the Empire we had given ourselves… We rebuilt the whole of Germany from North to South… We needed cities that harmonised with the capital we were building… And we didn't stop building… We are still building, bigger and bigger. The taste for colossal

---

1 Signed on 10 May 1871 in which it was agreed that France would pay five billion francs to Germany. The 'billion of the emigrants' was a payment made by Louis XVIII to emigrants who had been dispossessed during the Revolution.

statues, gigantic universities, fortress-like stations, Babylonian post offices, cathedral-sized shops, Valhalla-sized brasseries, monastery-sized barracks, all this hyperbolic monumentalism dates from the *Gründerzeit*... If the *Gründerzeit* gradually disappears from men's souls, it survives in the souls of the stones... And Wilhelm II, whose wardrobe only lacks the uniform of the Mercury, to which the herald's wand would be better suited than sabres and golden eagles on his helmets, dates however, entirely, from these years of megalomania, of the drunkenness of *parvenus*, with their swelling, their noise, their glitz, their false grandeur. He was very young in '70, but, when one does not possess the wherewithal to reform them, one keeps, all one's life, the ideas that were put into your head before the age of twenty."

Von B—— stopped for breath for a moment. I admired his stamina and ability to say so many words. He went on, with a smile:

"Old Wilhelm[1]... 'the unforgettable grandfather'... yes... Oh! I remember... In vain did we crown him Emperor in Versailles, he came back to Berlin as a good old King of Prussia as before... he was just a sort of lucky squire who, despite himself, Napoleon III had turned into a conqueror... One must say that he was well served... Roon,[2] especially Roon,—people only talk about Bismarck and Moltke—but you should read Roon... he pushed Bismarck forward, guided him, and only distrusted his drunkenness... A real genius!... Yes, Wilhelm was better than well served... This jaunty master had ambitious servants. They had already brought him some successes... I mean, duchies, Sadowa[3]... These successes were enough for him... for this decent man never looked like a conqueror, he

---

1 Kaiser Wilhelm I (1797-1888).

2 Field-Marshal von Roon (1803-1879) was Minister of War and of the Navy from 1859 and responsible for the reform of the army.

3 The Duchies of Schleswig and Holstein were acquired from Denmark in 1864. The Prussian army defeated the Austrian army at Sadowa on 3 July 1866.

did not have a savage, violent soul. Do you know that he only crossed the Rhine reluctantly?... It was too much... he was afraid... do you also know that for him the bombardment of Paris was an enormous mistake?... to bombard Paris!... He would rather have gone home... He had to be begged, pleaded with, dragged out of him by trickery, to give the order to fire the first cannon shot... Oh! He would have never thought of billions!...Moreover, it's only through Champagne—and that's the truth—that Bismarck gradually reached the figure, which was to astonish the world and which, to begin with, seemed fanciful to him... But yes, my dear friend, history has to be revisited... I can assure you... history involving these men and these times... and of all time, may the devil take me! If he hadn't been the absolute drunkard that he was, I wonder what Bismarck could have become... His only courage came from wine... Good squire Wilhelm allowed his servants to do the work;—the old servants finally took charge... But success did not change him... In quite a few families there are grandfathers like that who have made their fortunes, so to speak, despite themselves, and who continue to smoke the same pipes and to drink the same beers that they liked when they were young..."

He did not stop speaking as he poured me another glass...

"The curious thing, you see, was that our old 'unforgettable grandfather' only had very late in his life his 'daddy's boy'... He only found him in the third generation... The poor Fritz[1] did not have time, even if he had wanted to, to benefit from the adventure of '70, to enjoy it... He is little known, and that's a pity... An attractive man, in other words... He had modest tastes, was timid, very serious, cultivated, liked by writers and by artists... He did not really want to go to Sadowa and when he was there, almost despite himself, showed himself there to be a great captain... A curious fate!... From this humanitarian,—please excuse the horrible word,—from this man who

---

1 Frederick III (1831-1888) married the eldest child of Queen Victoria. He only reigned for three months.

hated war, fate turned him into a warrior… This simple and gentle man also carried out, in '70, more work than he made noise… He was the enemy of fuss, of pomp… And if it's true as is told, if a little dramatically, that a defeated woman, taking vengeance on him for her relatives, poisoned him, I bet that it will not have been a floozy, not even a *cocotte*… His wife, who had very noble feelings, had a lot of influence on him… As a good daughter of Queen Victoria, she only asked to live in a bourgeois manner…"

Von B—— spoke a little louder:

"For example, his son has never been very nice towards him. Have you seen?… He stuck his statue, as a sort of penitence, in front of the door of a museum… It looks as though Wilhem II only ever thought of belittling the role of his father, from Sadowa to Wissembourg… It looks as though he put him on this tranquil horse, between this alleyway and this bridge, only to leave him nothing else to conquer, in the face of posterity, than a picture rail… Frederick never spoke of his campaigns… Was he ashamed of them?… In any case the braggards of '71 were always reluctantly aware of this silence, of this restraint… Wilhelm himself can never accept that his father did not honour him sufficiently… He blushes at the thought of him, and pushes him from history, as other bad sons send away and shut away, in her bedroom, the old mother they no longer wish to see because she is not sufficiently well dressed. Unless it's a question of a worse resentment… and that he reproaches his mother for his breeding, his father for his recklessness, both of them for the rickets which makes his pride suffer cruelly… Oh! I have often felt it… This silent and reserved man, it was not the father needed for this blowhard son; this crowned invalid was not the Emperor that the *Gründerzeit* wanted… The nation, hurt in the worst of their pride, could not excuse the simplicity and cancer of this peaceful hero… And so, it is Wilhelm II who is truly, with the radiance and noise required by the *Gründerzeit*, who is the first new Emperor of Germany… He installs himself on the imperial throne, which he did not conquer… which was not even conquered for him… Beneficiary, without striking a blow, of an epic, he prances on the exercise grounds, to persuade himself and give the impression that the epic still continues… He really is… Do you understand? 'His Majesty Daddy's Boy'."

Von B—— stopped for a moment and, as though frightened by what he had dared say, he added, more slowly:

"My dear friend, there are, in Wilhelm, two very different and mutually exclusive beings: the charming man that I like a lot; and the Emperor, that I hate, for I find him hateful. I have seen less of him for a few years. He annoys me more and more… I fear that the Emperor will end up dragging me completely away from the man… that will make me sad. The man is pleasant, attractive, very cheerful, very simple, very loyal, very generous, and he is faithful to his friends… Yes,—he does have friends, real friends, among whom there are some, obscure, selfless people who, like me, expect nothing from omnipotence."

He said, and I quote word for word:

"He's a good boy… a good German boy!… Do you see that?…"

And he went on:

"If you hear him, in private, chatting informally, without haughtiness, without pomp, leaning back in a low armchair, his legs crossed, smoking his pipe and laughing loudly, you could never imagine that he is this formidable autocrat, cumbersome and lacking in colour, who fills, who overworks, who terrorises Europe and the world with the clatter of his personality."

He pushed the chair on which he was balancing a little away from the table and launched into another digression:

"Strange chap!… This intimate Wilhelm II, son of an Englishwoman, is still a young English patrician, who went to Bonn rather than to Oxford, and who does what he can to remain a sportsman. If he could, I think that he would take part in horseraces, or would compete for rowing prizes. But his

Britishness is too mixed up; it is really only Anglomania. The uncle[1] sniggers at these pretensions and this makes the nephew cross. And besides, sport? How could he do that?"

Here Von B—— dropped his voice:

"He has all sorts of ways of hiding the arm which is not fully grown… But mind you… Just look at him, look at his photographs, in vain does he take and have taken every precaution, so that it doesn't show… it's…"

And he whispered the word in my ear.

"He's a horrible cripple… a cripple!…"

He stopped for a moment on this word, to allow me to savour it. And from the way that his face lit up with joy, I sensed, despite his earlier statements, all the hatred he had for the Emperor… then he said, with a more detached tone:

"He has a broad intellectual culture but a rather vague one. Unlike that character in Molière who had clarity about everything,[2] Wilhelm has shadows about everything. The only thing that he knows about in a precise and detailed way—and this is an important trait of his character and his politics—is geography, for geography is business… In earlier times it was a joy to discuss a question of literature, philosophy, morality with him. He did not impose his ideas on us, and they were, as you can imagine, very reactionary and bourgeois; quite naturally he accepted that you did not agree with him. He even enjoyed lively arguments, and when he felt himself beaten, he never thought of throwing his imperial crown at us, as a final argument, to be in the right. I suppose that later he took it out on his generals and his ministers."

Von B—— sniggered and slowly chose an enormous cigar from the boxes that the head waiter had just placed in an imposing pile on the table. He lit it and went on:

"Recently he has changed a little… even quite a lot. His agitation is getting worse, the grimaces, his facial tics are

---

1 King Edward VII of England, son of Queen Victoria.
2 A reference to Clitandre in Molière's *Les femmes savantes*.

becoming almost painful. Now when he talks, he has a sort of convulsive movement of the hand accompanied by an annoyingly repetitive clicking of fingers. His laugh, formerly so bright, has a sort of false timbre which troubles and annoys you… Finally, he shows less tolerance, less kindness towards his friends. The Emperor is spilling over into the man. Our friendships are over… A few bright spots, here and there, but they don't last long. It was said of him, at the beginning, that in contrast with Fénelon, he had a velvet fist in an iron glove; he must still be the Maximilien Harden's[1] terrible child, who only criticises his Emperor because he expects too much of him, or the *Simplicissimus*,[2] the intimate enemy of Wilhelm, and who reproaches him mainly for not being Wilhelm the Taciturn. In reality too often now, his fist hardens so as to appear made of steel, and he changes his gloves more often than he does uniforms… I attribute this change to three main causes: the worries and disappointments from his foreign policy, his state of health that bothers him more than is thought, the quiet influence, but slow and tenacious, the Empress[3] has on him despite himself. The Empress has always hated this sort of Bohemian sloppiness, which, in the Emperor in whom two opposed worlds are in conflict, mingled sometimes with the stiffness of the feudal spirit that she accused us of perverting. Oh! She is not one of the most intelligent, nor the most pleasant of women. My Lord! I don't demand that a woman should be beautiful; I just ask her to be graceful. Well, the Empress totally lacks the most important attribute for her sex, what makes a woman a woman: charm. She has virtue… she is virtue itself and, like virtue, rather limited, surly, sectarian, and, as a result, lacking in kindness. More than to his religious education, and more than he takes to be political necessity, Wilhelm gets from

---

1 A German journalist (1861-1927).
2 A satirical weekly paper.
3 Augusta Victoria of Schleswig-Holstein (1858-1921) married Kaiser Wilhelm II in 1881 and was mother to his seven children.

his wife this sort of absurd preachiness which so often gives his speeches such a comic and false note. As a result, we greatly miss that old and gentle Augusta,—who was also virtuous but in a more human way,—to whom your Jules Laforgue told such pleasant things and read French poetry—Baudelaire, I think… he didn't go as far as Verlaine—which would have made today's Empress die of shame… Here is a fact which is not known in France… and which will amuse you. The Empress has awarded herself a state role, a rather strange bureaucratic mission… She is the censor of plays put on in the Berlin *Schauspielhaus*. I can assure you that she carries out this function conscientiously. For example… without pity she crosses out in all manuscripts the word: *Love*, which seems to her to be highly improper. She only tolerates it—probably through national resignation—in the plays of Schiller and also in the French works which are put on, at the Imperial Theatre, during Coquelin's[1] tours, for he is at the *Schloss* almost as national as Schiller. And perhaps, by being spoken in French, this indecent word holds out fewer dangers for German virtue… She has another foible, about which we laugh a lot amongst ourselves in Berlin… When, by chance, she is going to visit an art gallery, she demands that all the nudities of the paintings or the statues be removed or veiled, before she goes by…"

"She likes 'to cover up nudity in pictures[2]'" I declared.

To which Von B—— countered:

"But let's be fair to her, she 'doesn't like reality'… There are stories about her conjugal life, certain details of which would delight the puritan soul of your Monsieur Bérenger[3]… The story goes… But… how can one know?…"

He concluded:

---

1 Benoît-Constant Coquelin (1841-1909) was a famous French actor, appearing in plays and later in films.
2 A reference to a speech by Célimène in Molière's *Le Misanthrope*.
3 René Bérenger (1830-1915) was a puritanical French senator, known colloquially as *Père-la-pudeur*.

"With such a concept of life, of literature and of art, you can imagine that it wasn't much fun at court. Nothing could be more tedious than the galas, the receptions, of such a heavy and icy splendour, with such rigid etiquette, of such funereally gaudy ridiculousness. But this in no way prevents the most ferocious intrigues, the most frenzied passions... It is possible that, of all European courts, the Berlin court is the most corrupt... And you can see that we do not always manage to stifle the enormous scandals which burst out.... Oh! My dear friend..."

I was ready to hear amusing and very filthy stories. But von B——, possibly through nationalistic modesty, swerved away and then went on:

"What is needed to enliven a court like ours is a woman who has a little of this mixture, so difficult to define, of grace and pride... what you call... style... style."

As he repeated the word, he snapped two fingers in the air.

"The poor woman doesn't have it at all!... I can't tell you. But it's not something you find easily in the streets, not even in palaces... something very different from haughtiness, something which sits perfectly with simplicity, and is destroyed by the slightest affectation... a lively grace composed, above all, from naturalness... Even despite the guillotine Marie-Antoinette is ridiculous and especially tense, grating, exasperating... Genuine style is an air of authority never forgotten, but an authority which only reveals itself invisibly... Grandeur is needed with ease, character, a certain energy, and the gift of always finding happy attitudes, without ever making them up... It's rather like the laxity of a nature who senses his superiority and refusing to bow down to opinion, only yields in order to vanquish it... Education can compensate for it: it doesn't replace it... It is quite something to be able to keep oneself as much away from platitudes as from that pomposity that is called, in France, ham acting... Style? How many princes lack it whilst workers improvise it!... Look, your friend Stéphane Mallarmé had it in spades, whose charming dignity, indulgent towards everyone else was only severe on himself. Our old Augusta, who comes from the Dukes of Weimar, had it in her way, on that afternoon in July '70 when, beneath the decked-out Lindens, taking King Wilhelm to the Friedrichstrasse station, from where he would leave for the frontier, she wept, abandoned on the cushions of her state carriage, and hid beneath a handkerchief from the crowd shouting for her the tears that she could not hold back… Danish women also have style, who were brought up so simply in Copenhagen and Amalienborg: Dagmar,[1] terrible from time to time, wife of a dunderhead, mother of an imbecile; and her sister[2] from England, more gentle, more of a lady, impeccably elegant whose situation alongside a *bon viveur* was often difficult. They have a truly imperial grace that cannot be belied."

"And Princess Palatine,[3] so ugly!… She showed them, she faced up to her husband's lovers, to the mistresses and Jesuits of her brother-in-law… the slap in the face she gave her son, right in the middle of Versailles, when he accepted[4] to marry an illegitimate daughter of the King, that has style."

"I agree!… but the creole Joséphine, voluptuous, far better than pretty, often folksy, who was to everybody and to Barras, publicly, as well as to Bonaparte, had, even if she was not born an archduchess, more style than the colourless Marie-Louise… You can be badly dressed and still have it… Our Empress is badly dressed, God knows!… but she has no style… I know

---

1 Dagmar (1847-1928) was the fourth daughter of King Christian IX of Denmark. In 1866 she married Alexander III of Russia [Mirbeau's 'dunderhead'] and was mother to Tsar Nicholas II (1868-1918) [Mirbeau's 'imbecile'].

2 Alexandra (1844-1925) married King Edward VII [Mirbeau's '*bon viveur*'] in 1863. He died in 1910.

3 Princess Palatine Charlotte-Elizabeth of Bavaria (1652-1722) was rather masculine looking and had married in 1671 Philippe d'Orléans, brother of Louis XIV, and who preferred men.

4 The Duc d'Orléans (1674-1723) in 1692 married Mlle de Blois, daughter of Louis XIV and Madame de Montespan.

that it is not much more than a nuance… and yet it's a nuance that everyone feels, an air which is not lost on even the simplest of people, and which wins them over… Look, last year, the excellent woman spent several years in the castle of K———. No doubt to please her professional conqueror of a husband, she decided to win over the regions, squires, bourgeois and peasants… workers and poor people… She made visits, and received many, did not disdain from going into the village, speaking as kindly as she could to women, to children, to girls from the streets and the fields… You can't imagine the succour she brought to the sick, the gifts, the treats!… Well, she only received mediocre gratitude for her efforts… Nobody was won over… Towards the end of her stay, one morning, I happened to ask a gossip who was knitting at her door: 'Well then? Are you happy?… Did you see your Empress?… Did she talk to you?'—'Oh, yes she did!'—'She's a fine Empress, isn't she?' The woman stopped her knitting and looked at me: 'What?' I insisted… 'Isn't she a good Empress?'—'Good?… good?… Of yes, she is good… but an Empress…' She started knitting again: 'Empress…' she repeated, shaking her head… 'she hasn't a clue!…'"

By now we were almost alone in the restaurant where beneath the shaded lamps, the spires of the panelling, the helical coils of the ceiling took on the appearance of fantastic reptiles. The old general, whose face had gone from scarlet red to apoplectic violet, and who had had great difficulty doing up his belt, had just left his table. Outside, on the boulevard, we could hear the rhythmic step of a marching regiment. Von B——— who, until then had talked in a quiet voice, spoke louder.

"I won't say a word about Wilhelm's artistic taste… you are only too aware of it… and besides, it has made the whole of Europe convulse with laughter. Our good German folk, who do not however show brilliant taste, have not got over it. Berlin is a city without an artistic tradition. At least it had the merit of being ordinary, a fine, fat provincial city, hardly beautified in a few places by a small souvenir of our wonderful eighteenth century. Frederick the Great had had brought from Paris a few famous architects who built two or three elegant palaces, and a team of those brilliant gardeners who knew how to manage the seasons, and to assign their tasks, for eternity, to the green lawns and shrubbery. Why couldn't Berlin have remained like that?... Alas! Since the *Gründerzeit*, and especially since Wilhelm, we now have a national art which is a universal laughing-stock. We have the Wilhem II style, just as you have the Chauchard[1] style and the Dufayel[2] style. Furthermore, streets in which the houses look like huge organs, and of which your rue Turbigo and rue Réaumur have borrowed from our *Friedrichstrasse*, we have, amongst other architectures, amongst other monuments of an unimaginable ugliness, we have the giant porphyry sculpture of Bismarck, and, in the *Tiergarten*,[3] which was not so beautiful, this Alley of Victory, on which is often seen the Emperor reviewing the carnival crowd of his marble ancestors. I have to say that the city protested against the imperial plan, which consisted of contributing to the ugliness of our Bois de Boulogne with a regiment of statues.[4] Courageously it refused all the credits the Emperor was asking for... It did all it could to try to save Berlin from this caricatural and funereal horror. But, in the end, Wilhelm footed the bill himself—and he is not personally so wealthy—for carrying out this burlesque project, which was so dear to his heart, because he had all on his own conceived the plan and carried out all the designs... Would you believe that, in a country where they are the object of a

---

1 Alfred Chauchard (1821-1909) was the founder of the *Magasins du Louvre*.
2 Georges Dufayel (1855-1916) owned department stores which ceased trading in 1940.
3 The *Tiergarten*, literally Zoological Garden, is a park in the Northern part of Berlin. In it a Column of Victory celebrates victories over Denmark, Austria and France.
4 An allusion to thirty-two statues.

genuine religion, the Emperor hates flowers?… Yes, my friend, he detests them… Just seeing them, either in gardens or at the windows of houses, or even represented in works of art, creates an almost painful sensation in him."

"Why?… Does he think they are dangerous, like socialists?"

"No… he finds them ugly… Just as he finds ugly Rodin's statues, and the most glorious flesh colours of Renoir… he would prefer that we decorated our lawns and our parks with clumps of sabres, with baskets of shells, with flowerbeds of bayonets and cannons… I'm going to give you another anecdote… A very rich gentleman bequeathed to the city of Berlin the monumental fountain in *Schlossplatz*. I think it has a style, an elegance worthy of Puget;[1] its cast iron is very fine. The Mayor, according to ceremonial protocol, invited the Emperor to the unveiling. The latter, who had created all sorts of difficult squabbles, raised all sorts of administrative and legal difficulties so that the bequest not be accepted, refused the invitation brutally, almost coarsely. He could not accept that someone dared to erect in Berlin a monument of which he was the sole person to have had the idea, and, with his own hands, drawn up the plans and made the scale model. It seemed to him to be an attack on his authority, almost a crime of *lèse-majesté*. He was extremely irritated. I saw him a great deal at that time. Several times he spoke to me about this business which managed to exasperate him and which, for a week, took precedence over all the other affairs of state. One evening he cried out, in French, for every time that he swears it's always in French: 'You know… this bloody fountain… I don't give a toss… I don't give a toss… I don't give a toss… But I'm telling you, it's a socialist conspiracy.' I tried to calm him down, to reason with him… He told me to be quiet: 'Damn it!… I know… you as well, you are a socialist… Everybody is a socialist these

---

1 Pierre Puget (1620-1694) was a French Baroque painter, sculptor, architect and engineer.

days! Oh! But they should take care!' He nearly had me thrown out... The day of the unveiling, imagine the astonishment of the crowd when suddenly they saw the Emperor approaching, his face dark and menacing, his moustache more provocative than ever!... He rushed to the platform, interrupted the decent chap who, at this pathetic moment, was singing the praises of the donor, and said something like this: 'An evil spirit is blowing over the city... I will not tolerate it... I want you to know that, for this reason, I have had built in the very centre of Berlin a huge barracks, full of loyal troops and my faithful cannons... If the socialists make a move, I shall not hesitate, to save our German fatherland, to strike them down... Let them clearly understand... I shall strike them down... I have had enough!...' He looked at the fountain and, with a shrug, he murmured just loud enough to be heard by the dignitaries on the platform: 'As far as this fountain is concerned... it's ridiculous... ridiculous... phew!... ridiculous.' After this he rushed off, just as he had come, leaving the crowd stupefied by this extraordinary dispute... The strange thing is that news of the adventure scarcely circulated... even in Germany. It was discreetly talked about, quietly, amongst ourselves... It did not cross the frontier... The reason is that we Germans have a sort of national modesty, rather ridiculous when one thinks about it, which means that we throw a cloak over the ridiculous acts of the Emperor, as Noah's sons, over the indecent nudity of their father."

After a pause he added:

"One imagines that his antics have been planned well in advance, that he calculates them, that he works out their theatrical effect, coldly, the better to make an impact on the imagination of his subjects and of his people... That's not true... I'm not claiming that he doesn't think about abusing his power. In that respect, he's a man like other men. But I can assure you that he is far less of an actor than is thought. He only obeys the impulse of the moment—he does have some generous ones—and he is incapable of resisting them, only to regret them cruelly later… there is a great deal of neurasthenia in his case. And as with all neurasthenics the Emperor shows, in his most unbalanced acts, a certain logic, an upside-down logic… Thus, he is censured for example for an artistic decision: he immediately creates a journal. He is shouted at: he paints a picture. He is whistled at: he creates an opera. He is complained about: he disguises himself as a Muslim and sets off on a pilgrimage to the Holy Land. He is satirised in an illustrated magazine: immediately he orders that the remedy for tuberculosis be found the next day. You will probably tell me that these are dangerous games for a man on whom depends the security of a great Empire?… Of course… But there are even more dangerous ones and I'll tell you about them if you are not too tired…"

I was not tired; at least I did not feel tired. Wanting to benefit from von B——'s good humour that four bottles of Moselle and Rhine wine were inviting to the worst confidences, I encouraged him to continue. I was enjoying finding out what an enlightened German, without too much bias, without too much nationalistic self-deception, thinks of his Emperor and of Germany…

Von B—— lit another cigar, as do, at an interesting moment in their narrative, all experienced raconteurs and then went on:

"Do you want to know the truth?… the whole truth?… Well, the Emperor is no longer liked in Germany… He is no longer believed in… He is feared, that's all… and that's what just about makes him still tolerated. He tires us, he angers us, he discourages us, he overworks us, he annoys us… yes, there you have it… he annoys everybody, from the prime minister who is obliged always to carry out a policy of lying,—and bad faith finishes up disgusting even a prime minister,—down to the last of his soldiers who feels his rifle, his haversack weigh

more heavily on his shoulders and who is beginning to complain about it… Europe as well, where he sees himself more
and more isolated, has had enough of him, I can assure you.
And not only Europe, but the whole world, obsessed with
Wilhelm, undoubtedly, as in a nightmare. As far as we are
concerned, we are a people of decent folk, industrious, very
peaceful; at least we have become so again. We are sobering up.
For example, we have taken our prosperity seriously and, since
progress does not frighten us, we have endowed our country
with incomparable industrial toolmaking. In order to maintain
this prosperity, progressively to increase it, we want to be quite
at home. Well, we only live in the fear of the imbecilic, permanent complications that may be raised, any day, at any hour, by
the slapdash man, constantly agitated, and who cannot control
his nerves… It's intolerable… What we reproach, what the
young generation especially reproaches about the Emperor, is
that he is a false label, too garish, stuck, inappropriately, on
the good old German bottle. He no longer looks like it; it no
longer looks like him. People are beginning to laugh, now, at
the pretentiousness of the *Gründerzeit*, at the eye-catching,
megalomaniacal art, which comes from it and weighs on us. A
generation is coming to the fore, on whom Nietzsche will have
more influence than Wagner, a generation of more subtle men,
peace-loving, giving up impossible conquests, refined people,
and who can change a mentality inherited from the thugs of
'71… Force can only hold sway over right for a brief time, for
right always ends up being force… Perhaps our grandchildren
will avenge your grandparents… For the moment we are still
living perpetually as the flip sides of ourselves; I mean that we
must like what we hate, and hate what we like the best… We
like France, we like it all the more because from no point of
view,—I am talking about the essentials here,—do we fear
the country… And in the newspapers animated by Wilhelm's
spirit, it is only ever a question of grabbing it by the throat…"

"Lovers' tiffs!… You are only troubled because Wilhelm is Emperor."

"Of course," von B—— countered… "I don't reproach him for anything else… Note that he too… But when he is on a cruise, as soon as a French yacht is reported somewhere… it is stronger than him… he has to board it, that he invites himself onto it… My friend, if, during his marine journeys, he had met Gallay and La Merelli[1]… I believe, on my word of honour, that he would have gone to pay court to them!… Ah! what would he not do to dine at the Élysée Palace between the goatee beard of M. Milliez-Lacroix[2] and the wide, gleaming face of M. Ruau?[3]… Besides, the French—and this is the amusing thing—are sufficiently poisoned by their old monarchic blood!… I'm sure that M. Étienne[4] would enthusiastically abandon his Gambetta; the Prince de Rohan, his Duc d'Orléans for our Wilhelm… And M. Massenet, M. Saint-Saëns[5] and all? What fine old chamberlains they would make, at our court!… Humiliated, bent over, and so proud to have a clef in their backs… a treble clef, of course!"

He started laughing and went on:

"The most important thing, you see, is that we are beginning to become perfectly aware that with his feverish, hectic, incoherent activity, he will soon end up exhausting Germany, whilst we wait for him to push us into a gigantic economic crash, from which we will have the greatest difficulty to recover…"

"You are a pessimist…"

"I am clairvoyant… and I find it useless to close my eyes on purpose… When you have travelled through Germany, visiting our towns, our countryside, our factories, I'm sure that you

---

1 Alfred Gally wrote operettas and comedies. La Merelli was an actress.
2 A French senator and Minister for the colonies.
3 A former agriculture minister.
4 Eugène Étienne (1844-1921) was a French *député*. Mirbeau had accused him of dishonesty and had fought a duel with him on 7 August 1883.
5 Mirbeau did not particularly like the music of Massenet and Saint-Saëns.

told yourself: 'What a prosperous, happy, rich country!' And you envied us. It is certain that the facade is fine. But just go into the house, in no time at all you will see cracks, fissures, bulges. It is cracking up in many places. Why?... Despite all his faults the Emperor is intelligent, but he is no more than an intelligent man. When one takes on the absurdly superhuman task of making oneself the absolute master of other men, one needs more than intelligence, one needs genius; more than genius, one needs divinity. Well, for a long time our philosophers have been proving that there are no longer any gods. I have to be fair to Wilhelm for he has understood, as has everybody, that industry and commerce are, in a sense, the organs of life, the vascular system of a people. What he has not understood is that, for these organs to function well, you have to protect them from jolts, nervous disruptions, perpetual emotions, as well as too much food. One can die from not having enough blood; one can die, more brutally, from having too much. High blood pressure is worse than anaemia. And Germany at the moment is suffering from high blood pressure... The Emperor has alarmed German industry by making it rush, vertiginously, towards all economic conquests. So that Germany could be, as I've already told you, top of the class, he forced it to produce, to produce ceaselessly, to produce even more, to produce all the time. Products are piling up in shops, clogging up docks and attics, are moving with difficulty... Enormous stocks remain... I won't tell you about the disastrous business we call: Russian Steel[1]... It's too well known... Here is a more banal but just as characteristic an example. Jealous of the worldwide success of your Bordeaux, Burgundy and Champagne wines, you must know with what *furia* Wilhelm pushed our landowners and farmers into the cultivation of vines. In every way possible and in every region, he protected it... He even became an investor in wines, a broker, a public relations agent, a restaurateur... In

---

1 In 1900 there had been a crash in the price of steel in Germany.

Paris, in 1900, in the famous German restaurant, it was, can you believe it, the Emperor himself who—still in uniform!—a napkin under his arm, the shiny black apron covering his thighs, came to present the wine list to you… You must have certainly admired the huge hillsides which, along the winding course of the Moselle, layer their magnificent vineyards and, at this impressive sight, you have cried out to yourself: 'There's enough there to intoxicate the whole of Germany and also the whole universe!' The problem is that poor sales, which are happening in your country, are also happening here… Wine is filling up our crowded wineries. The landowners are getting worried, the farmers are complaining. In vain does the Emperor take tyrannical measures like, for example, restricting the sale of beer in certain restaurants, completely prohibiting French wines in officers' messes, it has no effect… Our economic situation may be summed up in one word: overproduction. In vain does Wilhelm sail the seas in his battleship, as in former times your Mangin[1] visited all French villages in his caravan; in vain does he dole out the most extraordinary blarney, does he multiply the most theatrical demonstrations and, sometimes, the worst threats, to attract buyers and place his products, overproduction increases, and we will soon be reduced to this painful choice: either stop production, which will mean ruin; or continue it, which will also mean ruin… Just note that our banks are engaged in this business up to the hilt; that we are not, like you, a nation of timid low earners, a nation of avaricious savings, that we enjoy life to the full, that we spend what we earn… As a result, we can't absorb, with sack loads of saved *écus*, the weight of a financial crisis… Unless…"

And here von B——— looked at me with a strange smile…

"Unless France, generous France, as it has done recently, comes to our assistance and re-establishes for a time the shaky balance of our finances…"

---

1 A travelling salesman who sold pencils throughout France from a caravan pulled by four horses.

Interrupting himself quickly, he slapped me on the shoulder:

"For you are good eggs[1]…" he said, with a hearty laugh that resounded through the empty room. "Admit that you are good eggs, aren't you?…"

I replied:

"But, my dear friend, we have nothing to gain from a German financial crash… We have everything to lose from it… A ruined Germany would be a universal misfortune… Let me tell you this: Because it's understood that we French are only lenders of money,—we are called the world's usurers,—because, on the other hand, through laziness, through timidity, through lack of toolmaking… and through excess of wealth, we have given up all conquests and even all industrial competition,—why shouldn't it be we who give Germany the money that it needs? Germany is honest, hardworking, tenacious; it's carrying out an immense endeavour, worthy of admiration… It deserves to be supported in this effort, which is a civilising effort. Apart from which it is immoral and shameful that our billions are being used, in our dear Russia, for the abominable work of which you are aware… it would be, I think, a good financial operation for us…"

"Gracious me!… you are right…" confessed von B——. "I've drunk too much. This blasted wine is making me say stupid things…"

Whereupon he refilled his glass and mine…

I asked him:

"Do you think there will be war? Do you believe the Emperor is thinking about war?"

"Not at all," replied von B—— in a loud voice… "That, never!… Despite all his uniforms, despite all the fanfares of his words, Wilhelm is not a warrior… He's a military man, which is very different… He's not even courageous… Like

---

1 Possibly an allusion to France's loans to Russia, criticised by Mirbeau since 1893.

your Napoléon III the noise of cannons brings him out in a sweat of terror…"

"Wait a moment… that's not a reason…"

"No, absolutely not… his speeches, his antics, his threats? Just a commercial… ploy… He terrifies Europe sometimes only to reassure our large factory owners who live from armaments… that to maintain a huge industry, to maintain a formidable toolmaking, for which a cloudless peace would mean ruin… then, what do you expect?… Wilhelm knows only too well that Germany cannot acquire more military glory than it already has… But…"

He started to chuckle.

"I wouldn't be surprised if he didn't dream a little of naval glory… Ho! Ho!… a naval war, is perhaps something he has thought about?… Fortunately, England…"

I could not stop myself from exclaiming:

"Ubu! He's Ubu!"[1]

Von B——, who was very up to date with our literature, strongly approved of this remark…

"But, yes, my dear friend,… he is Ubu… Moreover, Ubu is the most perfect image that we have been given of Emperors, of Kings, and let us say it, of those who, with whatever title, are involved with governing people… And if you would like, let's drink to the health of M. Alfred Jarry…"

Which we did… after which he thought for a moment and then said:

"There's another reason that will always prevent the Emperor from declaring war: he fears the result. Certainly, our army is strong, the strongest in the world… it has been exercised, trained, to the highest level… Our arsenals our full, our armament complete… our fortresses up to scratch: that's understood. Unfortunately, we no longer have any officers, or, rather, we only have parade-ground officers who resemble those ladies'

---

1 A reference to Alfred Jarry's *Ubu Roi*, first performed in Paris on 10 December 1896.

men of your Second Empire that we saw at Metz and at Sedan.[1] They don't work and are only occupied with their pleasures: gambling, women, and even men… You can't imagine the corruption that prevails in their ranks… From time to time, one sees the sudden disappearance of a lieutenant promised a fine future, a general well thought of at court, an impressive courtier, a minister who seemed sound… It's not a question of *cherchez la femme*… it is almost never a woman that has to be sought… As far as the high command is concerned, it is mediocre or even despicable. It is in the hands of generals well thought of at court, laden with honours and money, that the worst intrigues, the dirtiest bargaining, the filthiest debauchery have brought to fortune… And then, these generals, they don't count… Just think about this crazy thing: Wilhelm, if war breaks out, leaving to nobody the task of commanding his armies… For he also has war plans, as he has statue plans, picture plans, opera plans, plans for everything…"

Here, von B—— put on an expression of comic terror. He had been silent for a moment, but to allow his voice, which was becoming hoarse, to recover.

"Well, my friend," he cried, "we would be beaten by Switzerland… by Switzerland… I tell you… by Switzerland!"

My laugh indicated that I refused to believe such a prophecy:

"By less than Switzerland…" he insisted… "don't you believe me?… Think about it… On manoeuvres, where everything is planned, where the staging has been worked out in advance, where the Emperor always has to be the winner, well, these awful generals have enormous difficulty in not beating him. They work their guts out not to capture him, even in the plains… I was present at some of these manoeuvres… What buffoonery!… Oh! My friend, I have the most uproarious stories about them… From Switzerland if you understand me!…"

He was calmed by a sip of wine. His face became serious again:

---

1 Two catastrophic defeats for France in the Franco-Prussian war of 1870.

"And then, you see… there is an evil wind blowing today over Emperors and armies… Even here in Germany, the soldier is beginning to think, to experience disgust with his profession. Despite the harshness of the discipline, they are talking in the barracks; and it's not, I can assure you, to exalt the military profession and to glorify war. Caught between Russia and France, how could we avoid the great movement that is making the whole world tremble?… Oh! I'm not stupid enough to think… No… No…And yet!… I'm unaware of the parliamentary fate of German socialism, and really, not very bothered about it… There are so many flukes in elections, so many mysterious contingencies which falsify the outcome of them!… But I do recognise that it's making progress every day among the popular masses and also the enlightened bourgeois youth…"

"So, are you a socialist now?"… I thought I could ask him.

"Dear friend, I'm always a socialist, in the evening, after dinner," von B⸺ asserted solemnly.

And he went on:

"Once socialism decides to repudiate the sort of nationalistic sentimentality, which still shackles it to regrettable prejudices, it will accomplish wonderful things in Germany and in the world. Oh! It's a perfect time for disarmament! The folk who, today, would throw away their arms, would be blessed for all time. You have to be a politician, in other words understand nothing of the aspirations of his epoch, to dread the consequences of this outcome which will be greeted with enthusiasm—whether Emperors wish it or not—by every nation…"

He was getting carried away, and as he got carried away, his speech became slurred, had difficulty uttering the great sonorous words, and he struggled to pronounce them. With difficulty he ended his tirade.

None the less I agreed with him about the blind absurdity of politicians.

"It's true," I approved, "politicians understand nothing about what you are saying, and they will never understand anything. However, they do understand that they have an interest in the continuation of this terrible military mismanagement. If people die from it, they continue to live from it… What then?"

"Then… let's go to bed… and dream!…" said von B———, who stood up in a lumbering way, not without ascertaining that the bottle was empty.

He took my arm, which he needed for support and, as he walked, he started talking again. This man could not keep quiet:

"They don't even seem to know that the era of politics is over… You know that there are organs which survive the functions they were carrying out…"

"Survival, yes…"

"The whole evil comes today from the survival of sovereigns and politicians… I don't mean the King of England… But… even our Emperor is no longer in charge of leading his people… Maximilian Harden[1] is wrong to criticise him for his bark being worse than his bite… Really, do you think that he is free to realise his plans?… The Emperor of Austria… yes, the venerable Emperor of Austria… is less a sovereign in his empire than… than…"

"Than his cousin in Monaco, on his playground rock?…"

"Are you joking?… But much less… the Tsar of all Russia has scarcely more influence than the Prince of Bulgaria… the Mikado, himself… without going so far…"

And von B——— restrained himself with difficulty in the treacherous velvet of an armchair…

"Without going so far, your French politicians, those most aware of current progress, or should I say the least unaware, your socialists don't even know where they will be led by the mass of the working class of which they are only the embarrassed spokespeople… Two years ago, they were radically unaware—I mean like radicals—of the destiny of trade-unionism… The

____

1 Maximilian Harden (1861-1927) was a German journalist.

most cunning are those who manage, not to lead the flow of their electors, but to pick out, a few weeks in advance, from the currents in which the proletariat is seething, the one which they will vote for…"

"So what?… so what?…" I repeated as in my tiredness I could not find anything more meaningful to say… "So what?"

Truly, a barrel of Rhine wine could not have weakened the muscles of von B———'s tongue. He replied:

"Well, what's the point of useless organs?…this dead weight? What's the use of these appendices?"

And he burst out laughing…

His laugh made me laugh.

"Do you want us to have them operated on?"

"Hah!… Hah!… Medicine has had its day. Surgery is the future…"

He had a hiccup…

"Here's to surgery!… I don't believe any more in medi… ci… ne but… I… hic!…I believe in surgery."

"Dynamite-style antisepsis?"[1] I cried, pulling him along with my arm…

He forced me to stop and said slowly:

"The anarchist is a surgeon… a surgeon in spite of himself…"

"Weren't you saying you were a socialist?"

"After dinner I'm always a socialist… but…"

He pointed out to me, above the restaurant door, the dial of an illuminated clock, on which the copper hands were writhing…

"It's three o'clock in the morning, my friend…"

As we chatted, we had arrived in the foyer of the hotel… All its lights were out. The dawn light was beginning to recreate, in the half light, the frightening shapes of furniture and ornaments… Von B——— stopped again. The light of the dawning day brought tears to our tired eyes.

----

1 An allusion to anarchist attacks in 1892-1894.

"Ah!... And then..." cried von B—— suddenly, with a wide yawn, "all phrases are not worth a good anecdote... And we have said some stupid things... stupid things... pretentious, empty, useless generalities, so dear to the German mind!"

Another yawn made me yawn... As he stretched, he went on.

"The slightest thing... the slightest... provided that it is real and human... I prefer it to evolution, thesis, antithesis, synthesis of three eras of philosophy..."

He smiled and his eyes lit up.

"Listen!... I really like you... I'm going to tell you something that I have never repeated before... an extraordinary thing... do you want to hear it?"...

I sat down beside him, in a mahogany booth, on the leather cushions of a sofa, of which the daylight was softening the orange redness...

"It's a story that a disgraced Bismarck told me, one night, after we had been drinking, in Friedrichsruhe... That's just to tell you that we can trust it. Nobody was more brutal or more sincere when he had been drinking... Scarcely had the old chancellor told me the story than it seemed to me, from a contraction of all the lines of his face, that he would have liked to take it back... He was not a man to regret anything he had done, even something stupid... And since he did not like useless words, he didn't even ask me, in retrospect, to keep it secret... Yet, each time that I wanted to tell the secret, I saw again, in their hooded sockets, his burning eyes and I remained silent... This evening I feel that I'm letting it out... Good Lord!... take advantage of it..."

His hand grasped my knee:

"Do you know what was?" he asked slowly, "the first official act of Wilhelm II?..."

It could only have been to wait for my reply that he stopped.

"In any case, you are aware with what anxiety Wilhelm— then son of the crown prince and so far from the throne on which his grandfather was turning to stone—watched the progress of his father's illness in San Remo?... Do you recall his parricide fever of the Hundred Days of the reign of our Fritz, in Potsdam, to which the crowned cancer sufferer had been brought? Oh! Wilhelm had escaped his parents a long time ago... Bismarck had taken him from them... A game, wasn't it? For the old diplomat, in whom the fierce... energy, is linked to the finest craftiness... Bismarck excited the impatient ardour of the young man against the imperial couple... He had, for ever, ferociously hated and feared the woman he called 'The Foreigner' and her English ideas. He equally hated and no less feared liberalism, the loyalty of Frederick III... The funniest thing is that he could not foresee the appetite for omnipotence that would arise later in the imagination of his too-docile pupil that he was stimulating... Not an act, not a written or spoken word from the father that the chancellor did not teach the son to criticise... As for the influence of his mother, he was taught that it was evil... unpatriotic... The relationship between Empress Victoria and her son was extremely tense... and bitter. She was aware that he had his spies even in the bedroom of the poor sick man... A current ambassador had already been tasked, by Wilhelm, with a less ornamental, more delicate, mission at the bedside of the dying man, whose death agony was haggling over the throne in his favour... That is how he learned of the existence of a diary that his father had been keeping for years... Frederick liked writing. You will have read his letter to Bismarck, on his accession, his diary of '70-'71, and the account of his visit to Suez for the opening of the Canal?... I'm not saying that he had much talent, and that his writings are masterpieces... At least they bear witness to worthy intentions... The fear of this secret diary terrified young Wilhelm. Perhaps his behaviour might have been judged?... Perhaps dangerous wishes had been written in them?... All he could think of was how to get hold of these papers...But the Empress managed, before the end, to make them safe...

Deceiving the nevertheless minute surveillance of her son she had sent them to England… to the Queen, her mother, or to her brother the Prince of Wales… I can't quite remember… Scarcely had the dying man passed away than Wilhelm, as Emperor, demanded the *Memorial.* The Empress feigned ignorance… He insisted… He spoke in a masterful manner… He ordered his mother to obey him… She stuck to her plan… She had no idea… Wilhelm ended up angrily threatening her brutally… To his dry eyes his mother's tears seemed to be a ploy… The more she resisted the angrier he became, for it seemed to him that his mother's stubbornness proved the importance of the documents… The truth is that he could not stand that, in the first hour of this reign for which he had waited so feverishly, somebody, no matter how important, should dare to stand up against him… Anger drove this Emperor of one day to utter madness… He told himself that, after all, his mother was only a princess in the royal house of which he had become leader, the colonel in chief of one of his regiments, his subject!… 'Well then,' he ordered, purple with rage, 'you will remain under house arrest, Madame… house arrest… until you have obeyed me… yes… yes… I place you under house arrest.' Two hours later, when he arrived in Potsdam, Bismarck finds the palace surrounded by armed cavalry squadrons. The Emperor tells him how he has reacted to his mother's disobedience… He is still very exhilarated, thinks that it has been a brilliant idea: 'And let her not think that I will have a moment's pity, that I will soften… no… no… until she has obeyed me… do you understand, Chancellor?… until she has obeyed me.' The Chancellor admitted that he would have been very afraid if he had not used all his energy to find, at that very moment, strong enough arguments—albeit respectful ones—to prevent lasting one minute more this macabre stupidity capable of damaging the reign that was just starting. Later what astonished him the most was that he could stop himself laughing at his sovereign… 'I think,' Bismarck told me, 'that the young man wanted to impress me… Boot out the Empress… the Dowager Empress… the Empress, his mother, arrested, the same day as the Emperor died! That was colossal… *kolossal*!…' As it happens, the pupil had gone far too far. He had to use a deferential silence to indicate that he didn't approve, and then finally to show that there was a more rigorous and effective way forward… Why not reduce the allowances of the Empress?… suspend her prerogatives?… 'I know Her Majesty,' Bismarck said quietly… 'She's proud… House arrest will make her stubborn… she will accept it as a sort of martyrdom… but money, Sire,… money?… Doesn't money talk for everyone?' He also raised, with a great deal of tact, the probable representations that would come from England: 'Is it really a good moment, Sire?'… The Emperor who had finally calmed down, weighed up the advice… The Empress's house arrest was lifted… The officers took their cavalrymen back to their quarters… And Wilhelm became involved in the details of the funeral and the period of mourning, which he wanted to be lavish!…"

"But how does the story end?" I asked.

"The struggle between the Empress and her son lasted several months… At least six months…"

Von B—— got up to avoid the sun which had violently entered the foyer.

"It took at least six…" he repeated… "before the Emperor got his manuscript and the Empress her money… Oh! She was forceful!…"

I saw him tap his foot:

"There we have," he continued, "a worthy debut of this Emperor, who despairing that he would ever arrive at the glory of having created a Bismarck, perceived that the glory of daring to dismiss him was the only one that one could credit him with!"

He added:

"After all, what was he risking?… Germany had been created."

And suddenly:

"Tell me, dear friend?… What if we were to have our *café au lait*… with honey… with honey…? Here they have a honey from Westphalia!…"

The Dusseldorf School.

I owe an apology to Dusseldorf.

It is a very beautiful city. It offers no picturesque charm to lovers of old ruins, old Gothic churches, old tangled and stinking streets… It has only wealth and luxury. But it has a great deal of it; it even has too much of it. For example, the layout of its parks, its balconies, the grace of its gardens in which the greenery, the flowers and the pools combine into marvellous décor, make you quickly forget the *art nouveau* of the shops and houses. And the Rhine there is magnificently impressive. In the shopping districts the displays are of a rare lavishness. Fabrics, furs, jewels, silverware, victuals, adorned like the victims of ancient sacrifices stop you in your tracks, wherever you go. It is the city of great couturiers, great milliners, great tailors.

In the centre of this country of iron, so good at hiding beneath flowers the black and tragic effort of demanding work, one finds oneself truly at the heart of German wealth, at the heart of German abundance. The opulence sometimes appears tiring, of a rather heavy sensuality. But I often found in their demonstrative eagerness, in the welcoming honesty of these handlers of millions and of cannons, a sort of charm at one and the same time frightening and persuasive, and their vulgarity is neither unsympathetic nor banal. However, you feel they can be frightening. I have met there more than one Isidore Lechat.

Von B——, close friends with the majority of the region's main factory owners, introduced me to the houses of several families in the city and in the countryside. Their décor is in deplorable taste. It is very expensive; that, apart from the taste, is all that one can say about it. Moreover, that is all that is asked of it. The dearer an object, the more it noisily reveals that it is expensive, the prouder they are of it... in that they are like Americans; Americans as well in the way they dress and shave... Von B—— states that in business they are even bolder than Americans, and also of an unexpected cheerfulness. He tells me that, last year, he had taken one of his French friends to the factories of M. Ehrhardht,[1] the famous creator of Dusseldorf cannons, the rival of Krupp...

"Ahah!" said M. Ehrhardht, shaking the Frenchman's hand... You have come to see my pianos?"

"Sorry... your pianos?"

"But yes... Érard[2]... Érard... your Érard... Only, with me, it's a different tune... Ahah! Let's move on!"

He also tells me this anecdote:

Von B—— has an American friend. Like most Americans he is of German origin. Three years ago, this friend came to Paris... he went to see H——, the great upholsterer... He said to him, with no preamble:

"You are going to build me a hotel in London, a very fine hotel, the finest there can be. When, on 4 May next year I arrive in London, I expect to find everything ready: furniture, pictures, servants, horses, carriages, motorcars... even my dinner... I don't want to have to deal with anything... not even buying toothpicks... Have you understood?"

"Yes..."

"How much?"

"But," stammered the upholsterer, astounded... "I... I would like to know what you like... what..."

"I don't know what I like..." interrupted the American... "I haven't the time to find out... If I knew I wouldn't need your services... Hurry up...I'm busy... How much?"

---

1 Ehrhardht lost out to Krupp in obtaining Imperial contracts.
2 Sebastien Ehrhardht (1752-1831) was a piano maker.

"Ten million… or thereabouts," the great upholsterer risked who had regained a little if not a lot of self-assurance…

"Not… or thereabouts… Exactly… Quickly… How much?"

"Well, ten million!"

"All right[1]… here's a cheque for four million… When you need the rest… just send a cable! The fourth of May, just remember? Get it right… Au revoir!"

And von B—— told me:

"Here, they're not there yet… but they're getting close… Besides I believe that, despite the different mores of each country, the manias created by money are everywhere the same… There's a sort of moral uniform worn by all billionaire speculators."

I was astonished by the extravagant luxury of these houses. For a long time, I shall keep, amongst other memories, the memory of certain ceilings in which the whole Dusseldorf School has united to assemble the most improbable horrors… For there is still a Dusseldorf School. It is, as far as I can understand, a collectivity, a sort of painters' union, whose names are not known and who are working hard on the strangest works, in the houses in the city and in the châteaux in the countryside… If you ask:

"By whom is this picture?… this ceiling?… this large fresco?"

You invariably get the reply:

"It is the Dusseldorf School…"

In the office of a great metallurgist, I saw a portrait of Bismarck, as a general, helmeted, booted, immense, enormous, with mauve hints, yellow hints, green, pink, lilac hints, stuck, built onto the face, the tunic, the helmet, the boots… And thus, old Bismarck ended up looking astonishingly like that pretty Madame Roger-Jourdain[2], of whom Albert Besnard made such a shivering portrait…

---

1 In English in the original text.

2 A reference to a portrait by Albert Besnard (1849-1934) of his wife. Mirbeau quite liked the portrait but was puzzled by the 'yellow hints'.

I would have liked to know who had painted this Bismarck with the hints of colour.

"It is the Dusseldorf School…"

That is all I could get from my great metallurgist.

Why should not our Academy of Fine Art—you can never find the name of any of its members—turn itself frankly into a limited company of artistic exploitation?… It would greatly facilitate dealings between art lovers and would simplify the task of poor art critics…

The Emperor no longer comes to Dusseldorf. He is not popular there and he is criticised quite openly. His lack of gratitude to Bismarck is not forgiven for Bismarck is revered here, where everybody tells you:

"Bismarck, Monsieur, is the very soul of Germany!"

The Repopulating Theatre.

We went to the theatre. They were performing Maurice Maeterlinck's *Monna Vanna*.[1] You may know what a tremendous success this fine tragedy has been in Germany. There have been a countless number of performances, and its success still continues. It is performed with care but without verve. The staging is lavish but lacks taste. The colours shriek at you; the glitz of the props blinds you. It is not a walk-on part, it is fulguration.[2]

It was not at all easy to get tickets. A full house, a heaving house as we say. A reflective audience, more than reflective, in ecstasy as in a convent chapel, a choir of monks, on the evening of Good Friday. I have never seen such an almost religious attention, such prayerful looks, simultaneously turned towards the stage, as though towards a tabernacle, at the moment when

---

1 A musical play in three accts first performed in 1902.
2 In the original Mirbeau is playing with the contrast between *figuration* and *fulguration*.

the mystery of the Incarnation is resplendent... Never, in a theatre full to bursting, have I heard such an impressive silence.

Von B—— said to me, during an interval:

"You are present here, dear friend, at one of the most curious sights that can be seen in Germany... And what is happening here, in Dusseldorf, at this very hour, in more than forty towns, where *Monna Vanna* is on this evening... Do you know what is primarily responsible for the unprecedented success of this tragedy? I'll tell you... It couldn't be more German... In the second act, Monna Vanna goes into Prinzivalle's tent 'naked under her cloak'..."

He went silent.

"So what?" I said.

"That's it... 'naked under her cloak'... that's all... I'm not claiming that my compatriots are not sensitive to the supreme beauty of the drama, to its admirable, its incomparable lyricism... No, certainly... Whatever one says, the German likes grandeur in a work of imagination. Whatever he says himself, he is much more attracted than he thinks to romanticism, and this marvellous romanticism, with its old faults removed, delights him... In addition, he is crazy about theatre, especially French theatre. Yes, but here... there is something more... Monna Vanna is 'naked under her cloak'. Just take note of this. If, by a bold gesture she suddenly threw off her cloak; if an accident of the production—that the audience is not expecting—undressed her and that she appeared in her radiant nudity against the red background of her tent, amongst the animal skins on her bed... they would be deeply offended, would protest and the exaltation would drop immediately... Yes, but Monna Vanna is 'naked under her cloak'... That's enough... And believe me, for our good German, 'beneath her cloak', Monna Vanna is infinitely more naked than 'without her cloak'. Have you noticed the hypertension of gazes, dilated as though under the influence of belladonna, and so strangely fixed?… Have you noticed especially that, above all, a few men, the better to isolate themselves, the better to concentrate, the better to caress, the better to create the image, have shut their eyes?… All there is of veiled passion, of repressed and violent desires in the soul of the German, is excited by the fact that Monna Vanna is 'naked under her cloak'… Permitted licentiousness, allowed lust which multiplies, as though in a dream, the power of his internal vision!… And you are going to see, soon, an even more curious thing and which has never been seen, I think, in Germany… Nobody in the audience is thinking of going to supper, after the theatre. They have lost the taste for eating and drinking… They are going to go home hastily, their bodies on fire, and, full of the image of Monna Vanna 'naked under her cloak', they are going to endow the German fatherland with a little German, created according to the best recipes of Anthropogeny… Oh! Dear friend, one cannot know to what extent a woman who, besides, is not at all 'naked under her cloak', can increase in one evening, the population of a large country, like Germany… The statistics will prove it to us, perhaps, one day…"

And he added:

"I don't understand why, here as in your country, there are so many solemn idiots who wish to ban from the theatre, from books, from paintings, voluptuous images… Even what they call pornography should be respected, maintained, protected, as a force, as a national virtue, because it brings the sexes together… But the worst agents of depopulation are those Bérenger senators, protectors of sad and sterile masturbation…"

"So," I said, "are you also in favour of repopulation?"

"Me?" said von B——— quickly, "I couldn't give a toss, dear friend…"

An Evening at the Music-Hall.

An enormous crowd at the *Apollo Theatre* dominated by the military. You see nothing but uniforms; you hear nothing but the rattling of sabres.

On stage, it is the usual procession of tightrope walkers with sequins and jugglers in black jackets, Japanese acrobats, English families, Viennese ladies who sing, Spanish ladies who dance, living tableaux, cinematographs, French chanteuses, who parade in capital cities the means of satisfying the average level of the amorous and artistic aspirations of our contemporaries.

Our box is close to a large box, occupied by officers.

Long, slender, perfumed, slightly made up, in their tight tunics, their necks strangled by the red, blue or yellow straitjacket of their collar, they have insolent and effeminate expressions. Their way of prancing on too-wide hips recalls to a great extent that of the pretty little gigolos you see prowling, on our boulevards, before the Grand-Hotel and the Café de la Paix. They affect to have no interest in what is happening on stage, to show themselves blasé about everything. They are not drinking, not smoking, and are making tired gestures with their white gloves…

For a moment, they look at us with a snigger, eye up our ladies with such an exaggerated coarseness that one of us cannot help making a brief remark, but one as stinging as a slap in the face. Shouts, a commotion, provocation… Poor von B—— is obliged to intervene. He does it, moreover, with such authority that these gentlemen shut up and, shortly afterwards, leave the theatre, wiggling their buttocks…

"That is our army, for you!" said von B——

"Armies, in the plural!" I corrected him.

And I told von B—— about a similar scene, perhaps a more sickening one, that we had during the Dreyfus Affair, in a room in the Hôtel d'Angleterre in Rouen, where about ten French officers, hope of the country and pride of the salons, had no fear about coarsely insulting two ladies…

Memories and Daydreams in Cologne.

I will not say a word about Cologne except that the journey to get there was extremely arduous. Everywhere they were repairing something, they were connecting up, they were widening the roads. All we met were piles of earth and piles of stones, ruts and potholes. Three times—what humiliation!—I needed recourse to the help of a horse to rescue the bogged-down 628-E8. The roads into the villages, the market towns, the small cities were almost always blocked off. We were obliged to drive round them on paths, scarcely marked out on wet, loamy, uneven land, on which it is a miracle that the motorcar did not get stuck. On the parts that had been remade, the highway authorities,—with what devilish imagination!—had laid large, square cobblestones, from place to place and in such a way that, to avoid them and to avoid the plume of death, we had to carry out dangerous manoeuvres that I can only compare to dancing over daggers or over eggs. Confronted by all these obstacles Brossette's nationalism returned, even more sectarian and verbose. He did stop muttering between gritted teeth: "Filthy country!" and all that this exclamation conjured up of imprecatory remarks.

The fact is that his place behind the wheel was not a sinecure. The unfortunate chap had very painful wrists and was sweating profusely. But there were so many and such legitimate reasons to insult Germany that his hatred did not miss a single one, and he was rediscovering his courage and his skill in them.

To add to our misfortune, von B——, who, for reasons of friendship—ah! may the Devil take his friendship!—had wanted to come with us, ran out of petrol, that terrible, insoluble breakdown in Mercedes cars, and this immobilised us for two long hours, in the countryside, and for no reason: for, after two hours work, Brossette whose advice had been sought declared

that it would be necessary to strip all the pipework and, probably, all the coachwork… What should we do? Leave on the
road, without any help, this companion we had not invited?
It was very tempting but, alas, impossible. We decided to use
a rope to tow the Mercedes as far as Cologne which was about
twenty kilometres away.

✳

It was in a state of mind close to fury that we drove through
Bonn… I now regret that I was so unfair to this city. I ought
to pardon it for everything, even our tourists' disappointments,
for the always moving glory, the immortal glory of having given
birth to Beethoven. I never thought of it for a moment. Must
I also say that Bonn itself did nothing to bring it to my mind?
It is not a reason—not even an excuse—to have shown only
contempt for these streets, of which I mocked the glacial cleanliness, these gardens which brought to my mind the worst days
of the story of Le Vésinet, and its dull plains and ridiculous
fountains; for these monuments which I bitterly reproached
for sweating pedantry and boredom; above all for that university which, from so many young Germans, drunk with beer and
covered with duelling scars, makes so many old, bald doctors,
so many old doctors in God knows what subjects!

Deep in shame, in his motorcar that we were leading on
its leash, like a small dog, von B——— was not thinking about
Beethoven either. And he did not recognise his youth which was
saluting him as he went by, on the thresholds of pubs, which
was smiling at him, blond and fresh, leaning over the balconies
of windows with flowers… Ah! poor "Old Heidelberg"![1]

✳

---

1 The title of a popular play about student life.

360

It was late when we finally reached Cologne with our headlights on. In the evening details get closer together, merge into a mass. Of towns and landscapes all that remain are monochrome silhouettes. I had the impression that I was arriving at Pontoise, at dusk. The bridge, the river, the towers, the houses coming down the hillside, it was all there. But the bustle, the activity, the movement of the crowd, the absence of magistrates out for a walk with their families, bourgeois cooling themselves at the mouth of waterpipes, shopkeepers patting their stomachs in front of their shops, quickly dissipated this patriotic illusion.

We climbed out of the car in front of the Hotel du Dôme which is crushed by the shadow of the most colossal, the most colossally hideous cathedral in the world.

Dinner was unpleasant and perfectly dull. We had a von B—— transformed, refractory, quarrelsome, with the exclusiveness, the prejudices, the aggressive self-importance of an old German, with a subscription to the *Gazette de la Croix*. He bitterly jeered at socialism, defended Cologne's cathedral, "which is the finest cathedral in the world," Mercedes, "which are the best motorcars in the world", Kaiser Wilhelm, "who is the most brilliant Emperor in the world," the good taste of Berlin, "which is the most admirable good taste in the world", finally German virtue, "which is the most solid virtue in the world"... And he kept coming back to the cathedral, with a sort of comic hostility, his mouth spluttering and full of food:

"The finest... do you understand... the finest in the world!..."

For my part I insisted on replying childishly:

"The ugliest... the ugliest... the ugliest cathedral in the world!"

I did not even try to make an exception for the one in Prague which, at least, I proclaimed with a pompous lyricism, "has the beauty of erecting its enormous bulk on the heights of the Hradschin and being reflected, in the evening, with the surrounding palaces, in the blazing waters of the Moldau."

"The Moldau!" cried von B—— with a shrug… "the Moldau is only beautiful at Dresden, is only beautiful in Germany, when it is called the Elbe… And the Rhine? Ah!… the Rhine?… Why don't you talk about the Rhine?"

I felt arising in me, like a huge wind, the spirit of M. Déroulède.[1]

"The Rhine?" declaimed the spirit of M. Déroulède… But my poor von B—— it is no bigger than a glassful!"[2]

Even our gentle Gérald joined in who, with the insistence of a drunkard, was singing the praises of the supremacy of Westminster and the Thames over all other cathedrals and rivers in the world!

With the result that we went to bed, disgruntled the one with the other, furious with one another and with ourselves…

Oh, Goethe! If you could have heard us! And you, Heine,[3] what grimacing faces your superb and delicious irony could have added to the hilarious collection of puppets that compose your Schwabian School!

I slept very badly, annoyed, given nightmares by the proximity of the cathedral, of which—and it is what annoys me the most about it—the weather, which wears away everything, wears itself away without succeeding in more than scratching the surface of the hard stone. Neither the rain, nor the sun, nor the frost, nor the wind bringing corrosive dust, can soften its sharp angles and its straight lines, model its flat indentations

---

1 Paul Déroulède (1846-1914) was an author and politician and one of the founders of the League of Patriots to promote France's revenge against Germany for the Franco-Prussian War.
2 A reference to a poem by Alfred de Musset : "Nous l'avons eu, votre Rhin allemand, / Il a tenu dans notre verre", [We have had your German Rhine, it was no bigger than a glassful for us.]
3 Mirbeau was an admirer of Heinrich Heine.

and the horribly rigid flat surfaces. In my sleep its weight was stifling me, crushing me; and from the square right up to the point of its spires, a thousand sharp forms, a thousand faces with profiles of inquisitors, were breaking from it and entering me like so many instruments of torture… I woke up with jolt, panting, my temples frozen.

The following morning, I was in no mood to see Cologne again, its churches, its bridges, its museums and even its zoo where, however, I remembered having spent pleasant days, amongst splendid animals, and having espied an enormous bird, of the tribe of long-billed birds, looking astonishingly like M. Maurice Barrès in his Academician's uniform… I was tired of all that to the point of disgust.

When you are travelling there comes a point where even the most magnificent museums no longer interest you; moments when you would not take one more step to discover the most moving masterpiece. Art wearies you, gets on your nerves, like the caresses of a woman after you have made love. Leaving a museum where I have just gorged on art, just as leaving a bed where I thought that I had exhausted every joy—every joy?—of possession, I no longer have but one need, an imperious need: to walk, to walk, to smoke, to smoke cigarettes, in order to put distance and a cloud between these disappointing illusions and myself.

And again never, as much as this very morning, had I hated that traditional mania that impels us, scarcely arrived in a town, to hurry into museums, that is to say to worry about dead people, before mingling with living ones. As I walked, I said to myself, I said to myself repeatedly out loud, as though the better to firm up my resolutions:

"No… no… I will not go to the museum… I will not go…"

Just like a child who says to himself:

"No… I won't go to school today… No… no… I won't go."

Anyhow, I knew this museum… The idea of passing

again and again in front of the Bruyn the Elders,[1] the Master Wilhelms, the Grünewalds, even the Unknown Master, did not tempt me in the slightest. Even the *Virgin in Bean Flowers*, and the masterpiece of the *Passion* by Lyversberg, and the masterpiece of the *Glorification of the Virgin*, and the masterpiece of the painter of Saint Bartholomew, and the masterpiece of the head and shoulders portraits… and all the other masterpieces of the *Tomb*, of the *Crown of Thorns*, of the *Spear*, of the *Nails*, of the *Sponge*, of the *Reed*, of the *Olives*, of the *Calvary*, did not attract me either. It was not that I no longer liked these primitive painters of the old School of Cologne. I still liked them, but I did not like them at this moment of restlessness when I did not like anything. Or rather I no longer liked myself in them. I was truly as indifferent towards them as I was to modern masterpieces, the masterpiece of the *Woman in the Bath Tub*, the masterpiece of the *Passion and the Death of M. Félix Faure*,[2] the masterpiece of the *Immaculate Conception of the Virgin Otero*.[3] I preferred the docks on the banks of the Rhine and the farmers bringing to the town's market their droves of pigs and cartloads of cabbages.

I strolled aimlessly along the quaysides and in the streets, trying to become interested in life's movement in this opulent and active city, in which Catholicism, more aggressive than in Flanders, obsessed me with its towers, its spires, its crosses, its bells, no less than the monks you meet everywhere, dragging their brown habits, their sandals, on the cobblestones and

---

1 De Bruyn the Elder was from Antwerp but lived in Cologne from 1520 until 1560.
2 Félix Faure, President of the French Republic during the Dreyfus Affair, and attacked by Mirbeau, died in 1899 whilst making love to a 'woman of easy virtue'.
3 Caroline Otero (1868-1965), of Spanish origin, was a dancer and high-class prostitute.

seeking alms at houses… And then I stopped in front of a fine bookshop. Amongst many French books on display, amongst these authors unknown in France but who represent French literature abroad, through the illustrations on the cover which I find hideous, I noticed Balzac's *Correspondence*, in its in-octavo edition. I bought it and returned to the hotel. And straight away I felt that something positive had come from my walk. From now on, I had something on which my mind could feed, during this day that I foresaw as boring and joyless: I had Balzac, whose very name, in the shopfront of that bookshop, had sharply made Cologne's cathedral disappear, as well as Germany, the illusion of museums, and my phantasms. As I walked more quickly the rain began to fall, slow and fine, managing to give the city an aspect of funereal melancholy.

In the afternoon, I let my fellow travellers go out, and I shut myself in my room with Balzac.

What was Balzac's life? A permanent centre of creation, a perpetual, universal desire, a terrible struggle. Feverishness, exaltation, hyperesthesia, these constituted the normal state of his individuality. Thoughts, passions rumbled away in him like boiling lava in a volcano. He was simultaneously working on four books, plays, polemical articles for newspapers, all sorts of business activities, all kinds of love affairs, trials, travels, buildings, debts, bric-a-brac, fashionable relationships, an enormous correspondence, illness.

Once he had recreated the world, Balzac did not rest on the seventh day.[1]

---

1 In some versions of Mirbeau's work, there follow three chapters referring to the death of Balzac. Mirbeau was persuaded to withdraw these chapters from publication at the request of the daughter of Balzac's widow, Madame Hanska, who had been shown the chapters by the publisher. The three chapters are very cruel to Madame Hanska. They were reintegrated into the text in the 1939 edition. They are omitted here as they have already appeared in an English translation by Brian Stableford published by Snuggly Books in 2018, titled *The Death of Balzac*.

German Women and M. Paul Bourget.

That same evening von B—— took us to supper at the house of one of his friends who was a rich factory owner... It was by no means an event that we had expected. The only people there were intimate friends, six couples who were in the habit of meeting every evening. The men, a little clumsy in their manners, perhaps, but very intelligent and welcoming; the women, not very pretty, not very elegant, but totally charming, not like women in Paris, but charming, with a more serious, deeper, slower charm which arises not from their dress, nor their coquettishness, but which comes from themselves, from their naturalness and their wit.

The house is very attractively arranged, a little like an English interior, where luxury and comfort match so well with the needs of daily life... The furniture, some of it too large, some too small, did not always satisfy my taste for simplicity and styling. I must say however that they were reduced to the minimum of ugliness to be found in *art-deco*. It was just a momentary impression because items of furniture have this familiar mystery that they very quickly take on the face and the soul of their owners. For example, I was delighted to see on the walls only French paintings, chosen with a very bold and certain artistic taste: beautiful landscapes by Claude Monet, powerful still life pictures by Cézanne, the most admirable nudes by Renoir. The dining room is decorated with exquisite panels by Vuillard. In the study, decorations by Pierre Bonnard, sober, substantial, harmonious, with that so acute, so incisive, taste for the observation of forms in movement, and that quality of matter, that richness of colour, that are unique to him. Here and there, some van Goghs, Vallotons, extraordinarily expressive, some Roussels,[1] light, fluid, worthy of Corot and

---

1 Mirbeau helped to promote the work of many of these post-impressionist paintings.

Poussin. A large Courbet—a landscape of rocks in the Jura mountains—magnificently occupies the place of honour in the drawing toom. Whole line of pastels by Lautrec, some of them very racy, water-colours, drawings by Guys and Forain[1] lighten up the luminous staircase as well as the first-floor landing. On columns and plinths, on fireplaces and furniture, marbles and bronzes by Rodin, delicious wood statues by Maillol. I saw that this choice had been dictated neither by snobbery, nor by fashion, nor by the desire to astonish, but by a very reasoned aesthetic preference, very intelligently explained, especially by the ladies… And so, I had to come to Germany to have the joy of seeing, understood in this way, and lauded in this way, what I liked and for a whole evening, of feeling this so rare pleasure, even in France, of being in communion of tastes and of thoughts with those around you…

As I was taking my time to look at a very important picture by Valloton: *Ladies Taking a Bath*, our hostess said to me:

"I am shocked to see that M. Vallotton has not yet achieved, in France, the position that he deserves and is beginning to have in Germany. Here, we like his work very much; we regard him as one of the most personal artists of his generation. He is truly a master, if that word still has a meaning nowadays. His art, very reflective, very deliberate, very erudite, a little fierce, does not strain to move us by small sentimental means. One senses that he is hemmed in and ill at ease with intimate subjects. But how he develops, how he expands with large subjects! What I like so much in him is that constant and clear search for the outline, synthetic combinations of shape, through which he very often reaches great decorative expression. I find that he has the severe force, the powerful bearing of the great classics. The dryness of his lines, for which he is so unfairly criticised, in my opinion, is perhaps what impresses me the most in his work… It has something of the mural about it… In France, why don't you get him to paint huge frescoes? No other artist would carry

---

1 Mirbeau fell out with Forain over the Dreyfus affair.

them off so well... But it's a lost art, nowadays, I know... It no longer fits in with our complicated and tawdry civilisation.

Cultivated women, so-called intellectual women, are tedious. I avoid them like the plague. I find nothing more odious than their chatter, in which is displayed in comic fashion, a pretention to wit, to knowledge, to originality of thought, which is only most frequently the prerogative of ignorant, stupid people. It is impossible for them to have intelligence with simplicity. With them, talent is only the aggravation of stupidity... In France we have a woman, a poetess, who has wonderful gifts, an abundant and brand-new sensitivity, an outpouring which even has a little genius[1]... How proud we would be of her!... How touching, adorable she would be if she could stay a simple woman, and not take on this burlesque role of an idol in which she is cast by the so insufferable drawing room chatterboxes! Look! There she is, at home, completely white, immaterial, oriental, nonchalantly stretched out on cushions... Lady friends, I was going to say priestesses, surround her, in ecstasy at being able to look at and talk to her.

One of them says, holding a long-stemmed flower:

"You are more sublime than Lamartine!"

"Oh!... oh!..." says the lady, with tiny cries of a terrified bird... "Lamartine! That's too much! Too much!"

"Sadder than Vigny!"

"Oh! Darling!...darling!... Vigny!... Can that be possible?"

"More savage than Leconte de Lisle... more mysterious than Maeterlinck!"

"Be quiet!... Be quiet!"

"More universal than Hugo!"

"Hugo!... Hugo!... Hugo!... Don't say that!... You are talking about the heavens!... the heavens!"

"More divine than Beethoven!..."

"No... no... not Beethoven... Beethoven!... Ah! You are killing me!"

-----

1 Mirbeau is referring to Anna de Noailles (1876-1933).

And, almost in a faint, she passes her long, soft, undulating fingers through the hair of the priestess who is continuing her litany, lost in admiration.

"More! More!… Tell me more!"

This sort of behaviour is unknown to German women. With them you get the feeling that culture is not something exceptional, nor a profession, that it is not an adventure, a religion, and—if I may be allowed a not very gallant word—a joke. German women do not seek to surprise us, to dazzle us; they seek to educate themselves a little more, to understand a little more, through contact with others. They have sincerity, naturalness, passion, intelligence,—which is very seductive,—and, because they belong to a race, incredibly endowed with critical intelligence, it happens that, without wanting to, they often embarrass us even in things that we think we really know about. What I appreciate above all in German women, what I consider to be the most precious of all feminine refinements, is that women with the most profound education know how to remain women, without ever being pedants. Her duties as a spouse, a mother, mistress of the house do not humiliate her, cause her neither discomfort, nor tedium, nor disgust. She reconciles them very well with her desires, their passion for intellectual culture. I have even noticed that she puts more honesty, more rigour, more joy into fulfilling her duties because she understands their superior meaning; more grace too, because she has a greater sense of their penetrating, strong beauty. Never have I understood so well that an intelligent woman, who knows how to be intelligent, is never ugly. And I am certain that this is how I acquired that sort of hatred, or of pity, I am not quite sure which, for the very beautiful woman who persists in wanting to charm us uniquely through her useless beauty, and through her Doucet dresses and her Reboux hats.

This evening, in this house, was an absolute delight for us. The women knew everything, talked about everything,—even French things, both frivolous or serious,—with a precision, an accuracy, and with details that went as far as to stagger us. As I was still trembling from my memories about Balzac, I steered the conversation towards our great novelist, as naturally as I could, and no doubt with the hope of scoring a minor success. Oh! My surprise, and—why not admit it?—my disappointment in seeing that they knew him as well as or even better than I did!… Not about his life, perhaps, but about his works. They were not unaware of a single character of the *Human Comedy*… They commented on their significance, their character, their social significance, with a very detailed sense of human passions and without the slightest prudery.

One of them said:

"Although there is, in his books, a melodramatic hotchpotch which sometimes irritates me, and although he depicts morals—Parisian morals—with which we are not always very familiar, Balzac is, of all your writers—possibly of all writers—the one who seems to me to have depicted life—not only individual but universal life—with greater truth and greater power… Goethe seems to me to be small, even tiny, alongside this giant. Certainly, his intelligence is without equal. But what is the intelligence of Goethe alongside this prodigious imagination through which Balzac can recreate a whole society and the world?… It is rather hopeless… Moreover, life is hardly beautiful, even in our country, where we have hypocrisy instead of virtue… That is why he is not well understood in Germany… We boast about the fact that we only like experimental methods, but we are, more than one thinks, still subservient to the dogmas of the old romanticism of Schelling[1]… Despite our scientists, metaphysics has not completely died out in Germany… Whatever may be said, believe me, the new life brought by Nietzsche has not sprouted everywhere on German soil."

Then we turned to Renan, to Taine, to Zola, to Flaubert… to everyone and even—what a come down!—to M. Paul Bourget.

---

1 Friedrich-Wilhelm Schelling (1775-1854) was a German philosopher.

They were curious—rather like in a parlour game, I imagine—to know what I thought about M. Paul Bourget... Truly did I have an opinion about M. Paul Bourget? Oh well!

I replied:

"I knew Bourget[1] some time ago... I knew him well... We were close friends. I am a little uncomfortable talking about this... Then he took one path... and I took a different path... But all this was such a long time ago that I have the impression that he is dead..."

I took my time like an actor on stage, and:

"He was an intelligent boy..." I declared as if it were a eulogy.

They cried out... I insisted valiantly:

"I can assure you... intelligent... very intelligent... Listen, it is possibly Bourget who best understood Balzac... who spoke the most sensibly about him... He was very young then... and charming... He had a certain generosity of spirit... apart from the fact that, already, he did not like the poor... he did not find them worthy to be included in literature... or humanity... Being younger than I was he protected me, educated me, kept me away from what he called the rather too naïve and rather too coarse excesses of my nature... One day when we were walking up the Champs-Elysées, he said to me 'Abandon your poor people... they are not aesthetic... they will take you nowhere.' And, pointing out the fine houses on both sides of the avenue: 'There, dear friend... This is it!' Ah! If I had been able to benefit from his lessons... Well, he was charming... Since, well that's life, isn't it?... All sorts of ambitions..."

"He is so boring!" cried out a lady, with such conviction that we all burst out laughing...

"But what's he like?" asked another lady... "Is it true that all French women are crazy about him? I can't believe it..."

---

1 Mirbeau and Bourget were friends from 1876 to 1886. Their friendship ceased in 1889 when Mirbeau published an article criticising Bourget's realism without actually naming him.

"Good Lord!… They were perhaps crazy about him some time ago. Oh! Some time ago… Anything is possible. He certainly believed it… But Bourget believed so many things… in which he did not really believe!… Nowadays he is fat, a little chubby, and he is very, very old… He scarcely flirts with anyone these days except Joseph de Maistre, M. de Bonald, the monarchy, the Pope…"[1]

"Poor boy!" groaned the lady, with a compassion equally in her voice and in the expression on her face.

"Don't pity him… There must be some underclothes to rifle through… It is true that they are not those of the lady in the black corset."

Then a memory came back to me:

"Old father Augier,[2] who was an unrepentant bourgeois, made a remark to me about Bourget which characterises him quite well… It is picturesque, if a little vulgar… I'm not sure if I dare…"

"Come on… tell us!…"

"Well, Augier told me… he even told me in verse:[3] 'Your Bourget my dear friend is only a sad pig!…' I recounted this witticism to Bourget… he seemed to be delighted with it…"

"Because of the word 'sad' I suppose…"

"No… because of the word 'pig'… It is much more favourable for a psychological novelist…

"That's very funny… But you still have not told us what he is like!"…

"I shall, if you will allow me, tell you another story… The last time I saw Bourget, it was in Cannes, as you probably suspect… Maupassant had invited us for lunch on his yacht… Seeing me waiting on the quayside, along with him, for the

---

1 Bourget had moved closer to Catholicism and to these Catholic writers in about 1902.
2 Emile Augier was a dramatist, some of whose plays were written in verse.
3 The line that Mirbeau concocts for Augier is a twelve-syllable classical alexandrine.

rowing boat from the *Bel Ami*,[1] 'Fancy seeing you! How happy that makes me! It's been such a long time! I'm so pleased to see you again!... My whole youth!' And he embraced me, did my dear friend Bourget... And then: 'You know!... This will surprise you... You will find that Maupassant has changed... oh! Really changed!' Then he confided in me: 'Do you know?... I have finally brought him to psychology, yes, my dear friend, to psychology!' It was actually the year when poor Maupassant, alas, was writing *Notre Coeur*[2]... Bourget noticed my lack of enthusiasm... He reproached me for it: 'What?' he said... 'isn't it an enormous development... enormous?—'Yes, yes, I replied... 'Oh! Yes!' 'But it is the most important contemporary event... What bad luck that Taine is dead! How he would have liked that!' He added: 'It was hard work! But now, thankfully, it is finished!...' Aboard the *Bel Ami*, we found M. Jacques Normand, M. Henry Baüer, M. Valentin Simond, then director of the *Echo de Paris*, and good old Doctor Cazalis, who was already thinking of curing rheumatism in Aix en Provence using the pre-Raphaelite method[3]... The lunch was dull, dull... Maupassant did not utter a word... He was so terribly sad he was gazing at us with such strange looks that I could not help asking him: 'But what's the matter?... Are you sick?' He finally deigned to reply: 'No... I'm not sick... only... do you understand?... Yesterday... just imagine... at the very place where you are sitting, there was la Princesse de Sagan[4]... and there, where Baüer is sitting, there was la Comtesse de Pourtalès[5]... But there you are!' I was indeed very surprised... but it was not

---

1 *Bel Ami*, first published in 1885, was Maupassant's second novel and a great success.
2 *Notre Coeur* was Maupassant's last novel published in 1890. It has been published in English with the title *A Woman's Pastime*.
3 Normand was a collaborator of Maupassant, Baüer was a journalist for *L'Écho de Paris*. Dr. Cazalis had treated Alice Mirbeau, Mirbeau's wife, in Aix-en-Provence.
4 Considered to be an arbiter of fashion.
5 Noted for her wit.

the admiring surprise Bourget had promised me… Maupassant
had raised his arms towards the polished walnut ceiling, then he
had let them fall heavily… Now, with his elbows on the table,
his head resting on his palms, his red-rimmed eyes, and already
confused by the dim mist of the madness that was soon to carry
him off, he repeated, stammering: 'There you are… there you
are…' Then: 'I simply adore those women… because, old chap,
can't you see?… they have something that the others don't have
and that our grandmothers had… our dear grandmothers…
they are in love with love!' We were all heavy-hearted, except
Bourget who, addressing Maupassant, asked him: 'And *Notre
Coeur*?… How is it coming along?' And, as Maupassant was
not replying and just making a vague gesture: 'What a wonderful title!' cried Bourget, enlisting us as witnesses… 'You will
see… it will be the most marvellous book!… an extraordinary
book!' He then had the courage or the thoughtlessness to insist:
'It's down to me… for I brought him to psychology… didn't
I, Maupassant?… It was I, wasn't it? Tell them that it was I!'
Then Maupassant nodded and began to laugh, a painful laugh
that sounded to me like an electric bell going off… Never had
I heard anything more painful, more doleful… This is what he
had come to, this tough boy that, so many times, on the banks
of the Seine, with bare arms, a tight jumper, I had seen wielding
the oars with the enthusiasm of a joyful oarsman!… These were
horrible moments… I did all I could to bring this harrowing
visit to an end. We were put ashore at Antibes… Bourget tried,
as hard as he could, to accompany me to the train back to
Nice… As we were leaving one another, I slapped him on the
shoulder and I said to him: 'Ah, yes!… you have brought him
to psychology… And that's where he is, the poor blighter, in it
up to his neck!… My compliments, my dear Bourget…' Since
then, I no longer call him 'my dear Bourget,' not even 'Bourget,'
I don't call him anything at all… For I have never seen him
again… It was General Mercier[1] who saw him again…"

____

1 General Auguste Mercier (1833-1921) was Minister for War at the

Our Colonies.

The following day von B—— was returning to Berlin by rail as was his Mercedes… We were heading for Mainz…

In Mainz we met a certain Doctor Herrergerschmidt, the typical old German, as can still be found today in Swiss resorts, the German with a long frock-coat, a bushy beard, and round spectacles. But I note that the race is dying out more and more.

A professional epigraphist, the doctor has brought back very fine Punic stones, unless they were Phoenician ones… he is not quite sure… and which offer to the Historian a major interest since they are absolutely indecipherable…

"Indecipherable," he repeats with admiration… "That's the finest thing about them!"

He offered them to the Museum in Frankfurt which turned them down…

"Yes, Monsieur, turned them down… They are donkeys!…"

He offers to sell them to me for not very much… for almost nothing…

"Such fine inscriptions!… Possibly Syriac?… or perhaps, Persian?… Just a few marks, Monsieur!"

But I too refuse… The Doctor does not insist, shrugs his shoulders and:

"Stupid!" he says simply… "Stupid!"

He knows Morocco very well because he had sold in Tangiers, and even in Fez he assures me, a large consignment of sewing machines and typewriters… "not Punic, not Phoenician… no… German ones, Monsieur… Ah! Yes! Good old German manufacture!…" he cries.

---

beginning of the Dreyfus Affair in 1894. He had a major responsibility for the condemnation of an innocent man.

"Very beautiful, Morocco!… A very beautiful country… And the Moroccans, very decent people, Monsieur… excellent people!… really decent people!…"

We talk about the recent error of Kaiser Wilhelm, his arrival in Tangiers[1]… The doctor said:

"What's the point of such useless activities?… All these noisy demonstrations… theatrical ones… Oh, I don't like that… Yes, I know, national honour?… But national honour, Monsieur, is business… And German business gets on very well in Morocco… It gets on very well, very well indeed… because in Morocco we have admirable agents, Monsieur, truly admirable agents… Yes, Monsieur… the best agents in the world… the French!…"

His long beard is shaken in all directions by a laugh… He carries on in a tone which still retains a trace of irony…

"I really like the French… You French people… you have great… great qualities… brilliant qualities… enormous ones… you are… you are…"

He tries to define what we are, we French… to quote characteristic examples of our so brilliant qualities; and, finding neither definition nor examples, he sticks doggedly to his first, vague statement:

"Really… you have great qualities, oh!… But please excuse me… you are not always easy to get on with… Devilishly authoritarian… vexatious, aggressive, always seeking quarrels and arguments… slightly thievish… Hey! And even cruel… I am talking about you in your colonies, your protectorates… everywhere where you have an establishment, a degree of influence… you are detested! Hey! Don't you agree?… it's very sad…"

Noticing that I am not responding, he continues, the good doctor.

---

1 On 31 March 1905 Kaiser Wilhelm II landed in Tangiers wishing to assert his view that Morocco should be an independent country. However, the Conference of Algeciras in 1906 granted France a privileged position.

"So, the natives concentrate on freeing themselves from your authority… on ruining, if they can, your influence. And they find a good occasion—one can always find a good occasion—to annoy you, to massacre you, to suppress you… Damn! Just listen!… Don't get angry Monsieur… We are just chatting, aren't we?… I am telling you about history… I am telling you about your history… your colonial history… and even your national history… If it has often been glorious—but, Good Lord, what is glory?—It has not always been very generous… All these fights… all these wars… all that blood… throughout the centuries!… Finally, does it matter?… I like the French very much… To them we owe the greatness of Germany… One can't forget that!… Oh! And don't forget… I suppose… that in Morocco… that's it… in Morocco, there are also Germans… The Germans are heavy, stupid, ridiculous… They drink beer and eat smoked sausage… I know… I am only too aware… But they are kind to the Moroccans… They respect their values, their customs, their religion, their right to be a human being… They help them, occasionally, and, if need be, defend them without conspicuously exciting them against others. They give them confidence… and as there is always something to be done in Morocco, something to sell there… Hey, Good Lord, it's the German who naturally benefits from the positive attitudes of the natives and their hatred of the French… Don't you see, it's no more complicated than that!… Diplomacy, Monsieur… what a joke!… As for me, if I had been Emperor, I wouldn't have got involved in anything. I would have said, quietly smoking my porcelain pipe: 'Let the French get on with it… They are working for us…' And, thereupon, I would have taken a large glass of that excellent beer which makes us stupid and so heavy…"

Suddenly he ruffles even further his beard, whose golden strands stick out in all directions.

"Listen!" he proposes… "We are going to make a wager… That's it… a little wager… We are going to wager my fine Punic stones against anything you like… anything you like, ah!…

We are going to wager that, if the French left Morocco, and the Germans were the only people left in Morocco with the Moroccans… There would be no more problems… no more havoc, anarchy, wars, massacres… nothing… Morocco would suddenly become again a sort of Paradise on Earth… Don't you want to wager?… No?… You are probably right…"

Then, after a short silence:

"You really don't want my Punic, Phoenician, Syriac, Persian inscriptions?… Come on, Monsieur, a hundred marks? You really don't?… A pity… a pity!…"

Strasbourg.

After crossing the Rhine at Kehl, despite our letters of recommendation and our fine red seals, we had to go through long and costly formalities at the customs post. Although it is completely unrestricted in Germany, motorcar traffic in Alsace suffers from vexatious regulations, which result in great harm to Alsatian business. The hoteliers, the merchants, and especially the owners of the luxurious garages set up in the towns, are begging the government to rescind measures which are ruining them, by forcing motorcar drivers further and further away from these admirable regions, that were yesterday frequented for the joy and to the benefit of everyone. But the government remains deaf to these grievances. It still has a certain defiance, a sort of unspoken resentment against this area.

I had not been back to Strasbourg since 1876. Was it the case that I did not recognise it? With the exception of the area around the cathedral, and that so picturesque old district called Little France, nothing else from then remained. And soon these last remains, which we recognise, will soon disappear. The pickaxe is ready. Today Strasbourg is a magnificent, spacious and brand-new city, the city of fine white houses and balconies garlanded with flowers. There is not a similar one in France. The wide streets of the new districts, gleaming like Swiss parquet floors, huge universities, all these palaces built in honour of literature, sciences, and arms too, by means of which Germany has dug itself to the deepest depths of old French soil, these marvellous gardens, this busy commerce which flourishes in enormous banks, in luxurious shops, and this formidable army that watches over all that, must give grounds for sad thought to all those who still keep in their hearts impossible hopes. Oh! I pity poor Kléber[1] who observes, in his square, impotent and made of bronze, the continual development of a city into which all that was needed was an infusion of German blood for it immediately to acquire this strength and this splendour. At least, that was my first impression.

I do not claim that I can judge the mentality of a city by driving through it. A traveller may be taken in by so many appearances! And so many things pass him by!… But I had a lengthy conversation with a very intelligent Alsatian, who does not spout pious words. He told me:

"Strasbourg has been completely Germanified… A few bourgeois families are still holding out. But their resistance is limited to dwelling on old memories, in French, in the evening, around the lamplight… They have neither influence nor credence. And don't forget, either, that the priest, in this very Catholic area, quickly became the most ardent, the most listened to agent of definitive conquest. For personal and political reasons, the priest became profoundly, aggressively German. He did not even wait for the last crowing of the Gaulish cockerel to deny his fatherland!… To tell the truth, there are only very few Alsatians left here, drowned under a flood of Germans who after the annexation came to Alsace, as one goes to the colonies, to scout out business and to seek one's fortune. It is not the cream of Germany. Our civil servants, all German as well, are not the cream of civil servants either. Many had done

---

1 The Place Kléber, in the centre of Strasbourg, is named after the French Revolutionary general Jean-Baptiste Kléber born in Strasbourg in 1753.

bad things back in Germany… Instead of being sent to prison they were sent to Alsace… And they hope to be pardoned by showing exaggerated zeal… They are rigorous, legalistic, very harsh, and keep us in a rather humiliating tutelage… For example, we have the best army possible… In this respect, they have not skimped on expenditure, not haggled… twenty thousand men!… the best, the most reliable regiments of the whole Empire… Oh! We are not very proud about it… I should say however that the soldiers have lost a lot of their arrogance, of their arrogance and haughtiness… The officers are amiable, join in more with general life, live harmoniously with the civilian element… Many are wealthy and spend their money… And then the military bands, that we hear everywhere in the gardens and in the squares, are excellent…"

As I mentioned to him the enormous growth of the city:

"Yes!…" he said rather vaguely… "It's mainly a front, behind which there is a great deal of poverty… I don't exaggerate when I say malaise. Although Alsace possesses fertile soil and is, so to speak, the only agricultural province in the whole Empire, nevertheless it doesn't make us any wealthier. The economic crisis, which is hitting the industrial centres of the mainland, is also hitting us… We are crushed by taxes… The cost of living is horribly dear, forty-five per cent higher than in former times… So, materially we are not very happy… Morally, politically, we are still under the authority of Germany, in the same way as we were under that of France: obedient, passive and disgruntled… People make many mistakes in France about the mentality and the sentimentality of the Alsatian. He is not at all as you imagine him, as he is characterised in false legends, and a whole stupidly patriotic literature… The Alsatian hates the Germans, that is correct… From this you infer that he likes Frenchmen very much… A major mistake! If it's true that the expression of true feelings about a country may be seen and read in popular imagery and in familiar sayings, you will know for certain straight away when you know the rude and similar way that the Alsatian treats the Germans and the French. He says of the Germans that they are *Schwein*, pigs; he calls the French 'Welches!'"[1]

I though I had heard 'Belgians' and remarked on it.

"'Welches'… Belgians… it's the same word," he replied. And imagine that, in his mind, one is no less insulting than the other. Deep down, he does not care whether he is German or French… All he wants is to be Alsatian… And what does he dream of?… His independence… Only, would he know how to make use of it?… I fear not… A spirit of traditional, atavistic discipline makes him obey, grudgingly, obey nevertheless sometimes France, sometimes Germany… But, left to his own devices, I fear that he will get drawn into all sorts of internecine quarrels. I do not think that he knows how to, is capable of acting alone… He needs someone to lead him by the halter… When he loses his temper, he soon becomes aggressive, extremely offensive… And if you knew his patois?… Well, it is more colourful than Parisian slang… However, an excellent man who one has to like for his strong qualities…"

He smiled and I could see that that there was no bitterness in his smile.

"I am telling you my fears… idealistic fears, aren't they?… As for the independence of Alsace, that is a question not yet ready to be raised…"

He added:

"Perhaps by becoming German we have gained a small amount of human dignity… Listen, under the Empire, Colmar was sickeningly filthy, smelly, decimated by typhoid fever. It had no water and had been demanding it in vain for more than a hundred years. The very day after the defeat, the first act of the German government was to bring, from Honach, abundant amounts of excellent water with which they watered and purified the town… Yes, the Germans taught us cleanliness and hygiene, which is not negligible, and a lack of concern for the

---

1 The German word *Welches* translates as "Which?"

future which has given us a less sordid and less bitter mentality. The German—I don't mean the German Jew,—the German is unaware of economics. He is—not lavish—for lavish behaviour implies imaginative taste, or an ostentation of personality not possessed by the German,—but very profligate. He spends all that he has, and sometimes more than he has, according to his desires and whims, which are almost always childish and expensive. Here's a curious detail… in Berlin—I say Berlin, but I could have said the whole of Germany—on holidays more than two hundred thousand families leave the city… They go to settle a little everywhere, but particularly in Switzerland… You must have met them, beside all the lakes, at the summit of all the fresh air spas… These decent chaps, rather naïve, rather noisy, rather getting in your way, take with them all the money they have at home… You can be certain that they don't go home until they have used up their last pfennig… Therefore, the universities, colleges, boarding schools, who are aware of these habits, oblige the fathers to pay, before they set off, the future school year of their children… Without that… this famous education!…"

He started to laugh.

"Well, we are getting a little like that…"

"In essence? What?" I asked… "are you not too unhappy under German rule?"

He replied simply:

"Good Lord!… We go on living… When one can't be oneself… to be this or that… Turk, Laplander or Croat… well… it's not particularly important…"

"And Lorraine?"

"That's a different story… It has remained French to the depths of its soul… Smiles or threats, nothing undermines this old, obstinate, deep, feeling… like hope…"

Berlin-Sodom.

As we were about to leave Strasbourg to drive through Alsace, at the very moment that we were getting into the motorcar, we saw running towards us, comfortably well-rounded, always scruffy, twisting his beard and rubbing his forehead, my friend Albert D—— He seemed out of breath but delighted to meet us. He was travelling around in Germany in this outfit and hat which, for at least fifteen years, had been indifferent not only to different seasons, as I thought, but also to latitudes and frontiers, as I was surprised to determine…

"Finally," he cried after he had bowed to the ladies, "Finally!… I find French people… I find Parisians, simple, frank people… normal, virtuous people… Just let me look at you!"

His lips moved forward as if he was going to laugh; he was shouting no less loudly than when, in the rue Laffitte or the rue Richepanse, he was talking about art, and forced his voice into a falsetto.

"Yes, my friends, I have just arrived from Berlin… This time you haven't been as far as Berlin, have you?… Go to Berlin… Go there… You simply must go to Berlin… You must see it; you must see it again… It's tremendous… *kolossal!*… as they say… Go there!…"

And taking me by the arm as if to drag me there, he was still talking:

"Every time I go back there, I have a new surprise… I actually knew Berlin in '56… A large provincial city, full of soldiers, sad, poor looking. Nowadays it is luxury everywhere… brououu… And the moral degradation?… Brououu!… Ah!… *Kolossal!*…"

His eyes closed in the grimace he made as he laughed, and he lowered his voice as he took me to one side with Gérald.

"Pederasts! Pederasts!… All pederasts!… The highest born aristocrats, officers, ministers, artists, chamberlains… and generals, equerries, ambassadors… all of them!… All of them!… Scandal after scandal… trial after trial… disappearance after disappearance… *Kolossal!*[1] Besides, you must have read on the front page of *Le Temps*, which doesn't go into details but quotes official telegrams, relating to courtiers in Germany? It's more pornographic than the advertisements on page four of *Le Journal!…*"

He was jumping around in his old boots that were misshapen by his gout, and slapping his thighs like a child who has just played a *naughty trick* on his teacher:

"And did you know that a league of these gentlemen has been formed, for the purpose of obtaining the abrogation of inconvenient clauses in the law which prevent them from… from…"

And rubbing his nose and his forehead in turn, he began to burst out laughing, much to the inconvenience of my cheeks and my nostrils…

"Yes, my dear friend, a league… a League for the Rights of Man and of the Pederast… a league with its statutes, its commissions, its annual general meetings… brououu!… circular assemblies, I suppose… It's *kolossal*! You see they don't keep it secret… Quite the contrary… They have had successively comfort… wealth… luxury… All that was missing was depravation… Now they have their fill of it… they lack nothing… It is always how armed victory ends up, the crowning of the *Gründerzeit*… This is how they now surpass peoples who have a real history… Ah!… ah!…And they are quite proud about it!… I was scandalised by them… really scandalised! For a Parisian to be scandalised, that's really something!… and they were ecstatic to see my stunned expression!… You should have seen them!…*Kolossal!*… And yet, didn't they tell us many times

---

1 This is a reference to a scandal that had erupted in 1907, two years after Mirbeau's travels in Germany, in which a journalist had alleged that there was a homosexual ring at the court of Kaiser Wilhelm.

that we were Babylon! According to their pastors, they waged war against us to snuff out the germs of vice, to burn Paris that was poisoning the world!… Well, they've gone one better… They are Sodom… Sodom-on-the-Spree. Naturally the provinces follow the fashion; it is propagated by officers and senior civil servants… There is Sodom-on-the-Spree… But there is Sodom-on-the-Main, Sodom-on-the-Oder, and Sodom-on-the-Elbe, and Sodom-on-the-Weser, and Sodom-on-the-Alster, and Sodom-on-the-Rhine… Ah! ah!… on-the-Rhine, my dear friend."

As he never forgets to show off his nationalism, he added:

"When we were given over to vice, we Frenchmen—we are no longer, that fashion has passed—it was in a light-hearted, jolly way… But the Germans who are pedants, who are tactless, and are ignorant about good taste, they are—how shall I put it?—scientifically… They couldn't just be pederasts like everyone else… they have invented homosexuality… Where else, Good Lord, can science go? They do pederasty the way they do epigraphy. They know who Wagner's lover was, and of whom Alcibiades and Shakespeare have been the mistresses. They write books about the loves of Socrates and about those of Alexander the Great… On old stones, they have made an inventory of all the names of all the pretty boys of all the pharaohs of all dynasties… Pederasts with exaggeration, sodomites with erudition!… Instead of making love amongst men simply through vice, they are pedantic in their homosexuality… Just go to Berlin… go and see Berlin again… It's worth the trip…"

We had all shaken his hand in turn without him stopping to talk, to shout and to laugh, and we were already far away but could still see him jumping about and pointing towards Berlin, on which we were turning our backs…

The Two Borders.

For five days we drove through Alsace, through its barley fields and vineyards, its daisy chains of hop fields, its fine pine forests, its mountains, with their elegant contours, their soft slopes, with their very gentle tones of old velvet... What tender light! What light, moving skies! I seemed to be seeing again the infinite transparencies of Holland. Nature, happy to be unaware of the limits that separate men on whom, here and there, in front and behind, stupid quarrels are imposed, nature is just as she was before... We stopped in small Louis XIV towns, often guarded by even older gates, whose bell towers, with slim ridges of green tiles, and facades painted with pink frescos, are like souvenirs from that old Germany that they have become again despite being completely unaware of the fact...

In one of the towns, we run short of petrol... We are told:

"You will get some at the chemists."

But the chemist does not have any left... He has just sold his last litre to some Englishman...

"You will get it at the doctor's," he informs us...

The doctor is out, visiting patients. The only person in the house is a maid. She takes us to a cellar where I notice a barrel full of 'benzine' and a large drum of oil.

"Take what you need..."

She has no idea how much we should pay... When I insisted:

"Whatever you think..." she said with a smile...

She is not pretty, not even blonde; and she is not wearing the costume with which Henner[1] disgusted us and with which, after the war, today's racketeers of beer and women, dressed so many pretty girls in their brasseries in Montmartre and Montrouge.

---

1 Henner (1829-1905) was an Alsatian painter of nudes. Mirbeau did not like his work.

In a sort of restaurant where we had a very poor lunch, we were served with, I am not sure what:

"A German dish!" says one of us.

"Alsatian, Monsieur," the innkeeper retorts quickly.

And as another dish was brought:

"French dish!… Ah! ah!" I cry, with a Déroulède style gesture.

"Alsatian! Alsatian!" the innkeeper corrects me, in a ruder and more irritated tone, as he turns his back on us.

And I think that I saw his lips form the word: 'welches!'… although he did not say it.

And so, driving steadily, we arrived late one evening at the border, at Grand-Fontaine, I think, a pretty, spread-out village, with attractive little houses, in a green valley in the Vosges. It was half past eight… And we had the crazy idea to spend the night in Baccarat… Good Heavens, why? The customs officer went through the formalities. Despite the lateness of the hour he did not create any difficulty about repaying our deposit.

"It just so happens," he told us, "that I have some French money today. I imagine that you would prefer that…"

The office was very clean and tidy, the men very polished in their green jackets. They wished us *bon voyage*.

At Raon-la-Plaine, the French customs post, we were treated like dogs. A stinking hole, a foul cesspool, a pile of dung: that was our border, our French border What we saw of the houses seemed poor and sordid. People were shouting in a café…

Small, thin, his kepi on sideways across his neck, a blue tie knotted like a rope around his neck, his grease-covered jacket unbuttoned, a customs officer ran in front of the motorcar waving a lantern… He questioned us in an imperative almost coarse tone.

"What's in these trunks?… these packets?"

"Nothing… just our belongings."

"What are you saying?… We'll have to take a look at that!… But it's too late!… Good evening!… Tomorrow!"

I went into the office to complain to the boss... A room in total disorder... a wooden floor sticky with filth... there was no boss... A man was sleeping on a bench, his head on a sack... He let out a grunt, then a curse, at the noise of the door opening... Outside the people had come out of the café... they were standing around the motorcar, they were looking at us in a hostile manner, sickly beings, gritty, rotten teeth, sly eyes...

I decided to turn and head back to Grand-Fontaine to spend the night there...

The following morning, we had to undergo the examination. The customs officer did his best to make it as ignominious as possible. He rifled through our belongings in the trunks, broke a bottle in a casket, made an inventory, piece by piece, of the tools of the driver... Up to a camera that had to be taken out of its case to see what there was inside. It lasted an hour... I drafted a complaint... But where do complaints end up?...

Finally, he allowed us to leave... furious that he had not found anything suspicious, but happy that he had annoyed us...

As we were driving past the last house of this loathsome village, a stone, thrown from I know not where, broke one of the windows of the motorcar... I got off with a slight scratch on the cheek.

"Well!" I said... "There's no mistake about it!... We are well and truly in France..."

"Filthy country!..." grumbled Brossette.

But I think that he was only speaking of Raon-la-Plaine.

Paris, Corneilles-en-Vexin, 1905-1907.

A PARTIAL LIST OF SNUGGLY BOOKS

MAY ARMAND BLANC *The Last Rendezvous*
G. ALBERT AURIER *Elsewhere and Other Stories*
CHARLES BARBARA *My Lunatic Asylum*
S. HENRY BERTHOUD *Misanthropic Tales*
LÉON BLOY *The Tarantulas' Parlor and Other Unkind Tales*
ÉLÉMIR BOURGES *The Twilight of the Gods*
ADA BUISSON *The Baron's Coffin and Other Disquieting Tales*
CYRIEL BUYSSE *The Aunts*
JAMES CHAMPAGNE *Harlem Smoke*
FÉLICIEN CHAMPSAUR *The Latin Orgy*
BRENDAN CONNELL *Metrophilias*
BRENDAN CONNELL (editor)
 The Zinzolin Book of Occult Fiction
RAFAELA CONTRERAS *The Turquoise Ring and Other Stories*
DANIEL CORRICK (editor)
 Ghosts and Robbers: An Anthology of German Gothic Fiction
ADOLFO COUVE *When I Think of My Missing Head*
QUENTIN S. CRISP *Aiaigasa*
ALADY DILKE *The Outcast Spirit and Other Stories*
ÉDOUARD DUJARDIN *Hauntings*
BERIT ELLINGSEN *Now We Can See the Moon*
ERCKMANN-CHATRIAN *A Malediction*
ALPHONSE ESQUIROS *The Enchanted Castle*
ENRIQUE GÓMEZ CARRILLO *Sentimental Stories*
DELPHI FABRICE *Flowers of Ether*
DELPHI FABRICE *The Red Spider*
BENJAMIN GASTINEAU *The Reign of Satan*
EDMOND AND JULES DE GONCOURT *Manette Salomon*
REMY DE GOURMONT *From a Faraway Land*
REMY DE GOURMONT *Morose Vignettes*
GUIDO GOZZANO *Alcina and Other Stories*
GUSTAVE GUICHES *The Modesty of Sodom*
EDWARD HERON-ALLEN *The Complete Shorter Fiction*
RHYS HUGHES *Cloud Farming in Wales*
J.-K. HUYSMANS *The Crowds of Lourdes*
J.-K. HUYSMANS *Knapsacks*
COLIN INSOLE *Valerie and Other Stories*
JUSTIN ISIS *Pleasant Tales II*